Angels of the Ages

Book I

In the Beginning

Angels of the Ages

Book I

In the Beginning

Wilma Styles

Grateful Steps
Asheville, North Carolina

Grateful Steps Foundation
Crest Mountain
30 Ben Lippen School Road #107
Asheville, North Carolina 28806

Copyright © 2023 by Wilma Styles
Library of Congress Number 2023931777
Styles, Wilma

ISBN 978-1-945714-69-6 Paperback
ISBN 978-1-945714-70-2 Ebook

Printed in the United States of America at Lightning Source
FIRST EDITION

www.gratefulsteps.org

TO MY FRIEND, CAROLYN

Preface

When I was a little girl, I used to go outdoors, look up at the sky and wonder what was beyond the clouds. As I would make pictures in my mind out of the clouds, I could only wonder, *Is there really a God and are there really angels watching over me?* There were times when thunder and lightning would shake the house. I would run and hide in a closet. I was so afraid because I thought the thunder was God talking, but I couldn't understand Him. I was sure the lightning was God's light but only a small fraction of Him. I could only question, *Does God really hear me when I talk? Will He answer me, or does He really care?* I was filled with questions. But down deep, I really didn't care. I was lost as I could be.

My grandmother told me and my sister about God all the time. She prayed with us and for us with so much love. My grandmother was bed-fast with crippling arthritis and lung cancer. She died when I was 9. My heart was so broken. She was everything to me. *Now, who will pray for me and who will tell me more about the God behind the clouds?*

I was in my early 20s when I became serious about wanting God in my life. Desperation pulled me to that place. I urgently needed a sense of balance.

I had heard numerous depictions of God and how to serve Him. I couldn't make up my mind if I believed any of the scenarios presented to me. I prayed God would guide me to the Truth.

Twenty years after my grandmother died, a voice spoke to my mind and said, "It's been twenty years since your grandmother died." Scared me to death! The voice said my grandmother's prayers lived long after she passed. A short time after that, I gave my heart to the Lord. It was then I began to pray to the God behind the clouds. My prayer was simple: that I may know Him. I said I would serve Him, but I would not serve a God I don't know. I had to know if God was real. After that as I prayed, God began revealing Himself to me. He also let me know the angels were very real and were with me. As I studied the Bible, I learned it is filled with many infallible truths about angels being with us. That was when I was moved by the Holy Spirit to write the *Angels of the Ages* trilogy. I wrote the *Angels of the Ages* trilogy because of my own search to find God. I learned early in my quest not to believe everything I heard. Therefore, I put my life before God and prayed that He would guide me in my pursuit to know Him. After eight years of prayer, intense study, fasting, watching and listening, I wrote the *Angels of the Ages* trilogy.

I wanted to use this fiction trilogy sprinkled with truth to share parts of my journey. In my life, I went through many of the things I have penned in the trilogy. I faced daily the endless war between good and evil. The constant challenge of not being sure about what was right or what was wrong kept my mind in chaos, facing forces from the dark kingdom that were there to destroy me.

God sent me many angels from the Crystal Kingdom to help me fight and win my battles.

Learning about the two trees in the garden was essential. The Tree of Life, where I could go daily and be cleansed in the Holy Fire of God was one option. Or I could be lured by the dark magic to the Tree of the Knowledge of Good and Evil. There a deceptive fire burns that would have destroyed me had I not cried out for God's help. That fire still burns today with a passion that even lured Adam and Eve. What kind of power did the tree hold that could so easily persuade perfect human beings like Adam and Eve to yield to its powerful magic? I heard about an "apple" tree . . . could any fruit tree possess the kind of power it would take to affect a perfect bloodline?

***

The Beginning, Book I of the *Angels of the Ages* trilogy, narrates the struggle of two women. Rachel and Cordilia, in their quest to fulfill the destiny God had ordained for them. Many times at night, the angels would shake my arm and tell me to go write, and I did. I am now 74 years old and know that beyond a shadow of a doubt, God and the angels are real and they are still helping me grow spiritually. I still look to the sky and remember when I was a little girl, but no longer am I afraid. With assurance I pray to the God who lives behind the clouds, and He answers me.

Characters

Good People
John, Rachel and Stephen Daniel Harris
Best friends: Paul, Cordilia and Phillip Dawson
Jacob and Barbara Harris – John's parents
Clayton and Maggie King – Rachel's mom and dad
Harold and Amanda Collins
Pastor Kenneth, Leah, and Paula Miller
The Hermit – Mr Spook/ Mr. McKinney
Stella Roberts
Effie Brown – Princess Kaylee
Sheriff Allen Butler
Roy Adams
Matt – Sheriff's deputy
Dr. White
Willow Chandler

Good Angels
Doug Holland – Haleb
Carmon
Raptor General Eagle
Queen Deborah, Princess Tina, Princess Sandra
Prince Jacob, Prince David, Prince William,
King Rayon/Supreme Being

Bad Angels
Jerry and Emily Jackson
Dr. Fred Wells – Shemed
Peggy Welsh
Queen Jewel
Telmar, Delilah, Meric, Delmar, Elmore, Demise

Acknowledgments

To God be the glory!

Thanks Ray, for all your love and patience.

Debbie thanks for all your help and the wonderful poem, "Ancient Tree."

A special thank you and much love to my prayer partner Carolyn, for giving me the title to my trilogy: *Angels of the Ages.*

Thank you, Opal, for being with me from the beginning of my very first book and all the reading.

Contents

Contents

THE ANCIENT TREE

The veil between the worlds has opened
A misty forest I see
Stars and galaxies sing new songs
My heart slows its beat
A breath, a gasp, my eyes are fixed
Royalty stands before me
Diamond flakes on emerald leaves
It is the Ancient Tree
God of nature, man and beast
God of wisdom, God of peace
God of wrath, God of love
It is the Ancient Tree
A treasure chest in the midst
Hinged with silver and gold
The Ancient Tree holds the hallowed hall,
The hallowed hall of souls
On bended knee I bow my head
This sacred place I've seen
Was it all a dream?
Something in my hand I see . . .
It is the ancient seed.

– by Deborah Stanaland

Chapter One

In the Beginning

*I*t was a beautiful sunny day in Todd's Creek, Virginia. Birds were singing, and the flowers of spring were in full bloom. A gentle breeze had begun to stir, rustling the tender green leaves on the giant oak tree that hovered over the corner of a white, two-story house. The home at 59 Brush Creek Road formerly belonged to John, Rachel's husband, who died five years earlier, and Rachel, the parent of Stephen Harris—a home that once was filled with laughter, the smell of fried chicken and apple cakes. But this day, May 10, 1971, everything changed. The sun was shining outside, but Stephen Daniel Harris felt as though a dark blanket had been thrown on top of him, blotting out the light. The birds were singing, but Stephen's song had turned to mourning. He thought nothing could be worse than losing his father five years earlier; however, the death of his mother proved him wrong.

After the funeral, everyone went home but his best friend Phillip lingered. At Stephen's request,

Phillip also hugged his buddy, and said goodbye. The day felt endless. The realization of being alone for the first time had kicked in. How could time have passed so fast that both his parents would have already been taken from him? His eyes scanned the long covered front porch and stopped on his favorite place in the world to find solace, the porch swing. His great-grandfather had handcrafted the swing and brought it to America from Dublin, Ireland, in the summer of 1826.

The swing was passed to his Grandfather Jacob, then to his father, John, and now it belonged to him. He loved to push back and forth and let his thoughts take over. Just sitting in it comforted him. He recalled what his father told him, "If you really want to find peace and connect with your God, you must be outside."

Stephen took his father's words to heart and sought refuge with nature. He loosened his tie and unbuttoned the top button of his shirt. He closed his eyes, turned his head to the side and rubbed the back of his neck. He slowly moved his hand to his jacket pocket and removed a small piece of paper. With trembling hands, he opened it. His heart began to race as he stared at the name his mother had written the day he was born. He ran his finger across the letters and said, "Shemed!" Even speaking the name sent a chill down his spine. He folded the paper and put it back in his pocket. Looking out across the front yard, his mind drifted back in time. Again, he remembered . . .

Chapter Two
About the Family

Stephen Daniel was the only son of John and Rachel Harris. John was born in the small town of Creely, North Carolina, on June 23, 1907. His parents, Jacob and Barbara Harris, had moved to Todd's Creek, Virginia, when John was 14. Jacob went to work for the Jamestown Railroad as a brakeman. Hard work had promoted him to conductor. John's love for trains started at the early age of 3.

One day, Jacob came home with a surprise for John, an engineer's hat. The boy's heart leapt within him as he placed the blue and white pinstriped cap on his head. At night, John would lie in bed and listen for the lonesome sound of the whistle as the 9:30 p.m. freight train rumbled down the tracks. In his mind, he was the engineer of that train every night. Wanting to follow in his father's footsteps, John went to work for Jamestown Southern Railroad when he turned 21. Although John loved trains, his secret passion was swords. Many times he envisioned himself as David, taking Goliath's head, avenging the Army of the Living God.

John and Rachel met in high school. He fell in love with her the first time he saw her, and he asked her to go steady on their second date. On their eighth date, John asked Rachel to marry him, and they were married June 23, 1928, John's 21st birthday.

Rachel was born May 13, 1910, in Todd's Creek, Virginia, to Clayton Randolph and Maggie Louise King. They were a middle-class family; Clayton raised cattle and Maggie was a piano teacher. She taught Rachel to play the piano and gave her voice lessons. She saw that Rachel dressed like an upper-class person, adamant that her only child would grow up and enjoy many of the things that had not been afforded her as a child.

After their marriage, Rachel didn't work on a public job. Her title would normally be a homemaker, but Rachel far exceeded her station. She loved to sing, decorate and work in her flowers. She taught Sunday school and sang in her church choir. With all her titles, Rachel wanted more for her life, to be a mother. John and Rachel tried for several years to have a baby . . . with no results. Rachel consulted with Dr. Fred Wells, the town doctor. Due to cysts on her ovaries, Rachel was unable to get pregnant. Dr. Wells felt that she should have her ovaries removed. Rachel protested and sought a second opinion. She went to the most renowned hospital in Norfolk,

Virginia. After several tests and exams, the doctors there concurred with Dr. Well's findings; she and John would never have children. Even though disappointed, John wanted what was best for his wife, but Rachel refused to even consider having surgery.

Chapter Three
White Stone Kingdom

A great number of witnesses from White Stone Kingdom in the Third Heaven were invited to a special meeting of the high court. When special meetings were held, everyone knew something exceptional was about to take place. The vast halls echoed with laughter and curious conversations as the last guest hurried inside to be seated. A hush fell as the towering doors opened. Twelve Ancient Warriors entered and were seated behind the elevated platform. The judges had been hand chosen by the Most High God because of their faithfulness to the White Stone Kingdom. King Rayon, commander of the Ancient Ones, raised his scepter and quickly brought it down, bringing the court to order. The Ancient Ones towered head-and-shoulders over all in the First, Second, and Third Heavens.

The King held his head high, closed his eyes and declared, "Warriors of White Stone, the time has come! The Ancient of Days has stirred a holy wind with his finger, unleashing manna from the beginning of time! Let White Stone rejoice!"

Haleb, the high general of White Stone Warriors was summoned to appear before the high court. As he entered, the panel of judges lowered their heads when he neared the semicircle where they sat. Inside the circle, a colossal red stone that glowed continually rested inside a smaller, deep circle filled with holy oil.

Haleb hit his chest and lowered his head in respect to the high court. Rayon motioned for Haleb to be at ease. King Rayon's face beamed. His round eyes flickered like fire, and his long, white hair sparkled like stars on a clear night. His clear diamond crown was crested with large emeralds. His white linen robe glistened with gold. Long, gold tassels draped his enormous shoulders. A vast gold ring with the letters AOTA graved in the center hugged strong finger. The counsel and Haleb wore the same ring.

Rayon greeted, "Haleb, my brother, it's good to see you!"

Haleb smiled, lowered his head and replied, "And you, my King."

Rayon continued, "My General, have you chosen carefully your troops for the great battle?"

"Yes, my Lord. Boone's Crossing and surrounding areas will soon be infiltrated with soldiers from the three heavens."

Prince William, sitting beside Rayon, asked, "What of Shemed?"

"The Gray Stone Kingdom has been gathering their empts—demons—at the Crossing for days. I've witnessed personally many of the chosen of Queen Jewel's army."

"But has Shemed made an appearance?"

Haleb shook his head. "No. Thus far my spies have seen no sign of him in the region."

King Rayon tightened his lips. "He's on the scene! It's just a matter of finding out what disguise he's wearing."

Prince Jacob quickly questioned, "And what of Telmar?"

"Not yet, my Prince, but my forces say he will be in the area soon.

Princess Tina leaned forward and announced, "The Most High has informed us that Rehabiah has sent word that His servant is ready."

"Yes, Your Majesty, she is ready," Haleb said.

King Rayon stood, held the golden scepter in the air and declared, "The Most High King rejoices that the time has come to open the royal book of mysteries."

Immediately, the chamber exploded with shouts of praise to the King of heaven. Rayon raised his scepter and a hush fell. Queen Deborah stood and announced, "The time of the great prophesy to be unveiled has come. This great number of witnesses has been invited to view the release of the prophecy and the faithfulness of our King."

Again, the immense hall erupted in praise. Queen Deborah stood and called for Princess Kaylee to bring forth the guarded book from the hallowed hall.

Trumpets sounded as the gigantic doors opened. Gasps filled the assembly room. Carrying the large book, Princess Kaylee entered, surrounded by an elite host of angels all wearing gold rings with the letters AOTA stamped in the center. She brought the book and placed it on a table before the ruling body. Once she lifted her hands from the book, the gold latch on the side unlocked. The cover slowly opened, releasing a radiant light from the primitive manuscript. The cover of black leather had hardened with age. In the center of the cover, the words Angels of the Ages were written in crimson red. She bowed her head, stepped back and said, "Blessed be the Ancient of Days."

Prince David called out, "Princess Kaylee, you and your host have guarded very well the book from the Ancient Tree. The Most High has prepared a chosen vessel to receive the deep mysteries. The Holy Spirit has been working in Rachel Harris for several earth years. As these witnesses well know, an intense battle has begun at Todd's Creek to prevent her from obtaining the knowledge."

Princess Sandra stood and called for the Watcher Eri. Immediately he was standing in the circle. He bowed his head, hit his chest and declared, "Glory to the Most High God."

Princess Sandra spoke. "Eri, the prayers of the earthlings John and Rachel Harris have come up before the throne of the Most High God. He has ordered that you visit earth tonight and let Rachel know she will give birth to a son by this time the next earth year."

Eri lowered his head and said, "Yes, your Majesty."

King Rayon stood and touched his staff to Eri's head. "Eri, it's time for you to go down the ladder. General Rakar has also been commissioned to go down with you. You will be his Watcher and retain your memory of who you are. However, Rakar will have no knowledge of his past. He will have to find his identity in order to wear the mantel that is his. Now go from this place. Haleb will report to us on your behalf."

King Rayon hit his chest, lowered his head and announced, "Rejoice, you great assembly of witnesses! The prophecy of the ancient book is now opened!" Rayon pointed his rod toward Princess Kaylee and the paramount guards of authority, and shouted, "The Most High King be with you, Haleb and the White Stone Warriors, with you Princess Kaylee, and with you that wear the golden ring of authority." Rayon paused and raised his scepter. The congregation jumped to their feet and bellowed until the heavens shook. Rayon cried, "We give all glory to the Most High King. We praise Him for the release of the Book of Mysteries and the Angels of the Ages!"

Trumpets sounded. When the scepter came down, the courtroom was empty.

Chapter Four
Angel Eri

*T*hat night, nearing the end of summer in 1950, Rachel went through her nightly routine before bed. At the end of the day, she always made herself a cup of hot tea, sat out on the porch swing and reflected on her day in order to relax. On this night, the air was a bit chilly, so she wrapped herself in an afghan, slipped on her old pink terrycloth bedroom shoes, got her tea and went to the porch swing and sat down. Slowly she began to rock herself back and forth while sipping her tea. Rachel couldn't remember such a beautiful night. The sky was perfectly clear, and the moon was surrounded with what seemed like millions of stars. She closed her eyes for a moment and took a deep breath. A slight breeze caused the leaves to dance and twirl around. Thoughts of John filled Rachel's mind.

After finishing her tea, she decided to get back inside, lock things up, and get some sleep. As she took hold of the doorknob, she faintly heard someone call her name, "Rachel."

Startled, she turned to see who had called her. No one was there. Her eyes darted around the yard as her fingers gripped the doorknob. Feeling very uneasy, she heard the voice again, "Rachel." This time with her heart pounding, she rushed inside the house. She hurried to the bedroom window, pulled the curtain back and looked outside, still edgy about the voice she knew she had heard. She immediately knelt by her bed and prayed.

The moonlight beamed through the window and rested on Rachel's white, cotton gown, giving it a blue tint that glowed in the room. At first, her tears came slowly, and then, like a river, they began to flow. Her sobs echoed through the bedroom and spilled out into the hallway. Suddenly, she froze sensing a presence in the room with her. Restless, she slowly raised her head and opened her eyes. For a moment, she saw nothing. As she wiped her tears, she gasped for air and pushed herself backward. Before her stood a being unlike anything she had ever witnessed. Is it an angel? she thought.

She covered her face with her hands and bowed her head to the floor.

"Rachel, do not be afraid."

Unable to speak and afraid to open her eyes, she could sense the creature moving closer to her.

The being gently took her shaking hands and helped her rise from the floor. He tenderly placed one finger under her chin and raised her head. She could feel the warmth of his stare. Gradually, she opened her eyes. The magnificent being's brightness left her unable to see all his features. As her eyes adjusted, the brilliant blue of the angel's eyes pierced her soul. His blond hair glistened as if it was filled with oil and diamonds.

"Rachel," he whispered, "by this time next year you will have a son."

From deep inside her, she managed to mutter, "A son? Who . . . who are you?"

In a calming tone, he answered, "My name is Eri."

"E . . . Eri?" she stammered.

"Yes, Rachel. I am your Watcher."

Rachel took a deep breath, exhaled and thought. Am I dreaming? Are you really here?

Eri answered her thought. "You're not dreaming. I'm definitely here."

"You said that I'm . . . I'm going to have a son?"

"You will have a son. As I have been your Watcher, so will I be the Watcher of your son."

Before Rachel could speak, he vanished. Her eyes searched the room. Nothing. She hurried to the window and looked out. Nothing. She turned and walked to the bed to lie down. Her mind was spinning as she stared at the ceiling, wondering if he was the one who called her name earlier. A calmness coccooned Rachel as she lay on the bed. "I'm going to have a son," she whispered.

Chapter Five
Gray Stone Kingdom

A black horse and rider raced across a field consumed with a heavy fog. As the rider neared the towering castle of Gray Stone Kingdom, the watchman blew a giant ram's horn signaling the guards to open the drawbridge. The dark kingdom's army had been put on full alert anticipating the war that was sure to come against the White Stone Kingdom. The demonic army filled the courtyard as the rider came to a halt. The chamber doors flung open as Maric entered Gray Stone's throne room. Three mammoth gold dragon thrones sat under a crimson red canopy, occupied by the three top generals who headed Queen Jewel's main force.

Maric bowed on one knee and lowered his head. Delmar, the lord of death, cut his black eyes to the rider, giving Maric an audience. The spy raised his head and said, "Lord Delmar, I bring news from the high court in third heaven."

"What have you to say?" Delmar demanded.

Maric paused. Elmore, the lord of pain, shouted in a voice that shook the walls, "How dare you not speak immediately when the lords bid you to do so?"

Trembling, Maric stammered, "Forgive me, Master Elmore."

Demise, the lord of confusion, interrupted, "Elmore, hold your peace. Can't you see that Maric is under duress?"

Demise ordered one of the guards to bring Maric a glass of water.

He took the water and looked to the generals.

Elmore declared, "Drink up, soldier, and make known your report."

The soldier drank the water straight down and gave the goblet to the guard. He wiped his mouth on his sleeve and asked, "Sirs, may I be at liberty to speak freely?"

Delmar leaned forward, rubbed his bald head and growled, "It would not be wise to speak any other way. Now speak before you lose your head."

"Court in third heaven was in session. Haleb appeared before the royal counsel."

Elmore pounded the arm of his throne and growled, "Haleb? How could it already be time?"

Delmar raised his arm to silence Elmore. "What of the meeting?" he asked.

Maric took a deep breath and continued, "Princess Kaylee was ordered to bring out the book of mysteries."

Demise furrowed his brow and asked, "Who gave the order?"

"Queen Deborah, noble one."

Elmore stood and demanded, "Did she say who the order came from?"

Trembling, Maric lowered his head and replied, "She said the word came down from the Ancient of Days."

Demise placed his long fingers around his sword handle and muttered, "Was there more?"

"Yes, my General. The elite guards that wear the gold rings of authority came out with the book of secrets."

Elmore frantically questioned, "Does Shemed know about the book and the guards of authority being brought forth from the secret chambers yet?"

"Yes, my General. Word has been sent to him and General Telmar."

Demise stood, tightened his fists and snarled, "Go back to your troops soldier!"

Maric lowered his head and said, "Lord Demise, there's more."

Delmar promply ordered Demise to sit until the full report was given. Maric took a deep breath and said, "Princess Sandra summoned Eri to appear."

The generals were visibly shaken at the sound of Eri's name. Elmore tapped his finger against his lip. "The Watcher! Surely, it's not time. How could it be?"

"What were Eri's orders?" Delmar asked.

"Princess Sandra said it had come from the Most High God that it was time for Eri to go down the Ladder."

Demise gritted his teeth and roared, "I want him dead!"

"When was Eri commanded to go down the Ladder?" Delmar asked.

"Right after he visits the earthling, Rachel Harris, and informs her that she is going to have a son."

Delmar raised his hand and shouted, "Stop! I don't want to hear what I think you're about to say."

Demise grabbed his arm and insisted, "Delmar, we must hear." He motioned to Maric to continue.

"Sandra said, 'General Rakar had received his orders to go down the Ladder with Eri. Eri would be his Watcher and retain full knowledge of who he is—'"

Elmore interrupted, "—and Rakar?"

"He will retain no information of his position. He will have to find his identity in order to wear his mantel."

Demise uttered, "Queen Jewel's witch warned her the war was upon us and that the destination for the battle will be at Boone's Crossing. Our forces have had control of that land for many centuries—"

Elmore interrupted, "—yes, but the witch didn't mention the Book, the Watcher and the General."

Delmar muttered, "So that's why Haleb and the Eagle Troops from White Stone have been commissioned. The time of the prophecy has come. We must try and prevent General Rakar and Eri from coming down the Ladder."

The soldier again lowered his head and said, "Masters."

They nodded for him to continue.

"General Rakar and the Watcher have already descended the Ladder."

Elmore stood and shouted, "What of the book and the Angels of the Ages Guards?"

"They have entered Todd's Creek and are preparing to make known the secrets of the book."

"Which means Princess Kaylee will be with the book. What disguise will Princess Kaylee be wearing?" Delmar growled.

"That of Effie Brown. She has positioned herself by the tree line near three of the dark kingdoms' most faithful, the Jacksons. They are neighbors of the earthling Rachel Harris, the one who will receive the mysteries."

A blank expression covered Delmar's face, "I have wondered why Rehabiah, took the form of Cordilia Dawson and was sent to Rachel Harris, and now we know why."

Maric rubbed his chin and said, "My Generals, I have yet another new piece of information."

"Say on," Delmar ordered.

"The earthling Rachel Harris has inherited the prophetic mantel from a White Stone warrior by the name of Margaret Daniels."

Through clinched teeth, Demise growled, "She served with the Ancient Ones in the beginning. Raptor, ruler of the Eagle army and sworn defender of White Stone, counseled Margaret, teaching her about the priceless stones that fill the streams from Wisdom Mountain. Raptor not only lived in Wisdom fields but visited often the Garden of Fire. He walked in the holy fire where the Most High dwells."

Demise turned his sharp eyes to Delmar and muttered, "If Raptor walked with Margaret, you can be sure he has already introduced himself to this earthling Rachel. Damn him! Damn them all!"

Delmar pulled his sword and placed the point under the soldier's chin and declared, "Take these words to the commanding force of Queen Jewel's army, Shemed and Telmar. Tell them to gather every available troop and have them in place for the war that is upon Gray Stone."

Elmore laughed, "The soldiers of the Most High are no match for the Dark Kingdom!"

Demise snarled, "You fool! If the mysteries of the book are released, they will bring a total devastation to our queen and her kingdom."

Chapter Six
Raptor

*J*ohn would be home in three days, so Rachel wanted everything perfect. She placed his robe across the old rocking chair that sat in the corner beside the dark cherry dresser. Rachel glided her fingers across the back of the chair.

She folded the oak leaf quilt arrayed in a variety of brightly colored leaves on a white background, and she placed it neatly across the antique cedar chest that belonged to her grandmother. Inside the chest were stored the treasures she inherited from her mother and grandmother. Rachel knelt and took a quick look inside the chest. The sweet smell of cedar filled her nostrils as she raised the lid. Her grandmother's silver brush and comb set lay on top of her mother's faded flannel pajama shirt. Removing the shirt, her eyes fastened on what she considered the greatest treasure of all, her grandmother's mink cape. Both the lustrous dark brown fur and gray satin lining were hand stitched. Taking the cape from the chest, she draped it around her shoulders and hurried to the full-length mirror in the corner. It looked as though it was tailor-fit just for her. She ran the palm of her hand down the soft fur. For a moment, Rachel closed her eyes and embraced the thought that along with the cape, she also inherited her grandmother's strong faith in God.

She remembered her grandmother sharing with her the many visions, dreams, encounters with angels—good and bad—and about a giant eagle she called Raptor. Her grandmother would place the cape around her shoulder and pray the words she still heard so clearly, 'Most High God, I pray the anointing of Elijah rest upon Rachel. Allow her eyes to be open that she may behold the diamond flakes on emerald leaves that live on the Ancient Tree. I call forth Raptor and the White Stallion to lead her to the Ancient Stump that she may partake of the sweet nectar that flows from the root of that tree.'

Lately, Rachel felt her grandmother's prayers had been granted for she too had been seeing visions. The first vision had scared her beyond reason. She had put the cape around her shoulders and looked into a full-length mirror that sat near the foot of her bed. Rachel looked down at the beautiful brown fur, and when she looked back into the mirror, a giant eagle was standing upright behind her. He held his head high, as he spoke to Rachel's fear.

"Why are you afraid? I'm a servant of the Most High God as you are," the eagle said in a low voice.

Rachel could still hear so plainly as she remembered the first vision. Trembling, she had neared the great eagle who stood seven feet tall.

His wing-span was extraordinary. His eyes were a magnificent pale gray and his pupils, black as coal. The feathers on his head and neck were a brilliant white. His huge gold feet displayed his black razor-sharp talons. He slightly raised his wings flaunting his dark brown feathers that were the same color as the cape that covered her shoulders. His distinct eyes looked at her, then the door. "Follow me," he had said in a voice of comfortable authority. As he turned and walked through the door, his long white tail feathers spread like an exquisite fan.

She followed close behind.

As they stepped through the doorway, they entered a flourishing green pasture. Eagles and angels were everywhere. They all stepped aside as the towering watchful leader entered. Rachel gasped when she heard them calling the eagle a name she had heard many times before from her mother, Raptor. As she walked, a great company of angels and eagles followed her.

She quickly had asked, "Raptor, why are they following me?"

He replied without turning, "You think too highly of yourself. They're not following you. They are and will always follow the mantel."

She looked down at her grandmother's mink cape she had placed around her shoulders moments before. "The mantel," she said softly as she touched her fingertips to the fur.

Rachel gasped as the large mahogany grandfather clock in the living room chimed. Immediately, everything was back to normal. With no time to ponder what had just taken place, she hurriedly put the cape away and went to check on dinner. Rushing past the window, she caught a glimpse of John coming up the walk. In haste, she pulled at her yellow cotton dress, straightened her belt and adjusted the white lace collar. She gave a rapid glance in the mirror to check her raven black hair, took a deep breath and opened the door.

John stopped, removed his hat and locked his eyes to hers.

A smile spread across her face as John hurried to her opened arms.

She felt like a teenager, although she was 40 years old.

In the kitchen, John stopped and glanced around the room. Knotty pine cabinets filled the walls, and the green marble tile had a shine that would pass a military inspection. The aroma of fried chicken and apple cake filled the house. He closed his eyes and announced with sheer delight, "It's so good to be home."

After supper, they snuggled in front of the rock fireplace. Family pictures and tall candles sat arrayed the fireboard. Silky, floral paper covered the walls. the solid oak floors were graced with large, hand-woven, wool area rugs.

Enthralled by Rachel's beauty, John gently stroked her cheek and whispered, "I've never seen you more radiant. Something different? What is it?"

Her response caught John off guard. "Honey, you know, after Dr. Wells and the doctors in Norfolk told us that we couldn't have a baby, I wouldn't settle for that."

John studied her face and listened intently. Rachel licked her lips and continued telling the story about the angel Eri and the son that God promised.

"After he told me his name, he said, 'Rachel, I am your Watcher. I will be your son's Watcher as well.' Then he vanished. His eyes were so . . . so I don't know how to describe them. It was like he could see straight through me. As long as I live, I'll never forget his stare."

John gazed at Rachel. After a moment, he took a deep breath and quickly blew it out. "An angel? How do you know it was an angel? Did he wear a shining robe and have muscles everywhere?"

"Exactly!"

"Really?"

She nodded, "Yes. Light literally emanated from him."

John ran his fingers through his hair and sighed, "My God!"

Rachel started to speak.

He put his finger to her lips and whispered, "I don't understand it; yet it's so real."

Rachel looked into John's eyes and stroked his cheek. "I love you."

"I love you too. Honey, this is beyond belief."

Rachel gently kissed his ear and whispered, "One thing that is not beyond belief is tonight I will conceive our son."

Chapter Seven

Rachel Tells John What Happened

*J*ohn and Rachel rose early the next morning, wanting to spend as much time as possible together. He would leave in two days and be gone for two weeks. John stood in the doorway, looking at the beautiful flowers that lined the walk. Shadowy silhouettes sprang from the rolling hills that were dark only minutes earlier.

Rachel was at the kitchen table, pouring orange juice. Pausing, she looked at John's tall slender frame and his slightly graying, dark brown hair. His eyes were the color of the sky on a clear sunny day. It was his blue eyes that caught Rachel's attention the first time she saw him.

Setting the juice carton down, she walked up behind him, slipped her arms around his waist and whispered, "A penny for your thoughts."

Facing her, he replied, "I've been thinking . . . ," he sighed and continued, "about what you told me yesterday."

"About the angel?"

"Precisely."

He put his hands around her slender shoulders. "I need to hear it again."

Rachel wondered about the solemn demeanor that filled his countenance. She took his hands, pulled him toward the table and said, "Come sit down and drink your juice while I tell you."

After taking a sip of her juice, Rachel set her glass down but didn't release it. She looked at the half-filled glass, took a deep breath and repeated what had taken place. She went to the door and looked out. Her large, brown eyes filled with tears. "It's all like a dream," she uttered.

John put his hand on her shoulder. "Yes, and a scary dream. An angel doesn't announce the birth of an ordinary child." His mind filled with questions as he looked toward heaven.

She looked at John in wonderment.

***

Thoughts of a son swirled in their minds as John mowed the grass for the last time before winter and Rachel sat in the porch swing, replacing a button on John's shirt. She went to check dinner.

After finishing the lawn, John sat in the porch swing, pushing back and forth enjoying the cool fall breeze as he remembered his father and wished he could be there to see his son.

When Rachel saw that John had finished mowing, she fixed him a glass of iced tea. She opened the screen door.

John smiled and reached for the tea. "Honey, you read my mind."

She sat beside him and patted his leg. "Supper will be ready soon." Tilting her head, she teased, "Because you've worked so hard, I made you cornbread."

"That's my girl! You know how to spoil me." John squinted as he looked across the field. "I think someone is moving into that old house near the Jackson's."

"Oh, yeah, I forgot to tell you with all the excitement," Rachel said. "Sheriff Butler came by and said an elderly woman by the name of Effie Brown is moving in. She told him her only family is her mixed- breed mongrel dog named Winston. I want to go visit soon and see if maybe she needs some help."

"Where's she from?"

"Allen said she was from Benson."

John shrugged. "Why don't we go over now, say hello and offer our assistance?"

Chapter Eight
Agreement

As they neared the old plank shack, the loud, rapid barking of Effie's dog was continuous. The house had two small windows on either side of the door and a narrow, covered front porch across the front. Just as Rachel started to knock on the door, it came open causing her to step back.

Miss Brown looked at least 70 or more, with long, gray hair twisted up in a bun, a little overweight, and standing about 5'3". There was a pleasant aura about Effie, although she wasn't too eager to display it. Her eyes were a beautiful hazel color and her skin, pale. She was holding the dog leash in one hand and a stick cane in the other. The dog lunged at Rachel. Effie gave a quick jerk on his leash and growled, "Shut up you no-account dog, or I'll give you away."

The dog settled instantly.

Effie gazed at John and snapped, "It's hard to find a good dog nowadays. Do you have a dog?"

Taken by surprise, John stammered, "No . . . no we don't have any pets."

Holding her stare, she asked, "Are you afraid of dogs?"

He glanced at Rachel. "No, we . . . we just don't have one."

Effie leaned toward him and muttered, "You should have a dog. What if your wife don't want to talk to you? Who you going to talk to . . . yourself?" She patted the dog's head and laughed, "I've been threatening to give Winston away for ten years."

Rachel quickly introduced herself and John. Effie managed a partial smile, a hello, but did not bother to invite them inside.

John and Rachel offered their assistance with the move.

Effie declined. As they stepped off the porch to leave, Effie called out, "Thank you for your visit. Rachel, come back soon for a cup of coffee or something a little stronger, if you desire." She pulled the dog's ear and laughed. "I'll let John take Winston for a walk while we chat."

On the way back home, John muttered, "That woman doesn't even know me, yet I think she hates me!"

Rachel laughed aloud and assured him that she was just an elderly woman having a little fun.

John didn't agree. "She doesn't know me. I might add it was you she invited back for coffee and chit chat while I hang out with Winston. They both giggled about how Effie and Cordilia would hit it off.

After supper they retired back to the porch swing to enjoy their last cup of coffee of the day. The sun had set, and a full moon was peeking through the scattered dark clouds.

John tightened his brow and asked, "How long before you can tell if you're pregnant?"

"I'll check with Dr. Wells in about three months." Rachel crossed her arms. "I already know our son is in my womb without an examination."

John put his hand on her stomach and smiled.

Rachel's expression turned somber. "John."

"Yes?"

"Should we . . ." She paused and began to play with the zipper on her sweater.

"Should we what?"

"Should we tell anyone about the angel? The only one I would even consider telling is Cordilia."

John stood. In deep thought, he went to the edge of the porch, looked toward heaven and shook his head. "I don't know."

Later that night while lying in bed, John faced Rachel and said, "Honey, the angel bringing the news about our son is a very holy thing to us. Let's keep it between us and God."

"I agree."

Pushing the covers down, they got on their knees in the center of the bed. The room was dark with only a glimmer of light from the full moon. Eye-to-eye with Rachel, John said, "We vow not to tell anyone about the angel, Eri, except maybe Cordilia. Amen."

Rachel lowered her head and smiled.

After they made the vow, a sweet smell filled the room as a soft breeze swirled the fragrance until the aroma of hundreds of roses hovered over them. Just as fast as it appeared, it was gone.

"What was that, Rachel?" John whispered.

"I don't know."

Shaken, John said, "My God, what manner of child is our son going to be?"

It seemed they had barely closed their eyes when the alarm clock went off. Rachel sluggishly sat up, and squinted at the clock. "John, it's time to get up."

"I need ten more minutes," he moaned.

"No, come on."

He opened his eyes and playfully pinned her shoulders to the bed and said, "I need coffee."

She agreed, "I'll make coffee while you get a shower. Deal?"

"Deal. But first I want you more than I want coffee." John pressed his lips to Rachel's with a passion that made every desire come alive in her. His intimate touch never grew old.

Chapter Nine
John Has a Trip

$\mathcal{N}$oticing the clock, Rachel nudged John's arm. "John, it's 7:15. Your train leaves at 8:45. Hurry up!"

As they pulled into the station, the train was waiting. John promptly got his luggage from the trunk and checked the bags. One last kiss, I love you, and John ran to get on the train as it slowly moved away from the station.

As he hopped up on the first step, he waved goodbye.

Rachel took a couple of steps forward, raised her hand over her head and waved. Tears filled her eyes as the train pulled out of sight. "I love you, John Harris," she whimpered.

As she walked gradually back to her car, Rachel's emotions got the better of her. She frantically searched the bottom of her purse for her car keys. Unable to see for the tears, she snapped. "Great day in the morning, where are the keys? I should have never put them in my purse to start with. I should have left them in the switch." Finally relieved, her fingers felt the cool metal.

As she opened the door of her black, 1939 Ford, John's cologne lingered. She put the key into the ignition and turned it. The car started right away, but she wasn't ready to move yet. With both hands gripping the steering wheel, she leaned her head forward and rested it on the wheel.

Suddenly, her body jerked when a voice asked, "Rachel, are you okay?"

Looking up through her swollen eyes, she saw Pastor Kenneth Miller. Trying to grab a tissue with one hand and roll the window down with the other, she whimpered, "Pastor Miller, you almost scared the life out of me." Drying her tears, she responded to his question. "Yes . . . yes, I'm fine. John just left, and for some reason, my emotions are a mess."

The reverend gently patted her shoulder. "I think I know what will cheer you up; Leah made a chocolate cake this morning. I'll have Paula bring some over to you later today."

"Thank you, Pastor, that would be wonderful. Leah makes the best cakes I have ever tasted. Be sure to tell Paula to come later and have some cake with me. I want to get her opinion on some ideas that I have for the Christmas program. I'm going by Cordilia's, but I should be home by 4:00 p.m."

Pastor Miller smiled. "Paula will be glad to hear that. She thinks highly of you and John. If you're sure you're okay, I need to be going."

Rachel nodded. "Yes, thank you."

"If you need anything, just call. I'll see you Sunday if not before." Pastor Miller backed away from the car, and Rachel slowly pulled away.

Feeling better after a hefty cry, Rachel hurried to Cordilia's. Cordilia and Paul Dawson had moved to Todd's Creek three years earlier. From the day they met, Rachel felt as though she and Cordilia were kindred spirits. She was the brassiest woman Rachel ever met; she had a unique way with words and was the most straightforward woman in Todd's Creek. When wanting to know the truth about something, Rachel asked Cordilia. They were so different, yet perfect for one another.

Rachel grew up in the church and had a mindset toward the things of God. She never tasted alcohol. Cordilia had been to church only a few times as a child, and her mind was on everything but God. Alcohol was a friend to Cordilia for years. She was with too many men to count when she met Paul. However, the many years of hard living produced a mighty woman of faith.

The two women were very different in their physical appearance as well. Cordilia towered at least 6 feet tall while Rachel stood 5'6". Cordilia's long blond hair was a stark contrast to Rachel's ebony hair. Cordilia always smiled and remarked that she could have been a model or a movie star, with her Sophia Loren body. "I gave it all up," she said, "because Hollywood didn't want Paul to come with the package. Therefore, I stepped down from my glamorous life to keep Paul and move to Todd's Creek."

Although outspoken, Cordilia had a big heart, and she was first to reach out if a need arose. The two did almost everything together. Going shopping in Norfolk on occasion was a favorite. Above all, they learned from each other's strengths.

As Rachel pulled up the driveway, Cordilia opened the door and stepped outside. Rachel waved as she parked the car. Cordilia could tell that something was up from the smile on her friend's face. Cordilia hurried to greet her.

"Rachel Harris, what are you up to? I know John left for Washington a bit ago. I usually have to baby you for at least three days, but here you are with a smile the size of three bananas." Cordilia laughed aloud as she took Rachel's shoulders, jumped up and down and asked, "Rachel, what is it? Has somebody left you a lot of money? Are we rich?"

Ecstatic, Rachel replied, "No, something better."

Cordilia frowned. "Better than money? What's better than money?"

Rachel took Cordilia's hand and pulled her toward the house. "I want you to be sitting for this." Rachel opened the screen door and led her to the sofa in the living room. "Now sit!" she ordered.

"You sound like you're talking to a dog, Rachel."

"For goodness sake, Cordilia, hush and listen!"

Rachel put her hands in a prayer position at her chest and began, "What would be the last thing you would guess?"

Cordilia raised both hands in the air and exclaimed in exasperation, "Here we go! I don't want to guess. Just tell me!"

"Okay, okay, I'll tell you . . ." Rachel paused.

Desperately wanting to know, Cordilia stood, put her hands on her hips and exclaimed, "For heaven's sake, Rachel, tell me, or I'm going to pop."

Rachel blurted out, "I'm going to . . . to . . ." Suddenly shaken, Rachel gasped. With her head spinning and pulse racing, she pressed her fingers to her temples.

Cordilia grabbed Rachel's arm, and helped her sit down. "What's wrong with you, Rachel. You're white as a ghost."

"I . . . I . . . I'm just a little dizzy, that's all."

Cordilia squatted in front of her, took her hands, and asked, "You're seeing the soldiers again, aren't you?"

Rachel anxiously nodded. "Yes! Yes, I am."

"Have you told John about this?"

Rachel slowly shook her head no.

"All right, that's it! This has been going on for some time now, and not once have you talked about it. Today you're going to tell me what you're seeing, or you'll stay here until you do!"

Rachel frowned. "You're right. I want to tell you. I should have told you the other day."

"That's right you should have. Go ahead."

"I . . . I feel as though someone or something is chasing me; I'm running as fast as I can to get away. I can hardly breathe. I never see anyone chasing after me. I just know they're there. When I first saw anything, it scared me so badly I couldn't say anything. I've never experienced anything like this. At first the vision only lasted

37

a few seconds. But now, they're lasting longer and longer each time. What's going on with me, Cordilia?"

Cordilia rubbed the back of her neck and shook her finger at Rachel. "One of two things is going on. You're nuts, which you're not, or God is trying to tell you something through the visions. Does this happen only when you're awake?"

"No. Sometimes when I'm sleeping, I see the same things. I wake up in a sweat with my feet hurting so badly."

"Your feet?"

"Yes, my feet! The pain is excruciating; yet when I check them, they're fine. When the vision ends, the pain ends."

"Is that all?"

"That should enough, but no, there's more."

They sat down at the dining room table and Rachel continued, "It's all so scattered. I . . . I see soldiers traveling through a long field, heading for a mountain. They're rough and hardened, yet kind. They're fierce, yet have perfect peace. They're in full armor—a large sword in one hand and a gold shield in the other. I hear them saying with such boldness, 'We will stand with you.' My God, they're talking to me, Cordilia."

Cordilia leaned back in her chair. "It sounds like an all-out war is going to take place." Cordilia looked at Rachel and said, "Don't you worry. I'm going to be right there to back you up and stop some of those fiery darts from going straight through you."

Rachel embraced Cordilia and moved toward the old upright piano in the dining room, "Let's sing a song. Like Paul and Silas when they were imprisoned. In the midnight, they sang and caused the earth to quake."

Cordilia jumped up. "That sounds like the right thing to do!"

Cordilia joined Rachel who began to play. A couple of the keys were missing, and one didn't have full sound. Nevertheless, that didn't stop the glorious music as Rachel played.

Cordilia lifted her voice in "Amazing Grace." Tears rolled down her cheeks as she lifted her hands in praise. For a moment, she closed her eyes as Rachel continued to play.

Cordilia knew her sinful ways where God had brought her from, and this song always served as a reminder that it all began at The Cross.

Suddenly, Rachel stopped playing. "Cordilia, I almost forgot to tell you."

"You better tell me something. You almost scared me to death catching your breath like that."

"You know the old plank house that sits near the tree line just on the other side of the Jackson's property?"

"Yeah."

"Somebody moved in there yesterday."

"Really? Is that place livable?"

"It must be."

"Do you know who moved in?"

Rachel laughed, "Yes, John and I went to visit her yesterday."

"And her name is?"

"Effie Brown. She's not married, maybe a widow. I don't know. An older woman from Benson or near there."

Cordilia questioned, "Children or grandchildren?"

"I don't think so. She has an old mongrel dog that's about as big as she is." Rachel couldn't contain her laughter.

Cordilia began to laugh with her. After a moment she asked, "Rachel what am I so tickled about?"

She told her about Effie's conversation with John. "You should have seen the look on his face. It was hysterical. You and I have to go visit soon." They continued to sing when Rachel thought of the time. Again, she caught her breath so hard Cordilia jumped. "What's wrong, Rachel?"

Pushing the piano stool back, Rachel frantically asked, "What time is it?"

Cordilia looked at her watch. "It's 3:15."

Hurrying to the door, she explained. "I forgot Paula is coming over at 4:00. By the way, I'm going to ask her to help with the Christmas play."

"I'm glad. She's not been herself lately. I recognize some of her symptoms, and it's not good."

"I know, that's why I want to make this a special day for her."

Cordilia smiled and shook her head. "Does this mean the tea set?"

"You know it does." Rachel started out the door, stopped, turned and said, "What I was going to tell you earlier I'll hold until later. It must not have been the right time."

"Ah, come on, Rachel, you're going to leave me guessing? I can't stand that. I'll get all stressed out trying to figure out what it is."

Rachel replied as she hurried toward the car, "When the time is right, not until then, so don't ask. Call you later."

Cordilia shouted, "I have something to tell you too, but not today, maybe Sunday. What do you think of that? I hope you don't get all frazzled thinking about what it could be."

Rachel waved as she drove away, hoping to have enough time to get everything set up before Paula arrived.

Chapter Ten
Visiting Cordilia

When Rachel parked the car, she looked at her watch, knowing she didn't have much time. It was 3:25p.m. Hurrying from the garage, she saw Raptor standing near the porch.

He started walking toward her.

She stopped and waited for him to approach.

Raptor had visited Rachel several times, but still she was amazed each time he appeared. He stopped in front of her and said, "Rachel, follow me."

She had learned to follow without question. This visit, she hurried her pace to keep up with his long strides. As she moved, she felt something on her shoulders. She glanced down to see the mink cape.

"Where are we going?" she asked breathlessly.

Before he responded, they entered a thick fog. Raptor called out, "Keep up, Rachel, or you could get lost very easily." Suddenly, Raptor stopped, put his wings in front of him and pulled the fog apart like opening a curtain. He motioned for Rachel to go through first. Feeling anxious, she paused before entering. As she stepped forward, she saw seven magnificent doors. Rachel cut her eyes to Raptor and asked, "What are these doors?"

"Choose one and find out," he replied.

Rachel looked at the doors and then to Raptor.

"Choose, but choose wisely," he said. His watchful eyes observed as Rachel walked to one of the doors and looked back at him. "It's good to ask for help when you're not sure; however, this time you must make your own choice."

Rachel touched each door and then came back to the one in the middle. She touched her finger to the hard wood and said, "This one."

"Why did you choose that door?" he asked.

"Because it's the one I felt I should."

Raptor sighed and lowered his eyes. "Open the door and see what you have chosen."

Rachel slowly pushed the door open, anticipating what she would find. At first, she could see nothing. He told her to step forward. When she did, she found herself going down a staircase on the side of a mountain. They stopped and viewed the plush green valley with several gigantic brown eagles looking toward them. They continued until they came to the bottom of the stairs. Rachel walked out into the grass a little way. There she saw that several red eagles had joined with the brown ones.

The red eagles came from the hills, but they didn't fly to the valley. The eagles talked with each other. Then they spread their wings and started to fly away together. The red eagles went in front of the brown ones. As they flapped their vast wings, the force of the wind blew Rachel down. When the wind calmed down, Rachel was standing in her dining room. She looked at the clock, not knowing how long she had been gone. To her surprise, it was still 3:25 p.m.— almost time for Paula's visit. Rachel tried to clear her mind as she hustled to get everything ready.

Chapter 11
Paula's Visit

*P*aula was a beautiful young woman with long auburn hair, fair skin and large green eyes. She had been in Rachel's Sunday school class for the past two years. Rachel had watched her grow from a little kid with pigtails into a young woman who all the boys swooned over. Lately, Paula's interest was focused on Chris Jackson, Rachel's neighbor.

Chris was a clean-cut young man, very proper, polite and good-looking. He too was in Rachel's class. Lately, Rachel noticed Chris was paying more and more attention to Paula. Although chemistry was stirring between the two, something just wasn't right.

Tea would be served in the sunroom, which was made up of large full-length windows. This was Rachel's place to sit and watch the rain, snow or breathtaking beauty of the fall colors. Her favorite season was spring when everything brought new life. Perhaps Paula would feel the warmth of this special place too.

After all, Paula was at a new season in her life— graduating from high school in only a few months and going off to college. A new school and a time of new maturity would enter her life. Being away from her parents for the first time also meant new battles in her spiritual life. Rachel felt that battle had already begun.

A large floral area rug rested underneath a white wicker table with a glass top. The table seated four. A red linen tablecloth draped with white Victorian lace and a red poinsettia that sat in the center of table provided the final touch." Rachel thought aloud, "This is perfect!"

Admiring the table, her mind raced back to her childhood. Her mom often played tea party with her. She cherished those memories. Remembering, Rachel went to the highly polished, cherry china cabinet. There she removed her treasured porcelain rose pattern tea set, brought it to the sunroom and placed it on the table.

Rachel recalled running in the front door from school when she was 10 years old. Her mother had stopped her as she entered the house.

"Rachel, I have a surprise for you. I want you to have a keepsake that will always remind you of the special tea parties we have. Now close your eyes and no peeking!"

Rachel put her hands over her eyes, "What is it, Mama?

"Stay here a minute."

Rachel heard her mom putting something on the table.

"Okay, open your eyes."

Rachel's mouth dropped open as she clapped her hands. On the table sat a white porcelain tea set covered with red roses. Recalling, Rachel picked up the teapot and held it to her chest. In her mind she could smell her mom's perfume. Speaking aloud, Rachel said the words she said to her mom that day, "Mom, I'll keep it forever."

The teakettle whistled, clearing Rachel's mind. Paula, is not my daughter, but I want to share my tea set with her today. As she poured the hot water into the teapot, she heard a knock at the door.

Paula was right on time with the promised chocolate cake. Rachel took the cake and led the way to the sunroom.

Paula glanced around and said, "You shouldn't have gone to so much trouble."

"No trouble at all. May I take your jacket?"

"No thanks, I'm fine."

Paula sat down at the table as Rachel poured the tea.

"What a beautiful tea set, Rachel!"

With pride, Rachel said, "My mom gave it to me when I was 10. I've had it for thirty years. It's my most prized possession."

"I can see why it would be."

Sitting across the table from Paula, Rachel said, "I would like for you to help Cordilia and myself with the Christmas program this year."

"I guess I could help. What do you have in mind?"

"I want to bring out how Mary must have felt having an angel tell her that she was going to have a son, keeping in mind she wasn't married and was a virgin. Greater still, this baby would be the promised Messiah. I think you would be a perfect Mary."

"Sure, I'll give it a try. What an honor!""

"Great!"

Paula looked toward a window that viewed the Jackson house. "Rachel," she said without taking her eyes from the window, "Who did you have in mind to play Joseph?"

"I don't know. Do you have someone in mind who lives next door?"

"Yeah."

Paula began to rock slowly. "I love this room. I'm sure you did the decorating yourself."

"Yes, I did, and thank you."

"This is a big house for two people. Did you and John choose not to have children?"

"We've always wanted children, but until now we haven't been successful."

Paula turned her head slightly, "Is there a news flash in that statement?"

"What?"

"You said 'until now.' If I'm not prying, of course."

"No, no, you're not prying." Rachel stared at Paula. "John and I are going to have a baby." Rachel put her teacup down and stood.

"That's great, Rachel! I'm so happy for you."

Rachel smiled. "We're so excited." She quickly added, "Please don't tell anyone, okay? No one knows yet."

Paula moved to the edge of the rocking chair. "Rachel, your secret is safe with me."

"Thank you, Paula."

"When is the baby due?"

"In nine months." Rachel said with a closed-lip grin.

"Nine months? Can Dr. Wells tell that soon?"

"I haven't seen Dr. Wells. I just know in my spirit."

Surprised, Paula questioned, "So that's why the focus on Mary in the Christmas drama?"

"Well, yes."

"Maybe you should play the part of Mary." Paula fidgeted in her chair. She stood and walked to the window. "I'd better be going."

Surprised, Rachel said, "You haven't finished your tea or eaten your cake."

"I have some errands to run, and it's getting late. Mom and Dad want me home before 9:00 p.m. Do you believe that? I'm 18 years old, and they still treat me like I'm 12."

Rachel, wanting to take advantage of the moment, asked, "Paula, is something bothering you?"

"No. I have some things to do. That doesn't mean there's something wrong."

"Of course not. I just sense an agitation in your behavior lately. If I can help . . ."

"Thank you, no. The tea was lovely." Paula leaned forward and picked up the tray that held the tea set. "Let me help you clear the table before I go."

Shaking her head, Rachel replied, "No that's fine."

"I insist," Paula said as she headed down the hall for the kitchen.

As Rachel picked up the cake, she heard a crash resound down the hall. She put the cake down and hurried to see if Paula was okay.

Rachel halted as she entered the kitchen. Gasping, she put both hands over her mouth. On the kitchen floor in a million tiny pieces lay her treasured porcelain tea set. Every emotion in her was screaming in pain.

"I'm so sorry, Rachel, I tripped, and it flew out of my hands."

Rachel struggled to keep from crying out in pain. "That's all right, Paula. You're not hurt, are you?"

"No, I'm fine. Let me pay you for it."

"No, no," Rachel said, shaking her head.

"At least, let me clean it up for you," Paula whispered as she stooped down to pick up a broken piece.

Rachel put her hand on Paula's shoulder. "No, I'll do it," she said softly.

"Well, I better be going," Paula said as she headed for the door.

"I don't want you to feel bad about this Paula." Rachel extended her arms, hugged Paula and continued, "It's all right."

"Thanks, Rachel, and again I'm so sorry." Paula hurried out the door.

Cordilia passed Paula pulling into the Jackson's driveway as she pulled into Rachel's.

Rachel was devastated. Emotions of anger and pain were blooming. Tears rolled down her cheeks as she stooped, and began to pick up the pieces. With each piece, the tears fell harder until she could barely see what she was doing. Cordilia saw Rachel slumped in the floor. She hurried to her friend.

"Rachel, what happened?"

"It was an accident."

"Did you drop the tray?"

Sobbing Rachel replied, "No, Paula did."

They finished picking up the broken pieces, and sat down at the table. Cordilia consoled Rachel until her tears dried. Rachel drank a cool glass of water. "Cordilia, I'm so glad you're here. Did you come for a reason?" she asked.

"Yes, I did. I was praying for you to have a good visit with Paula. While praying, I saw glass breaking all around you, and you were on the floor crying. So, I rushed over to check on you."

Cordilia asked Rachel to come spend the night with her and Paul, but Rachel felt she needed some time alone and Cordilia left. With her energy drained, Rachel wanted to lie down for a few minutes.

She pulled John's pillow to her chest and whispered, "I miss you." Closing her eyes, she imagined John's strong arms around her. With that safe, warm feeling, sleep overtook her.

Chapter 12
Paula's Sarcasm

≠$\mathscr{P}$ aula visited with Chris for a couple of hours before going home. Emily and Jerry Jackson forbad Chris falling in love with Paula. The dark kingdom advised Chris his job was to take away young girls' virginity and then leave them. His parents were very concerned about Chris's actions toward Paula. Jerry, was the president of Todd's Creek National Bank and a member of the town council. Emily did volunteer work at the high school. Status meant everything to them. Chris could care less about status. He purposely played down his feeling for Paula to his parents. Their relationship developed into secret meetings where they became sexually active.

Paula and Chris discussed their beliefs in God at times, but found, to Paula's surprise, they had very little in common. Therefore, the subject was often avoided.

Chris invited Paula to a couple of meetings that

he and his parents attended at a little antique shop in Norfolk called "A Journey in Time." The first time Paula attended, she was surprised to see Peggy Welsh, Dr. Wells's nurse, playing such an active part in the gathering. However, the biggest surprise was Dr. Wells himself presiding over the meetings. Many red flags went up for Paula, one being, why in Norfolk at an antique shop? The owner, Delilah, was an elderly lady who wore a black wool turban even in the heat of summer. Paula was confused about who Chris truly worshiped, God or what he called the dark kingdom?

There were constant lies about where they were going; otherwise, her parents would have never let her go. Emily and Jerry also lied. They told Paula's parents they were going to Norfolk to visit Chris's grandparents. Paula's motive was never to worship anything or anyone, but to be with Chris. At the last meeting, Dr. Wells gave her a black velvet pouch with a gold drawstring containing a large emerald crystal.

When Paula arrived home, Leah, her mom, was sitting on the sofa reading the paper.

Leah was a beautiful woman. She looked more like Paula's sister than her mother.

There was times Paula resented her for looking so young and beautiful. Unknown to Leah, Paula felt in competition with her and hated it; not that she wanted her mom to be less attractive or have a sour personality. Paula couldn't put her finger on what her motives were. Rage would come over her at times. Was it jealousy? Or insecurities she had never dealt with?

"Hi, Mom."

"Hi, honey. How was your visit with Rachel?"

"It was wonderful," Paula said as she kissed Leah on the forehead.

Hurrying by, Paula said, "Mom, I would like to lie down for a while. Okay?"

"Of course. I'll call you as soon as your father gets home."

"Where is Dad?"

"He had a board meeting tonight."

Vindictive, Paula lashed out, "I should have known. He always has time for something, but never time for you and me."

"Paula."

Unrelenting, Paula continued, "Well, it's true. You sit here night after night right up until bedtime waiting for Dad to come home. It's not enough that I don't have a father, but you don't have a husband either."

Leah stood and threw the paper down, "That's enough, Paula! Your father has time for us, and you know it. Maybe he's not here every time we want him to be, but he's here as much as possible."

Standing firm, Paula declared, "No, he's not! Why do you always take up for him?"

Overwhelmed at her behavior, Leah questioned, "Paula, what's gotten into you lately? You've never acted this way before."

"Mom, I've wised up to the truth, and you haven't. You will deny it until the day you die, but down deep you know I'm telling the truth. You're not happy sitting here, just waiting for Dad to get home. I know you need him for more than a roll in the sheets!"

Shocked at the statement, Leah got in Paula's face and shouted, "Roll in the sheets?" Where did you get this, 'roll in the sheets?' Another thing, young lady, our sex life is none of your business. Do you understand me?"

Paula frowned, tightened her lips and gazed into her mom's eyes. "Sometimes you act like you're afraid of him. I can't think of any other reason why you would put up with him."

Furious and hurt, Leah shouted, "Paula, I don't want to hear another word, do you hear me?"

Paula squinted her eyes and shook her head, "Yes, Mother, I hear you, but did you hear me? I don't say these things to hurt you. I love you, Mom, but I can't live with a lie as well as you can." Paula ran up the stairs to her room, slammed the door and locked it.

Chapter 13
Getting Involved

*P*aula growled through gritting teeth as she pulled her jacket off, "I hate this," Still holding the jacket, Paula remembered the green stone Dr. Wells gave her.

I wonder if the stone will do all Dr. Wells said it would do. Paula thought about it, reached into her jacket pocket and pulled out the black velvet pouch. She held it tightly, not sure whether to open it or not. After a moment, she muttered, "What can it hurt? At this point, I'll try anything. I'm so sick of all this! I'd better call Peggy to be sure what to do." Paula paused then dialed the number.

Peggy Welsh was 25 years old and had moved to Todd's Creek right out of nursing school. Her long, sandy blond hair and figure were perfect. Peggy's free life style and bubbly personality worked like a magnet on the teenagers. The girls wanted to be like her, and all the boys had a definite crush on her. She took a particular interest in understanding Paula needs.

She invited Paula for sleepovers, and introduced

her to red wine and her first cigarette. They talked about life, boys and sex. Peggy encouraged her to attend the meeting at Norfolk. She vowed Paula would never be the same and went further, saying, "The dark kingdom will grant anything you desire." At this point, Paula desired to escape the chaos churning inside her.

Peggy's house was a place for Paula and Chris to be alone. When they came for a visit, Peggy would leave.

The house was a setup—dim lights, soft music playing, a blanket spread in front of the fireplace, a bottle of red wine and one long stem rose. The romantic setting, the wine and the warm glow of the fire proved too much for Paula. When Chris looked into her eyes, he began to passionately kiss her, and all her resistance surrendered to his touch.

She was a virgin and had shared this with Peggy. Chris felt there was nothing wrong with having sex with a girl. His duty for the dark force was to draw Paula into sin with his seduction and take her virginity away. The trap was set, and they both fell.

Peggy answered the phone. Paula asked her right away about the green stone. Peggy assured her using the stone would give her a high she would never get over. If she felt sad, it would make her happy. If she felt ugly, it would make her feel beautiful. If inadequate, it wiould produce a boldness that would withstand anything.

At Peggy's urging, Paula opened the pouch, a green mist radiated from the top. Frantic, Paula gasped, "Peggy, there's a green fog coming out of the pouch!"

"Good! Telmar is pleased with you. Hold the stone over your head and call for Queen Jewel to energize you."

Her hand shaking, Paula held the stone over her head and paused, knowing what she was about to do was wrong. Nevertheless, she called out, "Queen Jewel, I need your strength."

A swirling green mist came out of the stone and hovered over her. The fog started at her head, moved down her body and encircled her feet until there was a glow all around her. Although she didn't see anything but the vapor circling around her, it felt as though someone was touching her all over her body. The touch took her breath away leaving her unable to move or resist anything that was happening to her.

Sheer exhilaration and boldness filled her. Unhurriedly the fog moved in front of her and a life form like she had never seen came into sight. His beauty was that of a Greek god. His long, shiny black hair, fair skin and eyes like pools of blue water were captivating. He stood at least 6'5" with more muscle than she had ever could have imagined.

Smiling at Paula, exposing his perfect white teeth, the being said, "The dark kingdom is pleased with you." He slowly viewed her from head to toe and whispered, "So am I."

Paula was so scared she visibly trembled. She never saw anything so beautiful and yet so frightening. His strong hand brushed her cheek. At his touch, Paula stepped backward. He put his finger under her chin and said, "Here now, don't be afraid. I'm here to comfort you. If I don't do my job, I'll get in trouble, and we don't want that, do we?" he said as he moved his finger from her chin and put his hand around her throat. His piercing eyes stared deeply into Paula's, he grinned, and he moved backward. He continued, "I loved the way you crashed Rachel's tea set."

Boldness instantly came over Paula. Trough gritted teeth, she replied, "It was my pleasure. If I could have broken it into more pieces, I would have."

Telmar touched his cheek against Paula's. "You're my type of woman. Any time you need me, just call. I'll be here to accommodate you in any way you desire." He proceeded to glide his fingertips down her cheek and whispered in her ear, "I'll take you to the Garden of Fire and introduce to a pleasure you've never tasted."

Before Paula could move, he was gone with the mist. The stone lay cold in her hand.

Astounded by what had taken place, she barely heard the knock at her door. She hurriedly put the stone in a nightstand drawer.

"Paula, please let me in."

She opened the door, "Mom, I'm sorry I didn't hear you."

"Did I hear voices in here?"

"You . . . did, I . . . I was praying. Mom, I didn't mean to say those things to you. Will you please forgive me?"

Leah embraced Paula. "I love you, Paula, and so does your dad. Don't ever doubt that. Okay?"

"I just blew off some steam. I'm sorry."

"We all say things we don't mean at times. "I'm sorry I interrupted your prayer. I'll go and let you finish."

"Mom, I love you."

"I love you." Leah turned to leave. She stopped and sniffed. Puzzled she asked, "What is that awful smell?"

Wide-eyed, Paula asked, "What smell?"

Leah sniffed again and said, "It's repulsive!

Paula looked around the room, "Sorry, Mom, but I don't smell anything."

"Are you sure?" Immediately the smell was cleared. "Maybe it's my sinuses."

Paula closed the door leaned back against it, took a deep breath and exhaled, "That was so close."

She free-fell onto the bed. With great pleasure and fear, she thought about Telmar. Still high from the powerful feeling absorbed from the haze that encircled her, her excitement grew, thinking about the next time she would feel the rush of sheer pleasure and fear again.

Chapter 14
Rachel's Dream

*R*achel slept over four hours when she was awakened by the phone ringing. "Umm, hello," she groaned.

"Hi, honey."

Rachel sat up on the bed and was instantly wide-awake. "John."

"And who else would call you this late at night? Other than Cordilia, of course."

At once he asked, "Honey, have you been thinking about names for our son yet?"

Rachel chuckled. "Not really, have you?"

Without hesitation, he answered, "I have."

"And?"

Elated, he announced, "Stephen Daniel Harris. Is that a noble name or what?"

Rachel teased, pausing before answering.

"Well?" John said with anticipation.

"I love it. Stephen Daniel Harris it will be."

***

Rachel was thrilled to have a name for the baby, but still very tired. The adrenaline from her tea set being broken had taken its toll on her energy. She held John's pillow and prayed until she fell asleep.

Her peaceful sleep was soon interrupted as she began to toss and turn. Distant images began to appear. As they became clearer, she could see herself in a delivery room, ready to give birth to her son. Her pain was very intense. The nurses called the doctor to come to the delivery room. There were several nurses in the room. They all looked the same, dressed in white starched dresses, white stockings, and white tie up shoes. Each of them had long black hair slicked back in a bun and crowned with a white nurse's hat. One nurse was standing beside the birthing table, telling Rachel to push. While pushing, she saw the doctor come into the room. He didn't look up or speak. With a resounding cry and one final hard push, the baby delivered.

Rachel raised her head to see her new son. The doctor held the baby in his large, tanned hands. Sweat dripping from her brow, Rachel looked at the nurse standing beside her and stated firmly, "I want to hold my baby." The nurse was silent. She looked at Rachel, turned and left the room. In a military fashion, the other nurses turned and marched out behind her. The only one left in the room was the doctor who was holding the baby at her feet.

Rachel's raised voice echoed as she cried, "I want my baby."

Slowly the doctor rolled the stool he was sitting on away from the foot of the table. Rachel tried but still could not see his face. Standing, the doctor held the baby out in front of him.

"I want my baby!" she yelled.

Laughter ringed loud in her ears. Without looking up, the doctor growled, "The baby is mine." With that, he raised his head to reveal a hideous-looking being.

Unable to get up, Rachel screamed at the top of her voice, "Give me my baby!"

The baby was no longer in the doctor's hands but in the creature's, mouth. "Never," he roared, and disappeared out of the room with the baby.

Screaming and kicking the covers, she woke up. Her body shook from the reality of the nightmare as she cried uncontrollably.

Stumbling to the bathroom, she held to the sink with one hand and turned the cold water on with the other; she soaked a washcloth and held it to her face with both hands. She pressed the cloth to her face until the warmth of her skin took the chill away. Gradually, she looked into the mirror at her swollen eyes. Her voice broken, she cried, "Oh, God, please help me! What's wrong with me? I feel like I'm falling apart."

Taking deep breaths, she sat on the edge of the bed. She felt it was too early to even call Cordilia. She decided to make a cup of hot chocolate. Perhaps the taste of something warm on her scratchy throat would help. Her head pounded as the image of the hideous figure continued to appear. Seizing the edge of the kitchen sink she cried out, "You will not have my child! I've prayed for this baby, and no demon in hell is going to steal it away from me! In Jesus name."

Needing company. she turned on the radio as she drank her hot chocolate. Afterward she curled up on the sofa.

Chapter 15
Rachel Sees Soldiers

*R*achel awoke to the sun shining through the blinds onto her face. Rising up, she rubbed her eyes, glanced around the room and groaned. "I feel like I've been beat half to death," she said as she turned the radio off. "What time is it? Oh, my goodness, it's 10:00 o'clock."

As fast as possible, she put the coffee on and headed for the shower. There was no way to make Sunday school. Cordilia could cover that. However, she needed to attend the worship service.

"What to wear?" she muttered.

Frantically searching the closet, looking for anything that didn't need ironing, she whined, "I have to make the worship service at 11:00! It's my Sunday to read before Pastor Miller gives the message."

An edgy feeling sent a chill down Rachel's spine as she dressed. Like lightning, she scanned the room. At once, the room began to swirl, and gradually images of the soldiers she had seen for a couple of months appeared. This time they were in small groups. It still wasn't clear where they were all coming from; yet they continued to materialize. A lead soldier with large eyes as green as fresh spring grass stared at her, nodded and continued to march through a long, open valley. Staggered, Rachel held to the bedpost.

"My Lord, what's wrong with me? I'm becoming paranoid? God, what is it? Who is this army, where are they coming from, where are they going, and why am I seeing them? Make them go away if you're not going to tell me!"

With no time left, Rachel made her way to the kitchen and took a quick sip of coffee as she grabbed the car keys from the table. While making sure the door was locked, she heard someone call her name. Immediately, the creature in her nightmare flashed before her. "Rachel," the voice continued to call.

Suddenly, realizing it was Cordilia, she breathed a sigh of relief and rushed to the car. As she urgently locked her fingers around Cordilia's arm she moaned, "Cordilia, I'm so glad it's you."

"Well, who else would have been calling your name at almost 11:00? I was concerned when you didn't show up for class. Paul is covering the class for me so I could come and check on you. You're white as a ghost. Are you all right?"

"Yes . . . yes, I'm fine. I . . . I just overslept. I'm so glad to see you."

"Hmm," Cordilia replied as she glanced at Rachel. "For a minute, I thought you had gone stone deaf. Didn't you hear me calling you at the top of my voice? If I had gotten any louder, someone would have called Sheriff Butler saying I was disturbing the peace!"

"I thought I heard something . . . or someone," Rachel said.

"What's wrong with you, Rachel? Are you sick or something?"

"Cordilia, I started to call you this morning at 4:00 a.m."

Cordilia frowned. "Why would you do that?"

"I had a terrible nightmare. I'll tell you later."

Cordilia pulled into the church parking lot. "I want to hear every word after church, but right now let's go in and hear what's on Pastor Miller's heart."

Chapter 16
Rachel Reads a Poem

*H*urrying into the vestibule, they were greeted by Stella Roberts, the church secretary, and Chris. Stella smugly asked, "Did you ladies oversleep this morning?"

Cordilia grinned and stated, "Stella, darling, one of us did oversleep. If you had been on your toes, you would have known it wasn't me. I've already been here, left, and back again. Now if you will excuse me, I need to get my choir robe on." Cordilia leaned forward, kissed Stella's cheek and smiled. "Stella, I love you!" She nudged Chris's arm and winked as she walked by.

Rachel hugged Stella, and whispered, "I was the one who slept in."

With a tight lip grin, Stella responded, "So I gather."

"Rachel, who is your new neighbor?" Stella inquired.

"She's an elderly woman named Effie Brown. Cordilia and I are going to visit her on Monday."

Chris added, "Are you talking about the woman who moved in at the tree line?"

"Yes," Rachel said. "I'm sorry about missing class this morning. Did everything go okay?"

"Cordilia and Paul did really well. Are you not singing in the choir this morning?"

"No, it's my morning to read."

Rachel looked into the sanctuary, saw the music director taking his place in front of the choir and motioning the organist to begin playing.

"We better get inside. The music is starting," she said.

In the sanctuary, Chris sat beside Paula. Rachel sat on the fourth row from the front at the end of the pew.

Instantly, the church filled with the magnificent sounds of the tremendous pipe organ positioned in the loft directly behind the choir.

Todd's Creek Baptist was the biggest church in town. The Frank Todd family came to the United States from Scotland and built the church in 1854. A very wealthy family, they spared no expense. Frank had stained glass shipped from Germany, and the pipe organ, from Switzerland; both were still in mint condition. The oak floors had darkened from age. There were certain places in the floor that creaked, one of which was directly behind the pulpit. Pastor Miller knew that board very well.

The altar and the pulpit were made from imported mahogany. The acoustics were heavenly.

There was a staircase leading to the balcony. About halfway up the staircase, there was a hidden door once used to hide slaves and soldiers during the Civil War.

The church was not lacking for history or beauty in a town of eleven hundred people.

There had been some changes. Bathrooms were added and red cushioned pads were added to the pews. The church was designed to hold 350 people. The main attraction was the steeple that contained the original bells that were rung at least once every day and twice on Sunday.

As the organ sounded, the choir filed down the aisles, walked up the steps and took their places in the seats behind the pulpit. Pastor Miller entered from a side door.

The choir in place, Ron lifted his hands, the pipe organ sounded, and the choir sang "How Great Thou Art."

After the hymn, the custom was for one in the congregation to share a reading from the Bible or a poem of his or her choice. Rachel read a poem she wrote a couple of years earlier.

She stood, cleared her throat and began to read:

> If today, the road The Lord has chosen for me to travel
> Should lead through the lion's den, I will not be afraid,
> For I will forever rest, in knowing my God is with me.
>
> If I come to the Red Sea, the enemy behind me,
> The sea before me and no way to turn, I will go through
> On dry land, for I know my God is with me.
>
> If the fire of the furnace is hotter than ever before, and
> Smoke is so thick I cannot see my way, by faith I'll face
> The fire and not fear the flame, knowing God is with me.

If I come to the battlefield, and there's a giant in my way,
I'll use the rock of my very soul and strike the giant between
His eyes. I'll watch him fall to the earth, and I'll not be afraid,
   For I know my God is with me.

If today I come to a place where I've never been before,
All my battles behind me, standing at the Jordan,
With my race run, I'll not be afraid, for even then I know
   My God is with me.

Rachel closed her book and sat down.

Cordilia quickly prepared to sing her solo "Great is Thy Faithfulness." Her soprano voice would melt the heart. Again, a song witnessed to Rachel's spirit that God is faithful, no matter what the situation.

Chapter 17
A Surprise for Rachel

*P*astor Miller took his position behind the pulpit. Kenneth Miller had been the pastor at Todd's Creek for twelve years. He felt the call to preach when he was just 17 years old. He and his wife, Leah, had moved to Todd's Creek from Austin, Texas.

A tall, slender, 41-year-old man, fairly good-looking with lots of charisma, everyone loved and respected him. His voice was very smooth and deep.

For a moment, he stood in silence behind the pulpit with his head lowered. Leaning forward, he braced himself, taking hold of the sides of the splendid mahogany podium. The congregation wondered why a delay in starting the message.

After a lull, he looked across the congregation, shook his head and smiled. "I prepared a message this week, but I feel I should go in a whole different direction.

"I was going to speak on 'Giving,' but I want to change my topic to 'Angels.' I'll be taking my text from two different scriptures. The first is from Psalms:

The Angel of the Lord encampeth round about them that fear Him, and delivereth them. Psalm 34:7 KJV

"There are different kinds of angels with different kinds of duties. How many of you in the congregation this morning believe that there are angels encamped around us?" Pastor Miller paused and smiled. "I see some of you looking around to be sure I'm not seeing something you're not." He chuckled. "Don't worry, folks, I don't see any standing around the sanctuary with my natural eye. But with my spiritual eye, I see a host of holy angels standing guard to do battle on our behalf.

"You may ask the question, 'If they are really here, why can't I see them?' Because more times than not, the only way we'll know they're here is to accept it by faith. 'Faith is the substance of things hoped for and evidence of things not seen.'

"The word substance means, Something under the feet; to strew under the feet like a carpet. [needs footnote] In other words, faith is something we can stand on that won't hurt our feet. When doubts or fears come against your mind, I want you to take authority over that spirit and put it under your feet. Don't let the adversary walk on you, but let the substance of your faith, which is Jesus Christ, trample or crush the enemy under your feet. In conclusion, I want you to know you can face any situation with faith. Your faith in the Most High God will put your enemies under your feet. Know this, I've said it, but it's worth repeating:

He will give his angels charge over you, to keep you.
Amen! Matthew 4:6 KJV

Rachel was stunned. The angels Pastor was speaking about she saw standing around the sanctuary. Everyone stood for the closing prayer but Rachel. Cordilia looked at Rachel who remained seated. She put her hand on Rachel's shoulder. At her touch, Rachel gasped and quickly stood. Cordilia raised her brows, smiled and whispered, "That was some message, wasn't it?"

"Breathtaking."

Paul peeked at Cordilia, "Shhh!" he said quietly.

After the service, Paul and Cordilia could tell something was bothering Rachel. They wanted no sad faces when they shared their wonderful news with their best friend. They were all smiles when Rachel got into the car for the ride home. Paul drove past Rachel's driveway.

She put her arms on the top of the front seat, and stated, "Hey, did you forget me? You just passed my driveway."

He chuckled. "Oh, was that your driveway?"

"Yes. Where are you going?"

Cordilia faced Rachel, "Hush! We're going to take a drive."

"Okay, what are you two up to?" Rachel insisted.

Cordilia put her hand on the back of Paul's neck and began playing with his hair. "Honey, I ask you, are we up to something?"

Paul glanced at Rachel innocently as he continued down the road that was becoming quite curvy. "Rachel, dear, why don't you just sit back, and enjoy the ride?"

Still trying to figure out where they were taking her, Rachel asked, "I have one question for you two criminals, "Am I being kidnapped?"

Cordilia laughed. "I declare, Paul, did you hear her? She said, 'kidnapped.'"

Rachel crossed her arms. "Well, if you are kidnapping me, I have two demands . . ."

Cordilia frowned and growled, "For heaven's sake, Rachel, if you're being kidnapped, you don't make the demands, the kidnappers do. This time only will we, the kidnappers, allow the kidnapped, to make her demands known. So, what do you want?"

"The first demand is I need to use the bathroom. The second is I need some food. Now can you meet these demands? Or I will have to throw a fit?"

Cordilia asked, "Can you hold out for ten minutes, or do we need to pull over and find a walking trail?"

"Are you sure it will be no longer than ten minutes?

"I'm sure, so sit back, and stop whining."

In a couple of minutes, Paul slowed the car down as they approached an enormous scrolled iron gate with the initials E.V. on it. A guard stood at the entrance.

Rachel's jaw fell open. In only a whisper, she asked, "Are we going to Echo Valley?"

Cordilia was so excited. "Yes, we are! Is that great or what? We are going to hob-knob with the rich and famous today."

"John and I have always wanted to come here," Rachel said, "but for some reason we never have."

Cordilia chuckled, "The reason Paul and I never come is the prices. But today is a very special day, and we're celebrating."

"I wish John could have been here," Paul added.

After passing security, Rachel put her head over the front seat between them. "So, tell me, what are we celebrating at this influential place."

Before Cordilia could answer, Rachel's eyes widened. "Wow! It's beautiful!"

Cordilia quickly agreed.

They were greeted at the main entrance by valets who hurriedly opened the car doors.

Cordilia looked at Paul and demanded. "Honey, you better hurry and make us rich fast. I was born to live this kind of lifestyle."

Paul laughed. "I'll start on that tomorrow at the sawmill."

The red carpet led them up six steps onto a porch with twenty, white marble columns. The elaborate porch was lined with white wicker furniture cushioned with brilliantly colored floral patterns. Interwoven among the white wicker were lavish ferns on tall marble stands.

Paul, Cordilia and Rachel walked across the grand porch to the entrance. The vast, glass double doors were etched with E.V.

The main lobby was bountiful with extraordinary, deep, blue velvet drapes with gold fringe and wide sash tiebacks. Crystal chandeliers lined the middle of the vaulted ceilings. Imported silk wallpaper and tapestries draped the walls. The floor was covered with a deep, blue carpet in a magnificent floral pattern. The lobby furniture was very ornate. This grand resort was built at the turn of the century, and maintained the renaissance of that era.

Rachel and Cordilia were still looking around when they heard someone call out, "Dawson party of three."

The maître d led them to their table.

Paul spoke up, "Cordilia, have you forgotten there's a reason for the visit today?"

"Heavens, no! However, it doesn't hurt to enjoy the moment. Isn't that right, Rachel?"

As they began to eat, Rachel exclaimed, "Enough already, tell me why we're here!"

Paul looked at Cordilia and asked, "Shall I tell her? Or do you want the honor?"

Cordilia dapped the corners of her mouth with the linen napkin and replied. "Paul, you do the honors."

Rachel was growing impatient. "Will somebody please tell me?"

Paul smiled and cleared his throat. "We're going to have a baby."

The statement caught Rachel off guard. She stared at her best friends. "What did you say?"

"We're going to have a baby!"

"Are you kidding?"

Cordilia sighed, "At the cost of this celebration, never! You know how long Paul and I have prayed for a baby? It seems like forever! Finally, God said yes to our prayers."

Rachel sat stunned at the news.

Cordilia tightened her brows and stated, "Well, I expected a little more excitement than this from my best friend."

"As my best friend, you should notice I'm shocked."

Cordilia put her hand on Rachel's. "I'm glad it's shock, or else I would have to punch you out for spoiling our moment."

Through earnest eyes, Rachel expressed, "I would never try and spoil your excitement. Maybe the news I have for you will shed some light on my reaction."

"All right, let's hear it," Cordilia said. "It better be good!"

Rachel swallowed hard, licked her lips and said, "John and I are going to have a baby, too."

Paul and Cordilia glanced at each other. Cordilia's eyes widened. "Did you say . . . ?"

"Yes, I did."

Stunned, Paul rubbed his chin and muttered, "A baby! God is that why we came to this place . . . two babies? News like this can't be celebrated at Shirley's Diner. Wow! You and John are going to have a baby?" Paul sighed. "When did you find out?"

Before Rachel could answer, Cordilia frowned and asked, "Speaking of kidding, you're not, are you, Rachel?"

"I wouldn't kid about something like that. To answer Paul's question, the Holy Spirit told me that I would have a baby boy by this time next year."

Cordilia her brow and questioned, "What's going on here Lord? Rachel, I want to share with you how I found out that I was going to have a baby."

"Please do!"

"I was out raking leaves three days ago. It was 1:00 p.m. The reason I know the exact time I had just looked at my watch to see how long I had been outside. As I worked, I was singing, and praising God. Sat once, I couldn't move. The Holy Spirit spoke to my heart and said these very words, 'By this time next year, you will have a son.' I fell to my knees and began thanking God for answering our prayers."

For a moment, the three sat silently. The silence was broken when the waiter asked if they would like coffee and dessert on the balcony to enjoy the view. The resort was located on top of a mountain that overlooked a natural lake. Bright fall colors layered the mountains with red, gold, yellow, green-brown and orange leaves. A continuous breeze blew.

The waiter rolled a cart filled with luscious desserts to their table, and poured coffee.

Rachel took a sip of her coffee and muttered, "Do you believe this?" She began to laugh, which caused a chain reaction.

"You know, nothing is impossible with God," Paul said. "Isn't it just like Him to give us double joy?"

Cordilia looked at Rachel and wondered, "Why now and at the same time?"

Paul wanted to know what had been bothering Rachel earlier. Rachel shared her dream. "The creature had my baby in his mouth. It seemed so real."

Cordilia shared what had happened when she came in from raking the leaves. "I was elated at the promise of having a baby. I felt humbled and knelt at the sofa. I was weeping for joy when instantly, I felt exhausted. I was moving slowing because I had walked a long way through a heavy mist. At once, the fog was gone, and was standing in a vast place among a countless number of angels. I gradually moved through the host. As I walked, they stepped aside. When I came to the end of the line, there was a staircase. Compelled, I started up the stairs. As I moved upward, thunder grew so loud it hurt my ears. Sheets of lightning danced all around. Still, I continued on with my head lowered and my focus on the stairs. The higher I climbed, the color of the stairs changed from white, to a brilliant emerald green. Angels lined the stairs; their shouting voices and the thunder were as one. In unison, they cried, 'Holy, Holy, Holy!' Moving on, I found myself shouting Holy!

"As I moved, there were awesome beings standing in a circle. I stopped in front of one, and I felt my knees begin to buckle. Somehow, he touched me without touching me, renewing my strength. When I looked into his eyes he said, 'Rehabiah' (Ree huh bye uh). He stepped aside and said, 'You may enter.'"

"What did he call you?" Rachel asked.

"Rehabiah."

Rachel asked, "Why would he call you that?"

"No idea. I've never heard that name before."

"What happened next?"

"He said, 'You're a mighty warrior who has served the kingdom well. There's a great battle ahead of you. Don't fear, a host has gone before you and will war on your behalf.'

"Then he said, 'the child you carry will be as mighty a warrior as you. Now go!' I opened my eyes and was at home in front of the sofa."

After hearing what Cordilia had to share, it was hard for Rachel not to tell about the angel Eri. She wondered at that moment why she chose not to tell her about Raptor as well.

They stood at the railing to soak up as much of the beauty as possible before they left.

"Cordilia," Rachel said, "I want you to know how very happy I am for you. God has made it more special by allowing us to be carrying our babies at the same time." Rachel lifted her cup of coffee. "I would like to purpose a toast." The three lifted their cups and Rachel said, "To our God who answers prayers and to a new beginning."

Chapter 18
Morning Sickness

The day finally came for John's return. Rachel was elated with so much news to share, where she would start. Possibly, it would be about the morning sickness she was having. Of course, Cordilia was not going to let Rachel get ahead of her. She too had been very queasy for the past few mornings.

Rachel hurried to pick John up. The train came in early, and he was waiting in front of the station when she arrived.

Their trip home was filled with "I love you" and "I missed you." John pulled in front of the house, parked, and they got out of the car. Rachel went around to John's side and locked her arm around him. John glanced around the yard then to the sky.

"A penny for your thoughts." Rachel whispered.

"I was thinking about the day we made the covenant in the yard."

Rachel chuckled. "I have so much good news for you later."

Inside, John pulled Rachel to him, and kissed her tenderly. "I missed you so much." He said softly. "I just want to feel you close to me. Smell the sweet fragrance in your hair."

Pressing her cheek against his, Rachel whispered, "I love you, John." They stood in the center of the kitchen floor and held each other for a long while.

The evening was filled with catching up on all the events. The Dawson's going to have a son being the prevalent story. John grinned and stated, "Stephen Daniel Harris, what a great name!"

"No greater than the son who will bear that name," Rachel whispered as she snuggled in John's arms.

John added, "Not greater than the God who's giving the son to us."

The night evaporated into the shimmer of the sun as it came unhurriedly over the rolling hills of Todd's Creek. There was no sign of life at the Harris house. John and Rachel slept like babies in the comfort of each other's arms. The phone rang causing Rachel to jump. "John, it's ten o'clock!" she exclaimed as she put the receiver to her ear.

"For heaven's sake!" Cordilia said. "I thought of calling Sheriff Butler to come out and check on you two. What are you doing that you can't answer the phone at ten o'clock in the morning?" Cordilia laughed. "Have you two had breakfast yet?"

"No, we're still in bed." Rachel sat on the side of the bed. "Why do you ask?"

"I am making breakfast for you."

"That sounds great! I'm starved."

In the middle of breakfast morning sickness kicked in leaving John and Paul to clear the table and do the dishes.

"Ladies, we're going outside for a while," Paul said as he put his thumbs under his suspenders. "John, don't you think it's a little strange that our wife's have made a complete recovery since the dishes have been washed and put away?"

John grinned. "It most certainly is."

Cordilia strolled over, popped Paul's suspenders, and said, "Paul Dawson, you get out of here and take your friend with you."

Paul shook his head, and muttered, "I've spoiled her rotten, John."

As the men stepped outside Paul laughed, "Cordilia, here comes Sheriff Butler. What have you two done that would bring the good sheriff out here?"

"Ha, Ha, Ha!" Cordilia said as they went to the front porch.

***

Allen Butler had been the sheriff of Todd's Creek for twenty-five years, and his father, Roger, was the sheriff for the thirty years prior to that. Allen knew everybody and everything that went on in Todd's Creek. He drove a 1944 black and white Ford police car that was ready to be replaced. He faithfully wore a brow Stetson hat. Due to lack of activity, Allen was fifty pounds over-weight. He had a great personality, and almost everybody in Todd's Creek loved him. He joked if anyone ever ran against him they might win, but no one ever run against him in the twenty-five years he had been sheriff. He was married and had two grown sons. His wife, Molly Hightower, had lived in Todd's Creek all of her life. Jack, their youngest son, was an attorney in Benson. Their oldest son, Alex, had a farm in Todd's Creek. Sheriff Butler was a good friend to Rachel's parents. He had watched Rachel grow up with his sons. When he was nervous, he would pull at his left ear, and run his finger across his lower lip.

He got out of the car, laughed, and said in his country drawl, "I've not had a greeting like this in many a year. How you good folks doing?"

"We're doing fine. What brings you out on this grand morning?" John asked.

Before the sheriff could answer Rachel added, "John, I would like to think he just came by for a visit."

The Sheriff pulled his hat off, took a deep breath and said, "Rachel honey, I wish it was a social call, but not this time. You know I've been the sheriff of Todd's Creek a lot of years, and I'll be honest with you, I've not had ten important calls in all them years. I just sit around all day and draw my pay."

Paul laughed and said, "How would we have ever guessed that?"

"Did you get an important call?" Cordilia asked.

"I got two disturbing calls," he said as he pulled some papers out of his coat. He opened the paper to reveal a beautiful blonde-haired girl. "She's Willow Chandler from over in Marshall County. Her mother reported her missing three days ago."

Rachel looked at the picture. "Allen, how old is she?"

"She's only 13. Her mother said she saw her get off the school bus and watched her as she walked down the driveway to the house. Now here is the eerie part, her mother said she watched as Willow came down the driveway, she just disappeared right in front of her eyes."

"Disappeared?" Cordilia asked.

"That's what she said. The woman is a very respected, God-fearing woman. Nobody seems to think she would lie."

"How do you just vanish with someone watching you?" John asked.

"I don't know, John, but the mother is out of her mind with worry. The exact way she put it was, 'The girl stopped and just evaporated into thin air.' The sheriff of Marshall County asked us to join the search."

"You said you got two calls. What's the other one?" John asked.

"I tell you, John, this call was as weird as the first one. Some folks here in Todd's Creek, and over in Benson, have been reporting some strange goings on up around Boone's Crossing."

"What strange things?" Paul asked.

"Several people said they've been seeing glowing lights spanning over a mile radius. I talked to David Hart, he said the crossing had a green-colored glow. At times it would look like the whole Crossing was on fire, but most of the time it was covered with a smoldering green. Have you ever heard of such a thing in your life?"

"What would cause a green glow especially at Boone's Crossing?" John asked. "There's nothing remotely close to the mountain."

"I don't know, John. If you want to talk about green, Matt Wilson my new deputy is where to start. I tell you the boy is as green as they come. I'm sure not looking forward to investigating some weird green light at Boone's Crossing with somebody who jumps every time you cough. The Indians claimed years ago there was a curse on that Crossing. Something about young Indian girls disappearing every so many years. Then have a young girl vanish into thin air three days ago really makes you think."

"What does that make you think, Allen? About your soul?" Cordilia teased.

"Now you know I'm not into all that church stuff. I don't have anything against anybody that does, but I'm just not. Some of my favorite people in the world are standing right here."

Rachel took Sheriff Butler by the arm and said, "We love you, Allen."

Cordilia took his other arm and added, "Yes, we do love you, whether you're a heathen or not."

"Cordilia!" Paul said. "Sheriff, why don't you lock her up for about a week, and see if she talks to you a little nicer the next time."

"Hush up, Paul. Allen knows I am only kidding. Right, Sheriff?"

"Yes, I do, but we men have to look out for each other. Now, Paul, any other time I might lock Cordilia up, and give you a few days of rest, but not this time. If I have to go up to Boone's Crossing, I want these two women praying for me with the fervency of Elijah."

Allen put his hat on and said, "I better get these posters up."

Rachel hugged him and said, "You better take care of yourself, Allen Butler, and be sure to give Molly our love."

He was walking back toward his car when he stopped, looked back, pulled his left ear a couple of times and concluded, "How about you folks remembering the Chandler family when you pray. I can't imagine your kid missing like that."

"We will," John said.

Allen paused, lowered his head, and went to his car.

"You know, Rachel," Cordilia said. "I think the sheriff had a tear in his eye when he said that. God is going to have that man yet."

The women sat in the living room for a while, and talked about Willow Chandler and the strange lights at the Crossing. Rachel remembered how Eri vanished before her eyes.

The topic shifted to making an appointment to see Dr. Wells for a check-up, and discussing the names for the babies.

"Rachel, guess the name we've chosen for our son."

"Do I get a clue or anything? Like maybe the first letter in the name."

"No, just guess."

"Cordilia, how can I know? Just tell me!"

"Okay." Cordilia said as she sat in the newly painted rocking chair. "Phillip Ryan Dawson. What do you think of that?"

"It's a beautiful name."

Rachel moved to the edge of the sofa, with pride she said, "Guess our son's name?"

Cordilia snickered, "I know, I know. It's John, Jr."

Rachel frowned, "No, it's Stephen Daniel Harris."

"That's a powerful name? You have Stephen, who was a martyr, and Daniel, who was a prophet. That sounds like a winning team to me!"

"Rachel, now that we know the babies' names. Would you like to see the nursery?"

"I would love to."

"This is great, Cordilia," Rachel said as they entered the nursery. The room was sky blue with white fluffy clouds with curtains to match. Cordilia picked a blanket up from the crib and held it to her chest.

"Cordilia, you have the baby's room almost completed, and I haven't even started. Just look at all the things! Where did you get everything?" Rachel asked as she took a toy lamb from the crib.

"The lamb was mine when I was a baby and so was the crib. As fate would have it, Mama held on to them. Our neighbor, Margaret Stanley, gave them to me. She was a hateful woman, but very giving.

The rocking chair belonged to Paul's mom. Some of the clothes I bought, and some I got from my sister in South Carolina. She mailed them to me a long time ago. 'In case I ever got pregnant,' were her exact words."

Rachel put the lamb back into the crib and asked, "What do you think it feels like when the baby is born? You know, the labor part."

Cordilia put the blanket down and replied, "I think it will feel like you're in a fight, and you're not doing so well."

They looked out the window to see if they could see the men.

"Cordilia, I am seeing the vision more often."

"Are you kidding?"

"No! I wish I were."

Cordilia grabbed Rachel's hand and pulled her toward the door. "Let's don't think about it right now. After Allen's awful report let's try to think happy. Let's go see what the men are doing."

Paul and John were fixing a fence near the barn. They needed more nails to finish the job.

Paul asked if the women would go to Ray's hardware and pick up a pound of nails for them."

Chapter 19

Mr. Spook

The streets of Todd's Creek were virtually empty. After picking up the nails they decided to go up the street to the five and dime. On the way Cordilia grabbed Rachel's arm and whined, "Oh God, help us!"

Rachel didn't see the man coming toward them at first. "What's wrong with you, Cordilia?" Just as she said those words, she saw what Cordilia was talking about.

"Oh Lord in heaven, Cordilia! That's the hermit everybody calls 'Spook' for sure."

"How do you know, Rachel?"

"I don't. I'm only guessing."

"Rachel, if we keep walking down this street, we're going to be within inches of him. Look at him! He's talking to himself and laughing out loud when there is nothing to laugh about. Check the weird motions he is making with his hands. What should we do?"

Feeling apprehensive, Rachel wiped her upper lip. "Cordilia, he's almost at us. Let's just turn around and look in the store window until he goes by. We won't even look at him."

They turned and appeared to be checking the display as Spook drew closer. "I can almost smell him from here, Rachel."

Rachel nudged Cordilia in the side, "Hush up, Cordilia! You can't smell anything. Besides, I don't want him to hear you say anything like that."

Spook moved only a step or two away from Rachel and Cordilia and stopped. The girls wondered what he was doing. "Oh great granny, he stopped Rachel."

Again, Rachel nudged Cordilia's arm, and whispered "Hush up."

The old hermit lived in a makeshift cabin on a mountain about twenty miles away from Todd's Creek. Once a month, he would walk down from the mountain and come into town for supplies. No one knew exactly how old he was. His long bushy hair was a yellow and white combination. It was in desperate need of being shampooed and brushed. His fingernails looked like they had not been cut or cleaned in months. A dentist would have been stunned checking his neglected teeth.

He had on an old pair of blue pants that could have stood alone from the dirt on them, a ragged checked shirt, and coat held together by a giant safety pin. Yet, his feet were graced with a brand-new pair of high-topped boots. Rachel found out later that Ken Moore, who owned the one of the two gas stations in Todd's Creek, gave him a new pair every year about this time.

Cordilia and Rachel stood there trying to ignore him. They wished he would go on by, but he just stood there looking at them in the reflection of the window. He walked around them and in a voice that scared the life out of the girls, shouted, "You better watch out! The devils after you!" Afraid to move, they stood there like steel post.

Again, Spook walked from one side to the other, and laughed so loud Rachel and Cordilia almost jumped out of their skin. He declared, "The angels are coming! Satan can't get you! The angels are coming!"

With that statement, Rachel turned, and fixed her eyes on the old hermit dancing around clapping his hands.

Cordilia took hold of Rachel's arm, and tried to keep her from turning, but it was too late. Rachel gasped when she looked directly at the old recluse still laughing, dancing, and clapping his hands. Over and over he kept repeating, "The angels are coming! Satan can't get you! The angels are coming!"

Cordilia panicked. "Oh God, help us!" She said as she grabbed Rachel's arm and shouted, "Come on let's get out of here."

Cordilia felt her flesh get chill bumps. Through clinched teeth, she asked, "Rachel, what are you doing now?"

Rachel stared at the man. "I need to ask him something."

The recluse continued his routine in front of them repeating the same words over and over. It was as though he didn't even see them standing there any longer. Rachel shouted, "Mr. Spook?" With that, he stopped dancing, and stood there silent like a statue with his back to them. Rachel repeated softly, "Mr. Spook?"

The loner slowly turned his head to the side looking past his shoulder at Rachel and Cordilia. With the speed of light, he jumped around, and clapped his hands right in front of them. Looking directly at them, he laughed, and said in a voice only above a whisper, "The angels are coming! Satan can't get you! The angels are coming!"

Trembling, Rachel managed to speak although her mouth was as dry as cotton. "Mr. Spook, what do you mean the angels are coming?"

He looked at Rachel with a frown and growled, "Why are you calling me Mr. Spook?"

Rachel stuttered, "I-I didn't know your name."

Cordilia wasn't waiting for Rachel to say anything else, she quickly added, "She didn't mean anything by that Mr. Spook. No disrespect at all."

"No, no, I meant no disrespect. If you'll tell me your name, I'll be glad to call you by it. Just tell me."

With a frown, he replied, "How would you like it if I called you a spook?"

Rachel swiftly replied, "I'm sorry. As I said, tell me your name, and I'll never use that term again." Her mouth was so dry she could hardly swallow.

"Call me Spook." He muttered. "It don't matter what you call me." With those words, he clapped his hands together and repeated, "Ha! The angels are coming." Rachel and Cordilia jumped back. Again, the recluse went into a dance repeating the words.

Cordilia pulled on Rachel's coat. "Rachel, let's get out of here. He's lost it!"

"No, he hasn't, Cordilia. He knows exactly what he's doing, and I want to understand. I need to understand. Stop and listen to what he's saying."

Cordilia paused. "You're right, Rachel, he knows something. Just look at him though, dancing around like a maniac."

"Cordilia, I have to ask."

"Yeah, I know you do."

In a little louder tone, Rachel asked, "Mr. Spook, what do you mean by saying the angels are coming?" Again, he stopped, and faced them squinted his eyes, and said, "God in heaven is looking down from above." Quickly, he snapped his fingers in front of Cordilia's face. She let out a muffled scream and jumped back.

At that point, Rachel was getting irritated. With all that had been taking place, she knew down deep this man had a message for her and Cordilia and he wasn't as crazy as he was acting. She stepped forward and firmly said, "Mr. Spook, Mr. Spook!"

At this, the old man stopped and glared at Rachel. "What do you want from me?" He asked.

Rachel swallowed so hard it hurt her throat. "I want to know what you're talking about."

He leaned within inches of Rachel's face and said, "Have you not listened to a word I've said? I've been telling you Queen Jewel is as good as dead. Although she'll still try to bring you down. Stand firm in the Lord, and don't lose your ground! Why should you tremble at a defeated foe? The heavenly host is with you, and that's all you need to know."

With those words, he clapped his hands and danced in front of them. Then eye to eye with Rachel he growled, "The angels are coming, and I know where they are."

With a laugh, clap of his hands, he danced down the street repeating, "The angels are coming."

Rachel called out, "Mr. Spook, what do you mean you know where they are? Who are they?"

The man paid no attention. He continued down the street and out of sight around the corner.

Bewildered, Rachel and Cordilia looked at each other. "What do you think about all that, Cordilia?"

"Don't ask me anything right now. I can't think straight. I've never seen anything like Mr. Spook in all my life. Do you think he knows what he was talking about or is he just crazy?"

Rachel looked down the empty street. "He knows more than he told us and I want to know what it is."

"Rachel, let's go home, I want to lie down and regroup my thoughts. Besides, we need to get the nails for the men."

Rachel had forgotten all about the nails. "Cordilia, you're right. They're probably wondering where we are."

Chapter 20
Why Not Help?

*J*ohn and Paul were sitting on the steps when they arrived. As soon as they got out of the car, Paul stood and asked, "Where have you two been? We gave up on you!"

Cordilia pointed her finger at Paul and answered, "It's not too late for me to go to Hollywood without you. So, take the nails, finish the fence and join us for a cup of coffee. We'll be glad to fill you in."

Paul kissed Cordilia's cheek as he went by and said, "I love it when you show that fiery side babe."

Rachel added, "Please hurry. We've got something to tell you."

After finishing the fence, they gathered around the kitchen table, and shared what had happened with Mr. Spook. Paul and John laughed hysterically. At first Rachel and Cordilia didn't find it so funny, but it didn't take long before they were laughing too.

Paul was laughing so hard tears rolled down his cheeks. Wiping his eyes, he said, "My, my, you two! It's not bad enough that everybody calls him a spook you two come along, dress it up, and call him Mr. Spook. I guess he had a laugh himself as soon as he got out of sight."

Cordilia playfully hit Paul on the shoulder and said, "That's it! Have a good laugh when I could have had a heart attack! What you would have called him?"

Through the laughter, John said, "I wouldn't have called him anything, especially Mr. Spook. How about you, Paul?"

"There is no way I would have called him that."

Rachel asked, "What is his story anyway? What makes a person become a hermit, and who came up with the name 'hermit'?"

Paul replied, "I can't say who came up with the name, but I can tell you what I heard about him before he became a recluse.

Cordilia groaned, "By all means."

"He was a fairly successful farmer with several acres, a wife and two little boys. He had gone out of town to take some cows to market, and would be gone overnight. Two men broke into their house. They hoped to find money, but there was none there. It was in the bank. Enraged when his wife told them there was no money in the house. They needlessly killed his wife and two sons.

"In the meantime, the hermit finished his business and decided to come home without spending the night. When he came through the front door, he realized something wasn't right. He heard talking upstairs. Realizing it was men's voices, he got the shotgun from the closet, and quickly went up the stairs. The rest was inevitable.

Entering his bedroom, he saw the two men had not only murdered his wife, but they had raped her. The little boys were killed before their mother. He emptied the shotgun on them. After that, he just couldn't adjust. His neighbor bought the farm, and he went to the mountain, and has been there ever since."

Appalled Rachel asked, "Why didn't somebody help him?"

"From what I've been told, they tried. They even put him in the mental hospital at Pine Ridge. Everyone said he was doing fine when they let him out, but as soon as they let him out, he went back to the mountain. That's been thirty years ago. People just left him alone. He's harmless, even though he can scare people half to death when they see him coming."

Rachel was quick to say, "He's not as crazy as he acts. I can tell he's not. Do you think maybe somebody could help him if they tried again?"

John could tell what Rachel was thinking, "Honey, I want you to stay away from him. Do you hear me?"

With a very stern look, Rachel said, "I wasn't thinking about me. I was actually thinking about you and Paul."

John stood behind Rachel and rubbed her shoulders. "Maybe he likes things just the way they are now."

"John," Rachel said, "what do you think he meant by saying, 'The angels are coming, and I know where they are?'"

John sighed, "I have no idea."

Paul propped his elbows on the table and said, "You know, Rachel, I did hear somebody say once that he said an angel told him to go to the mountain after his family was murdered. But of course, I've heard so many tales, some of which are so far out, no one could believe them."

John remarked, "I heard that about an angel telling him to go to the mountain. After a while, you hear so much you just stop paying attention."

Rachel gasped, "How could you stop paying attention?"

John put his hand on Rachel's. "It doesn't mean I don't care. I know how you feel, but there's not a great deal we can do except pray for him, and ask God to deliver him."

Rachel quickly added, "Why would an angel tell him to go to a mountain? "

"Rachel," John said, "you've lived here all your life, yet you act as though you've never heard the stories."

Rachel thought a moment and muttered, "Mama and Daddy always tried to keep really bad things from me, but there is something I remember. Sheriff Roger Butler, Allen's dad, came by to tell Mama and Daddy about somebody shooting somebody. Mama screamed and cried. Daddy saw me standing in a doorway and hurried me back upstairs. He told me there was an accident, and someone had been killed. After that, no one would talk about it, and I just pushed it aside. On occasion, you would hear something about the spook on the mountain. It seems I would have heard something about it from the other kids at school. I remember Stella teasing about the spook on the mountain that come to her house trick or treating. Another thing," Rachel said, "I've lived here all my life. One would think in 40 years I would have at least caught a glimpse of him?"

Taking a deep breath John said, "Yes, Honey, you would think so, but if you haven't, then you haven't. So what is the big deal?"

"I don't know!"

Cordilia was watching Rachel. She could see the wheels turning. Cordilia spoke up, "If you two have heard so much about Mr. Spook, why is it Rachel and I have heard very little and never seen him before? Have you and John seen him?"

"Yes, a few times."

John questioned, "Did you two act like this when Stella mentioned him?"

Rachel frowned and replied, "No."

Cordilia glared at Paul and questioned, "Why haven't you told me about him? When I saw him today, I felt totally faint. It was Rachel who said he was the hermit." Cordilia cut her eyes toward Rachel. "By the way, Rachel, how did you know he was the hermit?"

"I don't know. I don't know anything anymore."

Cordilia looked at Paul and continued, "You should have mentioned him to me."

Paul raised his hands and stated, "Baby, I don't go around with Mr. Spook on my mind. I'm sure I speak for John when I say the next time I hear or see anything you two will be the first to know."

Rachel took her cup to the sink. "How could we live in a small town and never hear anyone express concern about this man? Including our husbands and Pastor Miller?"

Wanting to end the conversation John said, "Honey, we better be going. We've had a wonderful time, and let's end it that way."

My concern for Mr. Spook wasn't intended to dampen our spirits. If I did, I'm sorry."

"You didn't dampen anything." Paul said, "You've just got a big heart, and that's as it should be."

Headed for the door Cordilia remembered, "Rachel, I'll get John a jar of apple butter."

John hugged Cordilia and said, "I'm glad you thought of that."

Rachel went with Cordilia to the basement where she kept her canned goods. Paul and John waited outside.

At the bottom of the stairs Cordilia looked up at Rachel and said, "Rachel Harris, I can see what you're thinking. You get those thoughts out of your mind right now."

"What thoughts?"

Cordilia put her hands on her hips, and replied, "About helping Mr. Spook."

Shaking her head, Rachel said, "Nobody has tried to help him in Lord knows when!"

"Oh yes they have! Did you forget the new boots?"

"For heaven's sake Cordilia, you're the last one I would expect to hear that from. God delivered you from so much. Where is your compassion, anyway?"

Cordilia frowned and questioned, "Are you rebuking me?"

"No! I'm asking how can we not do more than just pray? If you're hungry and I send you away with 'I'll pray' instead of food, then I've done nothing except send you away to starve to death. If I have bread for you to eat and don't give it to you, than I'm a killer."

"That's right, Rachel, but he hasn't come to you for bread. He hasn't come to you for anything."

"Cordilia, we don't just wait for people to come to us. We're to go to them and compel them to eat the bread. Sometimes they don't even know they're hungry. After a person goes hungry for so long, the hunger pain goes away. By the time the hunger comes back, if it comes back, they could be so near death, they'll die before the food can do what it's supposed to."

Cordilia concluded, "You're right Rachel."

"Rachel." John called.

"I'll be right there." She replied. Quickly she asked Cordilia, "Did you get what Paul said about Mr. Spook saying an angel told him to go to the mountain?"

"How could I have missed that?"

Again, John called her. "I'll be right there." They quickly went up the steps. Rachel looked at Cordilia and added, "I need to talk to that old man again."

Cordilia hugged Rachel. "I know."

The kitchen door came open, and John started to call Rachel again but saw them standing at the door. John smiled, "What is it with you two today?

It's taking longer to do everything. That's not a sign of old age, is it?"

Rachel pinched John's cheek, winked and said, "Remember, you will always be older than I."

Cordilia, patted John's shoulder and added, "And I'm two years younger than she."

Chapter 21
What Does it All Mean?

Rachel and John headed home, with plans to relax the rest of the evening.

John stopped the car and let Rachel out before pulling into the garage. Rachel took a couple of steps toward the porch and halted in her tracks. Feeling compelled to look toward the sky she raised her head to view a huge fluffy white cloud hovering over her.

With her eyes fixed on the enormous cloud, Rachel saw what appeared to be a male figure inside the cloud. Light radiated around the form. Claps of thunder rang loud in her ears and a flash of lightning streaked through the cloud. Then it was gone.

Rachel began to hyperventilate. John came from the garage and saw something was wrong. He frantically ran to her. "Rachel, what's wrong?"

"I . . . I." Her words wouldn't form.

"Rachel, are you hurt? Is it the baby?"

"No," she whispered.

John helped her to the porch swing. "Can I get you a glass of water or something?" John anxiously asked.

"No, I'll be okay in a minute." She took a couple of deep, slow breaths.

Worried, John asked, "Honey, what happened?"

She told John about the cloud and the man in it. "The thunder was so loud, wasn't it?"

John reluctantly responded. "I didn't hear any thunder."

Rachel snapped, "Well, I did. How could you not have heard it? It was so loud."

"Okay, Rachel, I believe you, but I didn't hear anything."

Rachel was shaking. John put his arm around her. "Honey, you need to calm down."

Rachel closed her eyes and muttered, "After the thunder, there was a blinding light, and then it was gone. Just gone."

"Honey, are you sure?"

Rachel shouted, "Yes, John, I saw it, and I heard it."

"Rachel, you don't have to be short-tempered with me. I'm just trying to help. I can't help it if I didn't see or hear anything."

Feeling hurt, John lowered his head for a moment. Rachel stroked John's cheek.

"I'm sorry. It wasn't my intention to hurt you. It just scared the life out of me. I don't know what's going on. I've never encountered so much weird stuff in my life. It's been almost constant the last several weeks. I didn't mean to snap at you. I'm so sorry."

Still looking down, John asked, "Honey, forget being sorry. You're not the only one who needs to know what all this means. First you see an angel, then we're going to have a baby. You and I felt a breeze go over when we made the covenant about the angel. Not to mention the smell of roses that filled the room. Then, Mr. Spook saying the angels are coming and knowing where they are. Then this."

Rachel sighed, "John there's more."

"More! More what?"

Rachel told him about her dream with the being holding her baby in his mouth after it was born. She also told him about the soldiers that were marching through a valley.

John took hold of Rachel's hand. "Should we talk to Pastor Miller about these things?"

Rachel responded at once. "No, but we will talk to God about it. If God doesn't know, I'm sure Pastor Miller won't. Anyway, Pastor would think we're a couple of nuts!"

Rachel walked to the edge of the porch, looked up, and asked, "We're not crazy, are we, John?"

"No! I pray God will give us understanding, because as of right now, I don't have a clue about any of this. But this I do know: God is in control of our lives that are somehow being turned upside down."

Chapter 22
The Jacksons

They were sitting for almost an hour when they saw Jerry Jackson walking through the field toward their house. "John, why would Jerry be coming here? They never or call or visit. Do you think something could be wrong with Emily?"

John looked at Rachel and laughed. "Honey, why don't you slow down so I can answer you? Every time I go away on a trip and come back, you sound just a little more like Cordilia."

"And what's wrong with that?"

"Absolutely nothing."

Jerry came into the yard. John walked to the edge of the porch to greet him. "Hi neighbor, how you doing?"

"Hello, John." Jerry said as he stepped onto the porch and extended his hand to shake John's. "I haven't seen you in a while." Jerry said. "How have you been?"

"Staying busy and you?"

"Staying busy at the bank." Jerry looked around John. "Hello, Rachel. It's good to see you."

"Hi, Jerry. Is everything okay?"

"Yes, everything's great. However, I do know where you're coming from with that thought. We haven't been very sociable since we've lived here, but I want that to change."

John could see Jerry was a little embarrassed by Rachel's question and said, "People are so busy anymore. Seems like no one takes time out to visit like they should. I know that's true with Rachel and me. You're right, Jerry, that does need to change."

Rachel offered to get Jerry something to drink.

"Thank you, Rachel, but that was the reason I came over. Emily and I saw you and John sitting in the porch swing and wanted to have you over for some coffee and fresh homemade brownies. Emily just took them out of the oven a few minutes ago."

"That's really nice of you, Jerry." John looked at Rachel, "What do you think, Honey?"

Before Rachel could answer, Jerry added, "Come on Rachel, I insist."

While Jerry was speaking, Rachel was thinking, they had lived beside us for six years. They hardly speak to us, even at church, and suddenly they want to have coffee together. Rachel smiled and replied, "Of course, Jerry, we would love to. Why don't you guys go on? I'll make sure the door is closed and join you."

"We'll wait on you, honey."

"No, you go ahead. I'll only be a minute."

Jerry patted John's shoulder and said, "Come on, John, and I'll show you a couple of new guns I picked up recently."

All smiles, he looked at Rachel, "We'll see you in a minute, dear." She watched as they walked across the yard.

"I wonder what Cordilia would have to say about this?" she muttered.

Chapter 23
Jerry Jackson's Sword

*T*he fall leaves had peaked, making the rolling hills looked like an artist's canvas. As Rachel walked across the field to the Jackson's, she looked toward Effie's house but saw no one. She wished she could continue her walk and enjoy the beauty of creation. Instead, she would be forced to admire a man-made creation in Jerry's breath-taking home.

The Jacksons had a very elaborate, old, white Victorian, three-story house, which was in pristine condition. Outside, an enormous gazebo sat in the center of the amazing landscaping. Inside, the house was filled with rare antiques. Jerry had an antique gun collection, which he constantly raved about. Persian rugs covered the immaculate oak floors. The great room was designed with large bay windows cushioned with light pink imported silk. White icicle-shaped lace draped the tall windows. Exquisite Louis the Sixteenth furniture filled the room.

As Rachel approached the house Emily greeted her.

"Hi, Emily. I was just admiring your stunning home."

"Thank you, Rachel. Won't you please come in? The men are in the sitting room. Come, we'll join them."

Emily was the type of person that would fit in with the queen of England. Very elegant, tall with long strawberry-red hair, fair-complexion with a few well-covered freckles. However, she was not the type person you would think of as making brownies. Strangely enough, they did not have a maid.

Emily led the way to the sitting room. As they entered the room, Jerry and John stood as the ladies sat down. "We're so glad to have you in our home." Emily said.

"Thank you for having us," Rachel said as she found herself sitting a little more poised than usual. Emily had the coffee in a silver pot, and the brownies on a silver platter with a white lace doily. She served everyone and sat down.

"Jerry's been showing me his gun collection. It's incredible, Rachel!"

Rachel smiled and looked around the room, "I think incredible sums up my thoughts as well."

Jerry went on and on about wanting Rachel and John to make themselves at home. He was even talking about him, Paul and John doing a little hunting together.

The whole time Rachel was trying to figure out what this visit was all about! It was all so phony. They had nothing in common. Rachel felt totally uncomfortable. John, on the other hand, was eating it up.

"Have you met your new neighbor, Effie Brown, yet?" Rachel asked.

Emily straightened her posture and said, "No! I hear she's a strange one."

Rachel frowned. "I thought Effie was really nice. John and I met her the a few days ago.

Emily spoke up. "I'd stay away from her if I were you. Someone said she was an old witch."

Rachel frowned. "She didn't seem to be a witch to us, did she John?"

"Well!"

"He's only teasing." Rachel added.

John asked, "Did Sheriff Butler come by your house today?"

Looking appalled at the question, Emily said, "No, he did not! Why would he come by here?"

"He said a young girl in Benson vanished in front of her mother's eyes." John said.

"How ridiculous! People don't just vanish in thin air," Emily snarled.

"According to the girl's mother, she got off the school bus and was walking up the driveway and just disappeared," Rachel said.

"Who was the girl?" Jerry asked.

"Willow Chandler." John replied.

Jerry thought a moment and said, "I know a Chandler family in Benson. They came in the bank a month or so ago for a loan, but I don't know if it's the same family?"

John added, "He also said there have been strange green lights seen at Boone's Crossing."

"Really?" Jerry said.

Emily, in a nonchalant way, ended the conversation. "Could we please talk about something just a bit more cheery? I feel a bout of depression coming on if we don't."

It was then Rachel said something that struck a nerve in both Jerry and Emily, "I've noticed Chris and Paula are showing quite a bit of interest in each other lately. I think they make such a good-looking couple."

Emily's lips tightened as she sat her cup down, and with a look of pure hatred, responded, "Chris and Paula are not a couple. Where did you get such an idea?"

Rachel tried to cover it up as much as possible by interjecting, "I didn't mean like going steady or anything like that."

Without hesitation, Emily said, "I would think not. Chris is too young to think about anyone seriously. Paula isn't Chris's type."

They were startled when a voice from the doorway responded. "What type would you be referring to, Mother?" No one realized that Chris was standing at the door overhearing what had been said. At once Emily stood, and walked toward Chris without answering his question.

"Chris dear, look who's here, John and Rachel." Chris was looking at his mother in a dead stare with his lips drawn tight.

In a very stern voice, Emily said, "Come, say hello to our guests."

Under her breath Rachel heard Emily say, "We'll talk about it later."

Chris's expression changed to a smile as he turned to face Rachel. "What a pleasant surprise! It's good to see you two." Chris gave Rachel a hug and shook John's hand.

Emily took her seat. "Chris, I was just about to call you. What time are you to be at work today?"

"I'll be leaving in about an hour."

Trying to relieve the tension, John asked, "Are you still working at Jim Sloan's garage?"

"Yes, but I don't get that many hours. I'd like to find some odd jobs in the evening, so I don't have work at that garage."

"Chris," John said, "I have some jobs I could use some help with, if you're interested."

He smiled, "I would be very interested. What kind of jobs do you have?"

"I could use some help splitting firewood and stacking it. I don't usually have enough time when I'm home to get everything done. With winter coming on, it would be a big help."

"That sounds great. Just let me know when and I'll definitely help."

"I also have a tree out next to the shed that needs to be cut down. Every time there is a hard wind the limbs fly in every direction. I'd like to remove it before somebody gets hurt."

"How big is the tree?" Jerry asked.

"It's big enough that I need some help guiding the way it falls."

"We'll go over and take a look at that tree if you have time, son. Jerry said."

"Sure, Dad, I have time. All I have to do at the garage is a brake job for Margaret Jones."

"Is she the elderly lady who sits on the second-row pew on the left hand side of the church?"

"Yes, she is the one who wears the big hat pins in her hat?"

Jerry shook his head. "Yes, she is the one."

Emily walked over and locked her arm around Jerry's. "Dear, let John and Rachel finish their coffee first."

"Yes, of course," Jerry replied as he went back to his chair. "Besides, I couldn't let John get away without showing off my latest toy. John, you're going to love this! I'll be right back." Jerry returned holding a long slender black case trimmed in gold. He placed the case on a table and started to open it.

Curiosity got the better of John, and he started making his way to see what was in the case. Jerry opened the container, inside was the most breathtaking sword John had ever seen.

Eyes all but popping out of his head, John exclaimed, "Jerry, this is extraordinary!"

Jerry took two pair of white gloves from the case for them to put on before touching the sword. Jerry took the sword out and handed it to John.

Admiring it John said, "I've always wanted to collect swords. To see this is unbelievable!"

"It's gorgeous." Rachel agreed. "It must have cost a fortune! The price of a good sword is the reason John doesn't collect them."

"Rachel, you wouldn't believe what I paid for this sword."

"Where did you find such a rare jewel?" John asked. "This goes back farther than any sword maker I know of, and I know most of them."

"I found it at a small antique shop in Norfolk called "A Journey in Time." The owner is an aged eccentric woman named Delilah. I can't believe her prices. I don't think she knows what she has in that shop."

Rachel found that hard to believe. "Why would you own an antique shop and not know the value of what you're selling?"

"I don't know, but if you're ever in Norfolk, look the shop up. I'll give you the address. If you go, be sure to tell Delilah that Jerry and Emily Jackson sent you. Try not to forget to mention our names. It may help the price on the next sword I get from her if I send a customer her way."

"I would love to go sometime." John said as he pulled the gloves off and put them back in the case.

Jerry put the sword away and said, "Enough about my toy. Let's go take a look at that tree." Emily said goodbye, and gave an open invitation for John and Rachel to come visit any time.

Chapter 24
Effie Brown

$\mathcal{R}$achel decided to visit Effie while there. She was outside sitting in an old stick chair propped against a large oak tree. Winston was sitting on the grass beside her. When Rachel entered the yard, Winston stood, but didn't bark. Effie pointed her cane toward Rachel and said, "I see you decided to come back for that coffee. Rachel, isn't it?"

"Yes. I was visiting the Jackson's and thought I would drop by and say hello, and see if there's anything you need."

"No, it's all taken care of. The good thing about not having a lot of things, is it doesn't take long to get situated."

Rachel looked up at the huge tree. "That oak has the fullest braches I've ever seen. The colors are breath-taking."

Effie pecked the trunk of the tree with her cane and said, "If these old trees could talk, what a story they could tell! She pointed the cane toward the house. "How about we go inside, and I'll brew us fresh pot of coffee."

A little surprised at the invitation Rachel paused but readily agreed. Rachel was seated at a medium-size round table with two chairs as Effie put the coffee on the wood stove to perk. The meager house consisted of one bedroom, an open area where two rocking chairs, the table and chairs where she was sitting were across from a wood stove and sink with a curtain at the bottom instead of cabinet doors. Effie stoked the fire and then joined Rachel at the table.

Feeling heartsick for the aged woman, Rachel asked, "Effie, with winter nearing, would you mind if John and Paul, a dear friend of ours, brought you a load of wood?"

"Effie frowned. "That won't be necessary. I've been getting my own wood for a very long time."

After pouring the coffee, Effie excused herself while she and Winston went to the outside bathroom. Observing the room, Rachel's eyes fixed on a small table near one of the rocking chairs. However, it was the book on the table that aroused her curiosity. After glancing toward the door, Rachel hurried over to check the book out. As she neared the table, she paused and looked at the antique manuscript—a large volume with a black leather cover that appeared hardened from age. The scrolling around the edges was unlike anything Rachel had ever seen. The binding was worn, and the words of the title were cracked. Though splintered, the crimson letters were legible: *Angels Of The Ages*. Rachel reached out to touch the letters, but Effie closing the door startled her. She hastily jerked her hand back. Feeling like a child with the hand caught in the cookie jar, Rachel slowly turned back to the table. Effie stood for a moment staring at Rachel then gradually made her way to the table. Taking a sip of her coffee she asked, "Like my book, do you?"

Rachel blushed. "Yes, very much. I . . . I was just curious about the author."

"Let's just say, 'The author is a dear friend of mine.'"

Rachel teased. "Now, Effie, I'm sure you're nowhere near that old."

Effie chuckled. "I've just maintained my young girl looks, a gift from my father. He never seemed to age. Old, with wrinkle-free skin. Can you imagine that?"

"No, I can't, but I think that would be wonderful to have skin that never aged."

"I don't think you have to worry about that for a while, Rachel. You're a beautiful woman, with a beautiful spirit."

"Thank you, Effie. That's a nice thing to say."

"I say what I see. I say nothing just to flatter. Another attribute of my father."

After a moment of chit chat, Rachel said, "This is a red-letter day. In just the last two hours, I've seen two of the rarest antiques I've have ever witnessed."

Effie took a sip of her coffee and asked, "What do you mean?"

"Your amazing book and Jerry Jackson's sword are beyond belief."

Effie pushed herself up with her cane and looked out the small window beside the door. "What kind of sword does Mr. Jackson have?"

Rachel shrugged and replied, "It's a most elaborate jewel-crested sword. John knows all about swords and their makers. I mean, he's studied the history back about as far as sword-making goes, and he said Jerry's sword went back a lot further than that. When I saw your book, my thoughts went automatically to the sword."

"Did he say where he got the sword?"

Rachel stood and said, "Yeah, at an antique shop in Norfolk called Journey in Time."

Effie nodded her head. "I see."

"May I look at your book?"

Effie swiftly responded, "No, not today. I need to go into town. Perhaps another time."

Embarrassed that she had even asked, Rachel stammered, "Sure-sure-some other time. I need to be going as well."

As Rachel stepped off the porch, Effie called out, "Rachel, come back soon, will you?"

Rachel waved and assured her she would.

Chapter 25
Talking about the Book

*R*achel sat in the porch swing, watching the men check the tree. It was almost sundown, and Chris still hadn't gone to work. The sky was spectacular. It looked as if the whole sky was on fire. Immediately, Rachel's eyes were drawn toward the tree. Hovering above the tree, she saw the figure she had seen earlier in the cloud.

Unable to move, scream or do anything, Rachel watched the being in unbelief. Repeatedly, Rachel heard the Holy Spirit saying, "I am with you, Rachel. I have given my angels charge to watch over you."

She saw the figure only for a few seconds. Then it was gone. She could understand how Mrs. Chandler saw her daughter disappear right before her eyes. "Lord? Am I hallucinating?" She groaned.

Wanting to clear her mind, Rachel got her Bible, turned to Genesis and asked God for His wisdom and understanding as she read. She had been studying for about fifteen minutes when John came inside. She moved her feet from the sofa so John could sit beside her. "Did you men decide how to fell the tree?"

"Yes, I think we figured it out. Chris is coming over tomorrow after school to help. Jerry has a meeting. I think Chris and I can handle it."

"John, why don't you get Paul to help you? He knows about trees, and Chris is young. He can still split the firewood."

"Honey, would you stop worrying? Eighteen years old is not a baby. I promise, if I think we can't handle it, I'll call Paul. Okay? By the way, how did your visit go with Miss Brown?"

"It was a very nice visit. You should see this old book she has. The title was chilling: *Angels of the Ages.*"

"I've never heard of it."

"Me neither, but that book and Jerry's sword were quite thrilling in one day."

John's eyes lit up when Rachel mentioned Jerry's sword. "Wow! I've never seen a sword like that! There's no telling how old it is."

"It's is beautiful."

"Who knows?" John said. "Maybe one day, I'll have a sword like that."

As John and Rachel lay in bed, John was still hyped up about the sword. "That was an amazing sword," John said as he went straight into his next thought. "It was really nice of Jerry and Emily to invite us over, don't you think?" Before Rachel could answer, John continued, "We'll have them over next time."

John went on and on about the house and sword.

Rachel held her thoughts for a while, but could take it no longer. "John, are you just a little envious of that sword? I think I depict a tiny bit of jealousy."

"No, I'm not envious. I just think it's remarkable! There is a difference, you know. I saw you all but swooning over that house. Was that a touch of envy?"

"No, there was no envy. I think our house is wonderful."

John leaned over, put his face close to Rachel's. "Can you say that with a straight face?"

Rachel began to laugh. "No, I confess, I cannot. That house is gorgeous! There are a couple of things that bothered me. I wonder why they felt today was the day they wanted us to come over? I have invited them over many, many times, and they have been here only once."

"Honey, what difference does it make? The thing is they did ask."

"You're right. I just feel something's not right though. There are caution lights going off all through my spirit."

"Well, I thought they were very nice."

"They were, John. That's just it. They hardly ever speak to us, and now we have an open invitation to their home?"

"I know, I know. But you need to give them the benefit of a doubt, don't you think?"

"You're right, I do, and I'll try. I know one thing. I'll not say anything about Chris and Paula again. Now that I noticed. Let's close this subject." Rachel paused. "John, I . . . I saw the figure in the cloud again. I don't know why I'm saying figure; it was an angel. I know it was."

"What? When did this happen?"

"He was hovering over the tree while you men were checking it."

"Rachel, God is allowing you to see the angel, not to scare you but to show you that you have nothing to fear." John embraced Rachel and prayed for her. "I love you, Rachel, and I love you and our boy, Stephen Daniel."

Rachel laughed, "All kidding aside, that was some sword, and the house was breath-taking, wasn't it? It was a nice visit, John. We'll have them over for eggnog, and I'll try not to be negative."

John smiled and tenderly kissed Rachel. "That's my girl," he said as he turned out the light.

Chapter 26
A New May

*T*hat night, Rachel was restless and couldn't sleep. She drank a cup of hot tea and started back to bed, but instead she went to the porch swing. A cold wind was blowing and the scudding clouds overhead were the deep gray of slate. Rachel pulled her long, wool coat together and slowly pushed back and forth. "What am I doing sitting in the cold at 2:30 in the morning?" she muttered.

She gasped when a low voice from behind her replied, "I think you're waiting for me," Raptor said softly.

Rachel jumped to her feet. "Raptor!"

"I'm glad you have your warm coat on tonight. You'll need it where we're going. Come, I need you to stand beside me for this trip." He spread his enormous wing and wrapped it around Rachel, totally covering her body. She could feel the wind at her feet as she was gradually lifted. When her feet touched the ground, Raptor spread his wing releasing her on top of a mountain. It was dark and took a minute for Rachel's eyes to adjust. "Where are we?" she asked.

"Hold my wing and step forward. We're at a very special place."

When moving closer, Rachel recognized the mountain as the place where she saw the brown and red eagles before. She looked over the ledge into the valley. This time there was a big bonfire in the center of the pasture. She saw two women wearing flowing chiffon dresses of vibrant pastel colors. They had a crown of flowers on their long blond hair that swayed in the wind. They were playing flutes as they danced barefoot around the fire. There was another woman dressed in like manner. She too danced barefoot around the fire. Her long auburn hair swayed to the sound of the music. She held a long vine of flowers over her head as she swirled. Another young woman, dressed in pale yellow, swung her long dark brown hair as she danced holding a large, silver tray filled with red and white grapes. An older woman in soft green swayed her long white hair as she lifted above her head a silver and gold goblet encrusted with jewels. The goblet had a intricate design woven between the jewels. Three warriors joined the dance. Each one wore a gold breast plate and carried a gold shield. The shields were designed with gold lions standing in an upright position in the center. The blades of their swords were made of fine gold. The handles were T-shape with emeralds across the top.

They wore black, shiny, high top boots with their pants tucked inside. Rachel noticed the blades of their swords looked as though they had never been used. She watched as the embers ascended out of the fire to the sky.

Raptor watched the beam in Rachel's eyes as she began to sway to the music. "Why don't you join them in the dance?" he asked.

Wide-eyed, Rachel asked, "How can I? I'm here with you and they're yonder in the field."

Raptor wrapped his wing around her, and instantly she was standing by the fire, dressed in soft purple. Her ebony hair blew in the soft wind. Instantly, she realized that something was in her hand. She raised her hand to see what she was holding. Stunned by what she saw, she turned her eyes to the mountain where Raptor was now standing. Her hands trembled as she recognized the book she held was exactly like Effie Brown's Angel's of the Ages. She gradually held the book above her head and began to dance with all her might. Then one-by-one, the red eagles swooped down and began to pick up the dancers. The instant the red eagles' talons touched the dancers, the dancers became the eagles and continued flying. As Rachel soared with the eagles, she closed her eyes and breathed in the holy wind.

"Rachel! Rachel!" John said, trying to wake her.

Gasping for breath, Rachel opened her eyes and wildly scanned the room, finally stopping on John who was standing over her.

"Rachel, Rachel, you must have been dreaming. You were making a shrill screaming sound." He touched her bright red cheeks. "You're freezing!" He pulled the covers up on her. "Here. You get warm, and I'll fix you some breakfast."

Rachel stared at her hands. It felt as though she was gripping the book in her hands. She removed the covers and stared at her feet that felt as though they were still dancing. She closed her eyes, trying to recapture the instant the red eagle swooped and picked her up.

John put breakfast on a tray and brought it into the bedroom, but Rachel wasn't in bed. He found her in the bathroom, holding a cold cloth to her face. John set the tray on the bed and hurried to her. "Honey, what's wrong. Are you sick?"

Rachel groaned, "Very sick. I think Stephen Daniel is mad at me about something. I wasn't just feeling sick this time. I threw up."

John put his hands on his hips. "That's it, Rachel! You're going to the doctor."

Rachel raised her head. "Cordilia and I are going to make appointments with Dr. Wells tomorrow morning. I'll be fine until then."

"Are you sure?"

"I'm sure." Rachel took the cloth from her head and started to laugh.

John grinned, although he didn't have a clue why Rachel was laughing. Finally, John asked. "What's suddenly touched your funny bone?"

"I was thinking about making our appointments. Cordilia and I want to make our appointments at the same time, so we can blow Dr. Wells's mind."

"That man is strange, if you ask me. Don't you think, Rachel?"

"Now, John, you only say that because he doesn't have all your charm." Rachel looked at John standing there in his boxer shorts and tee shirt. She glided her fingertips down his cheek and groaned, "And he most certainly does not have your handsome physique."

John turned and flexed his muscles. With a look of sheer pride, he said, "Thank you, darling." He took her shoulders in his strong hands. "Honey, why don't you go back to bed and get some rest. By the way, that was some dream you were having this morning. You know you sounded almost like an eagle screaming. It was quite stunning. Anyway, I've got a few things to do before my next trip. Chris will be over after school to help with the tree. I'll need to get back before he gets here."

Rachel agreed, although her mind was filled with wanting to visit Effie again.

Chapter 27
The Position

*J*ohn got dressed and went into town to take care of some business. One of the men, Roy Adams, who had worked at Todd's Creek train station for thirty years, was retiring. So that he could be home with Rachel and Stephen Daniel, John put in for the position that had opened. The process of elimination would take a few months. Many had applied for the job, but John was praying he would be the one they would choose to fill the position.

Roy would be leaving his job in three days. A temporary replacement was to arrive in Todd's Creek at noon. All John knew about the temporary worker was that his name was Doug Holland, and he would be there until the railroad leaders made their decision on the permanent replacement.

Rachel tried to go to sleep, but to no avail. After tossing and turning, she decided to call Cordilia.

Cordilia was more than curious about John and Rachel's invitation to the Jacksons.

"Totally out of line for the Jacksons," Cordilia said. "Neighbors for years and all of a sudden they come on to you and John with the welcome wagon approach? Baking brownies . . . really?"

Then Cordilia shared something that helped Rachel realize she wasn't hallucinating when she saw the angel. "Rachel, you said when you saw the figure in the cloud, you thought about Pastor Miller's message about angels. I haven't told you yet, but I too saw the angels Pastor Miller was reading about in the sanctuary."

"What?"

"I saw the angels standing around the walls of the church."

"Why haven't you told me before now? How could you possibly keep that from me?"

"I've wanted to tell you, but the timing wasn't right. Now it is. The angels lined the walls of the church just like he read about. The circle of angels was unbroken. One thing I know for sure, the spirit world is very busy in Todd's Creek right now."

Rachel saw John's truck pulling into the driveway. "Cordilia, we'll talk later. John's home, I want to see what happened at the station. Be sure and tell Paul if he gets home soon to drop by about the tree. You come too."

"I wouldn't miss it. Who knows? If I hang around, I just might get invited to the Jacksons."

John hurried inside, pulled his coat off and gave Rachel a quick kiss.

Eager, Rachel asked, "John, what did you find out about the job?"

"Only that the temporary worker, Doug Holland, is in town, and it will be a few months before I know anything for sure.

Rachel looked out the window and saw Chris coming across the field. She patted John's arm and said, "Well, Paul Bunyan, here comes your accomplice tree cutter now."

"I'll be getting the saw," John said as he headed for the shed.

Rachel greeted Chris. "I'm sorry about saying anything to your mom about Paula. I hope I didn't get you in any trouble. I didn't know there was any friction about it."

"That's all right, Rachel. It would be the same with any girl, not just Paula. In Mom's eyes, nobody is good enough. If I'm dating every girl in town, that's fine, but never just one girl seriously."

"I'm sorry, Chris. I want you to know I'm here for you and Paula any time."

"Thanks, Rachel, but I'm fine." Rachel could sense a chill from Chris.

Without speaking, Chris looked toward the shed. "I better go help John." He ran down the steps toward the building. Rachel stood there a moment trying to decide if she helped matters or made things worse.

John saw he was about out of gas for the chainsaw. He decided he would go into town for more. He told Rachel he would be back in a few minutes with the gas. He told Chris to split some of the blocks he had already cut.

John started toward the truck as Chris picked up the ax to split a block of wood. As he drove out the driveway, he waved to Rachel, who was taking advantage of the beautiful weather and was working in her flowers.

Chapter 28
Fortuitous Invitation

On the way into town, John saw Roy Adams as he passed the station. He motioned for John to stop. John went back to see what Roy wanted. As he pulled into the station, he saw a man standing there with Roy. John got out of his beat up, black, 1937 Ford pickup. When he opened the door, it screeched loudly.

Roy laughed. "John, it sounds like you need to take a little oil to that door."

John laughed and patted the truck. "You know, Roy, a man gets used to the sounds his favorite things make. I don't think Black Beauty would run as good if I stopped that squeaking sound."

Roy shook his head. "You're right, John. It may fall apart if you stop the squeaks."

The stranger with Roy said, "I think you could make that truck a real beauty, with just a little fixing up."

"John," Roy said. "I almost forgot the reason I flagged you down. I want you to meet Doug

Holland. He'll be filling in for me until they choose the permanent person for the job."

Doug and John shook hands.

"It's a pleasure to meet you, John," Doug said.

"Likewise, Doug. Is this your first time for a visit to Todd's Creek?"

"I have passed through a couple of times before on a train."

"Are you going to be staying in the apartment above the station while you're here?"

"Yes. Roy has been kind enough to help me get my things carried upstairs."

"John," Roy said, "I thought you might show Doug around town and introduce him to some people. He doesn't know anyone. You know from working for the railroad that loneliness goes along with the job."

John paused and asked, "Doug, why don't you have supper with my wife, Rachel, and me tonight? I happen to know she has some homemade soup simmering in the pot right now." Without hesitation, Doug accepted the invitation.

John smiled. "I'm glad you made the right decision. Once you taste Rachel's soup, you won't regret it."

"I'm sure I won't."

John was thinking about Chris and the gas for the chainsaw. "Doug, I have to run into town and get some gas for the chainsaw. I have a boy that's waiting on me to get back so he can help me fell a tree."

"That's fine, John."

"Let me tell you how to get to my house. You can go ahead, introduce yourself and let them know I'm coming."

Roy cleared his throat. "John, I took the liberty and told Doug just a few minutes ago how to get to your house. I would have shown him the way, but I'm on call here at the station until midnight."

John, still conscious of the time, said, "I better hurry, or Rachel will be worried."

John said goodbye to Roy and headed into town.

***

Rachel was working in her flowers when she heard the chainsaw crank. She immediately shouted and ask Chris if he knew how to use a chainsaw. He assured her he helped his grandpa many times. She felt he should wait, but he said he would only saw the lower limbs off the tree.

After a couple of minutes Rachel heard a car horn blowing. At once she looked up and saw a car speeding up her driveway. The horn continued to blow. Rachel stood to see what was going on. The car skidded, and came to a stop. A stranger jumped out and screamed, "Rachel!"

Squinting, as the sun shone in her face, she tried to make out who was screaming at her. She felt her legs weakening when she thought she saw the angel that had hovered above the tree. The next thing she knew she was lying on the ground with a strange man on top of her, and a tree lying beside her.

Addled, Rachel gathered her senses as the man moved off her. In a kneeling position, he leaned forward, took Rachel by the shoulders, raised her to a sitting position and asked, "Are you okay, Rachel?"

In shock, Rachel took hold of the stranger's arms and screamed, "Chris! Where is Chris? Chris!"

Chris hurried to Rachel, knelt down and embraced her. "I'm so sorry! Rachel, are you all right?"

Trying to focus, Rachel grabbed hold of Chris's arm. "Chris, are you hurt? What happened?"

"I'm sorry, Rachel. I was just trying to help John."

"Help him do what? What is this tree doing beside me?"

"I wanted to fell the tree and have it finished when John got home to surprise him."

"Chris, how could you? He told you to wait until he got back. I thought you were only going to cut the low limbs."

Through all the hysterics, Rachel had forgotten the stranger who was standing beside her. She began to cry as she looked at Chris. "I didn't mean to scream at you, Chris. I'm okay. It just all happened so fast. I heard the car horn . . ."

When she said those words, she realized the man who had blown the horn was standing behind her. She promptly turned, "I'm so sorry. I . . . I can't think!"

Doug put his hand on her shoulder. "Forget it, Rachel, are you okay?"

Shaken, she turned, looked at the tree and back at the stranger. "How can I forget…you just saved my life!"

Chris took hold of Rachels arm. "Rachel, let's go sit down on the porch swing."

Rachel took hold of Doug's hand and said, "Please come sit down a moment."

He nodded. "Of course."

Chris went inside to get Rachel something to drink. Doug sat down in a rocking chair beside the swing. He leaned toward Rachel and said, "I suppose I need to introduce myself. I'm Doug Holland. I'll be filling the temporary position at the train station while they decide who will get the permanent one."

"I'm Rachel Harris."

Doug smiled. "I know."

Puzzled, Rachel asked, "You know? How could you possibly know?"

"I met your husband, John, at the station. He told me to come ahead, introduce myself and tell you he would be home soon."

"You met John?"

"Yes."

Chris brought three glasses of water on a tray, put the tray down and sat beside Rachel. "Rachel, I can't say how sorry I am. Are you sure you're okay? Do I need to call the doctor?"

Rachel patted Chris's hand. "Stop worrying. I'm a little shaken but fine."

Rachel looked at Doug as tears filled her eyes. "Doug, thank you for saving my life."

"It wasn't your time to leave this world, Rachel. You're very welcome, but all of the praise should go to God."

Rachel smiled. "That's certainly good to hear. You're right! All praise goes to God. I'm so thankful. I'm all right. Chris is fine, and I've met a new friend. Thank you, Jesus!"

Doug nodded at Rachel. "I'm more than happy to report that color is returning to your face."

Rachel introduced Chris.

Doug extended his hand to Chris. "Hi, Chris. You need to be more careful the next time you cut a tree down."

"I should have waited for John." Chris said.

Rachel looked up and saw John parking behind Doug's car. He got out slowly, walked to the front of his truck, looked at the tree and called out, "Who did this?"

Chris walked to the edge of the porch. "I did."

Surprised, John snapped. "You cut the tree?"

Chris lowered his head. "Yes."

"Well, it doesn't look good for Rachel's flower bed. Besides, I asked you to wait until I returned!

"And I should have." Chris said. "But there was more to it than just the flower bed."

"What do you mean? John asked. "Rachel can get pretty upset over her flowers. I can't think of anything worse than that."

Sober faced, Chris said, "Then you need to think again. Rachel was working in the flower bed."

A look of panic gripped John's face. "What? Oh my God!" John hurried to Rachel, "Honey, are you okay?"

"Yes, John. I'm a little shaken, but I'm fine. I may not have been if Mr. Holland hadn't blown his car horn and managed somehow to pull me out of the way of the tree as it fell."

John turned to Doug. "You saved Rachel's life! I don't know what to say." He shook Doug's hand.

"How can we ever repay you?"

"How about that bowl of homemade soup?"

John turned his attention to Chris. "Why didn't you wait?" he asked.

"I said, I'm sorry. What else can I do?"

"Nothing." Rachel said. "There is nothing to add, it's over, and no one was hurt. That's the important thing. Now why don't you guys get that tree out of my flowers while I finish supper?"

John put his arm around Chris, "She's right, Chris. Let's forget it."

Chris looked down and took a deep breath. "Does this mean I'm fired?"

"No, you're not fired. Now let's move the tree."

The men started off the porch. As Doug went by Rachel, she took hold of his arm, "Doug, thank you, again."

Doug grinned and nodded.

Chapter 29
Doug Holland

*R*achel had been in the house only a few minutes when she heard the kitchen door open and Cordilia call out, "Rachel, Rachel."

"I'm in the living room."

As Cordilia entered the room, she asked, "What are you doing, taking a nap?"

Rachel sat up. "No, not a nap. I just had a bad adrenaline rush, and I feel a little dizzy."

"Hmm! What kind of bad adrenaline rush?"

Rachel told Cordilia about the tree and about Doug Holland. "When Doug got out of his car, I looked into the sun to see who was screaming at me." Rachel paused.

Cordilia leaned forward and asked, "Well, and then what?"

Rachel still didn't say anything. Cordilia was getting agitated by Rachels silence. "Rachel, you're killing me here!"

Rachel stood and moved to the big picture window and gazed out without saying anything.

Cordilia stood beside her. With her friend still not speaking, Cordilia knew it must have been something bad. "Okay . . . let me ask you in a different manner . . . was this adrenaline rush life-threatening or something?"

Rachel lowered her head without speaking.

Cordilia squinted and ranted. "Rachel Harris, we've shared almost everything, good and bad with each other for a long time now. You know you can tell me anything. So please tell me what happened before I start itching and have to put that stinky cream all over my arms."

Rachel slowly turned and faced Cordilia. "I know. You're my best friend in the world. It's just hard to get the words out, but I'll try."

Cordilia took hold of Rachels hand. "Now that's more like it!"

Rachel took a deep breath and blew it out. "Remember when I told you about the sky looking as if it was on fire and about the figure, I saw hovering over the tree?"

"Yes."

"Right before Doug Holland pulled me out of the way of the tree, I looked up to see who was calling me. The sun was shining directly in my eyes, but for an instant, I could have sworn Doug was the man I saw in the cloud.

Cordilia looked out the window at the men working on the tree. "Hmm. First thing I want to ask is why do you think Chris was so irresponsible? He's usually very mature for his age." When Rachel didn't respond, Cordilia turned to see Rachel standing with her arms crossed and tears flowing down her face. Cordilia rushed to console her. "My dear friend, just cry until you get it all out of your system. Trust me it will help."

Rachel followed her advice. Cordilia helped her to the sofa. "You sit here. I'm going to get you a cold washcloth to hold on your eyes, so they won't get all swollen and you won't get a headache."

After a hefty cry, Rachel indeed felt better. Cordilia called the men to supper. Chris asked for a rain check. He said that he had homework to finish. Again, he apologized about the tree. Rachel assured him that all was forgiven.

Chapter 30
The Warriors

*A*t dinner, during in conversation, Rachel asked Doug if he was a Christian, and if he would like to come church with them. He answered yes to both questions.

Doug took a sip of his tea and said, "Rachel, John tells me you're very active in your church."

"Yes, I am."

Doug suddenly stood, and said, "The soup, and the company was exceptional. Thank you."

Rachel fixed her eyes on Doug. "No, Doug, thank you again for saving my life."

At once, John asked. "Doug, would you like coffee before you go?"

"Another time, John, thank you." Doug stared into Rachel's eyes and said, "May the peace of God be on this house and this family."

Paul and John walked out with Doug.

Cordilia nudged Rachel's shoulder and said, "He sent a chill down my spine when he said those words."

Rachel sighed. "Yeah, a chill, and fifty other things. I'm seeing some very strange things. For some reason, God has opened my sight to see into another dimension where soldiers are gathering, a man in the clouds, and a creature with my baby in his mouth. And how could we forget your visit to the throne room! How do I hold all that inside?" Rachel pressed her fingers to her brow and shouted. "I'm about to explode!"

Cordilia shook her head. "Then talk to me my friend about what you're seeing."

"Again, I saw the soldiers I had seen before. Only this time, I saw myself in the valley with them. They filed passed me on both sides. They held their heads high, and nodded to me as they marched passed. One of the soldiers with the most amazing green eyes stopped, held his sword in front of his face, and said, "The troops are here my lady. Then it ended."

Cordilia paused and put her hands on her hips and said, "I think God is reassuring us in unbelievable ways, that no matter how great the battle we are sure to face, He will be with us."

Chapter 31
Talking with Mr. Spook

Later that night, Rachel lay back in the tub of hot water to relax her muscles that were in knots.

John had paper work to do before his next trip. After her bath, Rachel opened her Bible to Genesis 1:1. She paused, and thanked God again for keeping her and her baby safe. There were times she feared for her baby, and knew the enemy would try and prevent her baby from being born. The tree may have been an accident on Chris's part, but the dark kingdom would have used it to kill her.

So many thoughts were running through her mind. Mr. Spook being at the top of the list for the moment. She felt so drawn to him and knew they would meet again soon. Rachel sighed and said, "God, I know he holds a key to some of what you have been showing me. I know he does."

Rachel studied for about an hour. As she finished, her study, John came into the bedroom and sat beside her on the bed.

Rachel pulled her ponytail holder from her hair and ran her fingers through it. "Your timing could not have been better."

John put his finger to Rachel's lips and gently outlined them. "Beautiful lips on a beautiful woman. Lips I love to kiss." John stared into Rachel's eyes and embraced her face in his hands. He whispered, "I don't know what I would have done if something would have happened to you and our son today. I was thanking God for keeping you both while I was working in the study." Tears welled up in John's eyes. "I love you, Rachel." He put one hand on Rachel's stomach, leaned forward and tenderly kissed her. He lay down and rested his head on Rachel's lap. Like a child, John cried and continued to praise God. She stroked his hair and joined in his praise.

***

The next morning John and Rachel had breakfast together. As they finished their coffee, John had an idea he was eager to share with Rachel. All smiles, John said, "Honey, it's only three and a half weeks until Christmas. Why don't you call Cordilia and see if she wants to go to Norfolk and do some shopping today. I'll get Paul, and we'll finish splitting the wood. Then we'll go pick out a Christmas tree."

Rachel was thrilled and knew Cordilia would love it.

It wasn't long until they were on their way to Norfolk. They went through Todd's Creek to get some stamps and mail some letters. As they came out of the post office, Cordilia got into the car and closed the door. Rachel sat down and started to close the door when, out of the side mirror, she saw the old hermit going up the street.

She quickly jumped out of the car and shouted, "Mr. Spook! Mr. Spook!" By that time, Cordilia had joined her.

Rachel called out again. This time, she and Cordilia moved up the street toward him. "Mr. Spook!" With those words, he stopped. So did Rachel and Cordilia.

To Rachel's surprise, Cordilia called out, "Mr. Spook, we just want to talk to you."

Rachel looked at Cordilia in total disbelief. With her eyebrows raised and her eyes widened, Rachel said, "Cordilia."

Cordilia lifted her shoulders. "Don't make a big deal out of this! I just want to ask him something."

Mr. Spook slowly began to turn around to see who was calling him. Rachel nudged Cordilia in the arm and whispered, "Look, Cordilia! He's turning around."

Cordilia again called out, "Mr. Spook, it's Rachel and Cordilia. We talked to you the other day, remember?" He tilted his head and squinted his eyes. Much to their surprise, he took two steps toward them.

Cordilia said softly, "Rachel, I think he's going to come to us." Rachel and Cordilia took a couple of steps toward him hoping not to scare him away.

Rachel said, "Mr. Spook, I would like to ask you something about what you said the other day. Do you mind?" He took another step toward them, and they too began to move closer to him. They got about three feet from him and stopped. He continued to look at them with his head slightly lowered and his shoulders slumped.

Cordilia again shocked Rachel as she asked, "How are you today, Mr. Spook? Rachel and I have been thinking about the things you said to us the other day and wanted to ask you about it. Is that okay with you?"

The hermit didn't take his eyes off Cordilia. He tilted his head and frowned as he held his stare. He raised his finger toward Cordilia and acted as though he was going to say something. Then stopped.

Rachel asked, "Mr. Spook, is something wrong?" With that, he raised his hand in a halt position toward Rachel and looked back at Cordilia.

Feeling a little uncomfortable at his gaze, Cordilia straightened her hair and asked, "Is something wrong with my hair? Do I look funny or what?"

Slowly he walked toward Cordilia. She swallowed so hard that Rachel could hear her. Eye to eye with Cordilia he began to shake his head.

Cordilia was turning her eyes from Mr. Spook to Rachel without moving her head. He wouldn't deviate from Cordilia's. Rachel wasn't sure what to do. With hesitation, Cordilia asked, "Will you tell Rachel and me where the angels are?"

Without breaking his stare, he asked, "Is it you?" Cordilia looked at Rachel and back at Mr. Spook. "Yes, it's me, Cordilia."

In disbelief, he said, "You're asking me where the angels are?"

Again, Cordilia shifted her eyes to Rachel and said, "Yes, we would like to know where they are."

Mr. Spook got so excited that he began to laugh and clap his hands. He raised both hands toward heaven and shouted, "Thank you, Lord."

Rachel insisted, "Mr. Spook! What did you mean the angels are coming, and you know where they are? Will you tell us?"

He quickly turned around in a circle and said, "Look all around, and what do you see? I see two angels standing in front of me." He turned and clapped his hands as he hurriedly walked down the street. He left Rachel and Cordilia stunned.

They watched him turn the corner and go out of sight. The girls looked at each other, turned and got into the car without speaking. They closed the car doors and sat looking straight ahead. Rachel broke the silence by asking, "What was that, Cordilia?"

Cordilia chilled thinking how close he had been to her face. "Rachel, if he had gotten any closer to my face his lips would have touched me. Hmm . . . the thought of it makes me feel a little sick. When he said, 'is it you? I felt my knees get weak."

"Cordilia, did you hear what he said? I see two angels standing in front of me."

Cordilia looked at Rachel with a frown, "Did I hear? He piped it right into my face. Of course, I heard it! I don't know what he meant, but I heard it."

Rachel started the car. Holding the steering wheel with both hands, she looked at Cordilia and said, "At least he was more sociable don't you think."

"To say the least."

"We've got to talk to him again. We've got to."

Cordilia took hold of Rachel's arm, and said, "Before we start, I want to tell you something."

In a voice barely above a whisper, Rachel asked, "What is it?"

"When Mr. Spook was looking directly in the eyes, I saw something. Besides sleep buggers."

"What did you see?"

Cordilia tightened her lips. "It was really bizarre."

"Tell me, Cordilia!"

"Okay. When I looked into his eyes, I felt as though I had looked into his eyes before. I know it sounds crazy, but I did."

"Rachel rubbed her neck. "That's it. We'll talk to Mr. Spook again."

"I just want to go to Norfolk and do some shopping." Cordilia whined. "I'm also starving. I've got to have food soon."

Rachel laughed aloud and said,. "Cordilia, you really came out today and talked to our new friend. I was proud of you."

"Well, I wanted to know what he was talking about the other day too. Rachel, I wonder what John and Paul would think about what happened today?"

Rachel laughed, "They would more than likely get a big kick out of us calling him Mr. Spook. And they'd tell us to stay away from him, but I can't stay away, not yet."

Cordilia and Rachel headed for Norfolk. Their minds were filled with so many different thoughts. At the top of their list was the new meeting with Mr. Spook, and the things he said.

Chapter 32
Christmas Shopping

When Rachel and Cordilia arrived in Norfolk, the streets were filled with people. The store windows were arrayed with every kind of Christmas decoration imaginable. Every two or three blocks they could hear the ringing of the Salvation Army bells as they heralded that Christmas was near. The weather was pretty-nice for the middle of December. The wind was cold, but at least it wasn't snowing.

Rachel and Cordilia turned off Main Street onto Niccolo Lane. They had only gone a short distance when Rachel pulled on Cordilia's coat. Trying to straighten her coat Cordilia growled, "What are you doing, Rachel? You almost pulled my coat off my shoulder."

"Cordilia, look what we found, and we weren't even looking for it."

Still straightening her coat, Cordilia asked, "What in the world have we found?"

Rachel fixed her eyes straight ahead. "A Journey in Time."

Puzzled, Cordilia asked, "Okay, what is 'A Journey in Time?'"

Still looking straight ahead, Rachel said, "You know the sword I told you Jerry Jackson showed to John?"

"Yeah, I remember. What about it?"

Rachel's face beamed. "This is where Jerry said he bought the sword."

Raising her brows, Cordilia chuckled, "Oh really?"

"Let's check it out!" Rachel said.

"I'm game if you are. Now, Rachel, I don't want you to be disappointed if you can't afford a sword. No whining! Do you hear me?"

Rachel smiled. "I promise. Besides, I'm not a kid."

Cordilia tightened her lips. "It's easy to promise." Cordilia squinted and held up her pinky finger. "Do you pinky promise? You know I don't want to hear whining all the way home cause something don't work out."

Rachel held her chin up, extended her pinky finger, wrapped it around Cordilia's and said, "I pinky promise."

One quick nod and Cordilia said. "Okay, let's go check it out."

As they drew closer to the shop, Cordilia noticed there were no Christmas decorations in the window. "The owner of this shop has gone all out on Christmas decorations," Cordilia chuckled. "They probably can't afford decorations due to lack of sales."

Rachel nudged Cordilia's side. "Hush up, Cordilia! I'm just going to look."

Rachel opened the door to the sound of soft music so soothing it was almost hypnotic. The first thing they saw upon entering the store was a suit of armor so tall that it almost touched the ceiling, and the ceilings were at least twelve feet tall. Rachel closed the door, but continued to hold the doorknob for a few seconds, in awe of all the amazing antiques. They stood just inside the doorway and slowly observed around the store. On the wall directly across the room from the entrance, Cordilia immediately saw a chair sitting on a platform. It looked like a medieval throne of some kind. The wall behind the throne was draped in purple velvet with gold tassels. Above the chair was a circular canopy draped with purple velvet and gold. A single spotlight shined from the canopy directly onto the chair.

Cordilia had to get a closer look. She strolled over to the grand chair and gasped. Holding her stare, Cordilia said in a low tone, "Rachel, come and take a look at this whopper."

Rachel joined Cordilia at the chair. "My word Cordilia! This is unlike anything I've ever seen." The detail work was breathtaking. The hand rest on the arm of the chair was magnificently carved with dragons' heads, and fashioned from rich mahogany. Dragon's bodies made up the arms of this great chair. Enormous eagles' legs extended to the floor. The backrest was in the shape of an angel with massive outstretched wings. The head of the angel was magnificent.

"Hey, Rachel?"

"What?"

Cordilia giggled. In a whisper, she asked, "Why don't you buy John this chair for Christmas?"

Rachel giggled and jokingly said, "I think I will. I wonder how much it is?"

Before Cordilia could say anything else, a grim voice came from behind them said, "This one is not for sale. Perhaps I could show you something else."

Caught off guard, Rachel stuttered, "W-we were just kidding."

Cordilia smiled, trying her best not to laugh aloud, as she asked, "Where did this chair come from anyway?"

"This chair, as you call it, belonged to a great king many years ago."

Cordilia widened her eyes and grinned. "Wow! I wonder who the king was, do you know?"

The woman raised her brows and said, "Rumor has it that this throne belonged to King Sargon. It's rumored that the king still visits his throne from time to time."

Cordilia jested. "Have you ever seen him?"

The elderly lady chuckled. "Many times." Again, she laughed out loud, "Allow me to introduce myself. I'm Delilah. I'm the owner of 'A Journey in Time.'"

Rachel spoke up, "I'm Rachel Harris, and this is my friend Cordilia Dawson."

Squinting her eyes, she looked at Rachel and Cordilia, "You are not from Norfolk, are you?"

"No, we live in Todd's Creek. We came up to do some Christmas shopping," Rachel said.

"Ah, Todd's Creek. I know that place." She put her long finger to her mouth, tightened her brows and added, "Hmm . . . I know. Jerry and Emily Jackson come here frequently. They're from Todd's Creek as well. Do you know them?"

Rachel smiled, "Yes, they're my neighbors."

The lady raised her chin and said, "Ah, wonderful!"

Cordilia was looking around the shop. Curious, she asked, "Where did you find all this stuff?"

Shocked, Delilah snapped, "Stuff? You call this stuff? My dear lady, I can tell you haven't been around rare treasures."

Cordilia smiled. "I guess you got me on that one. I like your analogy of rare treasures better than my raw analogy, stuff."

Rachel, wanting to get Cordilia out of her jam, interjected, "Delilah, don't mind Cordilia. She's full of stuff."

Surprised, Cordilia said, "Well, Rachel, what a thing to say!"

Rachel paid no attention to Cordilia, and continued, "My husband John was admiring a sword Jerry Jackson bought from you."

Delilah nodded her head, "Yes, that was a very recent purchase. I remember it well."

"Would you happen to have any more swords in stock?" Rachel asked.

"What kind of sword do you have in mind, dear?"

"I really don't know anything about swords, except that my husband loves them. He doesn't have one, mainly because they're too expensive."

"Your husband is a lover of swords?" Delilah asked.

Rachel smiled. "Yes, a big lover of swords. His dad got him started by reading David and Goliath and *Richard the Lionhearted.* When he was a little boy, he would get a stick and sword fight all over the house."

Delilah grinned at Rachel and added, "Well, my dear, this may be your lucky day. I have only three swords left. I'll be glad to show them to you. Follow me. I keep the swords in the back room."

In the meantime, Cordilia looked at a shield with two lions standing on their hind feet facing each other. As Delilah walked by her, she asked, "Delilah? How much is this shield?"

Delilah smirked, "25."

Cordilia eyes widened. "Wow! $25 dollars?"

Stunned by Cordilia's statement, Delilah shook her head and headed toward the back of the store. As she walked away, she firmly stated, "No! 25,000 dollars."

Cordilia quickly pulled her hand away, "My goodness! That's just a little more than I can afford today."

With yet another question, Cordilia asked, "Where are you from, Delilah? I love your accent."

"I am from everywhere."

Cordilia grinned, "Wow! I've never met anyone from everywhere."

"Why am I not surprised?" Delilah growled.

Delilah led the way to a small room in the back of the store. "There's a couple of steps at the door. So please be careful."

Delilah was very eccentric. She was a little heavyset, with salt and pepper hair. But you could see so little of her hair under the black turban with a gold trim. Her earrings were medium-sized, gold hoops. She was wearing a black dress with gold trim that perfectly matched her turban. She had on black leather shoes, which tied just above the ankle. To top off the wardrobe, she had on black stockings—so thick they looked like wool socks.

Cordilia muttered to herself, "She may be from everywhere, but her fashion statement screams Turkey or Russia."

Her shoulder was slightly slumped, and she was using a highly black-polished walking cane with a gold handle. Cordilia took mental notes on Delilah from head to toe. What caught Cordilia's eye more than anything was the size of the tremendous jade ring set in a wide gold band resting on Delilah's pointer finger.

Walking behind Delilah, Cordilia nudged Rachel's arm pointed to her ring, and then to the ring on Delilah's finger. Cordilia was all but bending over Delilah to get a closer look. Rachel pulled the sleeve of Cordilia's shirt, widened her eyes and silently said, "Stop."

As they reached the room, Delilah turned and said, "Wait here. I'll get the light.

Glancing around the room, Cordilia asked, "Is this room open to the public, or a storage room?"

Thinking it a bit nosey, Rachel hit Cordilia arm, tightened her lips, and frowned.

Only moving her lips, Cordilia asked, "What?"

Delilah turned the lights on, and answered Cordilia's question. "It's open only for ones that want to see special items like the swords."

There was a sword rack hanging on the wall directly behind a table covered with a cloth that went all the way down to the floor.

Delilah took the first sword from the rack and handed it to Rachel. "What do you think about this one, my dear?"

Rachel looked at the sword. It was just a plain sword with no character. She shook her head. "No, I don't think this is the one." Rachel handed the sword back to Delilah.

The old lady took down the other sword and handed it to Rachel. "What do you think of this one?"

Rachel looked at the sword, but shook her head. "No, this is nice but not what I had in mind. You said you had three swords. May I see the last one?"

"I'm delighted you asked." The old lady walked over to a table, bent down and took a case out from underneath it. After she laid the sword on the table, Delilah unbuttoned the top two buttons on her dress. Rachel and Cordilia wondered what in the world she was doing.

Using her thumb and pointer finger, Delilah reached just inside the opening, and pulled out a gold chain. On the chain was a rather large gold locket. Cordilia tried her best to see what kind of engraving was on the locket, but to no avail. Delilah carefully opened the locket and took out a little gold key. When she closed the locket, she put it back inside her dress and proceeded to unlock the sword case. When Delilah opened the case, Rachel eyes widened, lying on a royal blue velvet lining was a sword that looked as though it was used in many battles. The steel blade was darkened, there were nicks along the blade, and writings Rachel couldn't read. But the blade was not the part that caught Rachel's eye; It was the handle. Perfectly set in the handle were three beautiful stones. The top stone was red. In the middle was the most stunning emerald green stone Rachel had ever seen. The last stone looked like a diamond, but Rachel thought it must be a clear crystal.

In a voice only above a whisper, Rachel expressed her feeling, "Wow! I've never seen a sword like this one."

Cordilia looked at the sword and then at Rachel. "Do you like this one better than the first one?"

Rachel looked surprised that Cordilia would even ask such a thing, and replied, "Oh yes, much more than the first one. Just look at it."

"I am. That's the reason I asked."

Delilah took two pair of white gloves from underneath the table. She handed Rachel a pair and kept one for herself. Rachel put the gloves on as Delilah took the sword from the case.

Cordilia, who knew nothing about swords, asked, "Delilah, why the white gloves?"

With a blank stare, Delilah looked at Cordilia and replied, "To keep the oils from your hands off the sword."

Cordilia gave a halfway smile, "Oh, I see."

Rachel tried to pick the sword up with one hand but couldn't. "It's so heavy, and awkward to hold.

"Yes, every good sword of this quality is quite heavy," Delilah was quick to say.

Delilah put a white cloth on the table for Rachel to lay the sword on. Cordilia leaned down to look at the sword. "This sword looks as if it's been through a war. What era is this sword from, Delilah?"

"It goes back too far for me to even know."

Cordilia started to touch the tip of the blade, but was stopped by Delilah who firmly slapped her hand. "Don't touch it! I told you. You must have gloves on. Otherwise, you could ruin it."

Cordilia felt like a little child who had been scolded. She quickly pulled her hand back, "I'm sorry Delilah. I forgot."

Delilah looked at Rachel, who was admiring the sword, and asked, "Do you think John would approve of this one?"

Rachel took a deep breath and blew it out. "Oh yes, he would approve very much." With a nervous look, Rachel asked, "How much would a sword like this cost?"

Delilah surprised Rachel by asking, "How much do you have, my dear?"

"Not that much." Rachel chuckled.

Delilah smiled at Rachel and replied, "It's Christmas, and I feel very generous. So tell me what you have, and I'll see what I can do."

"I'm afraid. I only have three hundred dollars to do all of my Christmas shopping."

Delilah didn't speak. She only looked down toward the sword. After a few seconds, she looked at Rachel and said, "You can have it for 125 dollars, not a penny less."

Rachel and Cordilia looked at each other and then back at Delilah. "Are you kidding me?" Rachel asked.

"I'm not kidding. I told you I felt very generous."

Rachel turned and looked at Cordilia. She was so excited. "I'll take it!"

"You won't be sorry, my dear. I'm sure your husband will praise you for this purchase." Delilah placed the sword back into the case as Rachel was getting her wallet out of her purse.

Too their surprise, Delilah picked the sword up with one hand. Rachel and Cordilia insisted that she let them carry it to the counter. "Great day in the morning! Delilah, do you lift weights or something?" Cordilia asked. "This sword weighs a ton." Delilah didn't answer. She continued to walk toward the counter.

Rachel paid for the sword and thanked Delilah repeatedly for essentially giving her the sword. Rachel knew it was something she would never be able to afford. "Just enjoy it, my dear. I would rather you have it than anyone I know."

Cordilia was looking at the shield she had looked at earlier, "Hey, Delilah, while you're in a generous mood, what's the bottom dollar for the shield?"

With a sober look, she answered, "$25,000 dollars."

Cordilia felt in a joking mood, so she did what came natural to her. She walked over to the counter and put one hand on it and said, "Delilah, I feel pretty generous myself. I'll tell you what I'll do. I'll give you twenty-five dollars for the shield, and that's my last offer."

Rachel was trying not to laugh aloud, but she couldn't hold it. Cordilia was hysterically laughing. Not cracking a smile, Delilah stared at Cordilia. "Cordilia," Delilah said, "you have no taste."

That was all Cordilia could take. She leaned over the counter, raised her brows and growled, "You're wearing a hat like that, and you have the audacity to tell me that I have no taste?"

Rachel took hold of Cordilia's arm and pulled her back from the counter. "Cordilia, why don't you pull the car around, so we don't have to carry the sword so far?"

With sarcasm overflowing, Cordilia looked at Delilah and said, "It's been a pleasure. You have a great day." Cordilia stared at Delilah until she backed out of the shop. After putting the sword in the trunk of the car, Rachel said good-bye to Delilah, and thanked her again.

Chapter 33

A Slap on the Hand

On the way back to Todd's Creek, Rachel was elated that Delilah gave her the sword for such an unheard of price. Cordilia, on the other hand, was perturbed at Delilah.

Irritated, Cordilia firmly stated, "Did you see her slap my hand like I was a 2-year-old? I tell you, Rachel, it was all I could do not to pull that turban off her head, and tie it around her neck!"

"Cordilia, what's wrong with you? You were acting a little out of sorts yourself."

Cordilia widened her eyes in disbelief, "Me? I was acting out of sorts?"

Rachel grinned at her. "Yeah, just a little."

Cordilia shook her head. "Rachel, there's something wrong with that woman. How could she charge you $125.00 dollars for a sword that's no telling how old and want a whopping $25,000.00 dollars for a shield that could be easily dated? It doesn't make sense."

"I agree completely. The price floored me too. When she said the amount, I couldn't believe it. But I thought of what Jerry said about her prices, 'She doesn't know what she's got.'"

"Baloney!" Cordilia shouted. "She knows exactly what she's got. I looked around the store at some of the things she had priced, and trust me, she knows. To say she doesn't know what she's got is like saying she doesn't know how big that jade stone is in her ring. Furthermore, what's up with the key to the sword case? In a locket smothering between her cantaloupe bosoms? From the looks of the 'stuff' she has in her store, I'd say the old broad hasn't got a need in the world."

"For heaven's sake, Cordilia, must you always be a detective?"

Cordilia gave Rachel a tight-lipped grin. "Yes, Rachel, I guess I must."

The women were starving. When Rachel saw a diner just off the road, she pulled into the parking lot. She turned the car off and looked at Cordilia. "What is wrong with you? You're all to pieces over an old woman who wears a turban and smacks people's hands. What eating at you? I haven't seen you like this in a very long time. Now, confess, what is it?"

Cordilia looked down at her lap and said nothing. She began to play with the button on her coat.

"Are you going to tell me about it?" Rachel asked. "I'm going to sit right here until you do. So the sooner you talk, the sooner we eat. Stop playing with that button, or you're going to tear it off."

Cordilia gradually moved her hand from the button and looked at Rachel, "You better not slap my hand. I can't get over that. She had the audacity to hit me. Who does she think she is? There's something not right with her, Rachel. My spirit was a wreck the whole time I was around her. I don't know what it was, but it was something. Now I've said it. Let's eat. I'm starved!"

Trying to ease Cordilia's mind, Rachel said, "I wished I had a camera and could have caught your expression when she slapped you." Again, Rachel laughed aloud.

A smile crossed Cordilia's face. "Yes, Mommy. I was a bad girl, but that she-devil got to me."

The girls started toward the restaurant. "Rachel, I'm happy about the sword. I bet John will blow a gasket when he sees it."

"I know he will."

Rachel laughed and pushed Cordilia's arm. She recalled the way Cordilia nearly broke her back to get a look at Delilah's jade ring.

"I thought for a minute you were going to try and take it right off Delilah's finger."

Cordilia was almost back to her old self again. As they went into the restaurant, Cordilia chuckled. "The next time we see Mr. Spook I'll see if I can't fix them up for a date."

"Cordilia Dawson, you're awful!"

Chapter 34

A Christmas Tree

*W*hen Rachel and Cordilia arrived home, they found a Christmas tree in the living room on the tree stand but no sign of John and Paul.

"Rachel," Cordilia said, "since John's not here, do you want to bring the sword inside?"

Rachel thought a second and said, "You know, Cordilia, I think I'm going to leave it in the trunk of the car until John leaves tomorrow."

"Yeah, that sounds like a good idea," Cordilia said. "By the way, don't forget our appointment tomorrow morning at 10:00."

"How could I forget that?"

They had been home only a few minutes when they saw John and Paul walking across the field from the Jackson's house. When the men came into the house, John eagerly asked, "What do you think of the tree, ladies?"

"It's perfect!" Rachel said.

Cordilia straightened the collar of Paul's shirt. "Well, I see you have visited the big house."

Paul sighed. "Yes, and I liked it a lot."

Cordilia looked out the window and said, "You know, sweet cake, there is another place people call the big house."

"Oh really?"

Cordilia leaned against the sink, crossed her arms, and continued, "Now come on, honey, you should know this one. It's called prison."

Paul squinted at Cordilia. "Honey, what kind of off-the-wall statement is that?"

"Rachel, I have to be going. Paul gets way to brave around John. Much love, Rachel, and I'll see you later." Cordilia pinched John's cheeks and whispered, "You too, John." She then looked at Paul and said, "Are you coming with me, my dear?"

Paul said, "I have been summoned by the queen, so I better be going."

Chapter 35
A Talk with Chris

After Cordilia and Paul left, John asked about the trip to Norfolk. Rachel gave no hint that she found the gift John always wanted.

"Rachel, I asked Chris to help you with the Christmas lights, if that's okay with you. I got a call from Doug Holland, and I need to help him get settled in."

Cordilia and Paul had been gone only a few minutes when Chris knocked at the door. John told Chris that he and Paul had everything out of the garage."

"Well, Chris," Rachel said, "the lights are on the kitchen floor and a hammer and nails are on the porch. I guess we better get started before it gets dark."

Chris and Rachel went outside, got the ladder and the lights and began their task.

"How are you feeling, Rachel?" Chris asked.

"Fine. Thanks for asking."

Chris looked at Rachel. "You're doing fine?"

"Shouldn't I be?"

"Well, I just thought in your condition . . ."

"Chris, stop. What condition would that be?"

"Being pregnant, you usually don't feel good."

"Did Paula tell you that?"

"In a round-about way. So when's the baby due?"

Feeling betrayed, yet needing to respond, Rachel paused, and then said, "Not until May." She handed Chris a strand of lights. Silently, Rachel and Chris worked as fast as possible to finish before dark. On top of everything, it was getting cold. When the lights were hung, they went inside. "I'll fix us something hot to drink. Maybe it will warm us up a little. It's getting so cold!" Rachel said as she ran some water in the teakettle. "Would you like some hot tea or hot chocolate, Chris?"

"Tea would be great, Rachel."

Rachel took Chris's coat and had a seat at the table. The water will be ready in just a moment."

"Thank you, Rachel. Did you do a lot of Christmas shopping today?"

"Yes. How's your shopping going?"

"I think people make too much out of all of the gift giving."

Rachel poured the water in the cup and faced Chris. "You're right, Chris. Some people do make too much out of it. They spend money they don't have. They forget what Christmas is all about. It's not how much or how little we give; when we give, it's what's in our heart that counts."

"What's the big deal anyway?" Chris asked.

Surprised at Chris's demeanor, Rachel fixed the tea and brought it to the table. "Here you go, Chris. Enjoy."

"Chris," Rachel continued, "we celebrate giving at Christmas because God gave us the greatest gift of all, His Son. Life is all about giving because God gave and continues to give. He gave us life, and in turn, He wants us to give that life back to Him. You see, the big deal is really a big deal."

Agitated, Chris asked, "Then answer me this, Rachel. If God is such a giver of life, why does He take life?"

"Death is a result of sin, Chris. The rebellion against God started it all. It wasn't God. True, the first one to die was Abel when Cain murdered him. Adam and Eve also fell as a result of deception, and they died just as God told them they would. As a result of that sin, we're all going to die. You must remember, Chris, it was a choice that brought rebellion against God. The angels were made with choice, the same as you and I."

Chris gripped his cup so tightly that his knuckles were white, as he interjected, "God made us with choice and then forces us to choose."

"That's true, God gave us a choice, but the way we choose is up to us. He made us to choose, because He wants us to love Him. God won't force and cannot force anyone to love Him or serve Him. If you force someone to love you, it isn't love. Love is something that has to come from within each one of us individually. The angels were no different. They could choose, but each one had to choose on his own. I can't choose for you, and you can't choose for me."

Rachel reached over touched Chris's hand.

Pulling his hand away, he argued, "He gives you a choice, but if it's not Him, you die! Some God." Chris stood.

Rachel stood as well. "Chris, maybe you should talk to your father and mother."

"The way I feel is my choice, not my parents'."

"Chris, how long have you felt like this?"

"Like what, Rachel?"

"Like all the anger that is locked up inside you."

With a warm smile and a pat on Rachel's shoulder, Chris asked, "How did we get off on all this? We were talking about giving and end up on choice."

Rachel's heart broke as she looked at a young man she had taught in Sunday school. How could she not have seen this side of Chris before? "Chris, lets pray about this before you go. It's not good to let something eat away at your emotion. Prayer is a key weapon."

Acting very fidgety, Chris responded, "I don't have time. I've got to be going, Rachel. I'll see you later."

Not sure what to say, Rachel went to the bedroom and got Chris's money from her purse. "Thanks for helping, Chris. I couldn't have done it without you."

Chris took the money and with his avid charm, replied, "Anytime, and thank you, Rachel."

Rachel opened the door for Chris.

He stopped and looked at Rachel, "My coat."

"Oh, let me get it for you."

He put it on, went outside and called out to Rachel. "Come and look at the lights! They look great!" Rachel grabbed a sweater and stepped outside.

"They're wonderful, Chris. Thanks again for helping."

"Anytime," Chris called out as he ran to his car.

Rachel watched as Chris turned his car around. He rolled down the window and said, "You better get inside, Rachel. We don't want anything to happen to you and the baby.

Chapter 36
The First Kick

When John arrived home, he was amazed that Rachel and Chris managed to hang the lights so fast. Rachel wasn't going to let Chris spoil her night with John. This was his last night home before he had to leave for a couple of weeks. He would not be home until a couple of days before Christmas. John built a fire in the fireplace, turned the lights off and snuggled up with Rachel on the sofa. They wanted to absorb the red, green, blue, yellow, and clear lights as they twinkled on and off like a neon sign. Lights twinkled around the large picture window, the porch, the big, fir Christmas tree, shrubs and the two pine trees in the front yard.

As they relaxed, Rachel suddenly grabbed John's hand and placed it on her stomach and shouted, "John feel this."

"John, can you feel it, I think it's the baby." John didn't feel the movement, but Rachel knew it was Stephen Daniel's first kick. She was overwhelmed with amazement at the life that was moving inside her.

As they lay in bed that night, Rachel didn't have very much to say. John asked what was on her mind.

"John, I can't get Mr. Spook off my mind. I just can't."

John took a deep breath and blew it out. "Rachel, I know how you feel, but other than praying for him, there's nothing we can do."

"I just wonder how long it's been since he's had a real Christmas with somebody?"

John kissed her cheek. "Honey, please don't loose any sleep over this, okay?"

Rachel closed her eyes but sleep evaded her. The first visit with Dr. Wells was in the morning, and John was going out of town for two weeks. She was jubilant about feeling the baby move, but amid the joy Rachel was perplexed by the words of Mr. Spook. She wanted to ask him so many questions about the angels that he spoke about.

Chapter 37
Dr. Wells

As Rachel and Cordilia pulled into the parking lot of Dr. Wells's office, Rachel said, "Well, we're here, Cordilia."

"Yeah!"

Walking toward the office, Cordilia muttered, "I hate pelvic exams. What about you?"

Rachel furrowed her brow. "Great day in the morning, Cordilia! What kind of question is that? No woman in the free world likes a pelvic exam." Rachel was still shaking her head when she opened the office door.

They had just signed in when, Peggy Welsh, Dr. Wells's nurse opened the door leading to the examination rooms.

Peggy greeted them with a warm smile. "Well, hello, Ladies! It's good to see you. This is quite a surprise!"

Cordilia was quick to say, "Now Peggy, you know Rachel and I are always full of surprises."

Peggy chuckled. "I believe that."

Cordilia stared at Peggy, who was still smiling, and said, "You have the most perfect white teeth that I have ever seen. Who's your dentist?"

"Peggy, don't pay any attention to Cordilia." Rachel said.

"I'll try not to. Rachel would you like to come on back with Cordilia? You're the last patients until after lunch. We can be as informal as you like. Dr. Wells won't mind."

"In that case, I would love to." Rachel said as she pulled her coat off.

Cordilia sat down so Peggy could take her blood pressure. Peggy looked at her chart and shook her head. Immediately, she looked at Rachel's chart. In awe, Peggy laughed out loud and asked, "You both are here to be examined to see if you're pregnant? Are you kidding?"

Rachel pushed her blouse sleeve up. "No, we're not kidding."

"Have you missed any periods yet?" Peggy asked.

"Yes, I've missed three."

Peggy asked, "You've missed three already? How about you, Cordilia?"

Cordilia shook her head and replied, "Not a drop for three months."

Cordilia began to laugh causing a chain reaction. Rachel and Peggy burst out laughing too.

The women continued to laugh as Dr. Wells came out of his office. He looked over his glasses and said, "It sure doesn't sound like anyone is sick here today."

Rachel composed herself long enough to say, "You're right, we're not sick."

Dr. Wells went back into his office.

Peggy put Rachel and Cordilia in their examining rooms. In a few minutes, Cordilia heard a knock at the door. Dr. Wells came in and closed the door behind him.

"So, Cordilia, you think you may be pregnant?" Dr. Wells asked as he looked at her chart.

"No, not exactly." Dr. Wells glanced at her and grunted, "Not exactly? What do you mean, not exactly?"

"I mean, I *know* I'm pregnant, and I didn't have to go to school to know that. There are some things you just know by gut feeling, and this is one of them," Cordilia said adamantly raising her brows.

Peggy came in to assist Dr. Wells. After the exam, Dr. Wells pushed his glasses down on his nose. "Cordilia, I agree with your diagnosis about being pregnant, but we will let you know in a couple of days about your blood work." He closed her chart, put it under his arm. "Congratulations! Your heart and blood pressure are fine. If you need anything, just give me a call." he said as he exited the room.

The same report was given to Rachel. Dr. Wells looked at Rachel and asked. "How did you two get pregnant at virtually the same time?"

"Well, all I know is that God is the giver of life, and He knows when to give it."

"You and John better do everything you want to do alone, before next May."

Dr. Wells turned to leave the room, suddenly stopped, and said without turning around, "Congratulations, Rachel!"

Rachel got dressed proclaiming to herself, "Yes, yes, yes!" She joined Cordilia in the waiting room. Both Rachel and Cordilia were so excited. Peggy came into the waiting room, shook her head, and said, "I don't believe you two! Pregnant at the same time? Who would have thought? We'll have to do lunch one day soon to celebrate."

Cordilia was the first one to agree. "You know, Peggy, I'm so hungry all the time. I feel like we could do that lunch right now, if you like."

"I would love to, but I have some errands to run before I go home. Maybe one day next week."

"Rachel," Peggy asked, "when was the last time you saw Paula?"

"A couple of days ago, but only for a quick hello."

Rachel paused and said, "Peggy, I'm going to have a Christmas gathering for a few friends when John gets home. I would love for you to come."

Without hesitation, Peggy accepted the invitation. "Can I bring anything?"

"Just yourself."

"It will be very informal. Finger foods, punch and good conversation."

Peggy looked at Cordilia and asked, "Are you helping with the food?"

Cordilia walked by and patted Peggy on the shoulder. "Of course. Peggy, tell me something."

Peggy, uncertain of what Cordilia was going to ask, replied, "I'll do my best."

Cordilia put her arm around Peggy's shoulder and said, "You're a very fashionable person. Do you ever wear turbans?"

Peggy grinned. "Not with my hairdo. I couldn't get a turban on. Why? Are you thinking of buying one or something?"

Cordilia shrugged. "No, I just wondered."

Rachel got Cordilia by the arm and pulled her toward the door. "I'll see you later, Peggy."

Cordilia stopped and added, "Peggy, be sure to tell Dr. Wells to come."

"I'll do that."

Rachel said, "I don't know why I didn't think of Dr. Wells. That's a great idea!"

Dr. Wells, who was standing on the other side of the door listening, joined Peggy in the empty waiting room.

Peggy looked at Dr. Wells, crossed her arms and solemnly said, "What do you think about all this?"

"Well, they are pregnant just as Telmar said they would be."

Dr. Wells took his glasses off, put them in his pocket and watched as Rachel and Cordilia left the parking lot. "Peggy?"

"Yes,"

"It's time to call a meeting. Make sure Chris and Paula are there."

"Right away, Doctor."

Before Peggy got to the phone on the counter, Dr. Wells called out, "Peggy?"

Peggy walked back to where Dr. Wells was standing. She looked at him, she replied, "Yes? Is there something else?"

Dr. Wells put his open hand around the back of her neck and pulled her close to him and whispered, "Is Chris having sex with Paula as he was told?"

Peggy tried to move her neck from his hand, but he only tightened his grip. "Yes, they were at my place a couple of nights ago. Chris said they made love, and this time there was no resistance from Paula."

Dr. Wells let go of Peggy's neck, scratched his chin and said, "Tell Chris to be sure Paula comes to the meeting with him."

Peggy picked up the receiver to call the Jacksons. She put her hand on the phone and stared at Dr. Wells. "Are you planning a surprise for Paula?" she asked.

In a low-pitched growl, he answered, "Oh yes, Peggy. Telmar has informed me not to miss this one." Peggy had a very seductive look on her face. She took her hand from the phone, licked her lips, and smiled.

Dr. Well's black eyes followed every move she made. Peggy pulled the pony-tail holder from her long blond hair and shook it loose with her hands. Dr. Well's black eyes were fastened on her enchanting beauty. She kissed his cheek and whispered in his ear, "I'm here for you."

He grinned and said, "I think we have a jealous wench here, Telmar."

Peggy quickly turned to see if Telmar was truly behind her.

"Darling, are you jealous over Paula?" Telmar asked.

Peggy groaned, "Yes, I am. You can have me any time you want. So why her?"

Dr. Wells laughed, held Peggy's face in his hand, gritted his teeth, and pulled her face close to his and said, "Do you think you're all we want? The dark kingdom not only wants you, but every boy, girl, man and woman we can seduce. Don't you know that by now?"

She cried out Dr. Well's real name, "Shemed! You're hurting me! Please stop!"

Shemed's piercing, black eyes glared at Peggy, "Don't ever forget that you're here not only for our pleasure, but for seducing every man possible for the dark kingdom. And soon Paula will be available too." Shemed still squeezed her face as Telmar watched. "Do you understand me, Wench?" He shouted.

Shaking, she whispered. "Yes, I understand. You were talking about Paula while I'm standing in front of both of you. That's all."

Telmar put his arm around her, and said, "Enough, Shemed. Peggy has always shown her devotion to the dark kingdom. Now, let's show her our appreciation."

Chapter 38
The Book

*R*achel went by Effie's to invite her to the Christmas party she and John were having for their friends. She noticed that the front door was ajar, and she didn't hear Winston's loud barking. Scanning the area, Rachel called out to Effie. There was no reply. Smoke was spiraling out of the chimney, so she knew she couldn't have gone far. She leisurely made her way to the front door. After calling out a few times, she knocked on the door facing. When there was no answer, she slowly pushed the door open and called out again. Rachel's eyes were immediately drawn to the book. After glancing at the door, she was determined to get a quick look inside the cover. She gradually lowered her fingers toward the aged, black leather. As her fingers touched the cover, a stinging sensation jolted through Rachel's hand. Startled, she gasped and jerked her hand back. Unwavering, Rachel glanced at the door and hurriedly touched the cover again. This time there was no sting. Rachel glided her slim fingers down the splintered title. Just as she started to open the cover, the vision of the soldiers began to reappear. Again, she was standing in the valley with them. This time, she too had on the full armor.

The vision was interrupted as Effie spoke softly, "I figured you'd be back to see the book but not this soon."

Holding her breath not sure what to say, Rachel just stared at Effie.

"Catch your breath, child, before you turn blue."

Rachel anxiously stammered about calling out to her, and the door was open and being concerned.

Effie shook her head and replied, "You don't have to go on and on, just say that you were curious about my treasure."

Rachel blew her breath out. "You're right about the book. I was curious; however, I should have waited until you gave me permission. I'm really sorry, Effie."

Effie pulled her jacket off, hung it on the back of a chair and said, "Why would you be sorry? I would have done the same thing had I been you."

"I just came to invite you to our Christmas party."

Effie chuckled. "I can't imagine the Jacksons would be too delighted to see my pretty face."

"Do you know the Jacksons?"

"Mainly just hearsay things about them. They would more than likely tear this old shack down if they could get their hands on the deed."

"Exactly, who does own this place?"

"It's been in my family so long—since the turn of the century."

"Really?"

"Really, but enough about property. I think you would rather take a look at my book than chit chat, wouldn't you?"

Rachel blushed. "Yes, I would."

Effie gently touched the book and fixed her eyes on Rachel. "I don't allow just anyone to come near the book."

"Then I feel honored that you will allow me." Remembering the sting to her hand when she touched it before, Rachel giggled and said, "When I touched it, it gave me quite a jolt before. It must have been static."

Effie crossed her arms and muttered. "I'm sure it was static."

Rachel carefully lowered her fingers to the hard, black leather. She paused and sighed. Effie's sharp eyes followed her every move and response. "Where did you ever find this ancient writing?"

"And what make you use the word ancient, instead of antique?"

Rachel turned her eyes to Effie. "I can . . . I can feel that it goes way beyond just being antique. There's still a very odd sensation running through my fingertips. Where did you find such a manuscript?"

"It's been in my family for generations."

"You, said a friend of yours was the author, yet it's been in your family for generations. How could that be?"

Effie sat down in her rocking chair and replied, "You know, sometimes we say people in the Bible are our friends. Like Jesus, Abraham or Jacob.

They're our friends because of what their lives stood for."

Rachel chuckled. "That makes sense to me, Effie. What does the title Angel's of the Ages signify?"

"Why don't you open the book and gather that for yourself."

As Rachel gently pulled the gold latch and opened the cover, a puff of air hit her face. She swiftly looked at Effie who was stroking Winston's head. Winston began barking profusely. Rachel turned to see why. Suddenly someone pounded on the door. Rachel's eyes turned back at the book. Immediately the cover slammed shut and the latch closed. She jerked and turned to Effie who was opening the door. Rachel didn't see or hear anyone, yet Effie hurriedly said, that something had come up and she had to leave right away. Rachel glanced at the book.

Effie said she would come to the party if she got back in time. She hurried her out the door and locked it.

Rachel paused, wanting to say something, but her words wouldn't form for a moment.

"It looks like it's going to rain," Effie said. "Would you like me to drop you at your house?"

Rachel shook her head. "No, thank you, I'll . . . I'll walk."

Effie closed the truck door and grinned at Rachel. "See you soon, dear friend."

Chapter 39
Harold and Amanda

Rachel Cordilia, Paul and John worked hard to get everything ready for the Christmas party before their guests arrived. Rachel shared that she had invited Effie to the party but mentioned nothing about what happened with the book. Cordilia placed napkins around the tables. Rachel prepared the punch and coffee. The men brought the food from the kitchen and placed the food on the tables. Rachel wanted everything to be very relaxed.

When ready, they joined hands, asked God to bless the party and thanked Him for the babies who were becoming more active every day. More than ever, Stephen Daniel and Phillip Ryan had become a reality.

Doug Holland was the first to arrive. Soon all the chairs were filled. Peggy Welsh came in followed by Harold and Amanda Collins. Sheila Edwards, the church secretary, and some of the board members were also present.

Rachel looked around the room. Chris and Paula were sitting together, watched closely by Emily and Jerry. Peggy took the seat next to Doug Holland and tried her best to gain his attention with very little results. Harold and Amanda Collins captured John. Pastor Miller, Leah, Sheila and the board members were all in a group. The last to arrive was none other than Dr. Wells himself, which was quite a surprise to Rachel and Cordilia, even though they asked Peggy to extend an invitation to him.

Pastor Miller asked grace. Rachel stood and announced that Cordilia had made the snowmen center pieces. Everyone chuckled and applauded as Cordilia flashed her dazzling smile, stood and waved like the Queen of the Rose Parade.

"Okay, Cordilia, you may be seated," Rachel said.

Cordilia took one final bow and Paul gave one final whistle. Everyone chatted as they ate. The topic turned to angels when someone said they thought they had seen an angel in their room as a child. There was mixed feeling on the subject. Cordilia nudged Rachel and said, "I've encountered angels before."

Dr. Wells asked, "How do you know?"

"I know in my spirit."

Dr. Wells laughed aloud. "If you were to see a real angel, you would more than likely faint."

With a quick lift of her brows, she responded, "Oh, I don't think so. Did you see one and pass out or something?"

Dr. Wells placed his napkin in his lap. "These angels you saw, were they good angels or bad angels?"

Cordilia responded, "Both. Angels of light and darkness." Everyone laughed.

Pastor Miller added, "Speaking of angels, I'm reminded of the cunning used to deceive Eve in the garden by the ultimate dark angel."

Doug Holland spoke up. "Praise God, the ultimate darkness could never extinguish the ultimate light."

Harold Collins pulled at his ear and said, "There has always been a war between the children of light and the children of darkness. That battle will continue until the Light of the world returns and exposes the dark kingdom. I feel that time is upon us. Soon the Angel's of the Ages will be on the scene."

Rachel froze when Harold said, "Angel's of the Ages," remembering the title of Effie's book.

Her stare was broken as Cordilia nudged her arm and said, "Someone is knocking at the door."

Rachel told John she would get it, hoping it would be Effie. To her surprise it was.

Rachel introduced her to everyone. Effie tapped her cane in front of John and said, "I left Winston to guard the house. I'll bring him for a visit next time. Can someone tell me where the green lights over at Boone's Crossing are coming from?"

Some thought it had something to do with the weather, but Harold rebuked that thought and insisted it had something to do with the spirit realm.

Harold and Amanda said they had to be going. Rachel shifted her eyes to Cordilia who was stunned by their sudden departure. Rachel showed them out and asked why they had to leave so soon. Harold kissed her cheek. "Rachel, a mysterious wind has been stirred that's about to shake Todd's Creek foundation."

As they pulled away, Rachel saw Doug Holland standing by her side. "Doug, are you leaving too?"

He nodded and headed for his car. "Yes, I wanted to thank you for a delightful evening."

Inside, the topic of angels continued for a short while. Stella mentioned that her mother saw her deceased brother right before she died. Dr. Wells agreed by saying he too had seen an angel when he was a child playing in a field near his home. Rachel fought the urge to share about the angel Eri.

Emily Jackson spoke up and suggested that the subject be changed to something everyone knew about. There was a strange feeling in the air when Rachel asked Pastor Miller to close the night with prayer.

As the people were leaving, each one gave a comment on the events of the evening. Pastor Miller wondered where Harold Collins was going with his comments about angels being God's way of saving his sons. Jerry and Emily felt as though he was totally off track. As Dr. Wells passed by Rachel and grunted, "Your guests certainly have some strange ideas about angels."

As he passed Effie, their stares connected. Dr. Wells growled, "My, my, what a surprise to see you."

Effie frowned and responded, "I don't think you're surprised at all."

Cordilia asked, "Do you two know each other?"

Effie grinned. "We've met, but it's been a long while since our last encounter."

John and Paul walked out with Dr. Wells. Rachel took advantage of the moment and asked Effie if she and Cordilia could come visit soon.

Effie was elated.

Rachel also told Effie about Harold Collins saying something about "Angel's of the Ages."

Effie appeared surprised, but Rachel wasn't sure that she was.

Cordilia and Paul stayed to drive John to the station at midnight. Rachel saw to it that Paul was the one to put John's suitcase in the trunk of the car, not wanting to spoil his Christmas surprise.

Chapter 40
After the Party

*A*fter the party, Jerry and Emily pulled into their driveway to find Dr. Wells standing beside his car. Jerry and Emily were anxious about his demeanor. He was hitting his fist into the palm of his hand, and they knew it wasn't good.

Jerry got out of the car and said, "Dr. Wells, good to see you!"

He said nothing. Emily asked if he would like to come in for coffee.

To their surprise, Dr. Wells was furious at the statement. He groaned and shouted, "You make me sick!" He got in Emily's face and growled, "You better get your mind on something besides coffee, Emily!"

About that time, Chris pulled up. He could tell by everyone's appearance that it wasn't a social visit. No one spoke as Chris got out of his car.

Trying to be friendly, Chris said, "Dr. Wells. What a surprise!"

Dr. Wells frowned and through gritted teeth, replied, "Such an idiot! Why should you be surprised? You all should have been expecting me."

Chris tried to lighten the moment by saying how nice it was at Rachel's. Dr. Wells slapped Chris's face so hard that he knocked him down. Furious, the doctor shouted, "She's got to be stopped, or we are all going to be sorry!"

Emily ran to Chris. His mouth was bleeding.

With his fists clenched, Jerry took a step toward Dr. Wells. He extended his hand toward Jerry and fire came from the end of his pointer finger. The force was so great it knocked Jerry to the ground. "Don't you ever come toward me like that again, or the next time I won't aim at your feet. Do you hear me?"

Trembling Jerry replied, "Yes, Shemed, I'm sorry."

Shemed growled, "Our troops are gathering at Boone's Crossing. That overweight slob of a sheriff has been asking around about the light at the Crossing. We'll have to move before too long. I received word that the archangel Michael is releasing Chaldon to come and war with Haleb. Harold Collin's mentioning Angel's of the Ages lets me know things are moving fast. Who else was at the party, but Effie Brown, or should I say, "Princess Kaylee." She never leaves her post of guarding the book of mysteries unless the secrets of the book are about to be revealed. We must get that book before Rachel is enlightened. Effie Brown must be taken out. Delmar has sent word that Haleb has already bound Timna and most of his troops, which weakens the northern region where the battle will be fought. One of our generals, Teko, and his troops are assembling to reinforce the northern side. The last attempt to take that side failed. This time, we will not fail. The White Stone Kingdom will not be glorified in this region."

Shemed's eyes looked like fire as he stared at them. "There will be a meeting at Norfolk tomorrow night at 6:00 p.m. You better be there!"

Shemed stopped in front of Chris and added, "Bring Paula! That's an order."

Chapter 41
Dr. Wells' Anger

*C*hris called Paula as soon as he got to his room. Emily was upset because of Dr. Wells's violent temper. "Jerry, are you all right?" Emily asked.

Jerry, sitting on the sofa, leaned forward with his elbows propped on his legs. "No, Emily, I'm not. How do you think I felt when he hit Chris? When I started toward him, he threw fire out the end of his finger at me?" Jerry stood, placed his hands in his back pockets. "Emily, I can't protect you or Chris. Anything they want to do, they do, and I can't do one thing about it."

Emily embraced Jerry. She whispered, "You better be careful of what you say. If they hear you say something like that, who knows what they will do to all of us? If we get hit, then we'll get hit. We pledged to follow the dark kingdom, and that's what we will do."

Jerry grabbed Emily's shoulders and questioned intensely. "I wonder what Rachel knows about the ladder."

"I don't know, Jerry. We'll have to wait and see. Queen Jewel must think she knows everything because of the way Shemed acted tonight."

Jerry shook his head and replied, "By calling a meeting tomorrow night, there's definitely something going on."

"Jerry? What do you think they have in mind for Paula?"

"I don't know everything, but if I know Telmar, he will have her body."

Emily looked at Jerry and snarled, "I guess you won't have a problem with that, will you, dear?"

Jerry's jaw tightened, "If I'm told to take part, I will, just as you will." Jerry turned and went up the stairs.

Chris told Paula about the meeting and how important it was for her to go. "Chris, I don't know if Mom and Dad will let me go on such short notice," Paula said.

"Paula, I need you to go with me. We'll ride with Peggy so we can have some time together."

"Maybe next time. We can get together at Peggy's on Friday."

"Come on, Paula. I can't wait until Friday. I can't be without you!"

"You know I can't say no to you, Chris. So, I'll go."

Breathing a sigh of relief, he replied, "Great! You won't be sorry."

"What am I going to tell Mom and Dad?"

"Don't worry about that. Dad will tell them we're going to my grandmother's birthday dinner. The main thing is you're going."

When Paula and Chris hung up, Chris wondered what Shemed had in mind for her. He didn't want her hurt. Chris's feelings were getting so intense. He didn't like what was going on but didn't know what to do to stop it.

Chapter 42
The Ladder

$\mathcal{T}$hat night after the party, John got a call and had to go out of town for an overnight trip. Paul and Cordilia drove John and Rachel to the station. It had been a long day, and and after Paul and Cordilia dropped Rachel off at home, she was more than ready to settle in for the night. She felt extremely tired physically, yet wide-awake mentally. After Paul and Cordilia dropped Rachel off at home, she was more than ready to settle in for the night. She felt extremely tired physically, yet wide-awake mentally.

Missing John was eased by the activity Stephen Daniel stirred in her womb, reminding her that she was not alone. Rachel was keyed up over the party, and the conversation about angels that dominated the night. Her need to know more about what "Angels of the Ages" meant was ever present. Harold's comment and Effie's book were no coincidence.

Constant thoughts of Eri and Raptor flooded her mind. Pressing her fingertips to her temples, she prayed for understanding. As she lay there looking up at the ceiling, Rachel whispered, "Trust in the Lord with all of your heart and lean not to your own understanding. In all your ways acknowledge Him, and He will direct your paths." Rachel knew she would have to do that very thing. She didn't have the answers, but she did have the advantage. She knew the One who did.

Restless, Rachel snuggled up to John's pillow, and drifted off to sleep.

As she slept, or seemed to sleep, she felt her body weightlessly come up off the bed, although she could see herself still lying on the bed.

At once, the scene changed and Rachel felt her feet on a dirt surface filled with sharp rocks. Franticly she began running up a long, twisting mountain trail, which seemed endless—no longer in her flannel nightshirt, but in a long, white chiffon gown that flowed in the wind. On occasion, the pain in her feet was tremendous. A couple of times she fell, but her adrenaline pumped so fast she barely paid attention to her throbbing knees and feet. There was no time to stop. She must keep running, but she didn't know why. At one point, she again felt the pain in her feet that was now excruciating. For the first time since Rachel had been running, she looked down at her feet and realized what was causing all the pain. She was barefoot. At the top of her voice, she screamed out, "Where are my shoes? I can't stand this pain. I need my shoes."

Nevertheless, shoes or not, she knew this was the race of her life. Someone or something was pursuing her with a vengeance. It was so dark, and the terrain so rugged, she could not see the one hunting her. The pounding sounds of horses' hoofs echoed through the sinister realm. The chase ended abruptly when Rachel realized she had come to the crest of the mountain. Terrified, her lungs throbbed from sheer exhaustion. She grabbed her chest with both hands, expecting her pursuer to overtake her. After a moment, she realized the chase had ended. Trembling, she sat on the ground, pulled her knees to her chest and lowered her head. For the first time, Rachel felt the anguish of being so far away from the safety of her home and the comfort of her bed.

After a hefty cry, she raised her head. A brilliant full moon and an innumerable collection of stars filled the sky. Rachel eagerly surveyed shadowy silhouettes in the glimmer of the bright full moon. A blast of air hit Rachel and wrapped itself around her like a tightly tucked blanket. Her body jerked as she become conscious of something running down her arm and leg. Squinting, she tried to make out what was on her. The glimmering light of the moon revealed that it was blood. "Where is the blood coming from?" she aloud. "I must have cut myself when I fell."

Rachel's head pulsed with pain. Crying uncontrollably, she saw her tears spilling onto the rocky ground. Aware of echoing sounds that ringing loud in her ears, Rachel raised her head. She thought, Why would my tears make the sound of small hailstones hitting a tin roof as they hit the rocks? Groaning, she lifted her eyes to the sky and cried out, "Father, help me! I can't go any farther. I must rest. Dear God, I must have rest." Rachel looked around her to see if there was anything to lay her head on. At once, Rachel's eyes were drawn to a large white stone lying near her feet. Too tired to look any further, she placed her weary head on the rock.

As her eyes closed in sleep, Rachel saw lightning illuminate the sky and the heavens open. In the mist of the universe, a gold ladder unfurled and touched the earth. At the top of the ladder, she saw King Rayon standing looking down on her. Suddenly, angels appeared and came down the ladder to earth. Just as suddenly, they left the earth and went back up the ladder to heaven.

Rachel's body jerked in fright. Her breath was all but gone from her. As she opened her eyes, she knew immediately she was in no ordinary place. The holy aura of God's presence caused her to lower her head over the rock and worship. Gradually, Rachel raised her head as a radiant red glow emanated from the stone where her head had rested. Rachel pushed away from the rock when she heard a voice say, "Rachel, I will give you rest."

A sweet fragrance filled her nostrils. Something was dripping from her hands. She turned her palms up. Rachel gasped when she realized the sweet fragrance was coming from oil that now saturated her hands. Without being told, Rachel knew exactly what to do with the oil. She moved to the rock that now looked like fire. Slowly, lifting her head and her hands toward heaven, she cried, "My Lord and

My God!" Then she placed her hands on the rock. The oil covered the rock and saturated the ground around it.

Again, Rachel lowered her head to worship. Her praise was interrupted by a loving voice. "Rachel." Upon hearing the voice, she promptly raised her head. Standing beside her in glowing white raiment was an angel. In a gentle, yet powerful voice, the angel said, "Rachel, mighty woman of God, arise, and I will declare the mystery unto you."

Rachel was so frightened she couldn't speak.

The angel knowing this, spoke to her, "Fear not, Rachel. I'm a fellow servant like you. I've been sent by God to make known the mystery of the ladder to you. In turn, you will make the mystery known to many people." The angel took her hands and lifted her up.

Gazing into her eyes, the angel continued, "The place you have entered tonight is a chosen place for you. Of all the rocks on this mountain you could have chosen to rest your head on, you chose the right one."

"On the ladder, you saw the angels come down, and you saw the angels go up. But tell me, Rachel, where do they go when they come down the ladder?"

"I don't . . . know. Where do they go?"

The angel ignored the question. He looked at Rachel's feet. "Where are your shoes, Rachel?"

Rachel looked at her feet and back at the angel. "I don't know where my shoes are. My feet hurt so badly as I came up the mountain, I don't know how I made it to this place."

"Your shoes for this journey will only be found in the Word of God. Once you have your shoes on, the race won't be as painful. Find your shoes, and I will open the mystery to you."

Before Rachel could speak, the angel vanished, and she was sitting on her bedroom floor. Frantic, Rachel's eyes wildly surveyed the room. She pulled herself to her feet, hurried to the window and looked through the blinds toward the area light. She saw nothing. The dream was so real that Rachel still felt out of breath. She sat on the edge of the bed and looked at her hands, her legs and her aching feet, but there was no sign of blood or scraps from where she had fallen. She felt very sweaty, yet a sweet smell from the oil flowed from her hands.

Chapter 43
Calling Cordilia

After a hot shower, Rachel's first thought was to call Cordilia. She dialed her number, not caring about the time. The phone seemed to ring forever. "Cordilia, answer the phone."

"Hello," Cordilia said in a slurred voice.

"Cordilia?"

"Rachel, is that you?"

"Yes, it's me. Wake up."

"Rachel, what's wrong?"

"I don't know what's going on, Cordilia,"

"Did somebody break in the house?"

"No," Rachel replied as she fought back tears. "I just needed to hear your voice."

"Is something wrong with the baby?" Cordilia asked intensely.

"No, no. Nothing is wrong with the baby."'Well, what in the world is wrong? If you're going to wake me at 3:30 in the morning, I want a reason, so what's wrong?"

"I can't explain it, Cordilia."

"Rachel Harris, you have scared the life out of me. I am wide awake now, so you better tell me something."

Rachel told Cordilia about the dream. Cordilia insisted on coming over, but Rachel wouldn't allow it. She felt better after talking to her dear friend.

***

Christmas Eve had finally arrived. John was home, and Stephen Daniel was kicking up a storm. Rachel couldn't be happier as she prepared for their Christmas together.

The Jacksons and Paula were on their way to Norfolk for a meeting with Shemed. When they arrived, Delilah, the owner of the A Journey in Time shop greeted them at the door.

"You're late!" she snarled. "You know Shemed doesn't like to be kept waiting."

Jerry started to give a reason for being late, but Delilah interrupted him. "I don't want to hear it your excuses. Tell Shemed."

Tension was so thick that everyone was on edge. Paula held tight to Chris's hand. Delilah opened a door leading to a room just off the main floor. The room glowed with hundreds of candles. Paula couldn't believe what she saw. Dr. Wells was dressed in black with a long black cape lined with red satin. Everyone was calling him Shemed. Adding to Paula's surprise, Peggy Welsh was standing beside him in a very tight, black dress. The dress with its long slits was very revealing.

An old black book that Paula thought she had seen before was lying on the pentagram table beside an enormous sword. The room was filled with an eerie quietness. Finally, the silence was broken as Shemed picked up the sword, put it to Jerry's throat and shouted, "You dare keep me waiting?"

Jerry swallowed hard and tried to explain, "There . . . there was a wreck on the road."

Before he could finish his statement, Shemed pulled the sword down Jerry's neck, just enough to break the skin. Then he pushed him backward to the floor. Emily started to check on him but was stopped when Shemed pointed the sword at her, and growled, "No!"

Paula was frightened out of her mind. She was squeezing Chris's hand so tightly he couldn't feel his fingers.

Peggy spoke up. "Shemed, since I'm a nurse, let me check him out and make sure he's not hurt too badly."

Shemed laughed. "Go, you wench, do what you want to do!"

Peggy walked over to where Jerry was propped up on his elbow on the floor. Paula was about to see a side of her friend she didn't know existed. Peggy got on her knees in front of Jerry who was now sitting upright. She ripped the buttons off Jerry's shirt, pulled it off his shoulders, and began to lick the blood off his neck. Paula was stunned. Peggy got on Jerry's lap and pulled her dress off her shoulders, exposing the upper part of her body. She began wildly kissing Jerry, and Jerry returned the passion. Paula glanced at Chris, then Emily. Repulsed, Paula could not imagine how a wife and son could watch as their father and husband was intimate with another woman.

His eyes glaring, Dr. Wells shouted for Jerry to take her to the altar.

Paula was sickened as Jerry and Peggy moved to a huge, oval stone in the center of the room. There they completed their ritual. When it was over, Jerry took his place beside Emily. Emily took hold of Jerry's hand as though nothing had happened and smiled at him. At this point, Paula felt faint. The room was swirling as Chris held her arm.

Shemed looked at Chris and laughed. "I'm happy to see you brought our newest member. Paula, dear, you will have to forgive Peggy, she still thinks of herself as the altar slave. You know Chris and Peggy have performed many times on the stone, and I trust he is taking care of you."

Paula trembled in disbelief. The thought of Chris with Peggy on the altar made her sick to her stomach. Chris's face reddened as he fought back tears.

Shemed smiled at Paula and said, "The dark kingdom is so proud of Chris. He's brought many young women to the dark side. Can you believe he started out as an altar slave when he was only 13?"

Chris wanted to say something but was helpless. He wanted to scream but could not show any emotion. If he did, Shemed would take it out on Paula. He was trapped. Paula's hand loosened from Chris's, but he wouldn't let her pull away from him.

Shemed walked to the center of the room, took a green crystal from his pocket, held it above his head and cried, "Telmar!" A bizarre wind began to swirl around the room and settled into a funnel shape in the midst of them. As the wind spiraled upward, Telmar appeared before them. He first looked at Peggy and laughed. "You started without me?"

Peggy bowed her head. "I am always here for you, Telmar."

"Yes, you are, but first I have news from the dark kingdom. Soon there will be a meeting on the mountain. War has already broken out on the north side. I heard that Chaldon has been sent into the territory to war with Haleb against the dark kingdom. Our Queen said, 'The orders are the same.' Take Rachel, Cordilia and their babies out before the babies can even be born. We're running out of time. We must take the book of mysteries before the battle at the Crossing and make it secured in our kingdom forever. I will personally see to it that Effie Brown will be destroyed."

Shemed spoke up. "We have a plan for Cordilia as early as tonight. In addition, I have a plan of my own for Rachel. Soon, that thorn will be out of my side forever."

Telmar squinted his dark eyes at Shemed. "You better succeed with your plan. Your life depends on it."

"I will succeed! This territory is mine!"

Telmar looked at Paula and slowly walked to where she was standing. He put his face against hers and whispered, "If you need me, all you have to do is call."

Chris squeezed his fist together but dared not move for Paula's sake. Telmar put his arm around Paula's waist and pulled her tight to him. With his other hand, he ran his fingertips across her shoulder and down her breast.

Chapter 44
The Meeting

The next thing Paula knew was that she was coming to, lying in the back seat of the Jackson's car. Chris was holding her close to his chest. Jerry was driving home. Emily was in the passenger seat beside him. Paula was so depleted she couldn't pull away from Chris's embrace. She stared into his eyes. Though she didn't speak, Chris could see the pain in her eyes that said it all. Tenderly stroking her hair, he whispered repeatedly, "I love you." When Jerry and Emily heard Chris, they wondered if he meant what he was saying or if he was just putting on a convincing act.

Thoughts swirled in Paula's mind. She wondered, *What happened to me? What did Telmar do after I passed out?* Over and over in her mind, she cried, *God help me!*

At the Jackson's house, Paula went to Chris's bedroom to use the bathroom and freshen up before he took her home. She hadn't spoken since she gained consciousness in the car. Chris closed the bedroom door and got Paula a bathrobe and towels in case she wanted to take a bath before going home. Fury blazed from Paula's eyes as she glared at the boy she had fallen in love with. In sheer disgust, she knocked the towels out of his arms. Then, she violently slapped his face and would have slapped him again, but he caught her arm.

"Paula, I am so sorry."

Paula broke down and began to cry. "How could you, Chris? You made love with Peggy!"

Holding her hands, Chris replied, "Paula, please let me explain."

"Explain? How do you explain something as sick as what I saw in Norfolk? Your mother watched as your father made love to Peggy. Then Emily smiled and took his hand when he was through. How sick is that?" Paula pulled her hands from Chris. Through her tears she cried, "How many girls have you brought to the dark kingdom by saying 'I love you' and using their bodies as though it were nothing." She pounded his chest and screamed, "How many?"

Chris sat on the edge of the bed, lowered his head and with tears in his eyes, began, "You're right. I have had sex with a lot of girls to lure them into the dark kingdom, but I didn't love them."

"Love? I don't think you know what love is."

Chris stood and took Paula by her shoulders. "I didn't know what love was until you! I wasn't supposed to fall in love with you, but I did. Do you hear me? I did." Chris let go of Paula's shoulders, walked to the window and looked out.

"I love you too," Paula said. "That's why the pain is so deep. I don't understand any of this. You were the reason I went to the meeting. All I cared about was being with you. Peggy was a part of it all. Right now, I'm trying not to see you with her, but it's way too fresh." Paula began to cry.

Chris came to her. This time she wasn't fighting him. He stood in front of her and said, "The only girl I want is you, not Peggy, not anyone else. I have fallen helplessly in love with you. I couldn't do or say anything at the meeting, or they may have hurt you, to hurt me."

"Why did you call Dr. Wells, Shemed?"

"It's just another name he goes by."

"What did Telmar do to me when I passed out? I have to know."

"He picked you up, handed you to me and told me to take you home."

Relieved, Paula put her hands over her face and wept. Chris took her in his arms and gently held her until she stopped crying. While Paula went to freshen up, Chris went downstairs.

"Is Paula all right, son?" Jerry asked.

"She's going to be fine. Dad, tell me something."

"If I can."

"How can you have sex with Peggy, or any of the other girls, in front of Mom and never hesitate to do so?"

"Chris, I do what I have to do. Nothing more, you know that."

"For someone having to do it, you certainly seem to enjoy it."

"Chris," Emily added, "you know as well as I that we have no choice. If Jerry hadn't taken her, Shemed would have ordered him to. Like your father, when you make love to Peggy, you seem to enjoy it as well. So what's the difference?"

"Mom, there is a big difference. I'm not married. I'm not watching my wife!"

Emily took Chris by his arm and said firmly, "You better keep your head straight. For Paula's sake."

Chris stood silently as Emily continued, "You knew not to let your emotions get involved. Until this mission is over, any feelings you may have should be kept bottled . If Telmar finds out . . . or even suspects anything, he will take Paula to the altar himself. If you don't want that, do as you're told. Not only for Paula, but for all of us. You know how dangerous Shemed can be! He must make sure the mission with Rachel and Cordilia is accomplished. Trust me, Chris, he doesn't care what happens to you or any of us. Please promise me that you won't mess up or let your feelings get involved until this is over. Promise me, please, honey."

"Your mom is right, son. This battle is mounting, and I don't want even to think what could happen if someone does anything to make Shemed mad."

Chris looked at his mom and dad. "How did you ever get involved in this mess? I have been in it all my life, but why?"

"Look around you, Chris. The priceless antiques, this house, the car you drive, your father's job, the vacations we take . . . the only family around who has traveled abroad. That's why. We gave you to the dark kingdom when you were born, so we could enjoy life."

"Enjoy this life? Is that what we are doing? Then tell me why I'm not enjoying any of this?"

Emily turned and looked at Jerry. "You say something to your son."

"Chris, you serve either Satan or Jehovah. That's your choice. If you don't want Paula hurt, do as we say."

"You're right, and I will do whatever I am told, but only until this is over. But you have to promise me something in return."

"What is it, son?" Jerry asked.

"I want you to promise me that Paula won't have to go to the altar."

Jerry looked at Emily and replied, "We promise. Now you better take her home. After all, it is Christmas Eve."

Jerry and Emily watched as Chris drove away with Paula. "How is Chris going to respond when Telmar takes Paula to the altar?" Emily said. "I know he's saving her until we gather at the Crossing."

Chapter 45
Chris's Explanation

$\mathcal{T}$he emotions were high as Chris drove Paula home. He took hold of Paula's hand. "When this is all over, I want you to marry me, Paula. Will you?"

Once again, she was like putty in Chris's hands. She would do anything Chris asked. "Yes . . . yes, I will."

Paula wasn't thinking only of herself but of Chris's baby that she was now carrying. She wanted to tell Chris, but she didn't want him to marry her for the baby alone. Thinking of her baby, Paula asked, "What is the deal with wanting to kill Rachel's and Cordilia's babies?"

"Paula, it's complicated if you're not aware of the dark kingdom's rituals. Nonetheless, I'll try to explain. Whenever there are mighty angels dispatched from the dark kingdom or the White Stone Kingdom, it is noised throughout both kingdoms. The dark kingdom wars to stop elite angels from ever being born. The same thing goes with the heavenly kingdom."

"What do you mean angels are dispatched to be born?"

"One of the reasons Dr. Wells wants to stop Rachel is because he knows it's been ordained that the book of secrets will soon be revealed to her."

"What is the book of secrets?"

"It's a book that tells about the Angels of the Ages and the ladder that every angel must come down and then go back up at the appointed time. The king of White Stone's realm holds the time for each angel to descend and ascend what is called Jacob's Ladder."

"Jacob's Ladder? How does Shemed know about Jacob's Ladder?"

"He was there when the ladder was unfurled to the earth, and so were we. Sometimes there are things we can't explain, yet we know. I know we were there. My time to come down the ladder was almost nineteen years ago."

Before she could ask another question, Chris pulled into the Miller's driveway. Paula said, "I have to go in now, but before I do, I need to understand about the babies. You talked about Jacob's Ladder, but that made no sense and failed to answer my question about Rachel's and Cordilia's babies."

"Shemed said the babies were high-ranking angels among the White Stone warriors," Chris answered. When they're born, they will have no choice about their destiny. At the rebellion, those babies warred against Queen Jewel. When they're born, they will continue the fight for what is called the Most High God. I've heard your dad talk about the disciples like

216

Saul, having not been born as freewill people. They made their choice at the great war who their king would be. They're called the chosen ones by the White Stone Kingdom's ruler, King Rayon, because of what they did in the first earth age."

"Earth age? Did you know what Harold Collins meant when he said, Angels of the Ages would be here soon?"

"Yes, I did."

Paula looked down. "Does that mean you warred against the God? Does that mean I did too? Is that why I'm doing all these insane things to capture your heart? I didn't serve God at all?"

"I don't know, Paula. Sometimes it's all a blur. But one thing is clear to me, I love you."

Paula looked at Chris. "I love you too, Chris. I just don't want babies killed. Rachel's or Cordilia's."

"I don't want that either, Paula."

"How do you deal with knowing about it?"

"You have to block it out of your mind. If you don't, it will drive you nuts."

Chris leaned over and kissed Paula. While they were kissing, Pastor Miller came outside. Pastor Miller waved and told Chris he would see him at the Christmas dinner later.

As Paula got out of the car, she turned and said, "All this is so wrong. I want to hear more about this later."

Chapter 46
Stern Words

$\mathcal{T}$he church Christmas dinner was being held in the fellowship hall of Todd's Creek Baptist Church. The number of people in attendance was record-breaking high. Four-hundred people of the town's 1,200 population had attended. The tables were lined with every kind of food imaginable. John and Paul visited with all the guests to make them feel welcome. Cordilia and Stella filled the cups with ice and poured the drinks. Stella saw Chris and Paula talking to each other. Stella nudged Cordilia's arm and said, "I think Paula is doing more than talking to Chris, if you know what I mean."

Cordilia stared at Stella in disgust and replied, "No, what do you mean by that, Stella?"

"I mean you can tell by looking that something is going on between those two."

Cordilia couldn't listen to another word. She remembered her past and the many things that drove her to her past. She put one hand on her hip and stated, "Stella, may I ask you a question?"

Stella smiled. "Of course, you may."

Cordilia frowned at her. "Is Bob not giving you enough sex or something?"

Stella's mouth dropped open. "Cordilia Dawson, you're disgusting! Just what do you mean by that?"

"I mean exactly what I said. I figure it's either your home life, or that awful demon of gossip driving you. You know, Stella, you can do something about either one of those things. I'll tell you something else you can do. You can pray for Paula and for Chris while you're at it, but don't try to run my sister in Christ down. If you're a true sister, you'll try to help her, not kill her with your tongue."

Stella threw down on the table the towel she was drying her hands with and in a rage remarked, "How dare you talk to me like that! This time, Cordilia Dawson, you've gone too far." Stella stormed away from the table. Rachel hurried over to see what the problem was.

"Cordilia, what's with Stella?" Cordilia continued pouring tea and said nothing. "Cordilia, you answer me!"

"Rachel, I can't stand for someone to tear another person down as though they've never had to be saved from anything, when I know better."

"Hmm, did you say too much to Stella?"

"My spirit says maybe I did. My flesh says, Rip her hair out by the roots. I guess I'll listen to my spirit and when I settle down, I'll go talk to her and get things under the blood. I sure don't want this matter to hinder my prayers."

Leah forgot the cake she made and asked Paula to go pick it up for her. Chris was standing there and said he would drive her. The party helped Paula put everything behind her for the moment anyway. She was ecstatic over Chris asking her to marry him and just as adamant about never going to another meeting. When they went inside, Paula went to get the cake from the kitchen. Chris followed behind her. Before she could pick up the cake, Chris stopped her by taking hold of her shoulders. He put his face to the back of her head and smelled her hair, "I love you," he whispered.

Paula faced him. "I love you, and I want you to promise me you will never have sex with another woman. I can't stand the thought of it."

Chris gently stroked her chin with his fingers. "I told you I don't want any other woman. When I am away from you, you're all I think about. I can close my eyes and smell your hair, taste your sweet lips, smell your perfume, hear your voice. You're all I want."

The passion heated up, but Paula knew they had to get back.

Chris, on the other hand, didn't care if they went back at all. "I need you, Paula." Chris uttered. They went into the bedroom, and everything seemed to be going fine until Chris unzipped her skirt. She pushed him away and shouted, "No, not now! I can't!"

Surprised by her actions, Chris asked, "What's the matter, Paula?"

Paula quickly zipped back her skirt. "We need to go."

Chris took hold of her arm as she walked by. "What happened? Did I do something wrong?"

"I don't want to talk about it now, Chris."

"Yes, we need to talk about it now. I can't go back into the group and not know what's wrong. Please, Paula."

She pulled her arm away. "This has been a very traumatic day. I'm not ready to make love to you right now. I love you, and I want to marry you, but I need time. Are you going to have a problem with that? I don't know how to say what I feel right now. I can only be truthful about my feelings."

"Then be truthful. What are you thinking?"

"I'm thinking are you going to run to Peggy or some other girl in town, if I don't put out for you. Do they all think I am a fool, just like they were?"

Chris didn't say anything. He simply stared down at the floor.

"I can't help it, Chris. I wasn't the one who made out with a man in front of you."

Chris took a deep breath and said, "I know it will take time for you; it would me too. I won't rush you, and you don't have to worry about any other girls. I said you're the one I want; I mean that." Chris kissed Paula on the forehead. "We better get back, or your dad will come looking for us."

Chapter 47
Three Potato Salads

𝒯he Christmas dinner was a great success. Cordilia apologized to Stella not for what she said, but for the way she said it, and all was well. Rachel and Cordilia noticed the coldness between Paula and Peggy, but all and all, it went well.

"Rachel," Cordilia said, "I have stuffed Phillip Ryan with a vast assortment of food tonight. I just pray he will have mercy on me tonight when I'm trying to sleep."

"I know," Rachel said. "There was so much food, and I didn't even try half of it."

"Me too. That's why I'm taking home plenty of leftovers. I made sure to get a bowl of Stella's potato salad and Sandra Goldman's potato salad and a dish of Kayla River's potato salad."

"My heavens, Cordilia, you got three different kinds of potato salad?"

"I did," she said as she revealed a box that held the three bowls.

"I too made a small box of food to take home."

Rachel went out to put the food in the car. She closed the trunk and started back inside when she saw a mystifying green flash of light in the direction of Boone's Crossing. The mountain lit up like lighting in a thunderstorm. She rushed inside and told John, Paul and Cordilia. When they came outside, they were stunned at the vastness of the light.

"Great day!" Cordilia cried. "That gives me the chills. What is that?"

That night, Rachel went to take a shower while John was supposed to be studying, but when Rachel came into the living room, she found John on all fours shaking all the presents under the tree. "John Harris, you put those presents down!"

John fell backwards on the floor. "Honey, you could give me a heart attack!"

Rachel moved in front of him and put her hands on her hips. "And just what are you looking for?"

John looked like a little boy who had been caught with his hand in the cookie jar. "I was looking for the special present you said you found in Norfolk, but I don't think it's under here, is it?"

Rachel shook her head. "No, you're not even close." She smiled.

"Honey, please let me open it tonight. Please!"

"Oh, all right! Go in and look in my closet on the right-hand side." She laughed as she watched John get up and run to the closet. He found it, looked at Rachel and smiled. "Oh, baby, is this what I think it is?"

Rachel got down on her knees in front of John. "Why don't you open it and see?"

He ripped off the paper and saw the black case. He paused and looked at Rachel. She nodded for him to go ahead. He opened the case to reveal the beautiful vintage sword. He was speechless. John reached down and took hold of the sword. He quickly jerked his hands away. "My goodness, the static electricity is awful tonight!"

Rachel explained how it had the same effect on her and Cordilia. John picked up the sword, this time with no problem. He was elated. Rachel told him about the Journey in Time Shop and Delilah. She expressed her surprise when Delilah was able to pick up the sword with no problem.

John jumped around like a 5-year-old kid. His dream had come true. He was now the owner of a sword that any collector would give his or her eyeteeth for. He got on his knees in front of Rachel and said, "You have made me a very happy man, and I . . ." Before John could finish his thought, he noticed that the green stone in the center of the sword began to glow. John looked at her. "What's causing the stone to do that?" he asked. Instantly, stinging pains shot through his hands. He threw the sword on the floor. Suddenly a green mist began to emerge from the green stone. John and Rachel held each other.

"John, what's happening?" Rachel shouted.

"I don't know." John answered equally as scared. The mist went from the floor to the ceiling and hovered over them. After a few moments, the mist slowly descended and surrounded them. The light in the bedroom went out. The glow from the mist filled the room, and the odor of strong sulfur was almost unbearable. John and Rachel were unable to move as the green mist circled them while they remained on their knees beside the bed crying out to the Most High for help.

Chapter 48
Gathering

White Stone Kingdom was on full alert. At every point around the chamber, the Red Eagle elite guard stood at attention. Haleb made a request to speak to King Rayon and counsel. Immediately, he stood in the circle before the counsel. King Rayon joined him in the circle.

"Haleb, my brother," King Rayon said as he placed his right hand on Haleb's right shoulder.

"King Rayon, the war is intensifying against Rachel and Cordilia. As we know, Telmar has been summoned from the pit to assist Shemed. They are both in the battle area. Their mission ordered by Jewel is to destroy the babies before they can be born and kill Rachel and Cordilia as well."

King Rayon looked toward the counsel. "This comes as no surprise," he said. "Wisdom has informed us of the dark kingdom's plan to do so."

Concerned, Haleb continued, "My King, the enemy troops are mounting the attack on the northern side at Boone's Crossing. I saw the demon, Depression, sending out his troops. Telmar and his host have begun their assault. The sexual goddess, Iris, is destroying many in the churches and town. Her main targets are the young. She lures them into her house, sets the romantic stage and leaves them in the trap. Her cover is none other than Peggy Welsh, Dr. Wells' nurse. Grave darkness has stirred chaos. Delilah is using her witchcraft to send curses against the town."

"They are powerful demons, Haleb." Rayon said. "But no comparison for the Lord of the heavenly host. Our Father is using everything for His purpose. Allowing the good and the bad to grow together, ultimately fulfilling the prophecy of old."

Queen Deborah stood. "What of Princess Kaylee and the manuscript?"

"Princess Kaylee has befriended Rachel, and soon the secrets will be made known. Rachel saw Effie on Christmas day. This could very well be the time of revelation. Effie will know when it's time to make known the ancient mysteries to Rachel."

Princess Sandra stood. "Raptor is teaching Rachel how to wear the mantel at random without having to take it from the chest. When that happens, she will be ready to enter the holy place and view The Ancient Tree."

Prince William asked, "King Rayon, will Raptor and the White Stallion take Rachel to eat the sweet nectar from the stump?"

"Yes, the stallion will join Raptor." Rayon closed his eyes for a moment, as he recalled his visit to the enchanted stump.

In a blink, King Rayon raised his hand. "Haleb, Wisdom has informed me that Telmar is now in John and Rachel's bedroom terrifying them. The battle is fierce against them. Go help them and bring deliverance!"

Haleb raised his right hand and declared, "Glory to the Most High God!"

As Heleb turned to go, Rayon called out to him.

Haleb turned to respond. "Yes, your majesty?"

"When the time comes for you to bring down Shemed, Telmar and Delilah, I will send the Ancient Ones to war with you. Wisdom will tell me when the time is right."

"What about Paul and John?"

"Wisdom has already been sent to them. They will be the support that the women need. Now go."

Haleb bowed his head. With the speed of light, he was in the Harris's bedroom.

John and Rachel were paralyzed on their knees. The green haze had circled them. They heard laughing, jeering and growling, but could see nothing but the green mist. Suddenly a forceful wind with the sound of a freight train invaded the room. The deafening sound of steel blades clanging together, chilling groans and screams, caused the walls to vibrate. Immediately they felt a presence in the room surround them. At once, the mist was gone, and silence filled their home.

Again, John and Rachel were free to move. Shaken, John asked, "Are you all right, Rachel?"

Rachel exhaled. "I don't know. I think I am. How about you?"

Standing, John replied, "I think so." He helped Rachel up from the floor and stared at the sword lying on the floor. "Rachel, did that green stuff come from the handle of the sword?"

"I have no idea." John and Rachel sat down on the edge of the bed.

"I heard the roar of the wind and swords hitting together. My ears are still ringing. Did you hear the swords, John?"

John ran his fingers through his hair. "Yes, I heard the swords. Did . . . did you feel something brushing up against us while we were in the floor?"

Rachel looked down and closed her eyes. "Oh yes, I did," she said breathlessly.

John put his hand on her stomach. "Honey, is Stephen all right?"

"Stephen is fine. At this point, I think he's doing better than we are."

"Let's pray," John said. They bowed on their knees, held hands and faced each other. They lifted their voices in praise to God for sending warring angels to fight on their behalf, and for His faithfulness.

As they prayed, they didn't forget it was Christmas Eve. They lifted their voices and thanked God for giving His Son, that all mankind might have eternal life. Elated, in the midst of being shaken with fear, they thanked God for the special miracle that He had given to them, a son.

Chapter 49
The Complaint

*O*n Christmas morning, when no one sleeps in, John and Rachel were sleeping soundly. Suddenly, Rachel sat straight up in the bed, awakened by her telephone ringing. She stretched, yawned, rolled her shoulders and answered the phone. "Hello."

"Rachel?"

"And who else would it be? Merry Christmas, my dear friend!"

"I don't know if it's good or not, Rachel."

"Why would you say that? Is something wrong? Is it the baby?"

Cordilia whimpered. "It's not good. Not good at all."

"Is Paul okay?"

"Yes, he's fine. It's me, or a part of me."

"Well what part of you is it?"

In a high-pitched whining voice, Cordilia said, "It's my belly!"

"Are you cramping or something?"

"No, Rachel. It's not that."

In a stern voice, Rachel said, "I'm not playing, Cordilia. Now, what's wrong?"

In a voice so high-pitched that Rachel could hardly understand, Cordilia whined, "I have a stretch mark on my belly. It's the size of a number two writing pencil!"

"What? You scare me over a stretch mark?"

"Well now, Rachel, you know, I have always had a perfectly flat stomach. Now it's marked forever!"

"For heaven's sake, Cordilia, get a grip! Your stomach was flat but not flat enough to be crying like a baby over a stretch mark. You do have some bulges. Besides, baby Phillip must have room to grow and he will be worth all the stretch marks in the world. Now stop your whining!"

"Easy for you to say, Rachel. You don't have flesh that's separating. That's why you're so calm."

"Cordilia, I have three stretch marks. Do you hear me? Three!"

"Three? How could you keep something like that to yourself? I am your best friend, and you didn't share that?"

"It was easy not to share. Now, I am going to hang up. I'll see you later tonight. Merry Christmas!"

John got dressed and went to deliver a goody basket to Harold and Amanda Collins. Rachel wanted to go for a walk and take a present to Effie and wish her a Merry Christmas. She couldn't stand the thought of her being alone on such a special day. She opened the kitchen door, screamed and slammed it shut as fast as she opened it. Doug

Holland was standing on the other side of the door, hand poised to knock. Realizing what she had done, without delay Rachel opened the door. "Doug, I am so sorry. You startled me."

"I'm sorry."

"Merry Christmas, Doug!"

"And to you, Rachel."

"John has gone to deliver a Christmas present to the Collinses. He should be home soon."

"It's you, I'd like to talk with, if you have a minute."

"Sure. I was going to visit Effie Brown. You met her last night at the dinner. Would you like to walk with me?"

"I'd love to."

"What's on your mind, Doug?"

"Cordilia."

Rachel stopped and looked at Doug. "What about Cordilia?"

"Rachel, if you see any change, any change at all, I want you to get her to the doctor immediately."

"What do you mean get her to a doctor?"

A car pulled up beside them. It was Paula. She was on her way to the Jacksons. Paula wanted to ask Rachel a question. Doug said he had to be going. Rachel wanted to talk to Doug concerning Cordilia, and Paula wanted to ask her something. She didn't know what to do. "Just one moment, Paula. Why don't you pull over, and I'll be right there."

Rachel looked at Doug. "What do you think is going to happen to Cordilia?"

"Just trust me, Rachel. Listen carefully. Do not take her to Dr. Wells. Take her to Dr. White."

"I don't understand."

"You don't have to understand right now. Please do what I tell you. It could mean life or death for her."

"What?"

"Please trust me!" Doug turned and went back toward the house. Rachel couldn't go after him and leave Paula sitting. She called out, "Doug, wait!" But it was too late. Paula walked back to where she was standing.

"I hope I'm not interrupting anything," Paula said as she looked at Doug departing.

"No, Paula. You aren't. Where are you going on this cool Christmas morning?"

"I am dropping by to wish the Jacksons a Merry Christmas. Rachel, can I ask you a personal question?

Paula pointed at the present and asked, "Taking someone a gift?"

"Yeah. Effie's alone, and so I'm taking her something. Now what did you want to ask me?"

"Oh yeah. What . . . what does it feel like to be pregnant?"

Rachel looked at her and frowned. "Now why would you ask me that?"

"I just wondered. That's all."

"Paula, honestly, there are so many feelings that it's hard to describe. One minute you feel like you can jump hurdles. The next minute you could be throwing up in the toilet."

Paula laughed. "Rachel, that was a Cordilia statement."

"Hmm, John said that same thing the other day. Cordilia must be rubbing off on me. Paula, you know I'm here for you."

As Paula looked at Rachel, she could hardly stand the thought of something happening to someone who had shown so much kindness to her. How could anyone hurt an innocent baby?

"Paula. Paula," Rachel called. "What is it? I know something's not right with you. I pray for you every day, and you can't fool me all the time. I may not know exactly what the problem is, but eventually the Holy Spirit will show me . . . only because God loves you, not that it's important for me to know, but He will show me."

Paula turned to walk away but turned back briefly. "I have to be going now."

Rachel took Paula by the arm and compassionately said, "You can walk away from me, Paula, but please don't walk away from God."

Paula got into her car without a response. Rachel watched her drive away toward the Jackson's. Rachel prayed aloud, "Warring angels go forth, surround her and war on her behalf, in Jesus' name."

The air was extremely cool, with the wind picking up, so Rachel hurried on to Effie's.

Chapter 50
Effie and Rachel

*A*s Rachel neared the porch, she listened for Winston's bark, but heard nothing. Before she stepped on the porch, the screeching door opened. Effie was sitting in her rocking chair near the old stone fireplace. She called out without turning, "Merry Christmas, Rachel! Come join me at the fire and warm yourself."

Rachel looked at the door, wondering how it opened own its own. She took hold of the knob and closed the door. "Merry Christmas, Effie!"

Effie motioned to Rachel. "Come on around where I can see who I'm talking to."

Rachel stood before her and handed her the gift. "I wanted to bring you a special gift to celebrate our first Christmas as being friends."

Effie smiled and took the present. She carefully removed the paper as though she were going to save it. Rachel watched with anticipation. When she took the lid off the small box, she fixed her eyes on Rachel, and said, "You want me to have this?"

Rachel nodded. "Yes. When I went to buy you a gift, I could find nothing that was right. So, I decided to give you something personal that means a lot to me."

Effie took the mother of pearl cameo from the box. "Would your mother approve of you doing this?"

"How . . . how did you know it was my mother's?"

"You didn't buy it. Therefore it was something in your possession. Cameos are usually a mother's piece of jewelry."

"Effie, for some reason I feel very close to you," Rachel said. "We haven't known each other that long, yet I feel I have known you my whole life."

"The feeling is mutual." Effie handed the brooch to Rachel. "Would you do me the honors of pinning this on my sweater?"

After helping with the brooch, Rachel started to sit down, but Effie asked her not too. She pushed herself up on her cane, and said, "Because you chose to give me a gift that had great meaning to you, I want to give something very meaningful to me."

Rachel turned to the table where the book was lying. A tin candleholder held a thin white candle that had been burning for some time. Layers of wax were piled around the holder. On the other side of the book lay a small inkwell and a white-feathered quill pen. Effie pointed her cane at Winston and told him to guard the door. There was an extreme quietness that filled the atmosphere as Effie opened the aged book. To Rachel's surprise, the pages contained nothing but names written in antique script.

Rachel asked, "It's a manuscript filled with names?"

Effie turned her hazel eyes to Rachel. "Names indeed. Names that will forever be revered. *Angels of the Ages.*"

Effie asked Rachel to bring the book to the table where she was sitting. Rachel put the open book down and sat across from Effie, anticipating what she had to say. Effie smiled as she touched the names. "I'll start by saying, "The names on these pages go back to a time we call, The Beginning."

"The beginning of what?" Rachel asked.

"The Beginning of the Angels of the Ages. You see, Rachel, the beginning was a time, when all the angels of the Most High sang together in harmony. A time of peace and joy filled the universe. There was an archangel by the name of Tashmere. He was rewarded for his faithfulness to his Creator. Being an elite son, he was privileged to know how to work the deep magic. He was made high priest over a province called Emerald Shore. The Shorelyn loved him. Tashmere overflowed with joy. He was far taller than any that lived on the Emerald Shore. His face was noble and beautiful. His hair was as yellow as the sun. His wisdom shocked the Shorelyns. They knew he came from the place of the Most High God.

"There he served as high priest making sure that God's children were not having troubles. Tashmere, as the high priest encouraged the Shorelyns or lower angels to feel free to confess anything that may have been bothering them. We don't think of angels as having troubles. That was far from the truth. Tashmere was allotted a host that worked under his supervision. One of his most faithful was this name right here." Effie pointed her long, slender finger toward the middle of the page. "His name is Shemed. He, like Tashmere, had many titles. Emerald Shores was situated on the most beautiful of seas. The sea of Enchantment, because of its beauty and wealth. The land flourished with gold, silver, diamonds and above all, emeralds.

"Emerald Shore had a queen. Her name was Jewel. At first, she tried to hide that she was jealous because Tashmere had been sent to rule over her kingdom. Rage grew in Queen Jewel's heart against Tashmere. She set her mind to destroy him. Tashmere thought Jewel was the most magnificent woman he had ever seen. She took advantage of that weakness she saw in Tashmere. After a while, Tashmere grew comfortable at Emerald Shores. He forgot what the Most High had told him about guarding his heart. Although he knew the deep magic and the seduction it held, when it came to Queen Jewel, he felt helpless. She used powerful illusions to lure him to a place he would never escape."

Rachel blew out her breath and asked, "With his power, what place could possibly prevent him from recognizing her trap?"

"A special place called the Garden of Fire."

"What about Shemed? What was his role at the Emerald Shore?"

"He used trickery to prove the lower angels were authentic in loyalty . If he saw anything out of the ordinary, he reported back to Tashmere, who in turn told the Most High at the appointed times. He ..."

Winston growled and then barked repeatedly. The book slammed shut and the lock fell in place, as Effie stood and approached the door. "What is it, Winston? Do you smell what I do?"

Effie waved her hand and the door flew open.

Rachel held her breath, not sure what she was viewing.

There was no one at the door, but Effie hurried out anyway. She came back inside and looked at Rachel who was now standing wide-eyed, wondering what was going on.

Effie closed the door. "It's time to go now, Rachel. We'll continue another day."

Rachel moved to the door, stopped and asked, "What . . . what's going on Effie. How did you do that with the door? And the book slammed shut and locked by itself? Are you a . . . ?"

Effie finished her thought, ". . . a witch or magician? No, Rachel, I'm not, so put those thoughts to rest. You better go now, John's looking for you."

Just as Rachel started to the door, she heard John call her name. Rachel frowned and looked at Effie.

Effie chuckled. "I saw him coming across the field."

Rachel grinned and asked if she would like to have Christmas dinner with them. Effie said she had to go to Benson. Rachel assured Effie she would be back soon to hear the rest of the story and more about the book.

Chapter 51

A Warning

When Paula arrived at the Jacksons, she and Chris went to his bedroom and closed the door. Paula looked at Chris. "Chris, I can't do this."

Puzzled, Chris asked, "Can't do what?"

"I can't stand by and let anyone kill innocent babies, or Rachel, or Cordilia."

Panicked, Chris took Paula by her shoulders and demanded, "Listen to me, Paula. You can't say anything, do you hear me?"

"I am not a murderer. Those babies haven't done anything. Neither have Rachel and Cordilia. I don't care what you said about Jacob's Ladder."

Fearing Shemed would kill Paula for even thinking such a thought, Chris asked, "Paula, do you want to live or die?"

Paula shook her head. "What do you mean, Chris? Of course, I want to live."

"Then you better listen to me. Shemed will kill us both if he even suspects that you're thinking of telling anyone about this. When you joined the dark kingdom's army, it wasn't a game. You better not play around with this. I told you, when this is over, then we will get out, but not before. It's not because I don't want to hurt anyone. I can't help it. They could kill us all." Chris embraced Paula and said, "I couldn't stand for anything to happen to you. I love you, and I need you."

"I need you, Chris, and you know I love you, but this is like a nightmare, and I can't wake up."

"It will all be over soon. We'll leave Todd's Creek, and never look back. I promise."

Chapter 52
Rachel and Cordilia Visit Effie

$\mathcal{R}$achel couldn't get what Doug Holland had said about Cordilia out of her mind. She felt she had to call her friend. Paul and Cordilia were on her way to visit Rachel. When Cordilia arrived, she went straight for the refrigerator. "Rachel, do you have any cereal?" Cordilia asked as she looked through the refrigerator.

"Yes, but it isn't in the refrigerator. It's in the cabinet."

Cordilia took a box of cereal from the cabinet. "Ah, here it is, but not for long!" Cordilia poured the cereal into the bowl, looked at Rachel and asked, "Do you have peanut butter?"

"Cordilia Dawson, you're not going to eat peanut butter and cereal together. Now, you sit and eat your cereal and then you can have peanut butter."

"I am so hungry all the time, Rachel. Are you more hungry than usual or is Stephen Daniel having mercy on you?"

"Yes, I am eating more, but only on occasion, Cordilia," Rachel said as she played with a napkin. "Do you feel okay?"

"Rachel, honey, I feel wonderful in every way except hunger. Why? Do I look sick or something?"

"No. Let's just change the subject."

"Please do," Cordilia said as she washed her cereal bowl and put it away.

"Cordilia, have you mentioned to Paul my wanting to see Mr. McKinney?"

"Yes, I did, and he said you've lost your mind. Of course, I backed him up even though I didn't mean it."

"Cordilia, there's something God wants me to know about Mr. McKinney and the place where he lives. I don't know what, but after the New Year's Eve service, I will find out."

Cordilia giggled. "Rachel, let's just call him Mr. Spook. That is the way we first knew him, and I like it."

"That's fine with me. John has another trip on the second of January. With the help and grace of God, you and I will go to that mountain."

"What makes you think I want to go?"

"You wouldn't miss it for anything, and you know that."

"I know that if I continue to eat like this, I may not be able to go up a mountain."

Rachel laughed. "If you continue to eat like that, your Sophia Loren figure will look more like Maw Kettle."

Cordilia threw her napkin at Rachel and laughed. "Shut up!"

Rachel asked Cordilia to sit with her at the table for a few minutes. She told Cordilia about the things that had happened at Effie's.

Cordilia pressed her fingers to her temples. "How can all this be happening? How did the door open on its own? I am dying to know about that puff of air you felt when you opened that book. Is she a witch, Rachel?"

"No. I'm not sure at this point who or what she is, but she's not a witch. I want to hear the rest of story about the Angels of the Ages. Do you want to go with me and hear the story for yourself?"

Cordilia was picking out all the yellow jelly beans from the jar and making a pile in front of her. "She may not want me there," she said.

Rachel looked out the window toward Effie's. "Would you like to go now? Her truck is home, and it will be awhile before John returns."

Cordilia crammed several jelly beans in her mouth. "It's raining so hard outside. It's a rain like you would see in a horror movie, add some thunder and lightning, wow. Rachel, do you think it will be scary with all this rain at Effie's?"

Rachel put her coat on. "No, it won't be scary. Come on, I'll take my car."

Cordilia put the candy in her coat pocket and muttered, "Rachel, if a door or a book opens by itself, we're out of there." She laughed aloud. "Do you think I should I wear my garlic necklace?"

Chapter 53
Explaining the Book

*A*s they got out of the car, the two women could hear Winston's loud, fast barks. The porch was soaked from the substantial leaks in the tin roof. Cordilia nudged Rachel's arm, and teased, "It's not too late to turn back. Effie is old, and we might outrun her, but that mongrel dog might take our legs off."

Rachel tried not to laugh out loud.

Effie was taking longer to answer the door than usual. Rachel knocked again. This time, Effie opened the door. She looked around them into the yard. "You two better get in out of the rain," she said as she closed the door.

"Effie, do you remember Cordilia from the party?" Rachel asked.

"I do," Effie replied as she walked toward the fireplace. "Come, warm yourselves before you get a cold. This storm is quite unexpected. I believe the weatherman said it was to be sunny and cold."

Rachel asked Effie if she would continue the story about the names in the book. Effie fixed her eyes on Cordilia. "Because you have a pure heart before the Most High, you may hear what I have to say, Cordilia. Now where were we?" Effie asked as she sat down in her rocking chair. She pointed her cane toward a couple of wooden chairs and told Rachel and Cordilia to be seated.

Rachel spoke up and reminded Effie, "You were talking about Shemed using his cunning to prove all the lower angels."

"Yes, I remember now. Queen Jewel planned her time to destroy Tashmere. She lured him daily to the Garden of Fire."

Cordilia asked, "Why was it called the Garden of Fire?"

"Because there were two trees in the heart of the garden—that burned with eternal flames, that would never be consumed. One tree blazed with the flames of the Most High. The other tree carried the fire of knowledge of all things, both good and evil. Tashmere was well acquainted with the garden, because, as high priest, part of his duties was to guard the two trees."

"How could he guard flaming trees? I mean if they were burning, who could touch them?" Cordilia asked.

Effie frowned and said, "Fire can't burn fire. The only way one can be hurt by the blaze is to allow the holy fire within to be extinguished." A clap of thunder caused Effie to pause. Winston's hair raised on his back, and he gave out a low growl. "Be still, dog. It's okay."

Cordilia groaned and asked, "Should we come back another time, Rachel?"

"No. Maybe the storm will pass in a few minutes. I really want to hear what Effie has to say."

Cordilia nodded at Effie. "That makes two of us."

Effie grinned and continued, "Jewel enticed Tashmere to go to the garden with her. There she swayed constantly displaying her beauty and inviting Tashmere to take of her knowledge. He was so captivated by her. She aroused a feeling in him that he never knew existed. Jewel tasted the fire from the tree of knowledge. There was no turning back for her. Therefore, she intended to bring all she could with her into the fire that awakened every evil spirit. One never knew when partaking of the tree, which spirit would soak into the soul. The spirit of lust was waiting for the mighty man of God. Tashmere watched Queen Jewel daily cast her spell on him as she danced the forbidden dance. His resistance shattered. She explained to Tashmere how the fire of knowledge would birth an ecstasy unlike anything he had ever experienced. At his weakest point, she thrust the deep magic upon him, took his hand and led him into fire with her."

"What happened to him then?" Rachel asked.

"The Most High cursed Tashmere, and changed his name to Telmar, which means the lascivious god."

"And Jewel?" Cordilia muttered.

"Because of her sin, Jewel was already sentenced to be blotted out of the book in the end time. Therefore, she set up her own kingdom in the darkest region of the universe. She used the deep magic to illuminate the dark kingdom, deceiving many and pulling them into the fire of knowledge. You must understand, the Most High never intended for his children to partake of the strange fire. Yet, he left it up to his children to make their own choice as to what they would do."

"What about Shemed?" Rachel asked.

"Shemed followed Tashmere daily to the garden with Queen Jewel. At a distance, he watched what was taking place. Shemed's mindset was that before Tashmere could be persuaded to go into the fire, he would stop him. The deep magic was so powerful that even watching at a distance, he also fell into Jewel's enticement. In Shemed, the fire birthed resentment and hate for the kingdom of the Most High. Seeing this, Jewel made him a top general over her army."

Cordilia looked at Rachel and sighed. "Wow! This is some story."

Rachel looked at the book. "But this book is filled with names. Who are they?"

"The book carries the ancient names of The Beginning, both good and bad. The evil trinity of the dark kingdom, Jewel, Tashmere and Shemed led the rebellion against the kingdom of light."

Effie touched her finger to a name near the top of the first page, looked at Rachel and said, "This is one of the leading generals of the Most High,

General Rakar. A mighty warring angel, he led the Armor Bearers against Queen Jewel, and her evil empts. Because of Rakar's and the Armor Bearers' faithfulness, the Most High gave them a special gold signet ring with the letters AOTA stamped in the center."

Rachel spoke up, "AOTA. Angel's of the Ages."

"Exactly!"

Cordilia asked, "Where did you get this book, and how do you know so much about the names in it?"

Before Effie could answer, thunder sounded so loudly it rattled the house. "You two better get home before the road floods, and you wouldn't be able to get out of my yard. We'll finish the story another time."

When Effie opened the door, a tree limb landed on the porch. She asked them to stay, but Rachel felt because the house was in sight, they would be fine. They looked at each other. "I guess we better hurry." Rachel cried as the trees and shrubs bent before a forceful blast of wind like she had never seen.

The thunder was almost continuous now, making any conversation impossible. In a second, the road was covered with debris. A bolt of lightning found its mark on the huge oak tree just off the road. Tree limbs and twigs were flying all around. Water filled the dirt road. The car lurched, and a sheet of muddy water covered the windshield. The car sputtered . . . and then stopped. Unable to restart the car, Rachel asked, "What should we do Cordilia?"

Cordilia squinted and said, "We can hope the rain slacks, which doesn't look likely, or we can make a run for it. It's not that far to your house; besides we don't know when John will get home."

"You're right, it's not that far; let's just make a run for it."

They gathered their skirts around them and raced down the road. When they touched Rachel's porch, both the women were out of breath. After drying off, they discussed the book, the story and the storm.

"Where did she get that book, and how does she know everything about it?" Cordilia said.

"I can't answer either question. I wonder where John is. He should have been home before now."

Cordilia picked up the phone and said, "I better call Paul and let him know I'll be home when the storm settles."

Chapter 54
Chris Tries to Explain

The day after Christmas, John asked Chris to help take the Christmas decorations down before he had to go out of town. John had business at the train station in Benson and would be gone most of the day. Chris came around 11:00 a.m. Rachel had all the boxes out, so Chris could start when he arrived. After everything was taken down and put away, Chris knocked at the kitchen door. Rachel opened it to find Chris with his arms crossed, rubbing his upper arms.

"Come in, Chris. "I made us some hot chocolate."

He sat down and took a sip of the chocolate. "This is delicious. Thanks, Rachel. It's so cold outside."

"Yes, it is." As Rachel looked at Chris, she saw that something wasn't right, even his countenance seemed bizarre. So, Rachel blurted out, "Chris, do you love Paula?"

Shocked by the question, Chris stammered. "W-why did you ask that?"

"I just wonder."

Chris sat his cup down. "That really isn't your concern, Rachel."

"You know, Chris, it's obvious that she has feelings for you. I would hate to see Paula hurt, if you don't have the same feelings for her. I am going to tell you the same thing I told her. I know that something isn't right in your life. I've taught you in Sunday school for five years and Paula, a year more than that. Do you think I don't pray for you and ask the Holy Spirit to show me when you're in trouble? You know, God answers prayer, and he is revealing your heart to me. I just want you to know there is freedom for your life. Whatever you're involved in, you don't have to stay in that bondage."

Chris got up and walked to the sink, but said nothing. He stared out the kitchen window.

Rachel looked out the window with him. For a moment, there was silence. Rachel broke the silence by adding, "The truth will set you free, Chris. But you have to want to be free so much that nothing else matters."

Tears welled in Chris's eyes, and his breathing intensified as he began to weep. Rachel put her hand on his arm. "Let it out, Chris."

"You don't understand, Rachel. Some things you can't be free from, even if you want to be."

"That's a lie straight from hell, Chris. They're two ways to be free, the blood and the truth."

"Rachel . . ." Chris attempted, then suddenly turned, and headed for the kitchen door, "I've got to go!"

Rachel followed him out and called out. "Chris, your money!"

Without looking back, he said, "Just keep it."

Rachel couldn't figure out what changed Chris's mind until she looked up and saw Jerry standing outside looking toward her house.

Chapter 55
Thinking

*D*r. Wells told Peggy to call Chris and have him come to the office right away. When Chris arrived, Peggy and Dr. Wells greeted him. Chris felt very nervous. Dr. Wells had never called him in without his parents.

Dr. Wells put his arm around his shoulder and said, "Come in, Chris, and sit for a moment. I wanted to ask you a question."

"Sure," Chris said as he played with his fingers.

"Are you anxious about being here, Chris?" Dr. Wells asked as he stared at Chris with his piercing black eyes.

"No, why would I be nervous?"

"You tell me. Does he appear edgy to you, Peggy?"

"Yeah, he does. If he doesn't stop wringing his fingers, they're going to break off."

Chris placed his hands on his lap and assured them nothing was wrong.

Dr. Wells sighed . . . and muttered, "Good. I have a new girl who lives on Brush Creek Road.

Her name is Ginger Tally. She just moved here two weeks ago. Some of our soldiers report that she is ready for the taking. Telmar sent a seducing demon on her. By the time he's through with her, she will be ready for you."

Chris didn't know what to say. He didn't want another girl. Only Paula. He was afraid to say anything, so he played along with whatever Dr. Wells said.

"Are you ready for something new, Chris?" Peggy asked. "Is sweet little Paula getting old?"

"You know me, Peggy. I'm always ready for whatever my next assignment will be."

Peggy went over and sat on Chris's lap. She kissed his ear and ran her hand down his leg. "How about me, Chris? I haven't enjoyed your company in a long time. You know me. I need a young soldier like you after having Shemed. He's so rough. He growls like a dog the whole time, until the end when he howls like a wolf. You, on the other hand, can be so tender and slow."

Peggy knelt between Chris's legs. How could he stop her? He didn't want to do this! Peggy was taking his belt loose as Chris sat frozen, feeling scared and sick to his stomach.

Peggy stopped, looked at Chris and cried out, "Come on, Chris! Don't make me do all the work."

Chris couldn't move. All he could think of was Paula. Peggy took hold of Chris's hand and pulled it to her breast. When Chris didn't respond, Peggy growled, "Shemed!"

"Yes."

Peggy stared into Chris's eyes. "Something is not right here. He's not passing the test."

Chris set up in the chair, knowing he had to do something. His love for Paula could not be found out.

"Surely you're not trying to hide something from me?"

"No, Shemed, why would you ask that?"

Shemed stood and moved to the side of his desk. "Peggy is seldom wrong. She can read a man by his drive for her. Is she wrong or right, Chris? You wouldn't be breaking one of Queen Jewel's sacred rules, would you? Your emotions are never to get in the way of your duties."

"Of course not! I'm just tired, that's all."

"You wouldn't be thinking of betraying Queen Jewel, would you?"

"I pledged myself to Queen Jewel, and I have always been faithful, have I not?"

"As far as I know, yes, you have. So, satisfy the sex demon between your legs and prove it once again. Take her now."

Chris's heart filled with rage. He leaned forward and looked at Peggy in disgust though he couldn't show it. He stroked her long blond hair, clamped his fingers to the back of her neck, and kissed Peggy so hard her lower lip began to bleed.

Peggy pulled her long fingernails down Chris's neck. "So, you want to be rough?"

Chris directed all his rage to Peggy as he fulfilled his order.

As Dr. Wells watched, he growled. "Chris, you've been watching Telmar too long."

***

Chris drove around for a while and parked just outside of town at Lake Tamko. How could he ever face Paula and explain the scratches on his neck? He sat there for three hours. Repeatedly, he tried to think of something to say to Paula, but there was no way to express the excruciating pain that he felt inside. She would never understand. He felt like a trapped animal struggling to be free. He thought aloud, "I would rather be dead than to live the rest of my life like this. Paula you're the only person who has given me any desire to live."

As he sat there in deep thought, Sheriff Butler pulled up beside him. Chris didn't even notice. The sheriff got out of his car and walked over to Chris's car. He knocked on the window before Chris ever knew he was there. Chris rolled the window down. "Sheriff Butler! I didn't see you."

"So, I noticed. What in the world are you doing sitting out here for hours? I've driven by numbers of times, and you're still sitting here. What's bothering you, son?"

"I've just got so much on my mind . . . with school and choosing a college and so on."

"Bull, Chris! You don't sit like this over a college, but you would sit like this over a girl. Point being, I wouldn't recommend you sitting out here after dark. There have been some strange things going on lately. You know about Willow Chandler disappearing from over at Benson, don't you?"

"Yes, I did hear something about that."

257

"Why don't you go on home now and do the rest of your thinking there? Don't stay out here."

"I'll do that, Sheriff, thanks."

"Chris, whatever the problem is, you and the young lady can work it out."

Chris smiled. "I sure hope so, Sheriff."

Chapter 56
About Effie

$\mathcal{T}$wo days after Christmas, Rachel had heard nothing about Cordilia's health. She had been praying about what Doug Holland had told her. She didn't want to say anything to Cordilia, in case nothing happened. There was no need to worry her, but Rachel decided to call, just to make sure. Cordilia told her she was fine, and they begin discussing Cordilia's favorite topic as of late, food.

"You know, Rachel, I thought of fixing Paul a three-bean salad, but instead, I am giving him three kinds of potato salad. I decided I better use the leftovers from the church supper before it's too late. So I put a lazy Susan in the center of the table with the potato salad in three sections and crackers in the middle."

"My word, Cordilia, who would have thought of that other than you?"

Cordilia laughed. "So true, Rachel, I am unique. The only other person in the world who reminds me of me is Sophia Loren."

"Cordilia, it's getting just a little too deep for me, so I am going to hang up now."

Rachel felt much better knowing that she checked on her friend before she and John went to bed. She went into the bedroom in time to see John putting his sword back into the case.

"I love my sword," John said. "The only problem is it stings my hands so badly at times I can hardly pick it up."

"John, I would say that's very strange, but lately what isn't strange?"

As they lay in bed, Rachel talked about Effie and what she said about Queen Jewel and the dark kingdom." She paused, then continued about her study of Noah and the flood.

"There's something I saw while studying today that reminded me of Effie's story."

"What was that?" John asked as he put his arm under Rachel's head.

"The raven. After it rained forty days and nights, the rain ended. Noah opened the window of the ark, and sent the raven out. The raven went to and fro until the waters were dried up from the face of the earth."

"Okay."

"John, the raven was dark in color and went to and fro in the earth until the waters dried up. He also sent a dove out to check for dry land; the dove came back three different times, but the raven didn't come back at all."

"How does that remind you of Effie's story?"

"She told me about the dark kingdom, how Tashmere was cursed, and could never return to the elite position that he once held in the White Stone Kingdom. He was doomed on this earth, and he goes to and fro seeking whom he may devour. The raven couldn't go back to the safety of the Most High, just like Tashmere.

"You've told me about Tashmere and others in the dark kingdom. Has she ever mentioned the children of this White Stone?"

"She mentioned a General Rakar, who led the Amour Bearers in battle against Queen Jewel and her forces. They were given a gold signet ring by the Most High and knighted as one of the Angels of the Ages."

John laughed. "I wonder if this General Rakar had a sword as handsome as mine."

Rachel snuggled to him. "I feel sure it would be pretty close."

Chapter 57

A Visit to Dr. White

*J*ohn and Rachel had only been asleep for a little while when the telephone rang. Rachel looked at the clock and moaned. "John, who would be calling at 2:30 in the morning?"

"I don't know. You better get it."

Before she could say hello, Paul shouted out, "Rachel, something's wrong with Cordilia."

Now, wide awake, she said, "We'll be right there."

When they arrived, Paul was trying to get Cordilia's shoes on.

"What's wrong, Cordilia?" Rachel eagerly asked as she felt her forehead to see if there was any sign of fever.

"Have you called Dr. Wells, Paul?" John asked.

Before Paul could reply, Rachel shouted, "Don't call Dr. Wells. Call Dr. White."

Confused, Paul said, "Dr. Wells is her doctor."

Rachel grabbed Paul's arm, and pleaded, "Please trust me, Paul."

"Rachel? What's wrong with you?" John asked.

"Nothing's wrong! I know what I'm doing. Please pull the car around."

Paul called Dr. White. She agreed to meet them at her office.

Cordilia's short breaths and cold sweat scared Rachel. In the car, Paul asked Rachel, "Why not call Dr. Wells? He's easily ten minutes closer than Dr. White."

"Paul's right, Rachel. Dr. Wells is her doctor. She's never seen Dr. White. It's a good thing I know where her office is."

Panicked, Rachel defended her actions. "I know Dr. Wells is her doctor. I also know what I'm doing."

Cordilia groaned, "Hurry."

Dr. White saw right away that Cordilia was having an allergic reaction to something. The only thing she was allergic to was garlic. The doctor gave Cordilia some medicine to counteract the reaction. She looked at Paul and asked, "Why didn't you take her to Dr. Wells? A few minutes could have meant life or death."

Paul interrupted, "Dr. White . . . what about the baby?"

"The baby is fine. It has a strong heartbeat."

Rachel spoke up. "I am the reason we came to you, and I am glad we did."

"That's fine as long as she's okay. Tell me, Mr. Dawson, what did your wife eat tonight?"

"For supper, she ate a bologna sandwich, and a bowl of cereal."

"Paul, did she eat any of the potato salad she brought home?" Rachel asked.

"Not for supper. She did get up and eat something about ten minutes before I called you."

The nurse rolled Cordilia into the waiting room. She was feeling much better and very thankful.

Dr. White reminded, "You're a very fortunate woman, Cordilia. Can you tell me what you ate that had garlic in it?"

Cordilia thought and said, "It had to be the potato salad. I got up, and it was not long before I got sick that I ate a few bites. I don't understand it though. I asked all three women if their potato salad had garlic in it, and they all assured me they never used garlic." Cordilia giggled. "Rachel, you don't think Stella held a grudge, do you?"

"She may have thought of it, but I'm sure she didn't lie to you on purpose."

Cordilia's eyes filled with tears. Paul massaged her shoulders while Rachel held her hand. "Thank you, Dr. White, for pulling me and Phillip Ryan through this. Above all, I want to thank God."

"Amen!" Rachel agreed.

Dr. White concluded, "Get some rest, and check with Dr. Wells."

On the way home, Cordilia asked, "Rachel, why did we go to Dr. White and not Dr. Wells?"

Rachel shook her head and said, "We'll talk tomorrow. Tonight, you need your rest."

Chapter 58
Questions

The next day, Rachel and John went into town. John went to the hardware store while Rachel visited the five and dime. She really hoped to see Doug Holland or Mr. Spook. She knew Doug Holland went to Shirley's Diner quite often. As she entered the diner, she saw Doug sitting at a window table. Rachel walked over and said hello to Doug.

"Hi, Rachel."

"Hello, Doug. I need to talk to you a moment."

"Sure, why don't you join me." Doug turned to order Rachel a cup of coffee. She assured him she wouldn't be that long.

Rachel fixed her eyes on Doug. "How did you know about Cordilia?"

He sipped his coffee and answered, "I knew about Cordilia from the one who knows all things—God."

"Okay, I'll accept that, but why Dr. White? Cordilia had never seen her before."

Stern faced, Doug replied, "Wisdom told me she shouldn't go to Dr. Wells. You know, Rachel, things are not always what they appear." Doug wiped his mouth, put the napkin down and said, "I have to be going. Good to see you, Rachel."

Doug laid money on the table and walked outside. Rachel followed and called out to him. He stopped and faced Rachel.

Rachel blurted out, "Okay, Doug Holland, I want to know, who you really are? Are you a wizard or something? You seem to know everything, and I want some answers."

He chuckled. "Rachel, a wizard? If I were a wizard, you would know it in your spirit. If not, you better be praying for discernment."

Rachel tightened her brows. "Stop trying to avoid the question."

Doug replied softly, "Why, Rachel, don't you know I am your guardian angel? Here comes John."

"Hi, Doug. How you doing this windy morning?"

"Fine, John, and you?"

"Doing well."

"John, you applied for the job here at Todd's Creek station?"

"Yes."

"I've talked to some people, and I think your chances of getting the job are excellent."

"Really?"

Doug patted John's shoulder. "I'm sure it's yours."

Rachel and John glanced at each other, their eyes filled with excitement.

"Rachel, tell the Dawsons I am praying for them. I'll see you at the Watch Service."

Chapter 59

Peggy's Pain

*D*r. White's nurse called Dr. Wells about a patient of his being treated the night before for an allergic reaction to garlic. Dr. Wells was furious. He was standing at his desk when Peggy told him. She watched as he groaned, growled and knocked everything off his desk. He threw a paperweight and busted the picture hanging behind his desk. Peggy feared Mrs. Gentry would hear the commotion in the waiting room. Nervously, she managed to muster up enough courage to remind him that a patient was in the waiting room.

Shemed turned to face Peggy with a look in his eyes that scared her. He held his stare, tightened his lips and moved toward her. She began to step backward. Shemed followed her. She backed up against the sofa and could go no further.

She trembled as Shemed stopped in front of her. With fire in his eyes, he grabbed Peggy by her wrist, and squeezed it so hard she fought back screams of pain. "How dare you try to calm me down?"

He would have crushed Peggy's arm, but a voice from behind him ordered, "No, Shemed, turn her loose!"

Shemed turned to see Telmar standing there. Still enraged, he said, "Stay out of this, Telmar."

Telmar got in his face. "You should be thanking Peggy who tried to keep you from being exposed to the old lady in your office." Telmar stroked Peggy's hair and whispered, "Let me kiss it better." He kissed her wrist several times, "Later, I'll make you feel better all over, my sweet." He turned to Shemed, and said, "Queen Jewel received word that your attempt to stop Cordilia failed."

"Peggy made sure she exchanged her bowl with the garlic in it with the potato salad made by Kayla Rivers. But instead of coming here, Cordilia went to Dr. White."

"It appears you're hurting the one who did her job right. You better succeed, or Jewel will send you to the pit herself." Telmar put his face to Shemed's and continued, "By the way, Shemed, Queen Jewel sent me with that message just for you."

Shemed said nothing. Telmar turned his attention to Peggy. He put his fingertips to Peggy's lips. "Tonight, my sweet."

With a look of disappointment, Peggy whispered, "No, Telmar. Now."

Telmar looked at Shemed. "I don't have enough time right now. Why don't you try and soften Shemed so he won't get in trouble." Telmar laughed and vanished from of the room.

Shemed looked at Peggy and commanded, "Go tell Mrs. Gentry I'm not feeling well. Give her my apologies and make her my first appointment on January 2. Put out the closed sign and come back here."

Peggy walked out of his office not sure what to expect when she came back. When she finished her tasks, she returned to Shemed trembling. Shemed looked at her and said nothing. Peggy felt uncomfortable with his piercing stare.

Nervously, she asked, "Are we finished for today?"

Shemed tilted his head and repeated, "Finished for the day? What makes you think I am finished for the day?"

"We don't have any more patients, so . . ."

"Shut up! You got me into trouble today." Shemed took his jacket and shirt off, never breaking his gaze.

Even though she was a sex goddess, she wanted nothing to do with Shemed when he was in this frame of mind. As he moved toward her, she backed against the wall, her mouth dry from fear. Shemed pressed his body against hers so tightly it took her breath. "Shemed, please."

He held her jaw in his hand and growled, "Since I don't have your expertise in this area, you'll just have to forgive my crudeness. The good side is, I'm a doctor, and I can take care of your pain."

Shaking, Peggy begged, "Please, Shemed! Please!"

Chapter 60

Leah's Story

$\mathscr{D}$ecember 31, the last day of 1950, had arrived. Cordilia was back to her old self. Paula had not heard from Chris even though she called him many times. At one point she went to his house but was told he had gone out with his father. Paula doubted that story because she saw both Jerry and Chris's cars in the garage. She would see Chris at the Watch Service, but how could that help the problems between them?

Paula was lying in bed, thinking about everything when Leah called her to come down for breakfast. When she didn't respond, Leah went up to check on her. She knocked on her door. "Paula, may I come in?"

"Yes, come in, Mom."

"Honey, didn't you hear me calling you?"

"No, Mom, I'm sorry." She stood and tied her housecoat together.

"Your dad made breakfast with your favorite—bacon, eggs and cheese omelets with fresh-squeezed, orange juice."

Paula looked out the window. "I'm not that hungry, Mom."

Leah stood beside her. "When you talked to me about your dad, it cut very deep, but the reason the pain was so deep is that you were right. After that talk, I begin saying no to several things on your father's agenda. At first, he was startled that I said no to him; he didn't take me seriously. I told him I was tired of being a bed slave. Do you believe that?"

Paula giggled. "You did not!"

"Yes, I did. Your father almost fainted. I've never spoken to him like that in all the years we have been married. It felt awkward, but good."

Paula was so surprised. "How did he respond to 'being his bed slave'?"

Leah laughed. "First, he wanted to know where I had heard that statement. Then he wanted to know exactly what I meant by the statement. Also, I told him his daughter was a senior in high school and he knew nothing about her. Of course, he was defensive. I then told him some of the meetings and luncheons were going to end, or I was going to leave him."

Paula and Leah sat on the edge of the bed. "You told Daddy you would leave him?"

"Yes, I did. The scary part was, I really meant it."

"You would leave Daddy?"

"Yes, I was to that point; of course I prayed for God guidance. I love your father and the thought of life without him is the emptiest feeling I've ever felt. You were right. He spent his days with everyone else and came home for me to please him in bed. As a matter of fact, for more nights than I can count, I would already be asleep when he got home, and he would wake me up to serve his manhood. He never wanted to just hold me or talk to me. After I accommodated his need, he wanted to go right to sleep because of all his appointments the next day."

Paula put her arm around her mom. "Mom, you told Dad all of that?"

Leah nodded her head. "Every word. What do you think of all the truth you aroused in me?"

"I did all of that?"

"You did."

"So, how did he respond to you?"

"He wanted some time alone to digest all I had said to him. Stella canceled his appointments, and he drove around for hours. When he came home, he had been crying. He apologized for being so busy that he lost touch with the two most important people in the world."

"Do you think he'll change, Mom?"

"Time will tell. Stella canceled his appointments again today. He fixed us breakfast, and he asked me to help him decorate the church for the Watch Service tonight. He hasn't asked me to help him do anything since we left Texas." Leah stood and began to braid Paula's hair. "I'm sorry for all the time he's missed with you, Paula. We love you, and more than anything we want you happy. He said he saw you and Chris kissing the other day. Is that something you want to talk about?"

Paula stood and walked back to the window and looked out. "I don't know, Mom. Sometimes,

I am so happy, and sometimes I wish I never met him."

"Honey, why would you feel like that?"

"Sometimes, things can get so confusing."

Leah put her arm around Paula. "Paula, don't feel like you have to rush into anything. You don't. You have college and your whole life before you. Ask God for the guidance for this time in your life. You don't need a man to lean on, you need God. He'll be your help in time of trouble. Never forget that, Paula! It will save you a lot of mistakes and heartache." Leah embraced her daughter.

Pastor Miller came into the room, "How about a family hug?" he said as tears filled his eyes.

For a few moments, Paula's mind was at rest.

Chapter 61
Knowing Everything

*J*ohn, Rachel, Paul and Cordilia were going to visit Harold and Amanda Collins. John and Paul wanted to cut firewood and stack, but Rachel and Cordilia wanted to visit. Harold Collins really didn't need firewood cut or brought in. He cut firewood all year round, but John and Paul loved being around the couple. The Collinses never complained, even when justified. They always had a smile and worshiped God in the good times and the bad. They didn't have children and chose not to talk about why.

They treated John as their own and spoiled him rotten. Amanda made homemade fried pies and apple butter from their apple trees for John and Paul.

The Collinses were in their seventies. Amanda was a beautiful, white-haired woman, just a little on the heavy side. Usually around the house she wore a dress, thick stockings and an apron.

Harold's white hair was thinning, and he loved to wear a hat. An old Stetson hat graced his head around the house, and a new Stetson graced his head on Sunday morning. He was known to smoke a cigar on special occasions and shy about talking on a telephone.

He limped from a World War I wound. After the war, Harold went through a time of depression. He would sit in the woods all day and had little to say during that time. His faith in God helped him and in time healed him.

They lived in a log cabin nestled in an oak forest where they raised a garden large enough to feed ten families, only to give most of it away. As folks entered their home, it was like stepping back in time.

They were known around town as prophets. Some people at church had a hard time with that. Nonetheless, when they prophesied, everyone listened.

When the couples arrived at the Collins' home, they were greeted with hugs, a warm fire and hot apple cider.

Right away, Cordilia brought up the topic of Willow Chandler disappearing. She sat on the edge of the couch and asked, "Tell me what you two think about that young girl vanishing in Benson?"

Amanda spoke up. "I don't know the Chandlers, but I can guarantee you, those lights at Boone's Crossing are associated with the girl's disappearance."

"No doubt about that," Harold said.

Suddenly, Harold's countenance changed. He fixed his eyes on Rachel and Cordilia, who were sitting on the sofa. Aware of his stare, Rachel asked, "Is something wrong, Mr. Collins?"

"No, not at all."

"Why the strange look?" Cordilia asked.

"I was looking at the very big eagle standing behind you." Rachel and Cordilia immediately turned to see.

"You don't see him, do you?"

"No," Cordilia said.

Rachel said nothing, for she did see Raptor standing behind them.

"All right," Cordilia said, "Now, you said eagle. Did you mean an angel?"

Harold shook his head. "No, I mean a giant eagle from Wisdom's mountain."

Harold turned his attention back to the women, smiled and said, "You both are going to have sons, am I right?"

"Yes, we are!" Rachel replied.

"God has opened a whole new dimension of the spirit to you both, hasn't He?"

"You have no idea," Rachel said.

"Warfare is all around you. The boys you're carrying will be mighty warriors for the White Stone Kingdom. I see that very clearly."

"Rachel, your son will be as the prophet Daniel. He will preach to world rulers and be a leader for the Most High. Many times, he'll be betrayed. As with Daniel, the enemy will try to feed him to the lions, but he will prevail. The angels will protect him as they protect you. Queen Jewel is furious about this baby's birth. Guard yourself with prayer and the Word of God. Rachel, remember this, 'Faith comes by hearing and hearing by the word of God.'

People think the only way we can hear is through a preacher, but the Holy Spirit is the greatest preacher of all—"

Rachel interrupted, "How . . . how is it you know Queen Jewel?"

"My thought exactly," Cordilia added.

"I heard about her a long time ago from a friend. Of course, she is in all the mythological books. Anyway, let me continue. The Holy Spirit will open the veil and reveal the mysteries of the ages to you."

He faced Cordilia. "And you, Cordilia, are a mighty warrior for White Stone Kingdom. Until now, I never knew how much of a warrior you really are. I can see you in the third heaven with a sword in your hand, standing at attention ready to war for King Rayon. Your son is a high-ranking officer in Rayon's army. The dark kingdom will also try to stop his birth, but will fail."

Amanda frowned and asked, "Rachel, have you recently brought an aged sword into your house?"

Rachel's eyes widened as she moved to the edge of the sofa. "Yes . . . yes, I bought it in Norfolk, at an antique shop called A Journey in Time."

"I should have known," Amanda said as she looked at Harold. "Rachel, that shop is run by a witch called Delilah. She is one of the most evil of all dark stone's forces. Her witchcraft is so very powerful. She warred at the great battle with Queen Jewel against the Most High."

"How is that Delilah can fight with Queen Jewel ages ago and own an antique shop today?" Cordilia asked.

"You'll find out soon enough," Amanda said.

Cordilia squinted and shouted, "I knew something was not right with that woman. She hit my hand . . . like I was a child."

"This all sounds like a fairy tale," Rachel said.

"This is anything but a fairy tale," Harold added.

"Who are Cordilia and I that God would show us these things?" Rachel asked.

"You're His servants! But, let's go back to Delilah. If she sold you a sword, you can bet it's been laced with her evil spells. Have any strange things happened since you brought the sword into your home?"

"You cannot imagine how strange," Rachel said. "Even when John touched the sword."

"Yes, Rachel, I can imagine. I have encountered Delilah before; she's very dangerous. I know how she works. It's time for you to know."

Harold walked to the window, pulled the curtain back and looked out.

Amanda stood and asked, "what is it?"

"Something's not right." Shaking his head, Harold repeated himself, "Ladies, something's just not right."

"What do you mean, Mr. Collins?" Cordilia asked.

He faced the women and said, "Amanda, when have we ever known Delilah to make a move, like selling Rachel the sword, without Shemed being very close at hand?"

"Absolutely never," Amanda was quick to say.

"Do you two know about Shemed?" Rachel wondered aloud.

"He's one of Queen Jewel's right hand demons. You could call him the leader of Jewel's death force."

"You two need to talk with Effie Brown," Rachel said. "She knows about the people you're mentioning. All those names are in a book she has."

Amanda's eyes widened as she sighed. "Does the book have a title?"

Rachel responded, *Angels of the Ages*.

Amanda closed her eyes and smiled. "It's time Harold. It's time!"

"Praise to the Most High!" Harold said, "The time has finally come."

"What do you mean?" Cordilia asked.

"The time for the mysteries of the book to be released has finally come. The prophecy is about to be fulfilled. I could die right now and be satisfied. We've waited for so long for this time."

Amanda continued, "Warfare through the ages, Cordilia. Shemed comes in many different disguises. I don't know what his disguise is this time, but I know he's dangerously close. Rachel, you and John must destroy the sword to break the spell it carries. Describe the handle of the sword to me, Rachel."

"It's gold or looks gold with three stones."

"Is the stone in the middle green?" Amanda asked.

"Well, yes," Rachel replied in total surprise. "How did you know?"

"I have seen the sword before."

Amanda held out her hands to Rachel. "Join hands with me," she said.

Rachel took hold of Amanda's hands. "Rachel, I'm going to tell you how to destroy the sword."

"Please do."

"You and John must pray over your home, property and even your vehicles. When you're ready, have Paul and Cordilia come over and stand with you in prayer as you remove the three stones from the handle. Shemed and Delilah can call up a demon from the green stone. The demon's name is Telmar."

Rachel felt faint. "How do you know about Telmar?"

"It doesn't matter, just listen," Amanda said.

"Oh, my Lord," Rachel groaned. "A green mist came out of the green stone in the center of the sword the other night. It was awful! We were paralyzed."

"That was Telmar introducing himself to us," Harold said.

"That was a demon?" Cordilia asked.

Rachel spoke up. "How did a demon get into our house? I am a child of God and have covered my house with prayer."

"In deceptive ways, like the sword. You had no way of knowing about Delilah or the sword. That's why all this is being revealed to you now."

"Oh, Lord, help me!" Rachel exclaimed as she sat down. "There was a demon in my house. I can't believe it!"

"No, not there was a demon in your house, there is a demon in your house, if the sword is still there."

Rachel looked at Amanda. "It's still there, in our bedroom closet. How can we destroy it?"

"You must remove the stones and crush them into fine dust. Break the stones with the first blow of the hammer. Then burn the dust of the stones with the metal part of the sword. I know for sure you have a wood heater. Right?"

"Yes, in the basement."

"Build a fire. Get it so hot that the metal on the heater shows red. Then put the blade and the crushed stones into the fire. That sword will never be used again for the dark kingdom."

A light knock came at the door. Paul and John had finished with the firewood.

As they said goodbye, Harold thanked them for the wood.

Rachel hugged Harold and asked, "Do you know the old hermit Mr. McKinney?"

Harold and Amanda both chuckled. "Oh yes, we know Mr. McKinney. How do you know him?"

"Cordilia and I met him in town a couple of times. Can you tell me anything about him?"

Harold shook his head. "No, I can't help you there. That's something you'll have to find out yourself."

"Then there is something we need to know from him?"

"In time, Rachel, in time," Harold said. "Right now your main concern is destroying that sword."

"You're right. I'll see you tonight at the Watch Service," Rachel called out.

"We'll be there.

On the way home, Rachel and Cordilia discussed what Harold and Amanda shared with them about the sword. John quickly agreed that they would destroy the sword. Paul was very calm about the whole thing.

"You're not shocked about this?" Cordilia asked.

"No, I've been seeing into the spirit realm a little myself."

"Why didn't you tell me?"

"Honey, when it's time, I will tell you."

"Tell me what, Paul? You're killing me. Tell me what when it's time?"

"It's not time, Cordilia, so you know I'm not going to say another word until it is."

"Please, please, please, Paul."

"No!"

Cordilia knew she might as well be quiet.

Chapter 62
Pastor Miller

The church doors opened at 10:00 p.m. for the Watch Service. The sanctuary was decorated with red and white. Red and white candles lined the stage and the windows. The communion table was draped with white linen. A tall crystal candleholder held a lit red candle served as the center piece. Two long-stem red and white roses lay on either side of the center piece. A large chair sat at the backside of the table, draped with red and white satin. Soft music piped throughout the chapel. The glowing flames from the candles served as the only light in the sanctuary.

The cold, snowy weather kept no one at home; the church was filled almost to capacity. A holy aura filled the auditorium.

When Rachel and Cordilia entered the vestibule, they paused in awe of what they saw. The sanctuary was lined with angels, standing at attention, shoulder to shoulder.

For a moment, Cordilia felt as if she were back in the throne room.

When everyone was seated, Pastor Miller entered dressed in a long, white robe with a wide, red scarf around his shoulders. No one had ever seen him in such a light before; humble, yet standing in bold authority.

He paused as he glanced across the congregation. He turned his eyes upward and stated, "I know my Redeemer lives, and in the end, I will stand with Him. Tonight, we are surrounded with a great cloud of witnesses. He is the lily of the valley. The word 'lily' in the Hebrew means a straight trumpet used by a watchman. What is a watchman? A watchman is someone who guards and protects an area. He alerts others by sounding the alarm when anything out of the ordinary approaches, whether good or bad. A watchman is not to sleep at his post. In the United States Army in times of war, if the soldier on watch goes to sleep, he can be put to death. Why? Because others are depending on that watchman for their life. Going to sleep on duty can leave the gate wide open for the enemy to come through and kill everybody under that watchman's care."

"We are at war! As a child of the Most High God, I have been set as watchman over you. I want to confess I haven't watched as closely as I should have, but by the help and grace of God, from this day forward, I'll be alert at my post."

"Leah and I chose red and white for the service décor tonight. Red for the precious blood that frees us from sin and death. Life is in the blood. White for the purity and holiness perfected within us by the mighty Holy Spirit. He empowers us and quickens the spirit inside us and brings us alive. The Holy Spirit will light our path. The blood is our covering, and the sword of truth will destroy the enemy and set the captive free.

"As we prepare to take communion, God doesn't want us to take one bite and walk away. He wants us to eat and be filled, drink and be satisfied. Will everyone stand?"

When the bread and wine were served, Pastor Miller came to the front of the table and faced the congregation. "Tonight, I want us to put our focus toward the guest of honor's chair. Let us lift our heads, our hearts, our glasses and our bread toward the heavens . . . and partake."

Pastor Miller lifted his bread and glass toward the guest of honor's chair, and prayed, "Lord, we remember and commit our service to you."

When everyone had partaken, Rachel and Cordilia watched as the angels applauded the Most High God. A bizarre stillness filled the sanctuary. Everyone joined hands to pray. When Rachel closed her eyes, Doug Holland, took hold of her hand.

After prayer, only a few minutes remained until midnight. Pastor Miller opened the floor to anyone who would like to testify. At one minute until midnight, Pastor Miller said there was time for one more testimony.

Doug Holland stood, faced the congregation and, with a voice of power, declared, "There was a time known as The Beginning. A time of peace, joy and love. Then the ancient one that ruled over the Emerald Shores allowed pride to consume her emotions. The lust for power became her god. She had the full sum of beauty. Wisdom filled her soul with the mysteries of the deep magic. She lived inside Eden's gate, and bathed in the cool streams that flowed from Wisdom's Mountain. She was allowed free access to the Garden of Fire. She was warned by the Most High not to touch the tree of strange fire or she would surely be blotted out of the book. Up to that point, she stayed away from the tree of mysterious fire. However, she desired to have the knowledge that the evil fire held. She entered the zone of the forbidden tree and partook of its evil wisdom. After she received the forbidden wisdom, she used that wisdom and drew a vast number of the children of the White Stone Kingdom into the fire with her. Thus, she made her kingdom with the ones she drew with deception. Her army was sent to place a stone altar on top of Boone's Crossing generations ago. She and her soldiers have warred against the Most High and his Son King Rayon for ages. The war continues here in Todd's Creek today. This ancient one's name is Queen Jewel, and her kingdom is the dark kingdom. I'm here to serve notice on any of her followers that we are here to take back Todd's Creek and destroy the stone altar, thus breaking the demon power in Todd's Creek." Doug sat down and looked straight ahead.

Immediately, the angels who lined the walls were gone.

After service, Rachel went to Doug Holland and whispered, "You know about Queen Jewel and the dark kingdom?"

"Of course, I do."

Rachel asked, "Tell me, did you see anything in the sanctuary tonight?"

Doug smiled. "Are you talking about the cloud of witnesses."

"You mean angels?"

"I mean witnesses."

Cordilia joined the conversation. "You're one peculiar man, Doug Holland. How is that you know Mr. McKinney?"

Doug grinned and said, "I better be going. We'll talk later."

"Why not now?" Rachel asked.

Doug leaned forward and whispered, "If you knew my answer it would scare you to death." He nodded and left the church.

Chapter 63
Are You Kidding?

*A*ll the way home, John, Rachel, Cordilia and Paul were in intense prayer. They agreed to destroy the sword after the meeting.

John built a fire in the heater and waited until it glowed from the heat. When ready, John went to get the sword out of the closet. When he touched it, stinging pains shot through his hands, causing him to drop it to the floor. Boldly Paul picked up the sword, headed for the basement and laid it on a table. John got the sledgehammer while Rachel got the screwdriver to pry the stones out. Cordilia brought the pan to crush the stones in. John lifted the screwdriver and shouted the order, "I command you to come out of this sword in the name of the Most High!" He pushed the screwdriver to the side of the stone, and the red stone shot out. He followed suit with the clear stone. He took a deep breath as the others prayed. When he put the screwdriver to the green stone, high-pitched screams echoed through the room.

Sharp pain shot through John's hands again as a green mist smoldered over the sword, raising it from the table. A surge of electricity raced up his arm, knocking him to the floor.

Cordilia boldly took hold of the sword, pressed it to the table and screamed, "John, take the stone out."

With both hands John moaned, pulled the screwdriver down, and the stone popped out.

The screams continued as John put the stones in the pan, raised the hammer above his head and came down crushing the stones. A gale-force wind filled the basement as the green mist came out of the stone and swirled around and around. Then, at once, a calm filled the room.

Cordilia and John threw the sword and the crushed stones into the fire.

In silence, they knelt and thanked God for the mighty things He had done.

The next day, Rachel and Cordilia took John to the station at noon. He would be gone for a month. Afterward they had appointments with Dr. Wells at 2:00 p.m.

After John's train left, Rachel and Cordilia went to Shirley's Place for lunch. When they entered the diner, they saw Doug Holland sitting at a table near the door. Doug asked them to join him. When they were seated, the conversation turned immediately to the Watch Service.

"Did you enjoy the service last night, Doug?" Rachel asked.

"Very much."

Rachel frowned. "Why do you think we saw the angels when John and Paul didn't?"

Doug wiped his mouth. "God is trying to build your faith for things ahead."

"What things?" Cordilia asked.

"Maybe it's the battle you're going to face in the very near future—one like you've never imagined. You better absorb all the power the Most High is sending your way."

Cordilia took a deep breath and exhaled. "How do you know so much about what's ahead for Rachel and me?"

"You'll just have to trust me."

From deep within, Rachel said, "I trust you. I don't know why I do, but I do."

Doug stood. "I've got to be going, but before I do, I want to advise you there are some very powerful demons in your place of worship. They smile, hug you and say, 'God bless you,' but it's deception. Things are not always what they appear to be."

Before Rachel realized it, she blurted out, "Will you take us to see Mr. McKinney?"

"No, I won't."

"Why not?"

"I'll talk to you later. You better hurry or you'll be late for your appointment." Doug turned and walked to the counter to pay.

"How did he know about our appointment?" Cordilia wondered aloud.

Rachel whispered, "I don't know how he knew, but I'll tell you one thing, Cordilia, we will see Mr. Spook if I have to get Paul to take us."

Cordilia widened her eyes. "Paul! Are you kidding?"

"No, I'm not kidding. If Paul won't take us, then we'll go by ourselves. If you don't want to go, I'll go myself."

"That's it, Rachel."

"What's it?"

"That's how we can get Paul to take us. If we ask him, he'll definitely say no, but if I say you're going by yourself, then he'll go."

Rachel smiled. "Cordilia, you are so right!"

"I know. Just leave everything to me."

Chapter 64
A Visit to Dr. Wells

*P*eggy was looking out the window when Rachel and Cordilia pulled into the parking lot. She called out, "Dr. Wells, your favorite mommies are here right on time."

He sarcastically replied, "Good! If I have my way, their little bundles of joy will be dead by this time next month."

Dr. Wells took his stethoscope from his jacket pocket and hung it around his neck. "Call when you have them ready."

Before they signed in, Peggy opened the door leading to the examination rooms. "Hi, ladies, how are my two favorite mothers-to-be?"

Cordilia quickly replied, "Wonderful since the morning sickness has ended. My only problem now is I'm always hungry."

Since they were the last patients, Peggy took them back together. While taking Rachel's blood pressure, she asked, "Girls, is that Doug Holland handsome or what?"

"He is that," Rachel said.

"Do you think you could fix me up with him?"

Cordilia smiled mischievously. "Peggy, honey, come here."

Cordilia put her arm around Peggy's shoulder and whispered, "With your figure, which is almost as perfect as mine, I don't think you'll need any help with Doug." Cordilia pinched Peggy's cheek and said, "Now give me a big smile."

Peggy not only smiled, she laughed aloud.

Cordilia shook her head and continued, "Perfect teeth, perfect smile, perfect figure and great personality. So, what do you think we can do to help?"

Dr. Wells came into Cordilia's room. His glasses were pushed down on his nose as he studied her chart. He looked up over his glasses at Cordilia. "How are you, Cordilia?"

"I just told Peggy I'm doing fine since I'm over the morning sickness."

"Is the baby active?" Dr. Wells asked as he mashed on her abdominal area.

Cordilia chuckled. "He kicks like a horse."

With no expression, Dr. Wells asked, "How would you know that, Cordilia? Have you ever been kicked by a horse?"

"Not lately."

Cordilia began to giggle as he continued to push on her stomach.

Peggy started to giggle. Dr. Wells cut his dark eyes at Peggy and Cordilia. "Would you two mind telling me what is so funny?"

Peggy answered, "I was laughing at Cordilia."

Cordilia teased. "I was laughing at this mattress. Dr. Wells, if you had to sleep on this, you would be the one getting the exam today not me. Peggy might have to perform back surgery on you."

Dr. Wells showed no expression. "Well, Cordilia, I'll try not to keep you all night. The baby has a strong heartbeat, and I can feel that he's very active."

Dr. Wells closed her chart. "I got a call from Dr. White's nurse. She told me you were in her office a few nights ago for an allergic reaction. Why wasn't I called? I'm your doctor, not Dr. White."

Peggy took hold of Cordilia's hand and helped sit her up. "Actually, it was Rachel who told Paul to call Dr. White."

With fire in his eyes, he stormed at her, "What does Rachel have to do with who you call? Is that not up to you and Paul?"

Peggy stared at Dr. Wells, whose tone of voice was escalating. Peggy quickly added, "He was just very concerned, Cordilia, that he knows your history. Dr. White knows nothing about you."

Sternly, Dr. Wells said, "If you are going to see me, see me. If not, I would like to hear about it from you, not Dr. White's nurse."

Before Cordilia could reply, Rachel opened the door.

Surprised, Peggy said, "Rachel, Dr. Wells will be right with you."

Rachel entered the room. "I couldn't help overhearing the conversation. Nor could anyone else, had they been here. I'm the one who told Paul to call Dr. White."

Dr. Wells was furious, but was holding back his rage. "I couldn't help being upset when I heard that Cordilia had the reaction. That's a dangerous thing if you're not pregnant, but Cordilia, as you well know, is pregnant. It could have killed her and the baby. I have a right to know. After all, I am her doctor, Rachel. So why wasn't I called?"

Without blinking an eye, Rachel boldly responded, "The Holy Spirit told me to call Dr. White."

Dr. Wells took his glasses off and glared at Rachel. "So, the Holy Spirit told you to call someone else? Why?"

"I don't know. Believe me I wish I did. Regardless, I will do what the Holy Spirit says."

Peggy turned her big eyes to Dr. Wells and said, "It's good to hear it wasn't something else. Dr. Wells cares for his patients, especially you two." Peggy looked at Dr. Wells and smiled. "Right, Doctor?"

For the first time since he came into the room, he smiled, patted Cordilia on her shoulder, and said, "That's right. I don't want anything to happen to you or your baby. Rachel, if you will return to your room, I'll be right in." Dr. Wells exited promptly.

Peggy winked at Cordilia and whispered, "He doesn't have a way with words, does he?"

Cordilia raised her brows. "No, he does not. I was about to tear into him. Paul doesn't yell at me, and neither does anyone else."

"He didn't mean it the way it sounded." Peggy hugged Cordilia and told her to get dressed.

Dr. Wells told Rachel that she and the baby were fine, but he would have to check the cysts at her next visit. He said he wanted to make sure there would be no complications as her due date drew near.

Chapter 65
More about the Book

That evening Rachel and Cordilia made a point to visit Effie Brown. Wanting to know more about the contents of the book had become a driving force. As they neared the cabin, they saw Effie's old truck sitting beside the porch. They knocked several times, but there was no answer. Rachel called out to her, but there was no response. Concerned for her, they walked around to the back of the house, but saw nothing.

Seeing the padlock on the door, Rachel and Cordilia turned to leave. Effie was standing just off the porch staring at them. Winston was sitting beside her.

Rachel jerked. "Effie, I didn't hear you come up. Usually Winston calls alert to every movement."

Effie said in a low voice, "I've been expecting you." She glanced around the yard and said, "We better get inside."

They stepped aside for her to unlock the door. To their surprise, Effie turned the knob and went in.

Cordilia frowned at Rachel as they entered. Effie pulled her coat off, draped it on the back of a chair, sat down at the table and said, "Would you like to join me?" She straightened the book in the center of the table.

Cordilia squinted. "How did you do that with the door. It was locked."

"Things are not always as they appear. Now come sit." Winston stood and growled. Effie hit the floor with her cane and growled back at him. "Calm down, you ugly mutt, or I'll give you away, so help me!"

Cordilia frowned at Effie due to her brash reaction to the dog's growl. Without looking at her, Effie assured her that was her way of petting him for doing his job.

Effie cut her eyes to Rachel and asked her to open the book.

To Rachel's surprise there was no stinging of her fingers when she touched the latchet.

"Now where we?" Effie asked.

Cordilia spoke up and pointed to a name on the page. "You were telling us about this General Rakar."

Effie chuckled and continued, "Oh yes, General Rakar. He was one of the most beautiful of all the elites. He and Tashmere were best of friends. When Tashmere was sent to Queen Jewel's domain, Rakar was so happy because he knew if anyone could see through Queen Jewel, it would be Tashmere. Rakar got his orders the same time Tashmere did. The Most High wanted Rakar to take his military training in the Fields of Wisdom. His main objective would be to find true wisdom that would empower him to lead the Armor Bearers of the White Stone Kingdom."

"What is the Fields of Wisdom?" Rachel asked.

"It's a barren place filled with many gates. Once he chooses a gate and opens it, he can't change his mind. He would have to run the full course of what was behind the gate before it would open and release him back to the Field. His main goal was to find Eden's Gate without the knowledge of which gate that would be. Once he found Eden's Gate, he would gain entrance to Wisdom's Mountain—a mountain filled with waterfalls and streams. Not ordinary water though. The streams are filled with a mystical power that has been stirred by the Most High. Once Rakar stepped into the stream he would be empowered with wisdom, boldness and courage. However, there is a condition he must meet before touching the water."

Wide-eyed Cordilia asked, "What condition?"

Effie paused and lowered her head. "You must have a pure heart to be a leader of the Armor Bearers. There can be no lust in your heart. I'm not talking about love. I said lust."

"Did Rakar have lust?" Cordilia asked.

"Let me put it like this: before Rakar could draw near the streams, he would be tried.

One of the most powerful and beautiful generals in the White Stone Kingdom has been given the duty of trying every elite that tried to enter Eden's Gate. Her name is Queen Victoria. She, being one of the ancients, grew up in Eden. She bathed in the stream and was filled with pure wisdom. The Most

High knew his generals could not allow anything to dim or distract their vision. Rakar never dreamed that he had any such lust in his heart, not like his best friend Tashmere, but Victoria was about to prove him wrong. Her job was to bring Rakar to the place of admitting that he too wasn't above being tempted . . . though he thought he was. Such thinking breeds pride and self-righteousness."

"Did he find Eden's Gate?" Rachel asked.

"No, he didn't."

Rachel pointed at the book. "But here on the page he's called General Rakar."

Effie chuckled and tapped her cane on the plank floor. "That's just it; he was a general all along, he was born a general. He just didn't know it. His eyes weren't opened to that fact yet. Sometimes we have a way of not realizing what's on the inside until we go through the training fields."

"As a general, he not only had to have a pure heart, but eagle eyes. Behind the various gates, he would encounter beings that looked like you and me. Without training his eyes, he would see only the outside of a being, and that's okay, but not as a leader. After training his eyes, he too, would become like a mighty eagle. He would see the uniform underneath a being's exterior, whether a high ranking officer or a foot soldier. He could determine whether the being was a soldier of the light or of the dark kingdom. His ambition could not be his own, but that of the Most High. He had to be trained to lead in every area of kingdom authority."

"Did Rakar gain such wisdom?" Cordilia asked.

"Hmm. Let's say, he's still searching."

"Did Rakar and Tashmere every see each other again?" Rachel asked.

"Yes, but not as friends. After Tashmere became the god of lasciviousness, Rakar's orders were to lead the Armor Bearers against his former friend and in the end destroy him and the dark kingdom."

"Effie, what about the Angels of the Ages?" Rachel asked.

Effie scratched her nose and replied, "Legend has it that they're still very active today."

She pushed herself up on her cane. "That's enough for today. I'm old and very tired."

Cordilia sighed. "Can't tell us a little more?"

Effie closed the book and said, "Okay. The Angels of the Ages are still commissioned to come down the ladder."

"Ladder? What ladder?" Cordilia asked.

Effie squinted at Cordilia. "There is only one ladder! Now Winston and I are going to take a nap."

Chapter 66
Sheriff and the Mountain

The day John returned from his trip, Sheriff Butler came by to say hello and to ask the girls for a personal favor. Sheriff Butler stood beside the sink, staring out across the field toward the Jackson's. Just as they were seated at the table, Paul and Cordilia, knocked at the door. Paul laughed and asked if Allen changed his mind about locking Cordilia up for about a week.

"Yes, Paul, I better let her slide this time."

Rachel said, "You said you had something personal to ask?"

The sheriff rubbed his finger across his lip two or three times. "Rachel, honey, I know your mama and daddy tried to protect you from anything bad going on around you."

Surprised, Rachel commented, "We were just talking about that the other day."

Allen continued, "Did you ever remember hearing your parents talk about Alice Watts?"

"Hum, I don't think so. Why?"

"The Watts family lived over next to Boone's Crossing. Their daughter, Alice, disappeared in 1901 when my daddy was sheriff. You know my son, Jack, is an attorney in Benson. He was working on a case that took him into the old records hidden in the basement of the courthouse. He called and told me I might be interested in looking at some of the things he found in the transcripts. I drove over last night to check out what he was talking about. What I saw blew me away!"

The four listened intently. Sheriff Butler was pulling on his ear. Cordilia, who was sitting beside him, took hold of his hand and placed it on the table. "Honey, if you don't stop pulling your ear, there's not going to be any skin left on it. Here, hold my hand."

The sheriff smiled and squeezed her hand. "Thank you, Cordilia."

"Tell us what you found, Sheriff," John said.

"You know, we're still looking for Willow Chandler. There are no leads anywhere. The green lights are still being reported at Boone's Crossing and now this."

"Now what?" Paul asked.

"Alice Watts was 13. She had blond hair. Get this. Her sister said she vanished right in front of her eyes while they were playing outside. The very details Mrs. Chandler gave on Willow are exactly the same as the sister gave on Alice Watts. She was never found, so they said. In addition, green lights were reported at Boone's Crossing when Alice disappeared. Just like the Willow Chandler case."

"Could they be related?" John asked.

"I don't know how they could be related, but I want you to hear what else the records said. There was an old woman who died in the mental hospital at Benson in 1920. For twenty years, all she talked about was what went on at Boone's Crossing. My son got me the trial records relating to this, and I read over them. She said some kind of polished thing came out of the sky and landed at the top of Boone's Crossing."

Rachel eyes widened, "Like a spaceship or something?"

Sheriff Butler slowly shook his head. "I don't know. She said there were all kinds of soldiers, both men and women, gathered there. Their uniforms were from all different eras. These soldiers could disappear. She swore under oath that she saw thousands vanish into thin air."

Rachel and Cordilia looked at each other. "Were they spirit beings?" Rachel asked.

"I don't know anything about that stuff, but I figured you people would. That's the reason I came by."

"What else did she say?" John asked.

"She said that one night, there was a man, or something, who came down fro'm the sky to the Crossing. After this thing landed, a set of stairs came out. A man stepped onto the stairs and everyone bowed their heads. According to her, he stood at the top of the stairs, raised his arms over his head, and yelled out in a voice she could never stop hearing, 'We have come to take this territory!'

The crowd screamed for what seemed like hours, 'Glory to the dark kingdom!'"

"Why was she saying all of this in court?"

"I'm getting to that. She said after all the screaming ended, they brought Alice Watts out of the thing that came down from the sky. Two guards stood on each side of the girl, holding her arms. She was crying and screaming as they brought her down the stairs. According to the old woman, there was a huge rock in the center of where the soldiers gathered. After they tied the girl down on the rock, they danced and did many perverse things; however, they didn't touch her sexually. Now, listen to this. It gets more unbelievable as it goes on. The woman said silence fell. It was so still that she could hear her heart pounding. The man, whom everyone bowed to, stood on the rock where the girl was tied, held a green stone above his head and called out with a voice like thunder, 'Telmar!' When he shouted, 'Telmar,' the people of the Army screamed, 'Come now!'"

Rachel gasped, "Telmar?"

"Yeah, why?"

"Cordilia, that name is in Effie's book. The first time she talked to me about the book she said Tashmere's name was changed to Telmar!"

"What are you talking about, Rachel?" Allen asked.

"I . . . I'll tell you later. Finish your story."

Cordilia muttered, "My word. This is giving me the creeps! If you turned the lights out, this would be like camping in the woods and hearing ghost stories."

"Sheriff," Paul questioned, "how is it this woman got to watch all this without being caught?"

"That question was asked her on the stand. She was evidently homeless and stopped for the night at the Crossing. When she woke up, all of this was going on around her. They acted like she wasn't even there."

"What about this Telmar?" Rachel asked.

"She testified that a wind began to swirl, swaying the trees with a force. Up to that point, she said the sky was clear, and there was no wind at all. Then the Crossing lit up like the Fourth of July with an emerald green glow. A funnel cloud formed out of this green stuff. Suddenly the wind ended and on top of the stairs was the biggest man she had ever seen. All the soldiers cheered and chanted his name 'Telmar!' He went down the stairs and stopped where the girl was lying on the rock. She was struggling to get loose. This Telmar raped her repeatedly while all the others did whatever they pleased. The woman said Alice must have passed out because she stopped screaming before Telmar ever touched her."

Rachel pressed her fingers to her temples. "Effie said that Tashmere's name was changed to Telmar and was cursed by the Mist High to go through life as the lascivious god."

"Maybe I need to talk to Miss Brown," Allen said.

Tears welled up in Rachel's eyes. John massaged her neck. "What happened to the old woman?"

"They concluded that she was crazy and put her in the asylum."

"Wait a minute," Paul said. "Didn't you say they didn't find the girl's body?"

Sheriff Butler bowed his head and answered, "Yeah. The elderly woman said that they literally ate Alice. That's why they never found a body. After they finished, this Telmar vanished. The polished metal thing went back into the sky, and all the soldiers disappeared over Todd's Creek and Benson. One more thing really bothers me."

"What's that, Sheriff?" Paul asked.

"The woman said she recognized some of the soldiers."

"She recognized people who vanished into thin air?" John questioned.

"She pin-pointed the judge, four pastors . . ."

The sheriff paused and hung his head.

"What is it, Allen?" Rachel asked.

"She also pointed out the sheriff. My God! The sheriff was my daddy. My daddy never went to church or talked about God, but I sure don't want to believe this. The people at the asylum said that she never changed her story. Until she died, she swore the story she told was true, and never varied from it. My daddy was not a godly man, but he wasn't a purebred heathen either. How could he vanish into thin air?"

"I wouldn't worry too much about it," Paul said.

"We've seen the green lights at Boone's Crossing," Rachel added.

"I know," Sheriff Butler continued. "I've seen them too! I just wonder if this really happened the way that woman said it did. If so, it might be fixing to happen again!" Sheriff Butler stood and concluded, "I've got to be going."

"Please stay, Allen," Rachel implored.

"I would love to; maybe another time. I'll keep in touch." Rachel hugged him and told him not to worry.

Allen put his hat on. "How is it that Miss Brown knew this Telmar's name? I'll have to go by and ask."

John had a puzzled look on his face. Cordilia nudged John's arm. "What if your face were to freeze like that?" she teased. "The rest of your life, you would be doomed to walk around looking confused. People would say there goes that confused man."

John shook his head. "Oh, my Lord," John whispered.

"What is it?" Rachel quizzed.

"Rachel, everybody is talking about the green lights. We're not in Alaska where one would expect the Northern Lights to put on a dazzling display. We're in Todd's Creek for heaven's sake!"

John exclaimed, "Honey, that night in our bedroom . . ."

Before John could finish his thought, Rachel took a deep breath and stated, "The green mist."

"Exactly."

Cordilia gasped, "Right, you said it was green."

Rachel sat down at the table and moaned, "My God! I don't understand any of this. It's all so bizarre! What's going on?"

Paul joined her at the table. "There is only one way to find out and that's to pray." The four of them joined hands and asked for God's wisdom.

Chapter 67
Traps

*A*t church on Sunday morning, Rachel was confronted by a very personal attack. Half the people she spoke to hardly acknowledged her. Their cold stares and stern faces left her wondering what the problem was. As she entered her Sunday school class, there was less than half her class present. Chris explained that the others had gone to other classes.

"Cordilia, do I have the plague or something? Why this sudden coldness?"

"I don't know, but something's not right."

Rachel noticed that Chris and Paula weren't sitting together. Rachel tried to teach the class and ignore the circumstances. However, the pain was overwhelming. She stopped in the middle of a thought, fighting back her tears.

"Are you okay, honey?" Cordilia asked.

"Yes, I am," Rachel sternly replied. "I am not going to let anything stop me from teaching what's on my heart. The dark kingdom has many evil powers, one of which is called the Dragon. In the Greek, dragon means, 'entrapment, grasping, capturing.' He entraps us with trickery by seizing one's mind, thus forcibly holding us in his grasp.

"Under his power, he sets carefully hidden traps. When I came into church this morning, I received the cold shoulder by almost everyone. It hurt! I didn't understand why because I came to worship with these same people. Then I realized, the dragon tried to take possession of my mind by force. How? By using my surroundings."

"The last word I want to use to make my point as clear as possible is arrest. 'Arrest: when someone is arrested, they are put in prison.' He doesn't want you to believe that you can think for yourself.

"There have been traps set for some of you this morning, as were for me. He didn't want me to teach you this. Therefore, he set traps to discourage me and to hurt me. I could have wallowed in a 'poor me' mentality and be arrested or imprisoned, or I can do just as I did—recognize the trap, through the eyes of the Holy Spirit and put it under my feet. There are only two choices. You put the dragon under your feet or he puts you under his. It is up to you. Cordilia and I are here to pray for you and with you, but that choice is yours."

Paula raised her hand. Panic seized Chris's face. "Do you have a question, Paula?" Rachel asked.

"Yes, I do. Why is it so hard sometimes when you make it sound so simple?"

"What do you mean, 'Why is it so hard?'"

"Sometimes, you feel as though you can't break free from situations."

"Paula, fear is a strategic weapon the dark kingdom uses to keep us imprisoned. Fear brings terror and depression, which paralyze us. Fear takes our boldness away. In times of trouble, we are to come before the throne of God . . . with boldness. The enemy will tell you, 'You can't go before the throne for forgiveness, or anything else. Look what you have done.' He'll whisper, 'You can't be free. Things will never change.' The dragon is a liar!"

"The blood can cleanse any sin, change any situation and set the captive free. If you want to be free, all you have to do is ask. Don't be afraid or ashamed to ask."

Chapter 68
Cold Treatment

*A*fter church, Rachel asked Pastor Miller if he knew what was wrong with some of the people who did not acknowledge the fact she was speaking to them.

He assured her he didn't know.

Rachel and Cordilia passed Stella in the parking lot. "Hi, Stella, how are you today?" Rachel asked.

Stella raised her eyebrows and smugly replied, "Oh, hello, Rachel. Cordilia."

"Stella," Rachel said, "do you know what's going on? Almost everybody acts as though it's hurting them to speak to me."

With sarcasm, Stella raised her chin and replied, "So you just happened to think if anyone knew anything I would. Is that it, Rachel?"

Cordilia was fidgeting with a button on her shirt, trying not to explode.

Rachel quickly inserted, "Only in a good way did I think that, Stella. You know me well enough to know that."

Tilting her head, Stella snarled, "Do I really know you, Rachel? From what I have been hearing, I don't think any of us know you."

Rachel sternly mouthed, "That is exactly what I mean! What have you been hearing and from whom?"

Stella slightly grinned, and answered with a question, "Have you been getting lonely when John is away on all those trips?"

That did it! With rage in her eyes, Cordilia got in Stella's face and declared, "Look here, you old wind bag, trouble maker! You shut your mouth, or I'll be forced to send you to heaven or hell right now. At this point, I'm pretty sure it would be the hotter place." Stella backed up as Cordilia walked forward.

Seeing things were getting out of hand, Rachel took Cordilia's arm and said, "Cordilia, it's okay. Stella wasn't trying to imply anything, I'm sure."

"Not trying to imply? You're right! She's flat out saying it."

"Cordilia Dawson, you're nothing but a low life," Stella said. "If anyone should know what's being implied, it would be you. You've had plenty of experience."

Cordilia started toward Stella, but John interrupted, "What's going on out here?"

Rachel took Cordilia's arm and pulled her away from Stella. "Just a little misunderstanding. Everything will be all right."

Stella pulled at her dress and snorted, "You better keep Rachel away from this mad woman. Her influence is rubbing off on your wife, if you know what I mean!"

"No, Stella, I don't know what you mean."

"I don't think you'll have any trouble figuring it out!" Stella raised her head and walked away.

"Cordilia, are you all right?" Rachel asked.

"No, I'm not. She's straight from hell. There is not one ounce of godliness in her. I can see straight through her, and that is what kills me. She stood there and accused you of messing around while John's out of town. The dark kingdom's imps are spreading malicious lies about you. This war is turning ugly. All that God has been preparing us for is upon us Rachel. I feel it."

"I know, Cordilia, and I have a feeling it will get much worse."

"Wait just a minute," John countered. "Stella accused you of messing around?"

"No, John. Queen Jewel is the accuser. She only uses people to perform her tasks."

John sighed. "I am going to get Paul away from Pastor Miller, and we're going to Shirley's Diner for lunch. I'll be right back."

"Cordilia, don't let what Stella said hurt you," Rachel said.

"What she said about me doesn't bother me. God has forgiven all that long ago. However, when she comes against you with her implications, it's different. Everyone here knows that's a lie. Yet, they're acting as though you're a woman with the scarlet letter on her chest. When the only scarlet I see is the blood of the Lamb that covers you."

Peggy Welsh walked by while Rachel and Cordilia were waiting for John and Paul to bring the car around. "Hi, Ladies," Peggy greeted. "How are our moms-to-be?"

Cordilia nudged Rachel's arm and cheered. "Look, Rachel, there's a smiling face."

"Smiles have been very limited today," Rachel commented.

"Yes, I've heard there are some rumors floating around," Peggy said.

"What rumors?" Rachel quizzed.

"About you and the man I would love to be fixed up with."

Cordilia frowned. "Are you talking about Doug Holland?"

"He's the one."

"Are you kidding, Peggy?" Rachel asked in disbelief.

"No. I'm sorry to say I'm not. However, you don't have to pay any attention to gossip like that. Everyone should know better. Why, if they were saying it about me, people might believe it, but not you."

Rachel interrogated her, "Who started this lie?"

"Stella told me. I told her it wasn't true, but you know Stella."

John and Paul pulled the car around. Peggy was her usual flirty self. She leaned forward and smiled at John and Paul. "How are you two good-looking men doing today?"

Paul replied, "As good as we look. How about you, Peggy?"

Cordilia laughed and exclaimed, "Oh good grief! Peggy, don't encourage him. Paul knows he's good-looking, and if you say much, I'll have to hear about it all day."

Chapter 69
Chris Explains to Paula

On the way home, Cordilia told John and Paul what Stella and Peggy had said.

Rachel added, "I want to ask why, but I know why. I'm angry, but I need to direct the anger in the right direction. I can't believe that people are so eager to believe what they hear without asking me."

John put his hand on Rachel's. "Honey, I know better. Cordilia and Paul know better, but above all, God knows better. Now I want you to forget this, and let's enjoy our dinner."

Pastor Miller had asked the Jacksons to have dinner with them after church. Paula had not talked to Chris in a few days. She felt awkward and so did Chris. After dinner, Chris asked Paula if she would like to go for a drive. Emily Jackson insisted that Paula go with Chris while the grown-ups visited.

Chris and Paula said very little until Chris parked at the lake. Chris faced Paula. "I'm sorry I haven't called you."

Paula looked at Chris and said, "Are you sorry you didn't come out when I came by to see you?"

"Yes, I am sorry. I didn't think you would ever want to see me again after what I had to do."

Paula looked out across the lake and said nothing. In her heart, she knew it had something to do with Peggy.

"Don't you even want to know?" Chris asked Paula quietly.

Without looking at him, she answered, "No, Chris, I don't want to know, do I?"

"Well, you're going to hear it. I can't lie to you, even if it means losing you. I want to be honest with you. I love you, and these last few days have been torture. I can't eat, sleep or think straight. I wanted to call you, but I wasn't going to lie to you. At the same time, I didn't think you wanted to hear the truth, so I did nothing."

"I've felt the same way. I wanted to hold you so desperately."

"And I wanted you. Everything that is going to be done on this mission will have to be done within three months when the babies are due. After that, it will be over. Until then, it won't be. I want to ask you this up front. Please look at me, Paula."

Paula faced Chris. When their eyes met. Chris glided his fingers down Paula's cheek. At his touch she trembled.

"It's only three months," Chris said. "We can make it, but I need you to understand that I only did what I had to do, nothing more."

"Why did you have to do it?"

"Shemed called me to his office. Peggy was there. He said he had another girl for me after the mission was over. Peggy sat in my lap and was all over me. I wasn't responding to her. She told Shemed something was wrong. Shemed reminded me that I belonged to the dark kingdom, and I wasn't free to fall in love, or we both would regret it. I told him I wasn't falling for anyone. I was faithful to the dark kingdom, and I was just tired. He didn't believe me, told me to take her, and prove myself faithful. I did as I was told and left."

Paula put her hand over her mouth and groaned, "Do you promise it will be over in three months?"

Chris breathed a sigh of relief at hearing her question. "Yes, I promise."

"Then, we will do what we have to do for three months. No longer than that, and I mean it, Chris." They embraced and cried as the pain and fear they had felt the past few days seemed to fade away with the comfort of their touch.

Chapter 70
Believing God

*J*ohn was preparing for what he prayed would be his last trip out of town. If all went well, the railroad would have a decision on the job position in Todd's Creek. He prayed Doug Holland was right about the job going to him. John's train didn't leave until midnight on Friday.

Rachel asked a few people from the church to come over for a meeting. She wanted to confront the lies that were circulating. They also invited Doug. Doug and a friend of his, Camron, were the first to arrive. Paul and Cordilia had been there for a while when Pastor Miller arrived. However, none who had been snubbing her showed up. After Doug, Camron and Pastor Miller left, Cordilia and Paul tried to liven everything up. Cordilia and Rachel planned to visit Effie and learn more about her *Angels of the Ages* book.

At the station, they saw Doug and Camron. John had to hurry to get on the train. After the train pulled away, Doug told Rachel that Camron left his jacket at her house.

"Rachel," Doug pressed, "don't be discouraged, by those who didn't come tonight. I know about the rumors spreading through the church. That is a plan to distract you. Don't be discouraged!"

Suddenly, a green light filled the sky over Boone's Crossing. Camron looked at Doug and said, "We need to go now."

Doug put his hand on Rachel's shoulder and assured her, "God knows your labor, Rachel." He shook Paul's hand and put his hand on Cordilia's shoulder. When he touched her, a surge of the Holy Spirit radiated through Cordilia like she had never known. He proclaimed, "Mighty woman of God!" Before she could say anything, Doug and Camron were in their car, pulling away from the station. Paul and Cordilia wanted Rachel to spend the night with them, but she wanted some time alone to seek God.

$$***$$

Rachel knelt beside her bed, but all she could do was cry. There were no words that could express all the emotion she was feeling. She missed John! The timing for the trip could not have been worse. She needed to feel his arms around her. However, the abundant kicking she was feeling from Stephen Daniel would have to suffice. At that moment, she felt like a little child who wanted to climb into her heavenly Father's lap and feel His closeness. Rachel crossed her arms and hugged herself. She could feel His presence in such an awesome way as she knelt in the darkness beside her bed. The moonlight glistened through her bedroom window and illuminated her face.

She smiled, remembering the angel Eri who had stood at her bed almost seven months earlier. She wrapped her arms around her stomach that now held the child God promised. Rachel hummed, "Great is Thy Faithfulness" as she rocked her son back and forth. As she rocked she prayed for wisdom and understanding. She raised her hands and prayed this prayer, "For Your glory, Ancient of Days, fill me and use me. My God, who has been and will forever be, make my son and me a light to the hurting and hopeless. Give me the key to unlock those in bondage and set them free. Savior of our souls, I glorify Your name, Amen!"

Later that night, as Rachel slept, she had a dream. She came from a high mountain to a meadow with rolling hills. A path made up with stones led through the meadow and around the many hills before her. As she walked, she noticed Raptor walking beside her.

Rachel stopped and looked at him. "Raptor, where are we?"

The old eagle raised his head, "The Mountain of Promise." He looked down, and said, "We must follow the stone path to find the rainbows." His sharp eyes fixed on Rachel. "I'm glad to see you wore your mantel today."

Rachel looked down at the cape, not aware it was there.

"Let's move. The stone path is winding and exhausting," he said.

They walked for a long while around many winding trails woven through the hills. Each hill was higher than the other. Rachel had no idea how high the hills had taken her. The scenery all looked the same until they went around a hill that no longer was a hill, but a mountain. They stopped after rounding the bend. In front of her was the most beautiful rainbow she had ever seen. From the corner of her eyes, she could see one to the right of her and one to the left. She turned around and saw one behind her. Rainbows appeared everywhere. "Raptor, I want to stop here for a while. This place is so beautiful and peaceful, I could stay here forever."

Raptor squatted and watched as Rachel basked in the place of promises.

"Raptor, I know that the rainbows deal with the promises of God not to destroy the earth with water again, but I feel it has a much deeper meaning in this place."

"Wisdom has opened your eyes to that truth. The mantel you are wearing you used to have to take from the chest. Now you wear it because it has become a part of you. There are so many that need our help, but we can only help those that want help. We can only fight the battles that the Most High gives orders to fight. We can only help those who still believe in the prophets. So many have fallen because they do not yet have understanding. Many hidden prophets are waiting to be summoned for duty at this time. The prophet's eyes are very powerful weapons because we see what the Most High is doing and what the Gray Stone Kingdom is plotting to do. The red and brown eagles you saw before are the ones who scour the earth and see all that needs to be known for each battle."

As Rachel listened to Raptor, his thoughts became her thoughts. As he talked she could see the eagle's heart.

Raptor continued, "The Mountain of Promise assures us the Most High has his Watchers in place around the universe. We see, and we know."

As Rachel listened she saw Raptor not as a warrior, but as a compassionate father concerned for his children.

After a while, Raptor stood, straightened his feathers, and said, "Rachel, it's time to go. Come, there is more to see."

Rachel couldn't fathom how any place could be better than where she was. Nevertheless, she began to move forward as Raptor led the way. The mountain went higher and higher. Finally, Raptor stopped. Again, they were at the crest of a higher mountain. Raptor stepped aside and motioned Rachel to come forward. The apex of the mountain had surprisingly flattened.

When Rachel stopped, she couldn't believe her eyes. Rainbows were everywhere, but nothing compared to the sight she beheld in the midst of the rainbows. Looking over the edge at the end of the path, she saw a large natural lake in the center of the valley. One end of an enormous rainbow shot from the sky into the water. At impact, diamonds, emeralds and rubies cascaded into the air.

Stunned, Rachel looked at the Raptor. She could see him smiling, happy, because she had made it to this place.

Suddenly, the rainbow in the center of the lake began to spin. It came up out of the water and disappeared into the heavens. Gone in an instant. Rachel was left standing looking at the peaceful water.

She fixed her eyes on Raptor. In a gentle tone, he said, "The Most High is showing you things that are yet to come."

Overcome, she bowed, and worshiped. Raptor raised his head and screamed so loud the echo was deafening. When she lifted her eyes, she saw red and brown eagles on the mountaintop on the other side of the valley. They were screaming and cheering. She stood and looked for why they were celebrating. She asked, "Raptor, why are they cheering?"

He pointed his wing to the end of the valley. "The White Stallion has been summoned."

"Summoned for what?" she asked.

"To lead the way to the Ancient Tree." Raptor raised his wings and screamed. He gently flapped his wings, stirring a soft breeze.

The wind brought a refreshing unlike anything she had ever felt. She raised her arms and moved them up and down as the White Stallion pranced, raised his front feet and neighed. The stallion stomped his feet and ran like the wind through the valley.

Rachel opened her eyes only to find herself in her bedroom floor.

Chapter 71

Expected Guest

Rachel called Cordilia early the next morning to see if she wanted to go to Effie's with her. She said she would be there by 7:00 a.m. As they neared the house, Winston's rampant barking caused Cordilia to laugh. "The other day he didn't bark at all; today he's going wild," she said.

Before Rachel knocked, Cordilia took hold of her arm and teased "I smell coffee, so at least she's not asleep."

Rachel raised her hand to knock when the door slowly opened. Effie was pouring three cups of coffee at the table. "Come in!" she called out. "I've got our coffee poured, and the book is on the table."

"Good morning, Effie," Rachel said. "I hope we didn't come too early."

She put the pot on the stove, faced them, and said, "Too early? I was expecting you before seven."

"Expecting us?" Cordilia muttered.

Effie brought a plate to the table. "I made us a honey biscuit. I thought you better feed those babies."

"How sweet!" Rachel said. "Thank you."

Cordilia added, "I stay hungry all the time. Thank you so much."

After asking grace, Cordilia bit into her biscuit. "Wow! I've never tasted a better biscuit in my life!"

Rachel quickly agreed and asked if she used anything out of the ordinary in her recipe.

Effie smiled and replied, "I put a pinch of enchantment in the flour to make it bake faster."

"Where do you buy this enchantment?" Cordilia asked as she took her last bite.

Effie took a sip of coffee. "There are some things you can't buy."

Rachel told Effie about Alice Watt and the old woman's story. She also told that the old woman called the being Telmar who landed on Boones Crossing.

Effie wiped her mouth. "You sound surprised."

Cordilia and Rachel glanced at each other and made it clear that they were surprised.

Cordilia said, "The woman said Telmar was at the crossing at the turn of the century, yet his name is in this ancient book. How can that be?"

Effie opened the book and said, "Maybe I should continue the story."

Rachel spoke up. "You were telling us about Rakar searching for Eden's Gate."

Effie smiled. "You were paying attention." She cut her eyes to Cordilia. "And you?" "Yes, I was! I want to know more about the ladder."

"In time. I need to tell you about Grandly. Of course. he went by other names on occasions."

"Please do," Cordilia said as she picked the biscuit crumbs from the plate.

"Grandly was one of Rakar's closest friends and one of the upper elites. He had already entered Eden's Gate and bathed in Wisdom's streams. The streams empowered him to be one of the privileged of third heaven. Grandly's position was a Watcher of the high court to make sure everything went as designed. He also served as King Rayon's personal Watcher. After the earthlings were created, Grandly was assigned to certain individuals who were of old, called the ancients ones, or Angels of the Ages."

Cordilia threw her hands up and insisted, "Stop! What do you mean earthling and ancient ones?"

Rachel was about to explode, upon hearing the word "watcher." Eri had said that he was her Watcher. Remembering her vow, she said nothing.

Effie finished her coffee and continued, "A large part of the children of first and second heaven had entered the Garden of Fire and partook of the strange fire. Not all were sexual encounters. Each Highlander would be attacked at his or her vulnerable place. Greed, envy, murder, lust, hate and so forth. Third heaven wasn't exempt. At every level, Queen Jewel's dark forces used the deep magic to deceive at times even the elect. She could appear to be anyone, even King Rayon. You had to know by your spirit if it was really King Rayon or Queen Jewel in disguise. Many from first and second heaven were deceived and lured into Queen Jewel's clutch. Once the Highlanders of first heaven and the Shorelyns of second heaven partook of the fire of good and evil, they could no longer enter third heaven or the throne room of the Most High."

"Were they forced to stay away from the Most High forever?" Rachel asked.

"Oh no! The Most High would end the age before He would allow that. He still loved his children very much. The dark kingdom would have a set time to continue the wickedness before total alienation would be decreed upon them."

"Where does Rakar fit into all this?" Rachel asked.

Effie ran her long finger down the page. "Rakar is like all on these pages: the Ancient Ones. They have been since The Beginning. At the great upheaval, the Angels of the Ages on the right side of the page, fought side-by-side with the Ancient One. Jewel and her forces fought the children of light with a vengeance. They invaded the valley that led to the Beautiful Gate. The Highlanders and Shorelyns were prevented from going into the Gate because of the witchcraft of the dark forces. The valley rumbled as Shemed stormed the place that the Highlander and Shorelyns would have to pass through to reach the gate. When they arrived, they were arrested before they could reach the place of refuge. A thick smoke screen blocked the entrance. Shemed and his demons inflicted pain, guilt and hopelessness. Still the Highlanders and the Shorelyns held to the hope that one day help would come and set them free. That was the main reason Rakar had to take his military training. He would set them free if he found the Beautiful Gate. There were so many gates. Queen Jewel set her sight on Rakar, she wanted to do to him as she did Tashmere, lure him to the Garden of Fire and strip his mantel from him."

"Did Rakar go to the fire with her?" Rachel asked.

"We'll have to wait and see. I can tell you, the wickedness from third heaven, second heaven and first heaven, spilled onto the earth. The Most High had a plan . . ."

Suddenly the windows and walls began to shake as if an earthquake were taking place. The book slammed shut. Effie shouted at Rachel and Cordilia, ordering them out of the house and into the yard. Cordilia grabbed Rachel and pulled her toward the door. Rachel jerked loose and begged Effie to come with them. She said no and told them to go. When Rachel refused, Effie seized her arm and pushed her out the door. Once in the yard, the rumbling stopped. Rachel screamed out, but there was no reply. Cordilia shouted at the top of her voice, "Effie, are you all right?"

Effie replied without opening the door. "I'll be fine. Go home!"

Chapter 72
Stopped Teaching

*A*t church on Sunday, Rachel saw right away that Paula wasn't there. Leah reported that she hadn't been feeling well. She wanted to take her to Dr. Wells, but Paula flatly refused to go.

Rachel was getting the cold shoulder from even more of the people. She prayed and asked God to help her understand.

After church, Pastor Miller wanted to talk to Rachel in his office. Cordilia wanted to go in with her, and Pastor Miller agreed. "Rachel, some of the deacons want you to step down from teaching Sunday school."

In disbelief, Rachel asked, "Why? I've taught that class for several years now and never had one complaint. Now, you're telling me some of the deacons want me to step down."

"Rachel, I said some of the deacons, not the pastor."

"I want names so I can clear this matter up."

Pastor Miller looked down for a moment and said nothing. Rachel continued to probe, "Well, who?"

The pastor tightened his lips and looked at Rachel.

"They all do."

"What?" Cordilia put her hand on Rachel's shoulder.

"What did you tell them, Pastor?" Cordilia asked.

"With deep regret, that I would tell you."

Rachel looked out the window and paused before facing Pastor Miller. "They can't stop me from teaching the Word of God. If I don't do it here, I'll do it somewhere else, but I'll never stop."

Cordilia took Rachel's arm,and firmly stated, "Come on, Rachel. Let's get out of this snake den."

"Cordilia, please!" Pastor Miller pleaded. "You know I don't agree with them."

"It's all right, Cordilia," Rachel said. "Pastor, I know you don't agree with them, and that helps a great deal. If I thought otherwise, it would hurt, but it wouldn't stop me. Thank you," Rachel concluded as she and Cordilia left the room.

Chapter 73
Cordilia's Correction

On the way home, Rachel tried not to cry. She talked about everything except what Pastor Miller just told her. Cordilia let her chit-chat about Stephen, food, weather and John. About a mile down the road, Cordilia had heard enough and commanded, "Rachel Harris, shut up, cry and get this out of your system. How long do you think you can choke the tears back? I'm choking thinking about it."

That was all it took for her dear friend to sob. Cordilia was holding her hand and every once and a while, she would console her, "There, there, Rachel. It will feel all better in a moment." Cordilia was timing her, and after six minutes, she was going to tell her to stop. "Come on, kid, you have one minute left." Cordilia didn't say anything else until she began a count down. "Five, four, three, two, one. Now that's enough, Rachel, dry your eyes and get a grip. Half of this is from the hormones of being pregnant with Stephen Daniel. I suppose the old dragon is getting a good laugh out of all your tears. What did you teach last Sunday? The dragon is always setting a trap for us. You said either you're under his feet or he is under yours. Tell him, in Jesus' name, you're putting him under your feet. Now!"

Rachel blew her nose and concurred, "You're right, Cordilia. I know better than this. Thank you for reminding me."

"You're quite welcome."

Chapter 74

A Trip to Norfolk

The next morning Rachel went into Dustin's Market to buy a few things. As she turned down the aisle to get coffee, she ran into the Jacksons. The big surprise was that Chris and Paula were with them. It wouldn't have looked so bad, but this was a school day, and Paula never missed school.

Rachel wanted to scream out at Jerry and ask him why he voted against her teaching Sunday school; however, she did not. "Hello, everybody!" Rachel beamed.

"Hi, Rachel. What a surprise!" Emily greeted.

"No, the surprise seems to be here with you." She looked at Chris and Paula. "Are you two not going to school today?"

"We wanted them to go for a outing with us today," Emily explained. "Jerry has business in Norfolk and wanted us to go along with him and do some shopping afterward. Leah said that Paula could go with us. She is a straight A student and never misses school, but they agreed to let her go this one time."

Every red flag in Rachel's spirit went up. She knew Emily was lying about why they were going to Norfolk. "Do you feel better, Paula?" she asked.

"Yes, much better, thanks."

Jerry smiled and interjected, "We better be going. I don't want to be late."

Rachel felt sick as she watched them walk away. In her spirit, she knew that Chris and Paula were in some kind of danger. She left the buggy and hurried down the aisle to the door where she ran into Doug Holland and Camron.

"Slow down, Rachel. What's the big hurry?" Doug asked.

Rachel replied, "I really don't know yet."

"I'm sorry about the deacons asking you to step down from teaching your class," Doug commented.

"How did you know about that?"

"News seems to travel fast around here."

"I better go. I've got a lot to do today. Doug, Camron, it was good to see you."

Rachel headed out the door when Doug called out, "Rachel."

Rachel turned her head to see what he wanted.

"If you and Cordilia go to Norfolk today, be careful." Rachel was stunned for a moment.

Doug and Camron looked at each other, but said nothing.

Rachel nodded and walked away. She got into her car and looked back toward the market. "How did he know that?" she wondered aloud.

She hurried to Cordilia's house. Her friend answered the door in her curlers, a blue terry cloth housecoat and floral-design-boot bedroom shoes. Rachel laughed. "Hmm, what a picture of sheer beauty!"

"For heaven's sake, Rachel, what do you expect at nine in the morning. I haven't been up that long. Get in here. It's cold outside. What are you doing up and out this early?"

Rachel pulled her coat off and got some juice from the refrigerator. As she poured the juice, she asked, "What are you doing today?"

Cordilia squinted. "What's up your sleeve, Rachel Harris?"

Rachel shrugged and replied, "Oh, nothing."

Cordilia came back quickly, "Liar!"

"Okay, you're right, I confess."

"And just what do you have in mind? Does it involve me getting dressed?"

"Yes! How fast can you be ready?"

Cordilia smiled, raised her brows and declared, "I can be ready in ten minutes, if I don't have to press my clothes."

Rachel shook her head, "Okay, I'll press while you're working on the rest of you." Rachel plugged the iron and got the ironing board down.

Cordilia stuck her head around the door and asked, "Where did you say we were going?"

"I didn't. Where are your clothes? The iron is hot."

"Are we going to see Mr. Spook?" Cordilia probed as she threw Rachel her shirt.

"No, not this time, but we will before John gets home."

Cordilia clapped her hands. "Now this is more like it! I love the adventure."

"I've got your shirt almost ready. Hurry up!"

Cordilia called Paul and told him they were going to Norfolk shopping. On their way, Rachel shared what had happened at the market.

"Rachel, is Doug a . . . I don't know what to say about him. Is he a prophet or something like the Collins?"

"I don't know. I have a whole list of questions I've been asking myself for the past six months."

"Are we going to visit the woman with the turban on her head? Tell me outright, Rachel, if we are."

"No. I just have a feeling about something, and I want to see whether I'm right or not."

"Well tell me this, Robin Hood, are we going by The Journey in Time shop?"

"Yes, we are."

When they arrived in Norfolk, Rachel parked as close as she could to the shop, which was about a half block away. The wind was very cold, but they were determined. With their scarf's around their necks and wool gloves on, they were out of the car. They leisurely moved toward the shop. As they drew close, Cordilia took hold of Rachel's armand said, "Rachel, look! The Jackson's car is parked right in front of the shop."

Rachel shook her head. "Something bad is going on in there. Why would they bring Paula to this place?"

"I don't know, but I do know I'm freezing!"

"Wrap up. We need to get close enough to see if the open sign is out."

"What if they come out and see us lurking around the door?" Cordilia asked as she pulled her scarf over her mouth.

"Cordilia, we're not going to press our faces against the window. We're only going to see if the open sign is on the door. Now, come on!"

"Lord, help us, if we have to make a run for it, and us seven months pregnant!" Cordilia rubbed her stomach and continued, "Mommy's sorry, Phillip, but we have to do what we have to do."

Rachel and Cordilia drew closer to the door. They could see from the side of the shop that the closed sign was out. Rachel and Cordilia looked at each other. "Why would they be closed with the Jackson's and Paula inside?" Rachel wondered.

"So what do we do now?" Cordilia asked.

Rachel looked around and saw a park bench nearby. She took Cordilia by the arm and pulled her toward the bench. "Come on, we'll sit for a while on the bench."

"Well, that ought to be the smartest thing we could possibly do," Cordilia agreed sarcastically.

After sitting a moment Cordilia held her scarf over her mouth. "I am about to freeze to death, Rachel. I think I already have frost bite on my feet and nose."

"Stop whining, Cordilia. We'll wait another five minutes. Then we'll leave if they haven't come out."

"All right! Five minutes, and the clock start's now." Cordilia had barely those words when they saw the door to the shop open. They quickly stood and began to walk away from the shop. They went around the corner and stopped. Looking back, they saw the four of them getting into Jerry's car. Delilah came out of the shop and looked directly at them.

"Rachel, she sees us!"

"Turn and look into the store window. Point toward the glass or something to appear that we're window shopping."

Cordilia pointed toward the glass and whispered, "This is one of the most ridiculous things I have ever done. Is she still looking?"

"Okay, she is going back inside, and the Jacksons are pulling away. Come on, Cordilia. Let's get to the car."

"Rachel, surely we're not going to do a chase are we?"

"No, we can go home now. I saw what I came to see."

"What do you think we saw?" Cordilia asked as she turned the heater on.

"I'm not sure, but it's not good."

"Rachel, I'm hungry. Are you?"

Rachel laughed and agreed, "Yes. We'll stop at the next diner we come to." They stopped at a place called "Come and Get It." The food was good, and Cordilia had her eye on the chocolate cream pie. Just as she was about to order, Rachel exclaimed, "Oh Lord, help us! Cordilia, the Jacksons are pulling in here. What are we going to do?"

Cordilia quickly pulled a ten-dollar bill out of her wallet and gave it to the waitress. "Here. This will more than cover our meal. Can we go out the back way?

The waitress smiled and looked at the ten. "Sure, and thanks."

They went as fast as they could to the back exit, got into the car and drove away, praying they were not seen.

"Wow! What a rush, Rachel! I haven't done anything like that since Paul and I were married."

Frowning, Rachel looked at her. "Are you telling me you've done things like this before?"

"Heavens, yes! This wasn't anything."

"Well, maybe it was nothing to you, Bonnie Parker, but it's something to me. I've never done anything like this in my life."

Cordilia grinned. "Maybe that's why God put us together. He knew we would be doing a high-speed getaway. Do you suppose?"

"Quite possibly. I just pray they didn't see us."

"Do you believe how God has opened so many unbelievable things to us? One is Effie Brown. I can't wait to go back to and hear more about the book."

"I agree," Rachel said. "Cordilia, are there some things you feel you should tell no one about?"

Cordilia cut her eyes to Rachel. "Of course there are. Why do you ask?"

"If you feel that way, does that mean you would keep something big from me?"

Cordilia patted her leg. "Rachel, honey, some things are between you and God alone."

Rachel felt better hearing Cordilia's answer. She felt guilty at times about not telling Cordilia about Eri and Raptor.

Chapter 75

Here for You

*L*ater that evening, Rachel called and asked Paula if she would come over and help hang the curtains in the nursery. At first, Paula said she had other plans but changed her mind and said she would be right over. "Your nursery is great, Rachel. I love Mickey Mouse."

"Thank you, Paula. I figure any little boy would love Mickey Mouse."

"You're getting quite the stomach. That little man is really growing."

"Yes, and he moves like there's no room left for growing."

Paula's countenance changed as she picked up the stuffed Mickey Mouse and held it in her arms. "Paula, what's wrong?" Rachel asked as she put the tieback on the curtains.

Paula looked at the nursery and Rachel's stomach, filled with her baby that was due in one month. The thoughts of someone planning to kill her baby was overwhelming. She put her hand on

Rachel's stomach. What if something happened to her and Chris's baby? Rachel's baby would be loved so much—all the plans they had, even the name was picked out, and now the nursery was almost complete.

"Paula."

"Oh, I'm sorry, Rachel, my mind was in another orbit. What did you say?"

"I asked how your trip to Norfolk with the Jacksons went?"

Paula put the Mickey Mouse doll back into the crib. "Actually, it was pretty boring."

"Really?" Rachel asked. "What did you do, go shopping, or something, while Jerry attended to his business?"

"No. His business only took a short time, and we visited Jerry's mother."

"Cordilia and I go shopping there from time to time. A place that really stands out in my mind is The Journey in Time. It's quite the shop. Have you ever been there?"

Paula quickly answered, "No, I haven't."

Rachel felt sick that Paula would lie to her about that. "I figured Jerry would take you there for sure, but he hasn't?"

Paula acted very nervous. She began to fix the tieback on the curtain that Rachel had fixed already. "Why would you think Jerry would have taken me there?"

"Only because he highly recommended it to John and me. He raved about it. He said he went there almost every time he went to Norfolk, so I thought he may have taken you."

Paula continued to tensely play with the tieback and, with some irritation, responded, "He may have taken me there, I don't know. We've been to several places, but I don't know if that was one of them or not. What's the big deal if he has or hasn't?"

Rachel felt sick as Paula continued to lie. She walked over to where Paula was holding the tieback and looked at her. For a moment, she only stared at her.

Paula felt very uneasy with Rachel's stare. She turned the tieback loose and looked at Rachel. "Why are you staring at me?" she snapped.

Feeling irritated, Rachel wanted to shake Paula. Instead, she replied, "I'm trying to figure out why you would lie to me."

Paula picked the Mickey Mouse out of the crib and said, "Why would you say I'm lying to you? I'm not lying to you."

Rachel stood behind her. "You just lied again. I want to know why you feel the need to lie about something this simple? Why didn't you just say you've been to the shop?"

"I don't think it's any of your business where I've been or where I've not been, Rachel Harris. I don't appreciate you accusing me of lying."

"Paula, I told you I would always be here for you. That still goes. I'm praying for you, and I don't want to see you hurt or mixed up in something you know is wrong. I feel the same for Chris. You can lie to me, but you can't lie to the Holy Spirit."

Paula stormed out of the nursery, got her coat and snorted, "I've got to go!"

"Paula, you can walk out of this house, and you can walk out of what you're getting yourself into." Paula stood with her back to Rachel and said nothing. When she started to go toward the kitchen door, Rachel added, "Don't just think of yourself, think of your baby."

Paula's heart pounded. She looked at Rachel and responded, "I don't know what you're talking about. You know I'm not married."

Rachel was as surprised as Paula that she had said that. She surely had not intended to. "You don't have to be married, Paula, and you are pregnant," Rachel continued. "It wasn't me who said that about the baby. It was the Holy Spirit speaking through me. I had no intention of saying anything like that, but it is true, isn't it?"

Paula didn't reply. She stared at the floor. "Does Chris know yet?"

Paula glared at Rachel. "Who said Chris was the father?"

"Paula, for heaven's sake. I know you well enough to know you don't sleep around. When you started having sex with Chris, it was because you loved him. Which does not make it right. I'm not here to judge you. At times we all sin, but we don't have to continue in sin."

Paula was almost in tears. Rachel wanted to put her arms around her, but the timing wasn't right. "Does Chris know about the baby?"

344

Sarcastically, Paula snapped at Rachel, "You seem to know everything. You tell me!"

"No, Paula, I don't know everything. You're only upset because I can see the chaos churning in your life. What kind of teacher would I be if I didn't ask God to show me about the ones he has put in my care?"

Paula dried her tears and humbly answered, "No, Chris doesn't know, and I don't want him to know. I would appreciate it if you wouldn't tell anyone."

"I won't say anything, but I am going to pray for you. I love you, Paula, and I care what happens."

As Paula listened to those words, she wished Rachel knew what was planned for her and her baby, but said nothing.

Chapter 76
Needing Prayer

Sheriff Butler had been receiving more and more reports about the events taking place at Boone's Crossing. The townspeople wanted him to go to the Crossing, investigate the lights and sounds that were now being heard by the whole town. On his way to the Crossing, Sheriff Butler and Matt Wilson, his deputy, stopped by Rachel's. John answered the door.

"Why, Sheriff Butler, come in!"

"I don't have time, John. I just wanted you and Rachel to pray for my deputy and me. We're going over to Boone's Crossing to see if we can possibly determine what's going on there. I declare, John, I'm nervous as a cat about it."

Rachel came into the kitchen to see who John was talking to. "Allen, how are you doing?" Rachel asked as she hugged him.

"Rachel, honey, I want you to call Cordilia and Paul, and ya'll be praying for me and Matt. We're going to check out the Crossing. I told John I've got a bad feeling about this."

Rachel patted his arm. "We'll pray for you right away. Try not to worry. God proves Himself in a great way when our backs are against the wall."

Sheriff Butler exhaled. "I certainly am going to be depending on your prayers."

"Don't just depend on our prayers, but depend on the One we're praying to. Be sure and call us the minute you get back."

"I'll do that. Thanks." Sheriff Butler nodded a couple of times and walked away.

"John," Rachel said, "call Cordilia and Paul ask them to pray right away."

"Rachel, are you seeing more in your spirit than you told the sheriff?"

"Yes, I am. He's going to need our prayers desperately. I don't know exactly what's going to happen, but I do know his life is in danger and Matt's as well."

Chapter 77

Going to the Forest

When Sheriff Butler arrived at the foot of the Crossing, he was in a very somber frame of mind. From the moment he stepped out of the car, he felt as though his skin was crawling. He unlocked his gun holster and held his hand on top of his weapon. He told Matt to do the same. There were times he could hear laughter in the distance; yet at other times, it rang loudly in his ears. He could literally feel the breath from the one laughing. The trees were so thick and tall he could feel their branches grabbing for him and barely missing.

A slight fog rose as they entered the forest, but it grew thicker with every step forward. Sheriff Butler's heart was racing. He took his handkerchief from his back pocket, stopped and wiped his face. The fog had grown so thick he couldn't distinguish what he was wiping from his face—sweat or fog.

"Matt," Sheriff Butler asked as he continued to wipe his face, "how are you doing?"

Matt shook his head. "I don't care to tell you, Sheriff, that I'm scared as bad as I have ever been in my life."

Sheriff Butler looked around him. "I swear it all looks the same. I've been trying to look for markers, so we can find our way back, but I can't see any markers. Can you, Matt?"

"No, I can't. I just want to hurry and get out of here," Matt implored as he continuously wiped his face. Irritated, Matt added, "This fog feels like a soaking rain. How much farther are we going in, Sheriff?"

"Not much, but we will go a little farther. Stay close, Matt," Sheriff Butler ordered as he cautiously moved forward. They had taken only a couple of steps when they felt a warm gust of air hit them in the face. They froze in their tracks. In a few seconds, they felt it again. The warm air had a strange odor of something's breath. "I'm getting out of here, Sheriff!" Matt shouted as he ran away.

Panicked, Sheriff Butler yelled out, "Matt, come back! You're going the wrong way, Matt!" Up ahead he heard screaming. "Matt is that you? Matt!"

The fog was so thick he couldn't see his hand in front of his face. He heard a gun shot ring through the trees, followed by Matt, groaning in pain. Matt yelled out, "Sheriff, I'm shot!"

Sheriff Butler slowly moved forward and called out to Matt, "Matt, where are you? Are you okay?"

Allen's heart pounded so hard it hurt when he heard Matt screaming in agony, "Oh God! God, help me! Sheriff, the trees are killing me. Help me . . ."

"Matt, what . . ." The thing Sheriff Butler saw before him rendered him unable to call out to Matt, to God, or anyone. The tree limbs were like arms holding Matt and hitting him. He was screaming so loudly that the echo of his yells pierced the sheriff's ears. Matt was struggling to break free from the tree limbs but in vain. He still had his gun in his hand trying to shoot the limbs, but the bullets had no effect on the hideous arms of the trees that were tearing his flesh from his body. The last shot ricocheted, hitting Matt in his stomach, and then there was silence. Sheriff Butler stood there unable to move, as though he were a prisoner of the fog that was choking him. The silence was broken by laughter of the trees that echoed through the woods.

For an instant, the sheriff felt the freedom to move. He turned and started to run. He went only a very short distance when he ran into a wall that the fog had formed. Upon hitting the wall, the sheriff fell to the ground. He was addled, and his breath was knocked out of him.

Groaning, he put his hand on the back of his neck and turned his head from left to right. When he bent his head forward to stretch his neck muscles, he looked straight into the eye sockets of a skull lying beside him.

Terrified, he used his hands to scoot backward away from the skull. He felt something from behind him pick him up and stand him upright against a tree. The fog wrapped itself around him like a straight jacket. The arms of the straight jacket were so long they wrapped around the tree and tied him there. The wall of fog disappeared, and the sheriff could see clearly through the trees. As the trees began to move, he saw them lifting their roots out of the ground and moving toward him. He was so dizzy he felt as though he was going to faint. As the trees moved toward him, Allen knew he was going to die. For a moment he closed his eyes and called out to God for help. Then he said the words he had never said before, "Lord, forgive my sin." He could feel the ground rumbling under his feet from the enormous trees coming toward him. He opened his eyes and took a deep breath. Before he blacked out, he saw that the trees coming toward him were no longer trees, but giant men.

✳✳✳

When Sheriff Butler was found, he was lying beside his car. A man from Benson who was passing through saw him and took him to Dr. Well's office. Peggy met the ambulance driver at the door. She had everything prepared for Dr. Wells to examine him.

Jerry Jackson was in town when the ambulance came to Dr. Well's office. Several people gathered to see what happened. Paul and John were coming into town and saw all the commotion. They hurried over and asked Jerry what was going on. He told them all that he had heard. "Sheriff Butler is talking out of his head. He said the trees were walking and attacked Matt."

"Where is Matt?" John asked.

"I don't know, John. The sheriff said he was dead. He said that he shot himself trying to kill the trees. Have you ever heard such foolishness?"

"Matt's dead?" Paul asked.

"That's what he said."

"Where is Matt?" Paul probed.

"Allen said he was still at the Crossing."

"Is Allen hurt bad?" John asked.

"I don't think so. They said the main thing they were worried about was a blow to his head. He was coming to, though, when they brought him in."

Dr. Wells came into the waiting room and announced the sheriff was going to be okay. He wanted to go back, take some men with him, and try to get Matt's body.

"Is he able to do that right now?" John asked.

"I think he'll be fine. He may have a bit of a headache." As Dr. Wells was talking, Sheriff Butler came out of the room.

"Sheriff, are you okay?" Jerry inquired.

"We need to get Matt before dark, or we may never find him," Sheriff Butler said.

Dr. Wells tried to get Sheriff Butler to wait until morning, but he wouldn't hear of it. "We've got to go now. I need some of your men to go with me." Several of the town's men decided to meet in a half-hour and go with the sheriff.

John and Paul hurried home and told Rachel and Cordilia what had happened. "Oh my God! Matt's dead?" Rachel pondered in disbelief.

"How is Allen?" Cordilia asked.

"He's as white as a sheet, but he insists on going to get Matt's body before dark," Paul answered. Paul kissed Cordilia, looked at John and concluded, "We better go, John."

John kissed Rachel. "You girls pray for us."

"You both be careful," Cordilia called out from the porch. "Do you hear me, Paul Dawson?"

"John, call as soon as you get back in town, okay?"

"I will. I love you."

"You too," Rachel countered.

***

Rachel went to her bedroom, got her Bible and began to look up every reference to "trees."

"What are you doing, Rachel?" Cordilia asked.

"The Holy Spirit is saying something in all this. There's something about the trees. My spirit was quickened as soon as John said the word 'tree.' The Bible tells of a cedar in Lebanon with fair branches. His height was exalted above all the trees of the field. There was none like this tree in God's garden. He was tall, a vision of beauty and full of wisdom. His extravagant growth and beauty exceeded all the other trees. Pride was bred because of his grandeur. This tree not only placed himself above the other trees, but above God also—which spelled the grand tree's doom. God cut him down because of his arrogance and pride. He was cast down to the netherworld, among the other trees, who had similarly fallen. Does that sound like a male version of Jewel or what? Then when the Most High cuts the tree down, the chaos will end, and peace will be restored to Eden."

"Hum!" Cordilia said. "Rakar was searching for Eden's Gate. Rachel, do you think this has some meaning to the trees at Boone's Crossing?"

Rachel declared, "Yes I do! The Holy Spirit is showing me the trees that Allen and Matt saw represent a demonic stronghold in that region. They're not the cedars of Lebanon, which are referred to as the children of God. That once great tree is now referred to as a common box cedar. He stands out like a sore thumb compared to the child of God. A child of God will stand and not be moved by his tactics."

Cordilia raised her brows and tilted her head. "Do you think God is going to let us fell some trees?"

Rachel folded her arms and confidently replied, "Cordilia, I have no doubt." Rachel looked toward Effie's. "Effie also spoke of the two trees in the Garden of Fire. We need to visit Effie."

Chapter 78
Dr. Wells Attacks

Sheriff Butler and the other men arrived at the Crossing. He felt sick as he got out of his car and looked toward the woods. He paused, swallowed hard and exhaled. Dr. Wells was the first to get out of his car and ask the sheriff which way to go. Allen led the way to the tree line and paused.

"Well, let's go, Sheriff. Matt may still be alive," Dr. Wells demanded.

John spoke up on Allen's behalf. "Take it easy, Dr. Wells. The sheriff has been through quite an ordeal. As a doctor, you should know that."

Dr. Wells frowned at John. "I do know that! As a doctor, I also know if Matt is out there and still alive he needs assistance now!"

Allen pointed at a huge evergreen and instructed, "All right. We need to go in right here." He pulled his gun from his holster and led the way in.

The disturbed look on Allen's face was evident. He pulled his ear, and said, "I'm thankful there's not any fog."

Paul patted his shoulder, "Just take it easy, Allen. Don't let anyone intimidate you."

Some of the men from town had reservations about what the sheriff had told them. They weren't the only ones who wondered. So did Sheriff Butler. The forest was beautiful. There was no laughter, fog, tree limbs grabbing or walking trees.

They had walked quite a ways into the woods when Dr. Wells stopped and demanded, "Did you go this far in or not?"

"It don't seem like we did."

Sarcastically, Dr. Wells teased, "I don't hear any trees laughing or see any fog-building walls. Are we at the right place or not, Sheriff?"

John spoke up sternly, "Dr. Wells, why don't you lay off?"

He quickly responded, "John, why don't you wise up? There's nothing here like he said, including Matt's body. What do you say to that?"

Several of the men suggested they go in groups and see if they could find Matt. Sheriff Butler, John, and Paul stayed in one group. John asked Allen if he felt like going on. He insisted they go on to find Matt. All agreed to meet back at the entrance in one hour and to shoot into the air if they saw anything. After about thirty minutes, Sheriff Butler stopped and sighed. "I wish I could hear a shot go off. I declare I do. I don't understand. It was nothing like this. Nothing!"

An hour passed, and no shot had been fired. Back at the entrance, Dr. Wells said, "Sheriff, what are we to make of this? There was no of sign of Matt, dead or alive."

The man from Benson who found the sheriff spoke up. "I saw a dirty-looking mountain man run into the tree line on the east side over here. I don't know if he had anything to do with any of this, or if he just happened to be here."

Paul described Mr. McKinney to the man from Benson and asked if that could have been the man he saw.

The man replied, "Yes, the description fits him perfectly."

Allen concurred. "I saw so many things, but he's right. I vaguely remember seeing Mr. McKinney. I just wasn't sure until he mentioned it."

"It's getting dark. We need to be getting out of here," Pastor Miller said.

Sheriff Butler agreed. "The pastor is right. We don't want to be up here after dark. We'll search again tomorrow."

"If tomorrow doesn't turn up more than what we've seen here today, there's no need to come back," Dr. Wells concluded. He ignored the report of the missing body.

John asked Sheriff Butler if he would mind to drop Paul and him off on his way back to town. Rachel and Cordilia went out to meet them. Sheriff Butler thanked Rachel and Cordilia for their prayers. Then he shared with them the most important news of all. He was sitting in the porch swing beside Rachel. He barely pushed the swing back and forth. "I'm sorry, Rachel. You can hardly sit in a porch swing and not at least rock yourself, can you?"

"No, you cannot. If you hadn't started pushing, I would have," she replied.

Tears welled up in Allen's eyes. "I've got to call Matt's mama on the way home. I sure dread that—without even his body to give her."

He wiped his tears and started to pull his ear.

"Allen, do you want Paul and me to take you home?" John asked.

"No, but thank you, John. I have to take the official worn-out sheriff vehicle home with me. Tonight, we're both worn out. I do want to share one more thing with you before I go. When I was bound to that tree, and the trees began to walk toward me, for the first time in my life I really prayed to God. I asked Him to forgive my sins and come into my heart."

By this time, all five of them had tears in their eyes. Rachel put her arm around his shoulder and rejoiced, "I praise God for you, Allen."

"Today it was like my soul had entered hell. When I was tied to that tree, I thought I was going to die. I knew I wasn't ready to stand before any judge, especially God. I thought of Molly. I sure love that woman . . . and my boys, Alex and Jack. I also thought of you all praying for me. I can't thank you enough.

"Rachel, you've been like a daughter to me. Back before your mom and dad and before Molly and me were married, I used to think the world of your mom. She was one of the prettiest women I have ever met. You know, your mom introduced me to Molly. Speaking of Molly, I need to get home."

Sheriff Butler stood to go.

Cordilia said, "Sheriff, before you go, we want to pray for you." They joined hands, made a circle around him, and thanked God for the mighty work he had done in keeping Allen. They prayed for guidance to find Matt in the search tomorrow. Above all, they gave God praise for the blood that sets the captive free.

Cordilia hugged Allen and teased, "I love you, you old, used-to-be heathen."

Paul was quick to insert, "It's not too late to take her to jail for about a week, Sheriff."

Sheriff Butler started toward his car and stopped. "I feel worried about Mr. McKinney."

Rachel inquired, "Why would you feel worried about him?"

"I'll let John tell you about it. I've got to make a house call and get home. Molly will be worried to death. I love you all and thanks again for your prayers."

John told Rachel and Cordilia about the man from Benson seeing Mr. McKinney going into the other side of the forest.

"Why would he be there?" Rachel asked.

"I don't know, but Allen said he thought he saw him too. Everything was so blurred at the end, he wasn't sure."

"I don't believe he had anything to do with this, do you?"

"Honey, we don't know the man. How can we say what we think he would do or not do?"

Cordilia answered, "For some reason, I don't think he had anything to do with it either. Not in a bad sense anyway."

Paul raised his hand and agreed, "I'm with the girls on this. I don't know why, but I feel the same."

John raised his hand. "I make that vote unanimous. I don't think the men who went with us will feel as we do."

Chapter 79

A Mad Crowd

They found Matt's body, what there was left of it, the next day. The townspeople were furious and wanted somebody to pay. The one they wanted was Mr. McKinney.

The people of the town met after Matt's funeral. Almost every man in town wanted to hang Mr. McKinney without an arrest or trial. Dr. Wells, who did not even know Matt, emerged as the leader of the mob. Doug Holland and Camron were at the meeting. Rachel wondered where Doug had been. She hadn't seen him for a week and a half.

Sheriff Butler asked everybody to calm down. "There's not going to be any hanging in my town. Have you got that? Dr. Wells, I think you're getting out of hand."

With fire in his eyes, Dr. Wells stood. "Okay, Sheriff, we'll give you one week to bring him in, or we will bring him in ourselves."

The crowd was a mob of lunatics. John saw Rachel stand. He tried to stop her, but he was too late. "Dr. Wells! I want to know where you come off giving Sheriff Butler a time limit on something. Your position in this town is not the law. It's to give medical treatment to those who need your services. I know everyone in this place and have never seen any of you, except Howard Thomas, act like this."

With those words, the moment lightened. Every town has a town drunk, and Howard was the one of Todd's Creek. Everyone knew there were times Howard would get out of hand. When he did, his wife Meg would sometimes knock him out, or sometimes she would bring him to the jail to spend the night. Meg and Howard laughed along with everyone.

Howard responded, "Now, Rachel, you know I'm trying to do better. I've not spent the night in jail for two weeks now." Everyone applauded.

Meg added, "If he knows what's good for him, he'll keep it up."

Sheriff Butler was relieved that Rachel had lightened the tension.

Rachel continued, "As a town, we need to come together and pray—"

Before Rachel could finish, Dr. Wells interrupted, "I thought I heard Sheriff Butler say he heard Matt call on God to help him. Did God save him? The grave he is buried in cries out, 'No, he did not!'"

Peggy pulled on Dr. Wells's pant leg to get him to shut up. When he felt the pull on his pants, he saw the faces of the people and heard the hush fall over the room at his words. He lowered his head, and apologized, "I'm sorry, the sight of

Matt's mangled body pushed me over the edge. Please forgive my outburst. I just want justice for this atrocity."

Rachel stated, "If you feel that distraught just seeing the body, how do you think the sheriff felt after seeing the horrid event take place, without being able to do anything?"

Some of the other men agreed with Dr. Wells. They said the sheriff had one week, and then they would take the law into their own hands. Sheriff Butler sternly argued, "I'll not have any vigilante acts going on here. This is Todd's Creek, not Tombstone, Arizona."

Someone from the crowd yelled out, "There's only one of you, Sheriff."

Angered by the comment, Sheriff Butler shouted back, "There may be only one of me, but I'll call the state police in if I have to. Now go home!"

Allen turned and left the room. The crowd continued the crazy discussion. John looked at Rachel and said, "Come on, honey, let's go home."

Paul, Cordilia, John and Rachel were headed to the back door when they saw Doug and Camron. Rachel stared at Doug, shook her head and asked, "What do you think of this?"

Doug replied, "I think it's a mess."

"How are you, Doug? Camron?" John asked.

"Staying very busy, John. We're going to get a bite to eat. Would you like to join us?"

"Why don't you join us for a peanut butter and jelly sandwich?" Rachel invited.

"Yes!" John said, "Cordilia and Paul are coming by."

After everyone sat down for supper, John asked the blessing over the food and everybody ate as if they were starved.

"Cordilia, what's the matter with you?" Paul asked. "You're squirming all over the place."

"I'm not comfortable! Phillip is getting up under my ribs. Sometimes I think I can feel his head. It is like a softball in my tummy. I feel hungry, but there is no place to put the food because of mama's baby!"

Rachel was quick to respond, "A giant amen to that, sister!"

"I'll eat for both you and Phillip tonight, honey." Paul said.

Rachel looked at Doug and tears filled her eyes. John put his arm around her. "Honey, are you okay?"

With deep emotion, Rachel shared the feeling that had been eating away at her. "It seems so petty after what happened to Matt, but no, I'm not okay. I have lived in Todd's Creek my whole life. Almost everyone knew my mom, dad and me. I have never done any of the things that are being said about me. Teaching the Word of God is my life. I just need you all to pray for me. It hurts to be lied about! It hurts to know that where I've gone to church my whole life I'm being asked to give up my class. Those people know me!" Rachel looked up at Doug and apologized, "I'm so sorry you were lied about too."

Doug put his hand on Rachel's. "Listen closely, Rachel, the attack is very strong because God is preparing you for a mighty victory. You should expect nothing less from the dark kingdom. You know where the root of this originates. So let's all agree together and 'bind this force.'" They prayed not only for Rachel but also for each one.

Chapter 80

The Visit Finally

*R*achel got very little sleep that night: Repeatedly, she thought of Mr. McKinney and the things he had said to her and Cordilia.

"The angels are coming," rang loudly in her ears. "I see two angels standing in front of me." Looking into Cordilia's eyes, he had asked, "Is it you?"

Rachel got up and went to the living room. She didn't turn the light on, but the area light from outside glistened through the big picture window. She pulled the sheer back and looked outside. The full moon and the dark sky, filled with an untold amount of stars, was gorgeous. Her thought of Effie's story and the three heavens stirred her emotions. She wanted desperately to have a quick peek into that dimension. Though her eyes had been opened to see angels, warring eagles and Raptor, picturing the grander scale was her goal. Had it not been two o'clock in the morning, she would have gone to Effie's. As her eyes were being opened into the spirit realm, she found herself saying what the hermit had said. In only a whisper, she repeated Mr. Spook's words, "The angels are coming."

Needing to talk to her kindred, no matter how early it was, she dialed Cordilia's number:

Surprised, she answered on the first ring. "Hello, Rachel."

"Cordilia, how did you know it was me?"

"Who else would wake me this early?"

"Why did you answer the phone so fast?"

"I can't sleep! I've got a combination of things on my mind. The most important being Mr. Spook."

Rachel exclaimed, "Me too. I can't get him off my mind!"

Cordilia began laughing.

"What's so funny?"

"What are the odds of two gorgeous big pregnant women losing sleep over a dirty old mountain man. I bet Mr. Spook would step up his dance pace if he knew that."

Rachel laughed. "It just might push him to take a bath."

"Rachel, all kidding aside, it's time to go to the mountain."

"I know. Have you talked to Paul about it?"

"I have!"

"Really? He was okay with it?"

"I couldn't believe when he said we'll go tomorrow. We're so big pregnant. There's no way we can wait."

"John thinks we're nuts. He also knows if the Holy Spirit says go, I will. Besides, he has to go to New

York. He's leaving in the morning at 8:30. So Paul took the day off tomorrow?"

"Yes, Bob is filling in for him. We'll be at your place 9:30 sharp."

John had cautioned Rachel every way possible and assured her the only reason he agreed was the fact that Paul was going. Rachel was ready the next morning when Paul and Cordilia arrived. They prayed before they left the house and most of the way to the foot of the mountain.

They got out of the car, and Paul said, "Ladies, it's not too late to turn back."

Cordilia glared at Paul, tightened her lips, and asked, "Do you possibly think Rachel and I came out here for the drive?"

"Baby, I was only giving you the opportunity."

Cordilia pinched his cheeks. "Thank you, my love! Now, let's go."

Paul scanned the area. "Does anyone know how to go?"

Rachel pointed north. "Let's go this way."

They had gone only a short way when Cordilia took a deep breath and held her stomach. "Paul, honey! Are we doing a marathon here? I'm turning blue. Slow down."

Rachel agreed.

"Paul," Cordilia added, "I need some water!"

Paul got the water from a small pack and handed it to Cordilia. "Maybe this was a bad idea. We've not gone five hundred feet yet, and you sound like you're going to die. If you want to turn back, now is the time."

Cordilia grabbed Paul by his overall straps and demanded slowly, "Let's get going and no more talk about turning back. Okay?"

They went a long way up the mountain. Paul stopped often to allow the women to rest. Cordilia and Rachel sat down on a log. Cordilia's feet were beginning to swell. She whined, "Honey, look at my tiny ankles! They look like Pop Eye's arms. How are you doing, Rachel?"

"Stephen Daniel is giving me a fit. He's all feet. How about you, Paul?" Rachel asked.

"I'm happy to report that all is well. No swollen feet or movement in my belly. We need to get going if you're up to it. I don't have a clue how much farther to go or if we're even going in the right direction."

About twenty minutes later, Cordilia was just about to say "break time," when Paul proclaimed, "There it is!"

Rachel looked at Cordilia and cheered, "We made it!"

"Now listen to me," Paul said. "I want you to stay close and be careful. The only reason I came was I knew God would be with us. So let's go!"

"Paul," Cordilia chimed in, "we can't act like we're creeping in. We need to look like a legitimate visit is taking place."

Rachel was quick to add, "She's right, Paul. We can't try to sneak in. We'll just go up and knock. He doesn't know you, so let me or Cordilia lead the way."

Rachel got in front and started toward the old log house. As they drew near the porch, Rachel looked at Cordilia and knocked lightly on the door. No one answered.

"Rachel, knock a little louder," Cordilia ordered. Rachel knocked harder, but still no response.

Cordilia walked over and pressed her face to the window.

"What are you doing?" Rachel shouted.

"I'm trying to see if he is home."

"You don't press your face to people's windows. They may shoot you. If they're home, they'll answer the door."

Paul walked to the side of the porch. "Rachel, look over here! There's been a fire out back. He may be back there."

"Paul, should I call out to him?" Rachel asked.

"Whatever you think. This is your visit."

"What do you think, Cordilia?" Rachel asked. When Cordilia didn't answer, they turned to see where she was. "Oh my word, Paul, she's already in the house!"

They hurried to the door in time to see Cordilia coming out of the back door. "Cordilia!" Rachel screamed through gritted teeth.

"Honey, what in the world were you doing in his house?" Paul scolded.

"Don't panic! He's not in there."

"Cordilia! That's breaking and entering. You could get arrested for that," Rachel said.

"Let's get out of here," Paul added.

While discussing what to do, a stern voice startled them. "What are you doing in my house?"

Cordilia screamed.

Rachel inhaled abruptly and put her hand on her chest.

Paul jumped backward and apologized, "We're sorry. We must have the wrong house. We were looking for Mr. McKinney."

"What do you want with Mr. McKinney?" The man interrogated them.

Rachel stepped forward and answered, "We're afraid he's in danger."

The man standing in the doorway came inside. "Why would you think that?"

Rachel took a deep breath and put her hand on her aching back. "Because of the talk that's going on in Todd's Creek. Do you know where he lives? We're obviously at the wrong house."

The man moved closer to Rachel and stopped. "You're at the right house."

Cordilia moved in front of Rachel and said, "Can you tell . . ." She paused as she looked into the stranger's eyes. "Do I know you from somewhere?"

The man held his stare and replied, "Do you think you know me?"

Cordilia tilted her head. "Yes, I feel as though I do."

"Do you live here with Mr. McKinney, or are you a neighbor?" Rachel wondered aloud.

The man nodded his head and said, "You might say that."

Paul asked, "Can you tell us when Mr. McKinney will be back?"

Before he could answer, Cordilia, began to shake her finger at him and declared, "I do know those eyes."

The man quickly put his face to Cordilia's and said, "Is it you?"

Cordilia's mouth dropped open as she and Rachel looked at each other. Rachel moved closer and asked, "Mr. Spook? Are you Mr. Spook?"

"Yes, Rachel, I am."

Rachel shook her head. "You don't look like Mr. Spook."

There in front of them stood a clean-cut man, without slumped shoulders or matted hair. His teeth were clean. His clothes were clean, and he didn't smell bad. He looked twenty years younger!

"Looks can be very deceiving, Rachel."

The three were shocked. They almost forgot why they had come. Cordilia pushed his shoulder and exclaimed, "You nearly gave me a heart attack! Look here, Mr. Spook, we came ten miles up that mountain to warn you about the townspeople who want to lynch you. When we get here, we see a transformed man. Your eyes are the only reason I believe you."

Mr. Spook looked sympathetically at Paul, and shook his head. "She's a talker, Paul!"

Paul nodded and agreed. "You're only seeing a small part of the picture."

"Cordilia, I want to apologize for the walk. However, it's not ten miles, but a little less than one mile. As far as you being concerned, I appreciate it, but I'll be fine."

Rachel was listening and observing quietly. She stood in front of Mr. Spook and demanded, "What is all the big act with looking like a nasty mountain man?"

"I am doing what I was commissioned to do thirty years ago."

"Commissioned by whom?"

"The Most High."

Rachel frowned and probed, "God told you to live like this?"

"Yes, He did."

"I don't understand that. Why would He tell you to do this?"

"Rachel, that's like asking you why God would pull you to this mountain. You don't fully know. You just do as He leads you, whether you understand it or not."

Cordilia asked, "What did you mean that day in town when you said, 'Is it you?' That's been driving me nuts!"

"I recognized you."

"How could you recognize me? I had never seen you before, except the one other time with Rachel."

"Cordilia, when you looked into my eyes, you recognized me as well."

"I recognized you from where? Did you live in Ohio or something?"

"No! You recognized me from a lot further back than Ohio." Mr. Spook paused. "Rehabiah."

At that name, Rachel, Paul and Cordilia were rendered speechless. "How do you know that name?" Paul asked.

"The same way that I know your name is Jathniel."

"Is this some kind of joke?" Paul asked, unsure of what Mr. Spook was saying.

"Let me ask you this," Rachel continued. "How did you know the Holy Spirit was pulling me here?"

"I knew in my spirit, Rachel. Why don't we sit down?" He pointed to the straight-back wood chairs sitting around the room. They sat down and Mr. Spook put some wood in the old rock fireplace to knock the chill off the room. Paul looked at him but said nothing. Mr. Spook asked Paul, "Why don't you ask me what you're thinking, Paul? It's okay."

Embarrassed by the fact that Mr. McKinney could possibly be reading his thoughts, Paul began, "I . . . was just wondering about what happened with your wife and kids."

"What would you like to know?"

"I wondered if this was about the time you were told to come to the mountain to live."

"Yes, it was at that time. The Lord has mysterious ways to empty self out and allow His Spirit to fill the empty space. That's what happened, you know. I felt my whole world had been stripped from me because my wife and children were my life. Don't misunderstand me. God expects us to care and make our mate and children our life. The bad thing was I made them my whole life. I knew nothing else. When a catastrophe hit my life, I had no reason to live. I have learned my life is not given, or lost, as a result of my family being with me or not. Through the hardest lessons ever, I have learned my family made a difference in my life, but God is my life. I rediscovered that I am more fulfilled now than I have ever been as far as my spirit goes."

"What about the men you killed, did they have families here in Todd's Creek?" Rachel asked.

In disgust, Mr. Spook cried, "That I killed? I killed no one!"

"But . . ."

Before Rachel could finish her thought, Mr. Spook sternly rebuked her, "I know, they said I did it, but I killed no one."

"Who did?" Paul asked.

"Sheriff Roger Butler!"

"You mean Sheriff Allen Butler's dad?" Rachel asked in disbelief.

"Exactly! Of course, you won't read that in the old newspapers at the library, but he did it. I saw him shoot the men. He would have killed me too, but his gun jammed. He told the story that I walked in on the men, who raped and shot my wife, and I went crazy. I lost it, okay, but not before seeing Sheriff Butler shoot the men. He was there when I got home. When I came in the door, I could hear men's voices. I also heard my wife's voice. She wasn't dead when I entered the house. I heard her scream, 'Please don't shoot me!' Roger Butler shouted, 'Kill her!' There was a scream, and then a shot. I didn't hear my wife again. I tried to be as quiet as possible as I took my shotgun from the gun rack, but it wasn't there. I could still hear them talking as I got another gun from a closet.

"When I reached the top of the stairs, I heard one of the men say, 'Why did we have to kill them?' I heard the sheriff yell, 'For nothing! Where is the money you said was here?' The man said, 'I told you what I was told.'

"I didn't see him shoot the first man, but when he shot him, the other man cried, 'Sheriff, why did you kill Jack?' The sheriff cried, 'The same reason I'm going to kill you.' I stepped around the door as Roger shot him. I was out of my mind, not knowing about my boys and fearing my wife was dead. Sheriff Butler saw me and ordered, 'Mr. McKinney, you better get out of here. These men killed your wife.' The shotgun he was holding was mine. Again, he demanded, 'Get out of here!' I cried, 'No, you killed her!' He raised the gun to shoot me, but the gun wouldn't fire. He continued to say that they killed her. He tried to make me believe that someone heard gunshots out here, came to town and told him. Then he came as fast as he could. He had the nerve to point toward the bed where my wife lay naked. Blood was everywhere.

"The sheriff continued his lie when he pointed at m. 'I understand why you would shoot them after what they did to your wife and kids.' At that point, I really lost it.

"Everyone, including the doctor, said I was too distraught to even remember what went on. They put me in the asylum at Benson and performed shock treatments on me. That was supposedly what brought me back to my senses. I was the perfect patient. I did what they told me and kept my mouth shut. I knew if I was ever going to get out alive that I had to. The whole town was agreeing with the sheriff about what happened. They weren't there! I was. I know what I saw and what Roger Butler did to my family. All because he thought I had money in the house. My wife was a godly woman! The kids were about as perfect as kids can be. Anyway, after that, the Most High spoke audibly to me and told me to go to the mountain. And that's what I did."

Rachel, Cordilia and Paul were at a loss for words. "Does that answer your question, Paul?" Mr. McKinney asked.

Paul shook his head. "And then some."

"Mr. McKinney, what is it that you do here?" Rachel asked.

"I watch out for the demonic forces that hover over Todd's Creek. I wander into town every so often and check things out. I watched Sheriff Roger Butler's son, Allen, for a long time, but he's not one of them. I thought because his father was one of the demon powers here in Todd's Creek, he might pass it to his son, but he didn't."

Rachel stood. "Do you know what's going on at Boone's Crossing?"

"There is heavy fighting going on there even as we speak. The dark kingdom's forces have been gathering ever since the green lights were first seen. The Queen of the netherworld rules over this territory. Two of her top generals, Shemed and Telmar, have been sent to conquer and maintain this territory. The war is being fought because a great event is to take place very soon. Shemed and Telmar's main goal is to stop this event from taking place. The Most High has commissioned Haleb and the Eagle Army from the White Stone Kingdom to defend and take back this territory. The Highlanders and Shorelyns of first and second heaven are gathering to aid in the battle. Rachel, your feeling about coming to the mountain is right. It's just premature. You will be back soon and so will Paul and Cordilia. When the battle is at its peak, you will be summoned."

"What is the event? Do you know?" Cordilia asked.

"I wasn't told exactly what it was, but it would make a devastating blow to the dark kingdom. I do know it has to do with the ancient book that holds the mysteries of the *Angels of the Ages.*"

"You said we would be called back to the mountain. What are we going to be called back to do?" Rachel asked.

"Now Rachel, you know I'm not the one to ask that question. Seek the Most High! He will let you know when it's time. Now you need to go before it gets late."

Cordilia asked, "Mr. Spook . . . I mean Mr. McKinney, do you know what happened at the Crossing the other day?"

"Yes, I do. I pulled Sheriff Butler out of the forest before the trees killed him."

"That's what Rachel thought. The trees were like giants, Allen Butler said.

"There is going to be a showdown for this territory something like that of Elijah at Mt. Carmel. I'm excited about taking Todd's Creek back from Queen Jewel's grip. Now go! I don't want you here when the sun sets."

Rachel and Cordilia were stunned, not only at what Mr. McKinney had told them, but also at the names he said that were in Effie's book.

Rachel shook her head. "God never stops amazing me. You and Effie Brown."

Mr. McKinney interrupted, "Effie's here?"

"Yes, she's been here several months. How do you know her?" Rachel asked.

"I met her many years ago." He closed his eyes for a brief moment. "Then the book is here already. Which means the battle is upon us. Have you seen an exceptional old manuscript in her home?"

"Yes we have. Effie's been telling us about some of the names in the book. We're going to visit her again after our appointments with Dr. Wells."

"All praise to the Most High God!" He extended his hand to Rachel. "God bless you, my sister. Both of you have been honored by God to even see the book."

He hugged Paul. "It's a real pleasure to serve with you."

"Likewise, my brother."

Cordilia smiled as she looked into Mr. McKinney's eyes. "Well, come here, Mr. McKinney. I want a hug from you myself! And one more question please."

Mr. McKinney raised his eyebrows. "What would that be, Cordilia?"

"Even though you will always be Mr. Spook to me, I would like to know your first name."

"That's easy enough. I'll give you my full name. Thomas Edward McKinney."

"Great name!"

As they walked outside to start back down the mountain, Rachel turned. "Thomas, what are the green lights at the Crossing?"

"It has to do with the fact that green represents the earth. Queen Jewel is showing off that green color as her demons infiltrate the territory. It's Jewel's way of claiming victory at the Crossing."

"You be careful, Thomas. We'll see you soon."

"Sooner than you think, Rachel," he muttered.

Chapter 81
Cordilia's Anger

$\mathcal{T}$he next day, when John came home, Rachel filled him in on all that had taken place with Thomas. John was as shocked as Rachel was. "Rachel, do you think the end of the world is about to take place?"

"John Harris! I surely hope not. God is giving us a baby boy, and I want to enjoy him, watch him grow up and have children. No, I don't think it's the end of the world! I do think I had better be going. Cordilia and I have appointments with Dr. Wells. Do you want to go with us?"

"No! I just want to take a nap. I'm exhausted!"

Rachel picked Cordilia up and went into town on the way to their appointments. Rachel needed to pick up some envelopes. Jack Gregg was one of the deacons at the church. "Hi, Jack," Rachel greeted him as she entered the store.

Without a smile, or even looking up, he muttered, "Mrs. Harris."

Rachel felt as though she was doused with icy cold water.

Dismayed at the treatment Rachel was receiving all over town, Cordilia spoke up. "Hey Jack," Cordilia began as she picked up a spatula from a stand and went toward the counter.

"Yes, what can I do for you, Cordilia?"

Cordilia began to tap the spatula on the counter. "I want you to answer a question."

Smiling, Jack replied, "What's that, Cordilia?"

"When you were growing up did you get a lot of whippings?"

Laughing, Jack answered, "I think I got more than my share. How about you?"

Rachel watched, not knowing what Cordilia was up to. She continued to tap the spatula on the counter as she answered Jack's question. "Oh, I got way too many to count. You know, one of the worst whippings I ever got was with a spatula, just like this one."

"A spatula! Really?" Jack inquired.

"Oh, yes. Mama told me I better be nice to an old lady named Sally. That's not an old lady name to me, but nonetheless, that was her name. Sally was always rude to me, and I was always nice to her. One day, I decided if she wasn't friendly to me, I wasn't going to be friendly to her. I went in a room where she was standing. She spoke to Mama, and I said hello in my sweet little voice. You know what she did?"

"No, what?"

"She grunted at me like a big hog. Well, to make the story short, I asked her what her problem was. That didn't go well at all. Mama picked up a spatula that was lying on a table. First, she whacked me on my arm. That made me so mad, I could have spit. I blurted out, 'Why don't you whack that old hog? She needs it worse than me.' Mama was furious so she picked another site to whack. She carefully chose my head. Now you wouldn't believe this, but underneath this gorgeous blond hair lies a scar that required twelve stitches."

"Really?" Jack asked.

"Oh yes!" Cordilia tightened her lips, put the spatula in Jack's face and declared, "If you ever treat Rachel like you just did again, I'm going to choose my spot and whack you across that bald head . . ."

"What are you doing?" Rachel shouted as she took the spatula from Cordilia.

"I'm about ready to put a design on his egg head!"

Jack yelled, "You better get that maniac out of here, Rachel, or I'll call the sheriff."

Cordilia was furious. She shouted, "Go ahead and call him. He would arrest you for being so ugly in every sense of the word."

"Get her out of here, Rachel!"

"I'm sorry, Jack. Sometimes Cordilia just gets like that."

"She threatened me, and you're my witness."

Cordilia pulled away from Rachel and went back toward him. Jack backed up against the wall. Cordilia erupted, "You claim to be a deacon of the church. You're supposed to be an example and show Christ to others. All I see in you is the devil himself. You have the audacity to come against Rachel Harris who shows Christ to everybody, including you. All the lies that are flying around town you've helped spread! Even though you know Rachel hasn't been out with Doug Holland or anyone else. I wish I could say the same for you! How many times have you had sex with Peggy Welsh right in the back room here. If I hear, see, or if the Good Lord shows one more thing out of you, I'll take you before the church for your adultery. Better yet, I'll tell your wife. I wonder what she would think about that?" Cordilia backed up without taking her eyes from his. "Now you have a good day, Jack. Come on, Rachel, let's get out of this dump."

When they got into the car, Rachel didn't know what to say.

Finally Cordilia tilted her head back and said calmly, "We better be going if we're going to make our appointment."

Rachel smiled, then laughed aloud. Cordilia followed suit.

"How do you know Jack slept with Peggy?"

"I didn't know I was going to say that, so help me! Rachel, I saw something else while I was saying all that to him."

"What?"

"I saw that other men in our church have slept with Peggy."

"What? Are you sure?"

"Positive, and Chris is one of them."

"Chris! He's only 18!"

"I saw an unclean spirit working overtime in Peggy. My God, Rachel, this is a little scary! Now we're going into Dr. Wells's office and have to look at her knowing this."

"You know what else is scary, Cordilia, God opening our eyes to see these things. Why would He show us? I've served God most of my life, and I've never been exposed to anything like this. Yet I've hungered to see and know things like this for years. Even as a teenager, I asked God to let me see into other dimensions like Elisha, and now after all these years, to realize it is very humbling."

Chapter 82

Peggy's True Self

*D*r. Wells called Peggy into his office. "Jack Gregg just called and informed me that Cordilia knew you slept with him."

Puzzled, Peggy asked, "How did she know that?"

"Things are getting too close. When Rachel gets here, set the room up for a pelvic exam. It's time to induce labor."

"If Cordilia knows about Jack, I wonder if she knows about the rest of the men and boys I've given pleasure to."

"I don't know. It's time for the meeting on the mountain. Call the Jacksons and tell Chris to bring Paula. It's time for Telmar to do what he specializes in. Contact the soldiers holding Willow Chandler and have them prepare her for the sacrifice this Saturday night."

"Hmm, that sounds like fun to me. I'll make the call as soon as Rachel and Cordilia leave."

Cordilia felt a little strange looking at Peggy, knowing what the Holy Spirit revealed to her. Dr.

Wells checked Cordilia and told her everything looked fine. When he left the room, Peggy helped pull Cordilia up on the exam table. "Peggy," Cordilia said as she put her shirt on, "you're such a beautiful woman."

Peggy smiled. "Beauty knows beauty. That's why you recognize it when you see it. You also are a beautiful woman, Cordilia."

Cordilia wasn't smiling. She had fixed her eyes on Peggy.

"What in the world is wrong with you, Cordilia? You're not your cheery self. You look like you have lost your best friend."

"I do recognize beauty, Peggy. I feel so sad for you. For the first time since I've known you, I can see clearly that your beauty is only skin deep."

"What do you mean by that statement?" Peggy demanded as she stood in front of Cordilia.

"I mean you don't have to sleep with half the men at church, some young men like Chris and even younger."

"You don't know what you're talking about, Cordilia. If I were you, I would not be so quick to point out someone else's faults. You too have slept with many men. You know the fun of that. Don't deny it!"

"I don't deny it, Peggy, but God set me free from that spirit."

Peggy sternly stated, "I better go assist Dr. Wells." Peggy put her hand on Cordilia's shoulder. "Just pray for me. Don't judge me. I do have a problem with men, I confess, but I don't want anything to hinder our friendship. Okay?"

Tears welled in Peggy's eyes, "I love you, Cordilia." Peggy hugged Cordilia and asked her to help her.

Cordilia hugged her back. "I'll pray for you, Peggy. I will."

Peggy continued to hold onto Cordilia, even when Cordilia loosened from the hug.

Peggy whispered in Cordilia's ear, "I'm sorry, Cordilia. I have always wanted you more than I have wanted any man. I could make you forget all about Paul."

Cordilia shoved her across the room. "Don't you ever touch me again, Peggy, or they'll have to scrape you off the floor."

"It's your loss, Cordilia," Peggy declared as she went out of the room.

Cordilia felt sick to her stomach. "God, how could I have fallen for that phony 'pray for me, don't judge me' speech? I just want to go home and take a bath. Yuck!"

"Rachel," Dr. Wells began, "I told you at the last visit that we would need to check the cysts on your ovaries. Your due date is drawing near, and we want to make sure there will be no complications. Have you had any pain from them?"

"No, actually, I can't tell they're even there."

"I'm going to check only for a precaution." Peggy held Rachel's arm as she lay on the table and put her feet into the stirrups. Dr. Wells washed his hands and put the gloves on.

"This may be a little uncomfortable, but that's to be expected. Don't let it scare you." Dr. Wells pulled the stool up to the foot of the table and sat down. He began the examination. At first, it wasn't too bad. Then excruciating pain shot through Rachel's body. She groaned from the pain as tears began to flow.

"Hold on, Rachel, I'm almost through," Dr. Wells said.

Peggy took hold of Rachel's hand. "Here, Rachel, squeeze my hand."

"Okay, Rachel, it's all over with. I think everything will be fine. I don't anticipate any problems with delivery. You may have a little spotting from the exam, but it should end by morning. If you have any problems at all, call me." Dr. Wells closed her chart and concluded, "I'll see you next week, if not before."

***

Peggy told Dr. Wells that Cordilia knew way too much about her. Dr. Wells assured Peggy that it would all be over soon. "With any luck at all, Rachel will lose her bundle of joy before morning."

"How do you know that?" Peggy asked.

"Oh, my scalpel slipped and cut the mouth of her womb."

Peggy ran her fingers across his lips and exclaimed, "Shemed, you're so evil! Why don't we celebrate this event?"

"We will celebrate after Rachel calls."

Peggy ran her hand down Shemed's chest. "Come on, Shemed. Cordilia already rejected me. I can't take two rejections in one day. I need you or somebody right now."

Shemed took hold of Peggy's hand and ordered, "Not now! Call Jerry Jackson. Tell him we'll meet at his house later tonight. Then you can have your fun. Chris may be there, and you can enjoy both the father and son. Make it a family outing. Now call!"

Chapter 83
Rachel in Pain

*R*achel was cramping terribly when they left the office. Because Rachel wasn't feeling well, Cordilia didn't bother telling her about her run-in with Peggy and her advance toward her. Cordilia stayed a while with Rachel to make sure she was going to be okay.

John and Rachel both assured her they would call if there was any change for the worse. Cordilia felt extremely heavy in her spirit and went home to pray for what was ahead.

Just as Paul and Cordilia sat down for supper, John called and told them Rachel wasn't doing well. They had barely arrived at Rachel's when Doug Holland and Camron dropped by. Cordilia went into the bedroom with Rachel while the men talked in the kitchen.

"Rachel, how are you doing?" Cordilia asked.

Rachel was lying on the bed. She propped up on her elbows. Cordilia put a pillow behind her back to prop her up. "Cordilia, the spotting is not spotting at all. I'm bleeding and cramping something terrible!"

"That's it! I'm calling Dr. Wells."

"No, wait just a while longer."

Cordilia put her hands on her hips. "There's no time for waiting! You don't want to have Stephen Daniel early."

"No, I don't, but I just want to wait a few minutes." Rachel could hear men's voices. "Cordilia, who are Paul and John talking to?"

"Doug and Camron."

"I need to talk to Doug a moment."

Cordilia started toward the door and stopped. "Do you mean you want to talk to him alone?"

"No, not alone, you can stay. What would I say to him that I couldn't say in front of you?"

Cordilia raised her arms and exclaimed, "That's true! I'll get him."

Before Cordilia could open the door, Rachel groaned in pain. Cordilia rushed to her and called out to John.

Rachel was holding her stomach and groaning in pain, "I'm cramping so badly, and I feel so much pressure. I think I'm going to pop! Help me up, I have to go to the bathroom."

"Maybe you better stay down."

"Cordilia, I have to go to the bathroom now!"

Cordilia pulled Rachel up and helped her to the bathroom. When Rachel sat on the toilet, a gush of water came out. Her water had broken. Cordilia yelled out, "John, get in here!"

With that, John and Paul rushed into the bedroom.

"John, I think Rachel's water just broke. Paul, call Dr. Wells and tell him to get over here while John and I get her back to bed."

Paul went into the kitchen to call Dr. Wells.

Doug and Camron asked what was wrong. "Rachel's water broke. She's bleeding and cramping. I need to call Dr. Wells."

Paul picked up the telephone.

Doug grabbed Paul's hand and said, "Please hang the telephone up."

Paul frowned and asked, "What?"

"Let's pray for her now."

"We can pray, but I still need to call the doctor." Paul tried, but the line was busy.

Doug and Camron went through the bedroom door. "Rachel, can we pray for you?"

Crying from the pain, Rachel groaned, "Please do."

"John, Cordilia, join us," Doug said as he and Camron went to the side of the bed.

Panicked, John responded, "Of course. Did Paul get Dr. Wells yet?"

"Not yet," Doug replied. "The line is busy. Rachel is not going to need a doctor. Let's pray."

Doug pointed his fingers toward her and prayed, "I bind you spirit of death in Jesus' name. Rachel, be healed." The room quaked as a surge of healing power penetrated Rachel's womb and repaired all the damage. In awe of the miracle that had taken place, tears fell and praise went up to the Most High God.

Paul hurried into the room, "What just happened? I . . . I got Dr. Wells. He's on his way."

Paul stopped, looked at Rachel. Tears filled his eyes, "We don't need the doctor now, do we?"

There was great rejoicing! Once again, God was faithful. Doug and Camron said they had an appointment and left only moments before Dr. Wells and Peggy arrived. John heard a knock at the door. "It must be Dr. Wells," he said.

"John," Rachel called out, "let me answer it. I want him to see what the Most High has done!"

When Rachel opened the door, Dr. Wells and Peggy were visibly shaken. Dr. Wells declared, "Rachel, I thought your water broke."

Rachel hugged Dr. Wells and told him what the Lord had done. "God healed me! I'm sorry you made the trip out here for nothing. Would you like to have some coffee while you're here?"

"No thank you." Dr. Well's insisted, "I better check you to be on the safe side."

As he was speaking, Rachel's nightmare was standing before her. He was the hideous being with her baby in his mouth.

Rachel stood firm in her answer, "No! You're not going to check me. I'm fine."

Dr. Wells and Peggy left. They were meeting at the Jacksons' as soon as Dr. Wells got through at Rachel's. He was furious. Again, his plan failed.

He made sure everyone knew to be at Boone's Crossing Saturday at sundown. He emphasized that Paula must be at the meeting.

Jerry ordered Chris to bring her one way or another.

Fear gripped Chris's face. "Dad, you would tell me if they planned to hurt Paula, wouldn't you?"

Emily spoke up. "Chris, you know we would, so why are you asking?"

Chris paused. "I don't want her hurt in any way. I love her, and I'm going to marry her after this mission is over. Please don't ever keep anything from me."

Emily put her arm around Chris and consoled him, "Honey, just trust us, okay? Now call Paula."

He still felt uneasy about the meeting. Since it was at the Crossing, he was even more suspicious. Instead of calling, Chris decided to go to Paula and assure her it would be all right. Paula was thrilled to see Chris. They went to Paula's room. Chris held her in his arms for a long while. Just to feel her close brought him comfort and peace of mind. As he held her, Chris whispered, "It will all be over by Saturday."

Paula pushed back from him, looked him in the eye and asked, "Why do you think that, Chris?"

"Because this is the Grandfather Meeting. It's called that because Queen Jewel herself will visit this meeting. That would never happen unless something big was going to take place."

Panicked, Paula asked, "Does that mean something has happened to the babies?"

Chris shook his head. "Not as of tonight. Dr. Wells made a visit to report that his plan to abort Rachel's baby had failed. He was so upset!"

"If it's all going to be over by Saturday, does that mean they know something is going to happen to Rachel, Cordilia and the babies before then?"

"I don't know what the plan is or what they know."

Fear emanated from Paula's eyes. "Do you think Telmar is going to hurt me?"

Chris pulled Paula to him and consoled, "No! That's not what troubles me. The fact that it's going to be a gathering greater than any before is the only part that concerns me. As far as you're concerned, no one is touching you. I don't want you to worry about that. Do you hear me?"

"How can you be sure, Chris? I've seen the things they are capable of doing."

"Mom and Dad would know, and they assured me that nothing was planned for you." Chris closed his eyes and held Paula. Paula wanted to wait until after the meeting to tell Chris that she was pregnant.

Chapter 84
Cordilia's Whining

The people of Todd's Creek were in an uproar over Matt's death. They wanted to hang Mr. McKinney, although they still had no proof that he had done anything. Dr. Wells was the main instigator.

Rachel was again feeling the pull back to the mountain. She was sitting in the living room with only a glow from the street light beaming through the big picture window. John joined her after his shower. He could tell Rachel had something on her mind. She was very quiet most of the evening. He put his arm around her. "Do you want to tell me why you're so quiet tonight and why you're sitting in the dark?"

Rachel grinned. "No! I don't think so." Changing the subject, Rachel began, "You know, John, I used to be able to sit on the sofa and pull my knees to my chest. Now I can barely raise my feet off the floor. Stephen Daniel is under my ribs tonight."

John laid his head on Rachel's stomach and whispered, "Daddy loves you, Stephen, and Daddy loves your mama very much." He looked at Rachel. "You're such a beautiful pregnant woman."

Rachel started laughing at his comment.

"What's so funny about that?"

"You know, John, the mind is a strange thing. Instead of absorbing your gracious compliment, I thought of something Cordilia said yesterday."

John laughed. "Say no more. There is no telling what she said."

"She told me that Paul said she looked more beautiful than he had ever seen her. After that statement, Cordilia put him to the ultimate test."

John shook his head. "This has got to include Sophia Loren."

Rachel chuckled and continued, "How could you have ever guessed? Only Cordilia would pull Sophia Loren into this. She asked Paul to check her profile. She pulled her shirt tight from behind and asked, 'Do I still look as good?' Poor Paul said, 'Yes you do.' Then she opened her shirt, exposed her three stretch marks and said, 'Do I still?' This went on until Paul confessed. He said that he didn't care if her stomach wasn't flat or if she had stretch marks. Columbia Pictures in Hollywood may not sign her up, but he didn't care, he thought she was beautiful, no matter what."

"John, am I as pretty as Sophia Loren?"

Teasing, John bit his lower lip. "Well . . ."

They both enjoyed a lighthearted moment. "It's good to laugh," John added. "There has been so much going on until I'm not sure whether to laugh or cry."

"John, I know in my spirit that I am going to Boone's Crossing."

John was very quick to respond. "Have you lost all your sanity? No! You're not going to the Crossing. We just talked about Matt, and you say you're going. No way!"

"John, you're talking out of fear for me and Stephen."

"That's exactly right! You're almost full term, Rachel. You are not the only one you would be taking to the Crossing. You would be taking our baby. You couldn't even run if you had to, and I haven't even brought up how dangerous it is."

Rachel listened as John listed the reasons why she wasn't going to the Crossing. When he finished, she took a deep breath. "John, you know I have always respected and honored your opinion on almost everything. I've tried to allow you to be the head of this house. If I were not pregnant, you wouldn't be as fearful as you are now. I need you to understand that I'm not going off on some binge. I know I'm pregnant. I also know I'm going to the mountain for Stephen, not to hurt him. Laying all those issues aside, you know when the Holy Spirit speaks to my heart and tells me to do something, I will do it. Besides, I won't be going alone. Paul and Cordilia will be going with me. I would like to add your name to the list."

John went to the window and looked out. After a couple of minutes, John faced Rachel. "Add my name. I just want to know why we're going. Do you know?"

Rachel joined John at the window. She locked her arm around his. "I don't have a clue. The Holy Spirit said, 'The angels have been sent in advance to make the way safe.' I trust that. I also trust that He will show us what we will be confronting and why He is sending us."

"I'll tell you something I'm going to confront! That's the lie about you and Doug Holland. There's a men's meeting tomorrow night, and every deacon there will hear about it."

"No! Please don't, John."

"But why not?"

"Because God is going to clear up any doubts about me to the people."

Through gritted teeth, John replied, "I know God will, but you haven't been allowed to teach in two weeks now. It's not right, Rachel."

"John, I know more than anyone how that feels, but God is going to prove my character. I know it! It will be proved when we go to the Crossing. There again, I don't know what all that means, but it will happen at the Crossing. Please, just wait and see, okay?"

John ran his fingers through his hair and sighed. "Okay. It's hard not to stand up for you when I know it's all lies. After the Crossing, I won't hold back if the work isn't done."

"Thank you, honey, but it will be done. I have no doubts."

Chapter 85

The Collinses Pray for Rachel

*R*achel was surprised when Harold and Amanda Collins knocked on the kitchen door at 8:00 a.m. They went into the living room and sat down.

Harold looked around and asked, "Is John here?"

"No. He got a call from Doug Holland. He said he had some business to take care of and wanted John to fill in for him. What in the world brings you two out this early in the morning?"

Amanda proclaimed, "Rachel, there is going to be a gathering at Boone's Crossing on Saturday."

Puzzled, Rachel asked, "A gathering! What kind of gathering?"

"I suppose the only way to explain is to say a confrontation between the kingdom of light and the kingdom of darkness."

Rachel frowned. "A confrontation? When you speak of a confrontation, isn't that like saying there are two equal powers in the universe? There is a conflict that rages, but there is a sovereign God with absolute power. The dark kingdom may be the second most powerful in the universe, but it runs a distant second to the triune God who created the universe."

Harold and Amanda looked at each other and smiled.

Rachel asked, "Why are you smiling?"

"We're smiling, because you're almost ready."

"Ready for what?"

"Ready to go to the Crossing," Harold answered. "You do feel the pull to the Crossing, don't you?"

"More than I can express." Rachel rubbed her belly and said, "Why would God want to use two pregnant women in a war? I may not know the answer to that, but I do feel the pull to the crossing. I am going to tell you something I haven't told Cordilia. I feel the war. I hear the demons laughing and swords pounding together. As long as I can remember, there had only been silence at the Crossing. But for the past few months, I've had a vision of many soldiers marching through a vast valley to a mountain. I didn't know where they were coming from, but they continued to appear. At first I only watched them and then I was marching with them. There were so many soldiers I felt the ground rumbling under my feet as their boots pounded against the earth." Rachel walked toward the sink, leaned forward and gripped the edge of the counter so hard that her knuckles turned white.

She paused, then continued, "I've not only felt the rumble under my feet, but I am hearing the dry bones, spoken of in Ezekiel, coming together. I don't know how to explain it. The bones have been coming together, making up this great army that continues to march toward the mountain."

Rachel faced them and told about Effie sharing the contents of *Angels of the Ages.* "I feel at times I see the ancient ones, the Angels of the Ages, without really seeing them. Does that make sense to you?"

"All the sense in the world," Amanda said.

Harold asked Rachel if she had any oil in the house. Rachel got the oil and gave it to Harold. Only then did he tell her the reason for the early visit.

"God has sent us to anoint and pray for you. You are ready, Rachel. You will stand as Elijah and declare, 'If God be God serve Him.' Remember, Rachel, Jewel's power has limits. She and her demons work hard throwing up smoke screens to keep people from realizing their limitations. When the smoke clears, the light will be bright for all to see. There's so much darkness in this territory the light has hardly been seen. At the gathering, darkness will be defeated, and light will once again illuminate Todd's Creek."

Amanda and Harold prayed for Rachel and for the battle ahead. To Rachel's surprise, the Collinses said they would be at the Crossing.

Puzzled, Rachel asked, "You'll be at the Crossing with us?"

"You sound so surprised, Rachel. Of course, we'll be there. Our time here is almost at an end, but the end is only The Beginning."

"What you just said, do you think you won't be coming back from the Crossing?"

Amanda put her hands on Rachel's shoulders. "Rachel, honey, this is war, and people die in war.

If we don't come back from the Crossing, then you will know the Most High has called us back up the ladder."

"But . . ." Rachel began to cry.

"I would hope those are tears of joy."

"What do you mean God will call you back up the ladder?"

"You'll have to ask Effie about the ladder. We've got to go, but we'll see you at the Crossing."

Rachel called Cordilia and told her they needed to visit Effie right away.

Chapter 86
The Change

*R*achel shared everything with Cordilia as they walked through the field to Effie's house.

The sober realization of what awaited them at Boone's Crossing had instilled the desire to hear more about the ancient book.

About halfway across the field a harsh wind picked up as dark clouds raced across the sky. Rachel and Cordilia secured their coats and hurried on through the windswept field feeling they should have driven. Rachel knocked on the door. The wind was very strong and a hard rain had begun to fall. When no one answered, she pounded the hard wood to make sure she was heard.

Effie called out, "I'm coming. I'm coming." She opened the door and told them to hurry inside. Before closing the door, she stepped in the doorway and scanned the outside with her squinted eyes. The fear in Effie's face prompted Rachel to ask if something was wrong. She assured them everything was all right for the moment. They didn't understand what she meant by saying "for the moment." Winston was pacing wildly around the room. Effie told Rachel and Cordilia to sit at the table; she had something to share with them from the book. She pounded the floor with her cane and told Winston to sit down or she would toss him out the door.

She pulled the tin candleholder to her, took a long match from her pocket, raked it across the table and lit the short wick. Rachel and Cordilia were anxious about the wind that continued to send blasts of air against the house. Both women were unable to say anything. Effie waved her hand across the book and the latch fell, and the book opened. Effie glanced at Winston who had fixed his eyes on her. She scratched his head. "It's okay, dog. It's okay."

Wide-eyed, Rachel asked, "Effie . . ." Rachel paused. "Effie, I feel the evil outside these walls desperate to break through. Go with me and Cordilia to my house."

She fixed her stare on Rachel. "This is my post, and I'll not leave it!"

Rachel put her hand on Effie's. "For now, this is our post as well. We have to know more about the contents of the book."

Effie cleared her throat and continued, "I told you about Queen Jewel setting her sights on destroying Rakar. He led the Armor Bearers of the three heavens against the army Jewel formed."

Suddenly the house shook as the giant oak that sat beside the house gave way to the forceful wind and fell hitting Effie's truck. Rachel jumped up and cried, "We need to get out of here!"

Cordilia touched her arm. "Sit down, Rachel. No harm will come to us. Go ahead, Effie."

Effie ran her finger down several pages in the book and said, "After the battle, Queen Jewel and her army were sentenced to die in the end time. Until then, they were given a measure of time to do their evil. The ones who chose to go willingly with Jewel into the Garden of Fire and partake of the fire of good and evil would never be redeemed. The children who were seduced would have a chance to redeem themselves. The Most High set a ladder upon the earth, and the stairway ascended to the White Stone Kingdom. The Most High's Son, King Rayon, stands king over the Shorelyns, Highlanders and the White Stone Province. At the appointed time, the names in this manuscript are selected to descend the ladder that touches the earth." A loud force of wind broke the window, causing glass to fly over the floor.

Rachel and Cordilia jumped to their feet. "Effie, you're going with us!"

Winston raised his head and howled long and loud. Suddenly the wind died down. Effie rubbed his head and whispered, "That's my good dog." She looked at Rachel and Cordilia and continued, "I must hurry so you can get home before the wind starts again."

"Effie, what about the ladder?" Cordilia said.

"At certain times the Ancient One sends the angels of old down to help the ones being trained to war against Queen Jewel and her evil forces. Todd's Creek is stifled with her wickedness. At this time the earliest children have been sent and are about to fight in the war to free Todd's Creek. The enemies' strongholds have been established on top of Boone's Crossing. A stone altar was erected there centuries ago. The altar must be broken in order to regain the territory for the White Stone Kingdom. You will be in that battle."

Rachel spoke up, "Effie, what do you mean about the ladder? That only some of the angels come down at certain times?"

Effie cut her eyes around the room, placed her hand on the book and resumed, "This book tells of the ladder and the Most High's plan to save his children."

Instantly, the wind began to blow, lightning and thunder filled the sky unlike anything Rachel and Cordilia had ever encountered. Effie pounded her cane against the floor and shouted, "Winston, get them!"

Winston looked at Effie and leaped out the window. Effie grabbed Rachel's arm and said, "Listen to me! Every child of the Most High, except Queen Jewel and her followers, comes down Jacob's Ladder?" Effie cut her eyes to the window and called out, "I'm coming, Winston!"

"Jacob's Ladder!" Rachel shouted above the wind.

"The Most High showed Jacob this ladder and the angels ascending and descending. They came down the ladder to earth, stepped into flesh bodies. I look at you and see flesh, but that child of the Most High abides inside that flesh. When it's time, that child will leave that piece of flesh lying and ascend back up Jacob's Ladder to King Rayon." Effie trembled as she heard Winston's constant howls.

Effie groaned and screamed, "Get out of here before they have the power to come near you and your babies!"

"Come with us!" Rachel shouted.

The door flew open. Effie seized the book and handed it to Rachel, then pushed them onto the porch, grabbed their hands, squeezed them and declared, "The Most High be with you daughters of White Stone."

She let go and rushed inside, and the door slammed shut. Cordilia grabbed Rachel's hand and hurried off the porch. A freezing rain was pouring as they started across the field. Rachel pulled on Cordilia's coat and shouted, "We can't just leave her!"

They turned and raced back to the house and through the doorway. They froze as they entered, Winston was lying on the floor dead, and the most exquisite being they could have ever imagined was hovering in mid-air. On the floor below her lay the clothes that Effie had on moments earlier and the stick cane she used faithfully. Cordilia swallowed so hard it hurt her throat. "Effie, is that you?" she called out.

The beautiful woman smiled and said in a voice that echoed, "Rachel, Cordilia, use the things I have taught you from the book wisely. Tell of Jacob's Ladder and the *Angels of the Ages*."

In a blink she was gone, and so was Winston. As fast as Effie had disappeared, so did the storm that had so mysteriously arisen. Rachel held the book tightly as they went into Rachel's bedroom to dry off and change their clothes. Rachel put the book on the bed as she looked in the closet for something for Cordilia to wear. When they got dressed, Rachel started to get the book, but it wasn't on the bed. She looked at Cordilia, who was towel drying her hair. "Did you get the book?"

Cordilia grunted, "No, you put it on the bed."

"I know! It's not there."

They stared at each other in wonderment. They searched for the book, but it too had vanished like Effie and Winston. After much discussion about what had taken place with Effie, Winston and the book, Cordilia and Rachel prayed together. Cordilia went home, eager to tell Paul what happened.

Chapter 87
Haleb the Angel

*J*ohn had to stay at the station until the ten o'clock train made its stop. Rachel subconsciously looked for the book that she knew wasn't there. After a hot shower, she studied for a while, waiting for John to get home. She read until she realized that the only light on in the house was the lamp on her nightstand. She made her way down the hall with the reflection from the lamp beaming through the bedroom doorway.

She flipped the light switch at the end of the hall but nothing happened. She flipped it again and again. Still nothing. The light from the lamp in the bedroom had all but diminished, except around the doorway. Rachel thought the light bulb must have burned out. It was so dark! Usually, the street light would light the living room, but the living room was pitch black. Looking toward the bedroom, Rachel saw the light from the lamp, so she knew that power was on. "It must be the bulb."

Rachel took one step and froze. "What's that sound?" she whispered. It was the sound of water dripping in a stainless steel sink, only magnified a thousand times. A musty smell filled the hall. A very dim, gray light penetrated the vast darkness that filled her living room. Rachel called out, "Hello! Is someone there?"

She turned to go back to the bedroom. The light that had beamed from the bedroom was no longer shining. It was so dark she could not see anything. Rachel turned back. The gray light had grown a shade brighter. Afraid to move, she called out, "Raptor? Are you here?" She cautiously stepped around the corner to the entrance of the living room. "Oh God, help me!" she cried out. The gray light only shown on the floor. "Father, what is going on?"

"Rachel, don't be afraid," a soft voice said. When he spoke, it was as though a light came on from within the being, so she could clearly see him standing by the door. It was the same being she saw before when her feet hurt so bad, and when she poured the oil on the red stone. Again, Rachel could not see his face because of the white mist. The angel, seeing that Rachel was trembling, touched her shoulder, and instantly she was stilled.

He motioned for her to follow him. What should have been Rachel's living room was now a doorway to a dungeon. It was damp and so cold. The water dripped from the rounded ceiling. Torches in holders lined the long hallway. The angel stopped at a solid iron door.

Rachel could hear cries from the other side of the door. She listened intently thinking she recognized the voices, but she wasn't sure. It was a man and woman's voice screaming, "Help! Somebody, help us. Help!" The voices were growing weaker and weaker.

Rachel looked at the angel and asked, "Can't we help them?"

He pointed to the door and ordered, "Go through the door, Rachel."

Rachel stepped closer to the door and would have put her hand to it but was stopped by the angel who proclaimed, "Don't touch it with your hands! The only way to go through the door is by faith. If you're not ready to go by faith, then you're not ready to go at all."

Frantic, Rachel replied, "But the sound of their voices are getting so weak. We must go through before they die."

Again, the angel pointed to the door and directed, "Go through the door, Rachel." Rachel looked at him and faced the door. She stepped up and by faith stepped forward going through the door, which was now open. Her mouth dropped open and horror filled her spirit at the sight before her. "Paula! Chris!" She wanted to go forward but could not. She could see but was restrained from doing anything.

Paula and Chris were stripped naked with their hands tied in stocks above their heads. They were so near death that their arms were holding up the weight of their bodies. Bruises and cuts covered them from head to toe. Paula had blood running down the inside of her legs. At her feet lay a baby the size of her hand. On each side of them stood a guard with a whip in hand. Each time they cried out, the guards hit them. Two new guards were coming on duty to relieve the others. The two guards being relieved pulled the covering from their heads as they left their station.

Rachel put her hands over her mouth in disbelief. The two guards leaving were Emily and Jerry Jackson. Rachel looked at the angel and shouted, "That's Chris's mom and dad!" The angel nodded in confirmation. "Can't we do something?" Rachel asked.

"God has been preparing you for this time, filling you with His truth, light and power. God has allowed you to be confronted with the enemy many times. You have stood true. Chris has been beaten down and lied to all his life. Serving Queen Jewel, alongside Emily and Jerry, is all he has ever known. Paula, on the other hand, allowed her emotions and deep insecurities to arrest her. Chris fell in love, and she fell out of favor. Chris's heart is tender. He wants out of Jewel's grip that he has pledged himself to and so does Paula. It's time for you to lead them back to God."

"I've been praying for them. Please tell me how to get to them. How can I break this shield preventing me?"

"They will be at the Crossing, along with many others. You don't have to fear anything. The Ancient One has sent His angels before you to prepare the way. Tonight you read Acts 12:7, 'And behold the angel of the Lord came upon him, and a light shined in the prison: and he smote Peter on the side, and raised him up, saying, arise up quickly. And his chains fell off from his hands.'

"Yes, that is what I read."

"The Most High wanted you to see Paula and Chris's spiritual state and the bondage they're in. That includes being held prisoner by his mother and father. The reading about Peter makes clear three things. The church was praying for Peter. Their prayers brought the angel. The angel brought light to a dark prison cell. The angel shook Peter and told him to get up, setting him free. When you go to the dungeon at the Crossing, the Holy Spirit in you will bring light to the prison cell. You and the others with you will set the captives free."

Instantly, Rachel and the angel were back in her living room. Again, Rachel looked at the angel, wondering if perhaps it was Eri and asked, "What is your name?"

In response, the angel said, "My name isn't important. You can set no one free in my name."

Rachel lowered her head.

"Don't look down, Rachel, always look up."

As Rachel lifted her head. The white mist lifted from the angel's face. Rachel gasped and put her hands over her mouth. In only a whisper, she spoke the name of the man standing before her, "Doug Holland!"

"My given name when I was in a flesh body was Doug Holland, but my eternal name is Haleb. I was sent by God to war on your behalf, as I warred with you against at the rebellion against God. Your flesh name is Rachel, but your eternal name is Opal. A precious stone hewn by God's hand is its meaning. Now arise, Opal, and do that which you have been commissioned to do." Haleb vanished, and the lights returned throughout the house without anyone touching a light switch.

Rachel now realized that it was Doug Holland she saw in the cloud a few months earlier and by the house that night. It was Doug who saved her life and told her not to take Cordilia to Dr. Wells. It was Doug and Camron who led the prayer for her, and she was healed. She now understood how God used Doug to watch after her. When he said he was her guardian angel, he really meant it.

Chapter 88
The Ancient Tree

*R*achel praised God for His greatness, mercy and love. She wasn't sure how to tell John about Effie, Winston and Doug Holland, so she decided to wait until the time was right. She sat on the floor, wrapped her arms around Stephen and cried to God for help and understanding. As she groaned in the spirit, she had no idea that Raptor and a number of red eagles had gathered around on the floor, weeping with her.

After a while Rachel felt Raptor's big wing wrap around her. "Rachel, the thing you saw today with Effie isn't a sad thing. She accomplished her God-given mission."

"But the book is gone! I put it on the bed, and now it's gone. I should have guarded it."

"No worry, the book is where it needs to be." Raptor stood and helped her to her feet. "Why don't you come with me?"

Rachel quickly agreed.

All the red eagles stood, and one by one they disappeared out of the room. Raptor knelt and said, "This time, I think it would be better for you to ride. Climb on and hold tight."

Raptor flapped his wings and instantly they were flying high above mountaintops, observing the beauty of plush valleys, rivers and lakes below. The red eagles flew in a V formation with Raptor leading the way. They quickly began to descend and landed beside the clearest stream Rachel had ever seen. She fixed her eyes on the brilliant substance inside the water. Instead of sand, the riverbed was lined with gold dust. It sparkled as the sun's rays beamed on the water. Emeralds, rubies and diamonds glistened as the stream gently washed over them. When Rachel turned to ask Raptor about the stones, her eyes widened as she looked into the eyes of the White Stallion standing beside Raptor. She held the stare until Raptor muttered, "Come, Rachel, there's more to see."

The magnificent stallion pranced down the trail toward a colossal gate made up of extraordinary grape vines. The guardians were as extraordinary as the vines themselves. Rachel stopped in awe of the ten-foot-tall beings. Their long straight hair was oiled and shimmered like the clear stream she had viewed. They were draped in long white cloaks with scarlet tassels on their broad shoulders. Their faces were pleasant, yet stern, their eyes were round and flickered like fire.

Rachel touched Raptor's wing and asked, "Who are these creatures?"

Raptor put his wing to his chest and replied, "These are the primitive ones. They have stood guard at these vines since The Beginning. They're the guardians of the Ancient Tree."

Rachel frowned. "The Ancient Tree is behind this gate?"

The White Stallion shook his head causing his long mane to swing. The Guards lowered their heads as the gate opened on its own. Inside the gate, a long line of gold eagles stood shoulder to shoulder and lowered their heads as the White Stallion led the way onto a trail made up of large white stones. Rachel stayed close to Raptor as they marched down the trail. She hadn't noticed when she entered the gate that her mantel was no longer brown but gleamed a solid gold. As she walked, her feet were gradually covered with gold sandals.

Raptor said softly, "Your Majesty, the eagle guard has missed your presence."

Rachel paused and asked, "Where did the gold shoes and mantel come from?"

"The same place the gold crown came from."

Rachel quickly raised her hand to feel the crown that rested on her ebony black hair. The stallion neighed and motioned with his head for them to keep moving. As they moved forward, they came to a glittering white veil. Raptor nodded at the guards as they took hold of the veil on each side and pulled it back like a curtain. Inside the veil, a misty forest filled with trees more grand than the giant redwoods. In the midst of the forest, Rachel heard singing and music like she had never imagined. "Who's singing that wonderful song?" she asked.

"The stars and galaxies are singing a new song to the Most High God on the other side of the mountain."

Suddenly, Rachel's heart felt as though it slowed its beat. She gasped as she fixed her eyes on Royalty who stood before her. Their heads held high, Raptor, the White Stallion and Rachel quickly bowed. When Rachel raised her head a glow of all the colors of the rainbow illuminated the forest from a colossal tree that reached far into the sky. The leaves were magnificent emeralds covered with diamond flakes. Rachel breathlessly asked, "Raptor, what is this tree?"

Raptor raised his head and declared, "It is the Ancient Tree. In the midst is a treasure chest hinged with silver and gold, the Ancient Tree holds the hallowed hall, the hallowed hall of souls."

On bended knee, Rachel, Raptor and the White Stallion bowed their heads. When Rachel stood, she was no longer at the Ancient Tree but in the valley with the soldiers she had seen before. This time Raptor walked with her and the army toward the mountain. Rachel stopped and seized Raptor's wing.

"Raptor, where are all these soldiers going?"

"To Boone's Crossing."

"Where's the Ancient Tree?"

Raptor stopped and said, "This is not the time to ponder the Ancient Tree. It's time to consider the lost souls that need to be freed at the battle. You know the wealth of being set free, and you have been through many trials, yet in this age, you've not yet suffered as these soldiers have. You're ready for the tests that will release the highest levels of spiritual authority into your life. Rachel, I have witnessed many wonders since The Beginning. You and Cordilia volunteering to go to the Crossing to fight without hesitation illustrates great courage and a manifestation of immense faith in the Most High. You'll be taking light into a place of darkness and evil. Such light and faith will set the captives free. It won't be easy, but the Most High never promised that His way would be easy. Many will die at the battle. Many will be wounded, but we must remember our King was wounded for our iniquities."

Raptor slowly shook his head and groaned, "How many are willing to suffer for the sake of truth? We can rest assured that any suffering we do for the kingdom will be greatly rewarded."

"Will you be at the battle?" she asked.

"I've been at every battle since The Beginning. I'll see you there!" He cut his eyes to Rachel and said, "King Rayon has summoned me." Raptor lowered his head. "Your majesty."

Rachel gasped when she realized she was lying in bed with John.

John asked, "Rachel, did Doug get back from the business he had to take care of?" When she didn't respond right away he said, "Honey, are you asleep?"

"No . . . no. I . . . I don't know. I suppose he did."

Rachel turned on her side. "Honey, Harold and Amanda came by today."

"Really?"

"Yeah. They said Saturday would be the time to go to the Crossing."

John didn't say anything. He blew his breath out. "I don't know about all of this. I really don't. I was praying today at work. Everything was quiet, not a soul in the place, and the Lord spoke to me, 'You will know when to go, and don't fear.' So whether I understand it all or not, I am ready to do what the Lord would have me do. If you say Saturday, Saturday, it is!"

Rachel got up and went to the bathroom. She looked in the mirror and touched her hair where the crown had sat, her shoulders where the gold mantel had rested and the gold sandals, all gone. Rachel smiled and admired the sprinkles of gold dust stuck to her toes.

Chapter 89
The Meeting

Sheriff Butler came by Friday morning. He had found out more about the incident that took place at Boone's Crossing at the turn of the century. Rachel called Paul and Cordilia to join them. Sheriff Butler wanted them to hear what he had to say.

Everyone sat at the kitchen table, and the Sheriff began, "I don't hardly know how to start. I went to Benson a couple of days ago, and my son Jack pulled some more old court records for me. After what took place at the Crossing, I wanted to know everything I possibly could about that time. When I went through the transcripts, I found the name of someone who was at the Crossing with my daddy."

"Who was it?" Rachel interrupted.

Sheriff Butler paused, looked down at the table and began pulling at his ear.

Cordilia took his hand and held it in hers. She implored, "Here, you hold my hand. Squeeze it if you have to, but stop pulling at your ear. It's so shiny the reflection off it may blind me."

Sheriff Butler smiled at Cordilia. "Cordilia, you always manage to make me smile. What a gift you have!"

"Did I ever tell you that I could have gone to Hollywood . . .?"

Paul cut in, "Lord help us all! Honey, Sheriff Butler is trying to be serious."

Cordilia raised her brows, squeezed Sheriff Butler's hand and said, "Yes, my love, I know. He was just having a hard time getting through, so I was helping him."

"Sheriff Butler, I strongly suggest you take her to jail for a week or so. Right now!" Paul teased.

"Just continue with what you were saying," John said.

The sheriff proceeded. "The name is someone you will recognize, Rachel."

Surprised, Rachel asked, "Who is it?"

"Luther Donald King."

Rachel frowned, "Are you talking about my grandfather?"

The sheriff nodded. "I'm afraid so, honey."

"Why would my grandfather be there?"

"Why would my daddy be there?"

"What did it say about my grandfather?"

"He was one of the leaders of what they called Queen Jewel's Army."

"What?"

"Rachel, honey, I know how you feel. My daddy was one of the leaders too. All this came out in the trials and hearings that went on. I brought copies for you to see if you would like."

"Wow!" Cordilia exclaimed. "Is it me, or is this whole thing getting bigger and bigger, all the time?"

Rachel looked at John, then at the sheriff. "What happened that his name would be in the files?"

"It would definitely seem that a 13-year-old girl was sacrificed and consumed by all who were there. The story gets greater. The old files indicate that this event at the Crossing has happened two times before. At first, I thought it had only happened once before, but the more I searched, it became plain that it happened at least twice. My daddy was there, in 1902, but not at the one that took place on April 15, 1848. Your grandfather was at the one held in 1848. A couple testified that they saw everything that went on. Like the woman who was in the asylum, they too testified that some kind of shiny carriage came down from the sky. A woman came down the steps of the carriage, and everyone there bowed to her. They said that she had come to have a child, a very special child. The report stated that your grandfather was to be the father of that child."

"What? My grandfather?"

"I know how you feel, Rachel, but I'm just telling you what the files said."

"I'm sorry, Sheriff," Rachel said. "It's just hard to believe. Please go ahead."

"There was quite an orgy going on. When your grandfather came to the big rock they called an altar, this woman . . ." Sheriff Butler blushed as he lowered his head. "This is embarrassing to talk about in front of you ladies."

In a stern voice, Rachel demanded, "I need to hear what you have to say about this. It could be very important."

"The woman stripped right there in front of everybody on that rock. Your grandfather came and did the same thing. He was only 18 years old at the time. And they . . ."

Cordilia squeezed Sheriff Butler's hand and encouraged, "Come on, Sheriff, don't be shy on us now. What happened?"

Sheriff Butler shook his head. "This is hard to talk to females about."

"Cordilia's right, Sheriff. We need to know exactly what went on. Everything," Rachel added.

"They . . . made out on the rock. When they started doing that, all the couples did too. The file said they were planting seeds for the Gray Stone Kingdom. To fill Todd's Creek with their offspring."

"What about my grandfather? Why him?"

"He was called 'the chosen.' He was handpicked by Queen Jewel to bring forth this special child in the flesh. Have you ever heard of such a thing?"

Rachel was quick to respond, "Yes, I have heard of such a thing. What happened next?"

"After everything took place, the woman put a gold robe on and went back into the shiny carriage. It lifted up from the earth and went into the sky."

"Was there a child by Rachel's grandfather?" John asked.

"Yes, there was. According to the reports, at the meeting in 1902, a member of this Queen Jewel's trinity brought her down from the sky on the same kind of carriage. He presented her to all gathered there as Jewel's daughter."

"My grandfather had a child with Queen Jewel? Why would he do that?"

"It said that Jewel trusted him with the seed because of his faithfulness to her."

"Wait a minute now," Paul stated. "What happened to the girl if she was brought back? If she was still alive, she would be 100 years old."

"From what my son found out about this child, she is still alive. She lives in Norfolk."

"My word, Rachel, that would mean you have a 100-year-old aunt living in Norfolk."

Eagerly, Rachel asked, "Would you have a name and address on her?"

Sheriff Butler took a small piece of paper from his shirt pocket and unfolded it. "Yes, here it is. Jack wrote it down for me. It's strange, but she goes by only one name. She doesn't use her last name at all. Her name is Delilah, and her address is a business she owns in Norfolk."

By this time, Rachel and Cordilia stared at each other in utter shock, afraid of what Sheriff Butler was going to say. Rachel stood and shook her head. "Allen, is the name of the business A Journey in Time?"

Surprised, Sheriff Butler asked, "How in the world do you know that?"

Bewildered, Rachel walked to the window and looked out. Paul, John and Cordilia could not believe it either.

Allen didn't have a clue what he had said that sent everyone into silence. So he asked, "What in the world is wrong with everybody?"

Rachel cried out, "Are you sure about all this?"

"Yes, I am. Jack had a private investigator check it out for me."

Cordilia spoke up, "Harold and Amanda said that Delilah fought with Jewel at the rebellion against God."

Rachel added, "They also said she was as evil as they come. She sold me the sword for John. Oh my God! Cordilia, we were right there with her. We talked to her . . ."

"Yes, and she slapped my hand. I told you something wasn't right with that woman."

"Jerry was the one who told us about the shop, the swords and Delilah."

"I'm a little lost here," Sheriff Butler said. "I don't understand what you're talking about."

"Maybe it's not her, Cordilia. This Delilah is not 100 years old. She may be in her 60s, but not 100."

Sheriff Butler said, "As far as knowing about age, all I can tell you is that Luther was 18 when this thing at the Crossing took place, and 81 when he died." He stood and put his hat on. "I'll leave you with this last bit of shocking news."

They all turned to hear what he would add to the most bizarre story they had ever heard. "My daddy was also conceived at that meeting." He walked toward the door, took hold of the knob and added, "This is the wildest stuff I have ever heard of!"

John said, "By the way, Sheriff, have you heard any more about McKinney?"

"Only from Dr. Wells, who is ready to string him up. I'll see you good people later. Be sure and pray for us."

Rachel didn't know what to think. Neither did anyone else. Rachel made the announcement, "We're going to the Crossing at sundown on Saturday. Let's be prayed up and ready to face whatever Queen Jewel may have in mind."

Chapter 90
The Leader

Saturday arrived. The weather was beautiful. All the wonderful flowers said spring had arrived. Only one month until Stephen Daniel and Phillip Ryan would be due. With spring came new life. Rachel's prayer for Chris and Paula was that they too would find new life in the Most High.

The day was spent in prayer, seeking God for wisdom and boldness greater than they had ever experienced. They were to meet at dusk and go to Boone's Crossing together. The car was filled with silence as they approached the entrance to the forest. For over three miles they could see the green glow hovering over the peak of the Crossing. As they got out of the car, they surveyed the surroundings. "God be with us!" Paul exclaimed as he glanced across the tree line. They joined hands, and one last time John thanked God for what He was about to do, although they weren't sure what that would be.

Rachel would be the one to lead the way. John only agreed to it because the Holy Spirit assured him that it was God's plan.

"How do you feel, Rachel?" Cordilia asked as she looked around.

With her face set toward the entrance, Rachel answered with boldness, "It's not what I feel, Cordilia. It's what I know that counts. I know great victory will be given today. So what have we to fear? Fear says, 'God is not with us.' Boldness says, 'Let's take back Todd's Creek for the White Stone Kingdom!'"

To that, they all agreed with an "amen." With Rachel leading the way, they came to the entrance. Stepping onto the pathway, they heard jeering, screams and thrashing all around them. The trees took on a different appearance. They were transformed into people clothed in every style. Some of the dress went back so far in time that they couldn't distinguish in which era it had been worn. People lined the pathway. Their hands were filled with sticks, swords and bows and arrows. Hideous sounds filled the forest as people tried to strike the four of them as they proceeded down the path. Furious, some were trying to force through into the path, but could not. There was a protective hedge in front, behind and on either side of them as they marched forward. Wisdom opened their eyes so they could see the four angels guarding them. The angels were literally taking their hands and pushing the demon spirits away, preventing them from charging Rachel, John, Cordilia and Paul.

Suddenly, a hush fell throughout the forest. Rachel stopped as they approached a clearing at the top of the Crossing. When the angel moved from in front of her, she saw three empty thrones on a mound of rocks. At the foot of the thrones lay a huge, oval-shaped rock worn smooth across the top. On the rock, naked, with her hands tied to pegs, was the 13-year-old girl, Willow Chandler.

The Holy Spirit told Rachel to take authority over the ropes holding Willow against the altar. John, Paul and Cordilia chanted in unison, "We come against every demon and bind them in the name of King Rayon."

As Rachel stepped forward, a voice thundered, "Leave this place! You have no authority here." Rachel searched for the voice; to her surprise, it came from Dr. Wells. He no longer wore a white jacket, glasses, and a stethoscope around his neck. His long, black, oiled hair with a white streak down the middle was pulled back in a ponytail. His skin was pale and his eyes were round, black holes. His sword was as tall as he was. He held it up in one hand and said, "You have no business here, yet you dare trespass."

"Wrong, Dr. Wells! The Most High God has given us all authority here. I command you, in the name above all names, to loosen this girl!" With those words, the girl's hands were set free, but her feet were still bound.

Dr. Wells was furious. He could feel his power fading. His black eyes scanned the area, and he shouted the command for the trees to take them, but the eagle guards held them back.

Rachel stretched forth her hand. "Go back to the pit from whence you came."

"Telmar!" Dr. Wells cried out. A green mist swirled from the ground and took the form of a man. His black eyes glared as he stepped forward. "Shemed, what is the problem?"

Cordilia said, "You're Shemed?"

"Raptor is taking my strength from me." Shemed was shaking and began to disintegrate. He screamed to Telmar, "Take her out!"

Rachel saw Raptor standing behind her with his eagle eyes sending forth streams of light onto Shemed. As Telmar started toward her, Cordilia and Rachel raised their hands and shouted, "To hell with you, Telmar."

With that, Telmar fell to the ground and began to evaporate. When the smoke cleared, Telmar was no more. Only fragments remained of Shemed as he groaned for Delilah to come forth. Instantly, Delilah was there. She looked at Rachel and began to laugh so loudly that it hurt their ears. "How dare you come against your own flesh and blood, Rachel? You have the same blood in your veins as I do. After all, I am your aunt. Let's not fight. Why don't you join us and take your place alongside me?"

"Wrong, Delilah. Your blood doesn't run in my veins, and you're not part of my family."

"Wrong, Rachel. Your grandfather was my father. Would you like to hear it from him?"

Delilah waved her hand, and a man appeared who looked like her grandfather, Luther King. Rachel's chin began to quiver, and tears welled up in her eyes. She loved her grandfather very much. It wasn't the appearance that griped Rachel's heart, it was when he called her by his pet name for her. "Princess! Your Papa loves you. Don't do this to me!"

He opened his arms toward Rachel and cried out, "Come to Papa, Princess! I would love to have a hug. It's been so long—come."

With her emotions running wild, Rachel softly whispered, "Papa!"

Harold Collins appeared on the right hand side of Delilah and said, "Rachel, don't be deceived by what you see!"

Luther called to Rachel, "Princess, don't listen to him. Here, ask your daddy. He wouldn't lie to you."

Luther raised his hand in the air and brought it down. There standing beside him was her daddy. Trembling, Rachel put her hand over her mouth.

"It's so good to see you, baby."

Shaking, Rachel cried, "Daddy!"

Delilah spoke up. "See, Rachel darling, all your family is here. We want to hold you and have you with us."

At that moment, Amanda Collins appeared on the other side of Delilah and said, "Rachel! Don't be distracted by her magic."

Rachel's daddy said, "Honey, your mama is here too." Rachel wanted to feel the arms of her family around her so desperately. She stepped forward. Her focus had been drawn away by

Delilah's witchcraft. She took another step, and John shouted, "Rachel! No!"

She turned to see a man stab John in the hip. John screamed in pain. Blood was spouting from the wound. Rachel turned to go to John, but Cordilia called out, "Rachel, don't turn back! Go forward!"

Before Rachel could turn around, she heard swords clanging, and the cry of the battle. Rachel turned to go to her mother, father and grandfather, only to behold hideous creatures battling with Harold and Amanda. Rachel heard screams of death all around her. Delilah moved toward Cordilia with a sword in her hand. "Rachel!" a voice shouted, "Take the sword from her."

Rachel looked and saw Camron and Haleb fighting with Emily and Jerry Jackson. It wasn't the dainty Emily she knew, but a daunting force to be reckoned with. Haleb thrust a sword through Jerry and ordered, "Rachel, get the sword from Delilah!"

A surge of power shot through Rachel. With a voice like the sound of a freight train, Rachel yelled, "Delilah, don't touch, Cordilia!"

Cordilia had her back to Delilah, attending to John's wound. Upon hearing Rachel's voice, she turned and saw Delilah coming at her with the sword. Cordilia stood, looked Delilah in the eye, and screamed, "I'll teach you to slap my hand!" A sword appeared in Cordilia's hand. She brought it down, hitting the blade of Delilah's sword. They fought hard, but finally Cordilia knocked the sword from her hand and ran her through. Delilah froze and melted to the ground. All that was left was the sword and the turban she wore on her head. Cordilia ran her sword through the turban, pinning it to the ground, and nodded at Rachel.

Paul was warring against Sheriff Butler's father. Many had fallen since the battle had begun, including red and brown eagles. Rachel commanded the ropes holding Willow Chandler to be loosened in King Rayon's name, and they fell away. She pulled Willow to her feet. Hurriedly, she took the long sweater she had on and gave it to Willow to cover herself.

Suddenly, a rumbling in the ground grew stronger and stronger until the ground erupted like a volcano. Smoke belched from the opening in the earth. Lightning streaked, and the wind was gale force. When the wind and smoke calmed, Queen Jewel stood in the middle of the altar. She slung her head from side to side, growling like a lion and hissing. Cheers went up from the trees in the forest. They chanted, "Praises to Queen Jewel!" When she spoke, it was sinister. She looked at Rachel, Cordilia, John and Paul. Addressing Rachel, Jewel roared, "Look what you have done here! How this brings back memories, Opal. Shall I call you Rachel or Opal?"

Jewel looked beyond Rachel and saw Paul, Cordilia and John. "Look here, you've brought your playmates with you." She glared at Cordilia and growled, "Rehabiah! You call yourself a warrior. You have committed more sins than most, and now you dare stand to war against me?"

Cordilia boldly proclaimed, "I stand here innocent! My sins forgiven! I wish you could say the same.

I'm sure when you stand before the Most High God to be blotted out, you'll wish you had chosen to stay out of the strange fire."

Jewel gritted her teeth as she looked at Paul and hissed, "Rayuel, you could have been great in my kingdom alongside me. It's not too late. Join me, and I'll give you riches beyond anything you can imagine."

Paul stepped forward. "There is one I serve, and one alone—the Most High God. My knee will never bend to you."

Jewel fixed her stare on John and shook her head. "Jathniel! Are you hurt? I can heal you instantly. Your God allowed you to be wounded. What kind of god would do that to his soldiers? He couldn't even protect you. I'll protect you. I'll let you sit on one of my thrones. I'll give you every pleasure you can dream of. I'll use the deep magic to fulfill you. Only worship me."

"Look around, Jewel, at your dead soldiers," John said. "Were you able to save them? My allegiance is, and will always be, to King Rayon! I may be wounded, but at least I'm here. Where are your leaders, Jewel?"

Rachel stepped forward with the sword in her hand and demanded, "Where are Chris and Paula?"

Jewel laughed aloud. "What's that to you? They have pledged themselves to Gray Stone. Chris was one of my faithful servants . . . until Paula. He had the nerve to disobey me. As for Paula, Telmar took care of her and her baby. Chris should have never tried to stop him."

Rachel raised her hand. "Enough talk! I serve notice on you and the Gray Stone Kingdom. King Rayon has sent us with full authority to take Todd's Creek out of your power. I command you, relinquish this territory!"

Jewel snarled, "You dare command me?"

Cordilia, Paul and John chanted, "We take back this territory in the name of King Rayon."

Rachel held the sword above her head and added, "We come against every stronghold and every foul spirit you have sent against Todd's Creek, and command them to leave."

Through gritted teeth, Jewel cried out, "Never!"

Rachel pointed the sword at Jewel. "I command the darkness that has covered Todd's Creek for years to leave."

Jewel frantically looked around her. To her right, Raptor stood, his talons raised ready to take the prey. To her left stood the ancient guard. Behind the four of them stood the brown and red eagles. Trembling, Jewel stepped back and shouted, "No!"

"I command you, Jewel and your imps, to go back to the pit," Rachel demanded. "You have no more authority here. I command the land to be healed from every curse."

Jewel screamed at Rachel, "I may not ever have you, but I'll be back for your son!"

With that said, she vanished into a green fog. All the warring ended. The trees were again trees. The thrones were no longer there. Haleb stepped forward and handed his sword to John. John raised the sword, brought it down hard on the altar, and yelled, "For the White Stone Kingdom!" On impact, the earth rumbled and the wind blew as the Gray Stone altar split in half. When the cheering stopped, Rachel looked at the opening in the rock where the thrones had been. She could hear water dripping, the same sound she heard when Haleb took her to the dungeon where Chris and Paula were chained. As she stepped up to the entrance of the cave, Haleb stood beside the opening and motioned for her to go inside. Rachel looked at Haleb and asked, "Are they here?"

He nodded and pointed toward the rock wall in front of her. "Opal, mighty woman of the Most High God, go through the wall."

Rachel stepped forward to the rock wall. When she did, the wall vanished. In front of her, Chris and Paula remained hanging with their hands tied in stocks above their heads. They had been beaten, and Telmar had raped Paula. On the ground at Paula's feet still lay the tiny baby that she had miscarried.

Haleb turned to Rachel. "Go, do that which you have been called to do."

With tears, Rachel looked into Haleb's eyes.

Haleb put his hand to his forehead and proclaimed, "Our King be praised forever!"

He was gone. Rachel knew he had accomplished what he had come to do. Cordilia, Paul and John entered the cave. They went with Rachel to free Chris and Paula, but the chains fell off as they approached. Rachel lay Chris down as Paul and Cordilia lay Paula down. They were barely breathing. Paula had lost quite a bit of blood. Rachel looked up toward heaven and cried out, "I speak healing to Chris, Paula, and John's wounds. Be healed in the name of our Lord!" Immediately, Chris and Paula began to come to.

"Chris? Paula? Can you hear us?" Rachel asked.

Rachel and John were cradling Chris, and Cordilia and Paul were helping Paula. Chris whispered, "Rachel? Where's Paula?"

John pushed his hair back and consoled him. "It's okay, buddy. Paula's right here."

Paula was in shock. She called out for Chris.

"I'm here, Paula. I'm right here."

"Rachel," a voice whispered at the opening of the cave.

Turning to see who called her, Rachel was surprised to see Mr. McKinney. "I brought medical help from Benson." A doctor and three emergency workers were there with gurneys to take them to the hospital. John and Paul went with the doctor, while Rachel and Cordilia stayed to bring the car.

Outside, Rachel and Cordilia were amazed that the doctor and the others didn't seem to notice the dead lying all around. Rachel looked at Jerry and Emily's bodies lying near Peggy's. They felt sick as they neared the bodies of Harold and Amanda Collins. Rachel looked at Cordilia and cried out, "Amanda told me she hoped my tears would be tears of joy. She said that if they didn't come back from the battle, they would be going back up Jacob's Ladder."

When the four of them got back into town, they heard that Harold and Amanda were killed in a car accident. Dr. Wells and Peggy had left town together, but Dr. Cole was expected back the next day to continue to care for Dr. Well's patients. Emily and Jerry Jackson moved to Europe for a permanent position at a bank there.

The four of them knew better. "Where did these stories come from?" Cordilia asked.

Rachel sighed. "I have no idea! I'm stunned at the magnitude of God and His faithfulness, Cordilia."

Chris and Paula recovered completely. They would have more children in the years to come after they were married. Paula recommitted her life to God on Sunday morning. Chris accepted the Lord as his Savior for the first time.

Pastor Miller blamed himself for what happened to Paula. He recommitted to Leah and Paula.

Three new people attended the service that Sunday morning—Sheriff Butler, his wife Molly, and, to everyone's surprise, Mr. McKinney. Looking like a million dollars, he took the end seat on the third pew. Rejoicing and praise filled the town.

Chapter 91
Ready for Babies

$\mathcal{T}$he middle of May finally arrived. Dr. Cole announced the good news that both Rachel and Cordilia were dilating, and that either one of them could go into labor at any time. They were more than ready for the baby boys to be born.

John got the permanent position at Todd's Creek station, just as Haleb had predicted, and Rachel could not have been happier. The timing was perfect, with their babies' births expected.

Rachel began to study the Bible more after the incident at Boone's Crossing. The Holy Spirit had blessed her with many revelations. Cordilia and Paul, too, had been studying. After all their experiences, Paul wanted to know more about the mighty God he served. Everything seemed like a dream. At the Crossing, Rachel was amazed to hear John and Paul referring to King Rayon and the White Stone Kingdom.

Chapter 92

Going to the Doctor

Cordilia knocked at Rachel's door at 8:30 a.m. on May 15. Rachel had not rested well the night before . . . or the night before that. She and Cordilia were miserable. With swollen ankles and a belly that felt as if it could pop, Rachel waddled to the door.

"Cordilia, what are you doing here so early?"

"I thought you might want to cook breakfast for Paul and me."

Rachel shook her head and joked, "By all means, come in, and I'll have the maid start breakfast right away." She looked past Cordilia. "Is Paul with you?"

"Yes, he went to get your paper."

"You ladies, go sit in the living room, and I'll put the coffee on," Paul ordered playfully as he picked up the coffee canister.

John came down the hall into the kitchen. "Good morning, everybody. I wondered if Rachel was out here talking to herself."

Cordilia went to the sink where John was running a glass of water, took him by the arm, turned him around, looked boldly into his eyes and asked, "John, did you get any sleep last night?"

"I slept like a rock, Cordilia. Did you sleep well?"

"You hush up, John Harris. Do I look like I got any sleep last night? No, I didn't sleep. My belly and back hurt all night long."

"You can say that again. She's not the only one who didn't sleep," Paul concurred. "I was rubbing her back and her belly, not to mention the peanut butter on the spoon that I had to get up to get several times. Cordilia wanted to come over, so I thought we would fix them breakfast. What do you think of that, John?"

"That sounds great to me."

Paul chuckled. "I may show those two up, John. I make pretty tasty biscuits. Cordilia, on the other hand, does pretty well—but nothing compared to mine."

"Yeah! Talk is cheap, Paul Dawson. Rachel and I need proof of that boast. Right, Rachel?"

"Sorry, Paul, Cordilia's right. I think I need that proof ASAP!"

"I can't do anything until you two are out of the kitchen. Now go!"

Rachel and Cordilia sat and talked while John and Paul made breakfast. Rachel was feeling a lot of pressure and was losing some amniotic fluid, so she called Dr. Cole.

"John, I think Cordilia just might have our boy today," Paul said as he turned the bacon.

"I wouldn't be surprised if Rachel had our boy today, too. She's been having some awful pain in her back."

"Cordilia has been like a wild woman. She cleaned all day yesterday, up into the night. You know old people say a woman will do that right before she starts labor."

John laughed and agreed. "If that be the case, Rachel is for sure going today. She cleaned until she almost killed me."

Just as John was taking the biscuits out of the oven, Rachel called him. "What is it, honey?"

"John, I think we need to go to the hospital."

John, not thinking, asked the most ridiculous question. "Why?"

Rachel groaned. "My back is killing me, and you ask me why? I called Dr. Cole, and he said it sounded like it was time to get to the hospital."

Jokingly, Paul asked, "What about my biscuits?"

"Oh my word! We'll eat them as we go," Cordilia replied, rubbing her back and walking like a duck toward the door. "You know what would be great, Rachel?" She wondered.

"What?"

"If I would have Phillip while I'm there and not have to make another trip."

"Well, we are due at the same time, and I think we both are in some stage of labor."

"All things are possible," Paul quoted as he took a big bite of biscuit.

By this time, John had Rachel's suitcase, and Paul put the bacon in the biscuits and wrapped them.

Cordilia quickly filled the thermos with the coffee, and they were out the door on their way to the hospital.

John was so excited, knowing that when Rachel came home, they would have the baby they had waited so long for. Paul and Cordilia were praying the same thing would happen for them.

Chapter 93
Finally Babies

When they arrived at the hospital, Cordilia's labor pains were three minutes apart. Dr. Cole admitted both Rachel and Cordilia. Stephen Daniel and Phillip Ryan were born only eight minutes apart.

Dr. Cole made sure Rachel and Cordilia shared a room. When settled in their room, Paul and John were allowed to be with them. They had only been in the room about thirty minutes, when the moment they had waited for finally came. Two nurses brought the babies in and gave them to their mothers. Tears, sighs, laughter and hallelujahs filled the room.

As Rachel, John, Cordilia and Paul looked at the two boys, they wondered what God had in store for them. What road would they travel down that would bring them to their destiny?

Rachel held Stephen to her breast, looked at his little hands, the perfectly round little head, and whispered, "Cordilia."

"Yes, Rachel."

"When you look at Phillip, do you think about the fact that you are holding an angel?"

"I'm way ahead of you, Rachel. From the first time I laid eyes on him, I thought about it. I asked myself, 'What position did he hold in heaven? Was he a warring angel? Is he a worshiper? Did he side with God at the rebellion? Is he an ancient one who helped protect the White Stone Kingdom?' I could go on and on." Cordilia rubbed her cheek against the baby's head.

"I've asked myself those same questions. Could this baby be one that rebelled against God? Maybe God put him in my care to lead him back home. Whatever be the case, I'll do my best with God's help to point Stephen to his destiny."

"Are you going to tell Stephen about all the things and events that took place in an attempt to stop him from being born?"

"Without a doubt. I think it's essential that we tell the boys everything. We must never forget the threat made by Jewel. She said, 'I may not have you, but I will be back for your son.' So to prepare the boys for that time, they need to know everything. They need to know who they are and why they're here. They must understand the first earth age and the time when all the children sang together. They need to know about the rebellion. They need to understand Jacob's Ladder and the ascending and descending angels. Cordilia, we must share all the things we were never taught. The enemy will come again, but by the help and grace of God, Stephen Daniel and Phillip Ryan will be equipped with the full armor, and be able to stand against the deception of Queen Jewel and the Gray Stone Kingdom."

And that's exactly what Rachel, Cordilia, John and Paul did. Chris and Paula also joined in and told the boys of their experiences of being lured with deception.

Stephen Daniel and Phillip Ryan grew up together. Everywhere one was, the other would be. Through school, the boys excelled in every subject. Stephen was the valedictorian of his graduating class. Phillip graduated with honors as well.

Both the boys received scholarships to Duke University. It was very hard to let the boys go. The day they left them at Duke, Rachel and Cordilia cried all the way back to Todd's Creek.

The house seemed so empty and quiet. Rachel would go into Stephen's room, get a shirt from his closet and hold it. At times she took his baby clothes out and remembered the first time she saw him. Above all, she would cover him in prayer. Cordilia did the same for Phillip.

Rachel and Cordilia filled the void with God's word. John, being at home every night, helped so much. Twenty-two years had passed since the angel Eri stood at the foot of her bed, announcing her son's birth. How could it be? It seemed like only yesterday.

Chapter 94
John Ascended Jacob's Ladder

*O*ne summer night in 1972, to take his place in the White Stone Kingdom, John was set free from the flesh body that held him as he slept. Rachel felt as though her world had ended. Stephen and Phillip took leave from school and came home. Stephen knew that his mom would need him nearby.

John was only 65 years old when he died. It was very sudden. The shock and loss of her beloved only brought the reality of Jacob's Ladder closer to home. Rachel thought about ascending Jacob's Ladder herself. She too was getting older, and knew everyone had an appointed time to ascend the ladder. She was no exception.

After a couple of months out of school, Rachel and Cordilia, talked to the boys about going back. Without discussing it, they both decided to transfer to a small collage in Benson. Of course, Rachel didn't agree with that. "Stephen Daniel Harris! I want you to go back to Duke University and finish school there."

"Mom, I love you, and I know you need me closer home."

"Honey, Duke is one of the best schools in the country. Do you realize the opportunities it can offer you?"

Stephen looked at his mom and said words she did not expect to hear from him. "Mom, God has been dealing with my heart since I was a little boy to be a minister for Him. In addition, I feel God guiding me to live closer to you."

Rachel's mouth dropped open, her eyes widened, and in a whisper she asked, "What?"

"Mom, even when Phillip and I were little boys, I pretended that I was a preacher. Even in my sleep, I dreamed of preaching. I've known for a very long time. It came so natural to me. It was just a part of me that I could never shake. Nor did I want to shake it. It's like it has been engraved in my heart.

"God, in so many ways, confirmed my calling to me repeatedly. There were times when playing at the barn, Phillip and I saw angels. One time we heard them talking. It was as though they had gathered in the barn to hear me preach."

Rachel didn't know what to say. Stephen continued telling of the many times he and Phillip had encountered angels. "Do you want to hear a strange thing, Mom? Phillip was never afraid of the angels. I was always afraid and ended up shaking in my shoes, but not Phillip. Phillip talked with the angels like they were his friends. I don't think he's afraid of anything."

"Stephen, I'm at a loss for words. You saw angels?"

"Yes, many times."

"Stephen, did Phillip ever tell Cordilia about these things?"

"If you didn't know about it, I'm sure Cordilia doesn't, or she would have told you."

Surprised, Rachel said, "I would hope so. Cordilia and I have shared things for a very long time. This would be a very big thing, and we would have shared it. Why didn't you ever tell me? All those times I told you about Raptor, Dr. Wells, Telmar, Shemed and Delilah. Would that not have been a good time to jump in and tell me about this?"

Not giving Stephen time to answer, Rachel continued, "How many times did I tell you about the angel Haleb? I was even on the subject of angels, and you still didn't tell me."

"No, Mom, I didn't. It wasn't the right time. You've always taught me that timing is everything. When the Holy Spirit says move, you move, but not until then."

Rachel's mind ran back in time to the place it all started when the angel Eri stood at the foot of her bed and proclaimed that he was sent by the Most High to tell her she would have a son. "You know, Stephen, your father and I told you everything about the events that took place before and after your birth, except for one thing."

"What would that one thing be, Mom?"

Rachel tried to speak, but the words would not come out of her mouth.

"Mom what is it?"

"This must not be the time for me to tell you. You're right, timing is everything."

"That's okay, Mom. When it's time, God will loose the words."

Rachel walked to a table beside the big picture window. She picked up a picture of John and her, held it with one hand and touched the picture of John ever so gently with the other. Just looking at the picture, Rachel could feel John's arms around her. Remembering his touch, she held the picture to her chest. Looking out the window and holding the picture, Rachel remembered and said, "Stephen, this picture was made only a few weeks before you were conceived. I missed him so desperately when he had to go out of town."

Putting the picture back on the table, Rachel turned to face Stephen.

"Cordilia has helped me through so many lonely times when your father was away. We have done it all together. She and I always talked about what God would have for your life and Phillip's life. Does Phillip feel he too is called to be a minister?"

"Not in the same sense that I do. I don't know how to explain what the call on Phillip's life is. He is different than I am, Mom,"

"In what way do you mean?" Rachel inquired.

"Phillip can see things."

"What things?"

"He can see things that are going to happen before they happen."

"Explain?"

"For instance, there have been many times I would start to go somewhere or do something and he would advise, 'Stephen, don't do this,' or 'don't go here or there.' I would ask why. He would say that there's danger, or there's a trap set for you."

"Like a prophet?"

"Yes, exactly."

Rachel put her hands on Stephen's shoulders and said, "I want you to obey God over everything. Obedience is everything when you're a child of God. So, what do you feel you should do, go to a seminary or a Bible college?"

"I want to go to a Bible college. I want to know all I can know about God. I don't want to be a minister for money or profession. I want to be a minister, because God has called me. A true shepherd would never do it just for money or a name but because the fire of God has been kindled in his soul." Rachel looked at her son and wondered what position he held in *The Beginning.*

Rachel no longer wondered why Jewel and the Gray Stone Kingdom would bring such an attack to stop the birth of her baby. Jewel knew the great damage Stephen and Phillip would bring to her domain. Rachel agreed that Stephen should do as God was leading him. So often she had wondered where his destiny would lead him.

Of course, Rachel and Cordilia had much to talk about. As it turned out, Phillip told Cordilia now about the call of God on his life too. He too wanted to go to a Bible college with Stephen. While Stephen and Phillip were checking out colleges, Rachel and Cordilia went into the Word of God as never before.

The boys were accepted at the college near Norfolk. It would be only an hour's drive away from home. Stephen knew Duke had a highly respected seminary, Duke Divinity School, but he wanted to stay close to home to look after his mom. Two years had passed since John had died. Stephen and Phillip were at the top of their class in everything they did at seminary.

The call on Stephen's life to preach was almost more than he could contain. He was invited to a couple of churches to speak, but this only fed his desire. Rachel assured Stephen that when the time was right, God would move him into position, and nothing could stop that.

Chapter 95
Remembering

The Holy Spirit revealed *many* revelations to Rachel during her life. All of which she shared with Cordilia, Phillip and Stephen . . . except two. She hadn't shared about the angel Eri or the voice she was hearing.

As Rachel prayed one day, she began to hear a voice in the distance call to her. When she first heard the voice, it was the sound of only a very soft whisper. Over a period of time, the voice grew louder and clearer. It was the calling for Rachel to ascend Jacob's Ladder.

Rachel knew that it would be only a short time. She couldn't bring herself to tell Stephen. She knew he would want to put everything on hold and stay home with her. Rachel was pulled between her flesh and her spirit. The flesh wanted to live and stay with Stephen. Her spirit, that occupied the flesh body, wanted to go back to the Creator.

Rachel wanted to go for a walk and get some fresh air. She found herself walking across the field toward the old plank shack that Effie Brown once called home. She smiled as she neared the porch, thinking about Winston barking and Effie's firm scolding. As Rachel walked, a familiar voice spoke her name. She turned and smiled as Raptor stood beside her. "I hope you're not still looking for the *Angel of the Ages* book," he said.

Rachel smiled, "No . . . I just wanted to . . ."

"To remember."

"Yes," she said softly.

"What is it you want to remember?"

"The way I felt when I was around her. It was as though our spirits were one."

"That's because they were one."

Rachel stopped and faced Raptor. "All that's happened is like a dream. Sometimes it's so real, and sometimes it's like a fairy tale. Like how many people would believe that I'm standing in a field talking to a magnificent seven-foot-tall eagle? One that says he's been alive since *The Beginning*."

"Only the ones who can see into that dimension will believe it. Otherwise how can they?"

Rachel looked at the old house that appeared not to have been touched by the storm they encountered the last night she saw Effie. The oak tree was standing tall and the windowpane wasn't broken. Rachel pointed to the tree and asked, "How can that oak tree possibly be standing when I saw it split by lightning. The window broke and went all over the floor. I saw it, and now it's like it never happened."

"It happened only in that dimension. In this dimension it's still just as you saw it before Effie ever moved in."

As they entered the house, Rachel scanned the room. All that remained was the table in the kitchen. She recalled the sweet taste of the honey biscuits Effie made. She sat at the table and lowered her head.

Raptor placed his wing on her shoulder and asked, "Why the solemn face?"

"I've been hearing a voice for some time now." She paused.

"You know, Rachel, King Rayon has allowed you to see Jacob's Ladder first hand. You saw the river filled with gold dust and precious stones. You heard the stars and galaxies singing and saw your mantel turn to gold. Your feet were shod with the golden sandals, and you wore a crown of gold on your head. Very few earthlings are granted such privileges. Fewer still have access to the Ancient Tree. You've faced Queen Jewel at the Crossing, brought victory to Todd's Creek, and you have a son who will excel in the work for White Stone Kingdom."

Tears welled in her eyes. "It's just the thought of leaving him."

Raptor placed his wing on her shoulder again. "Rachel, you should know by now that you won't be leaving him; you'll be promoting him. You see, the gold mantel you wear will be passed to your son. He will carry on your legacy."

Rachel cut her eyes to Raptor. "What of Cordilia, Paul and Phillip?"

Raptor chuckled, "Trust me, they'll carry on."

"Raptor, what happened to the book?"

Raptor stood and replied, "Effie Brown is guarding it along with the other books that contain the mysteries of old. When it's time, King Rayon will issue the command and Effie will again visit the earth and make another secret known to a vessel ready to receive it."

Rachel stood and dried her tears, faced the old eagle and said, "I'll miss you."

"There's no need to miss me. I'll see you in White Stone Kingdom. There you'll find—on the street that leads to the Ancient of Age—a white stone with your eternal name engraved on it. You see, Rachel, there's so much more to the soul inside you than you can possibly know until the command is given, and then the flesh body sets the real you free. Before you go back up the ladder, there's one more place I want to take you."

Rachel eagerly smiled. "I'm ready!"

"You most certainly are, or the invitation would not have been extended."

Raptor spread his enormous wing and wrapped it around Rachel. Instantly they were standing in the valley where she had first seen the White Stallion. The mountain on both sides of the valley was filled with the brown and red eagles interwoven with the ancient ones. They stood at attention as Raptor and the stallion escorted Rachel through the valley that was covered with gold dust. In the center of the valley was a gigantic stump with a white fog swirling over the top. Rachel and Raptor stopped as the white stallion continued. When he approached, the stump, he neighed and lowered his head into the haze. When he raised his head, his mouth was covered with gold dust. He motioned for Raptor and Rachel to join him. She waited for Raptor to eat first. He lowered his head and came up with his mouth filled with gold dust.

"Eat, Rachel," Raptor uttered.

Rachel lowered her head into the mist and filled her mouth with the substance inside. What she had thought was gold dust wasn't gold dust at all. She quickly cut her eyes to Raptor. He nodded, answering her question without speaking. Again, she lowered her head and filled her mouth with the sweet substance. She lifted her head, faced Raptor, and breathlessly asked, "What is this remarkable tasting . . . stuff?"

He smiled and replied, "The Most High has allowed you to taste the sweetest part of him. It's the nectar of the Most High."

Rachel remembered the honey biscuit. "Cordilia asked Effie if she put something special in the biscuit to make it so good. Effie said she put a pinch of enchantment. Is this the enchantment she spoke of?"

"I'm sure it is. This is a place of enchantment. It's time to go, Rachel," Raptor said.

She looked one last time at the mountaintops where the eagles and Ancient Ones had gathered. She smiled as she looked at the stallion with gold dust still on his mouth, and said, "I'll be back soon."

Raptor touched her head with his wing. "I'll be waiting for your time to ascend Jacob's Ladder."

She hugged Raptor, gently stroked the stallion's face and instantly was back at her front porch. The sweet taste of nectar from the ancient stump lingered in her mouth.

Chapter 96
True Friends

*O*ne warm spring day, as Rachel sat in the porch swing that she and John so often shared, Cordilia drove up, got out of her car and sat down by Rachel in the swing. After saying hello, Cordilia and Rachel sat in silence for at least thirty minutes before speaking.

Cordilia broke the silence by saying, "I was praying for you today, my kindred spirit." Cordilia put her arm around Rachel's arm and held it. "You've not told me everything. You know how that gets to me. You and I have been through so many things together, and we will go through this together as well."

Rachel still had not spoken. Her eyes were fixed straight ahead.

"When did you first hear the voice calling you home?" Cordilia asked.

Rachel grinned and squeezed Cordilia's arm. "I could never hide anything from you, could I?"

Cordilia shook her head no, but said nothing.

"I remember thirty-five years ago when you first moved to Todd's Creek. You were such a mess! Yet, I felt God brought you here, just for me. Like Stephen and Phillip, we were like glue from the beginning."

"Hey! What do you mean, we 'were' like glue? We're still sticking." Cordilia teased as she squeezed Rachel's arm.

"Yes, we are," Rachel said. "We had so much in common to be so different. We both sang in the choir and taught Sunday school together. We became prayer partners only a month after you and Paul moved here."

"Yes, and remember . . ." Cordilia reminiscenced, "how John and Paul became best friends in only a few weeks?"

"Yes, and we prayed together for me to have a baby, even when Dr. Wells said I couldn't have one. Not only did I have a baby, we had Stephen and Phillip on the same day. We confronted Queen Jewel herself with God as our weapon and the Word of God as the cutting edge."

Rachel looked down and then at Cordilia. "Now I've come to a place that you can't go with me. The flesh is fighting the spirit, and the flesh can be very strong when it comes to this place, but I'm not afraid, Cordilia."

Suddenly dark clouds appeared, and a wind blew so strongly that it was leaning the trees. "What in the world is happening, Rachel?" Cordilia asked as she moved to stand.

"Don't get up, Cordilia," Rachel answered, as she held firm to her arm.

Cordilia sat back down.

"It's not regular rain clouds gathering around us. There is a war going on right over my house in the spirit realm. The Holy Spirit told me I would be leaving very soon. Do you remember the day when Effie Brown was about to go back to White Stone? She was in midair. She was so beautiful."

"How could we ever forget that day? I loved the stories you told me about Raptor taking you to the Ancient Tree."

The girls continued to swing until the clouds disappeared as fast as they came in. When Rachel stood, she grabbed her chest and groaned.

"Rachel," Cordilia called, not knowing what to do. "Rachel, are you all right?"

For a few seconds, Rachel could not move. The pain eased and Rachel breathed easily again.

"Rachel, let me call Paul and get you to a doctor."

"No, Cordilia, it's not my time yet."

Sternly, Cordilia demanded, "Well, what if you're wrong, Rachel?"

"I'm not, Cordilia. Stephen will be home soon, and I don't want you to say a word."

"Lord, help me! Rachel, don't do this to me!"

"Promise me, Cordilia."

"I promise, but I don't like it."

Rachel looked at Cordilia and smiled. "Do you pinky promise?"

Cordilia managed to smile back although her heart was breaking. She held her little finger up and took hold of Rachel's. "I pinky promise." Cordilia helped Rachel get into bed, so she could rest for a while before Stephen got home.

Rachel patted the edge of the bed and beckoned, "Cordilia, come and sit by me."

Cordilia sat down on the bed and took hold of Rachel's hand.

"I want to tell you what I saw in the Word last night . . . about being changed from glory to glory. "

Excited, Cordilia responded, "You know me well enough to know I like that verse a lot."

"I know."

"You're ever the teacher, Rachel. So, tell me about this verse?"

"I saw the passage in a whole different light."

"Share."

"While studying, I got up and looked into the full-length mirror." Rachel pointed to the mirror at the foot of her bed. "I have looked into that mirror for forty years, and nothing out of the ordinary has ever happened. This time as I viewed myself, so many things raced through my mind. My first thought was, Look at these wrinkles! And how my eyesight has gone downhill. Not to mention how gravity has flattened my bosom. I looked at my black hair that has turned mostly gray. When I tried to pull away from the mirror, the Holy Spirit said, 'Not yet.' So I looked in the mirror for almost an hour. Just when I thought I was free to move, a breeze swept through the bedroom. I turned to see if the window was open. It wasn't. When I turned back to the mirror, a white haze covered the glass from the inside."

Cordilia tilted her head and asked, "The fog was in the mirror?"

"Yes."

"And then?"

"I still couldn't walk away from the mirror. Curiosity pulled me to it. I all but put my face against the glass, but I still couldn't see anything. I put my hand against the glass and started to wipe it off. With the first movement of my hand, I saw a white fluffy cloud billowing in the mirror. By then my stomach was in knots. As I continued to wipe the glass, the cloud grew bigger and filled the mirror. It was as if I was looking at a motion picture screen. As the cloud moved, it began to separate. I could see something through the fragmented cloud, but I wasn't sure what it was until the cloud evaporated. Then, right in front of my eyes, in that mirror, angels were looking at me."

"My, my!" Cordilia exclaimed as she hung on every word.

"You must remember, Cordilia, I was looking in the mirror at the foot of my bed, not some trick mirror. As I looked, I saw heaven and earth the way they were before the great rebellion."

Cordilia questioned. "You saw this in your mirror?"

"In that mirror!" Rachel exclaimed pointing to the foot of her bed.

"Continue."

"Something you don't have to believe, if you choose not to."

"Rachel honey, how could you ever think I wouldn't believe what you tell me? No matter how far out it may seem. Have you forgotten 'The Journey in Time' shop and Boone's Crossings where we saw Queen Jewel herself."

"As I said, the mirror was like a movie screen. It moved as if I were walking through it, but I wasn't moving.

"Then the scene was at the first level of a mountain and just like a camera, zoomed in on one angel. The angel was shouting. As I looked at the angel, I saw my face, and I was so young. The scene pulled back from where it had taken me all the way to The Beginning. I saw myself at all different ages and stopped when I was a newborn baby. In the last scene, I saw a young me wearing a white robe, made of fine linen, lined with purest gold. As I watched, the girl in the mirror slowly disappeared."

"Rachel, God is so awesome! At times like this, how do you come up with words to express your feelings? Like my visit to the throne room?"

Rachel inhaled and exclaimed, "How could I ever forget that?"

As Rachel finished, Cordilia heard a car pull up. She looked out the window and shouted, "It's Stephen!"

Rachel hurried to get up. "Cordilia, don't forget that we pinky promised."

"Rachel! Stephen needs to know."

Rachel sternly reminded, "No, Cordilia. You promised me."

Through tight lips, Cordilia agreed, "Okay, but I don't like it."

"Let's go to the living room before he gets inside."

Rachel had barely sat down when Stephen barreled through the kitchen door.

"Mom," Stephen called out.

"We're in the living room, honey."

Stephen entered the living room so excited with Phillip on his heels.

"How are the prettiest ladies in Todd's Creek?" Stephen complimented as the boys leaned down to give their moms kisses. "Cordilia, I want you to come see the new wheels I put on my car the other day."

"Hmm! So that's why all thirty-two teeth are showing today." Cordilia looked at Rachel and raised her eyebrows. "I'll be back, Rachel," she said.

Cordilia and Stephen hurried out the door. Cordilia came back to the door and asked, "Phillip, do you want to come?"

"No, Mom. I'll visit Aunt Rachel."

"So what have you and mom been up to today?" Phillip asked as he sat down beside Rachel.

Rachel took hold of Phillip's hand. "We visited the heavenly places today. Places we've visited for many years now. It's hard to believe at times that such places exist."

Rachel paused and squeezed Phillip's hand. "Phillip, you know you're like my own son. I've watched you grow up and become a very handsome young man."

"Why, thank you, Aunt Rachel. That's the nicest thing anyone's said to me today."

As Rachel looked into Phillip's eyes, she tightened her brows.

"Is something wrong?" he asked.

"No, there's nothing wrong. It just that there's times when I look at you, you remind me of someone."

"You have told me that since I was a little boy. Tell me! Who is the blessed person?"

"That's just it. I don't know. You're so like your mother. I love you, Phillip. I don't want you to ever forget that."

"I love you too, Aunt Rachel. You're like a second mother to me. Some people don't even have one, but I have two. Is something bothering you, Rachel?"

"I . . . I feel very sentimental today for some reason." Rachel stood when she heard a car pulling out of the driveway. "Is Stephen going somewhere?"

"It's Stephen's car, but Mom's driving. She probably wants to burn a little rubber and impress Stephen just enough that he'll buy her some ice cream at Kelly's drug store."

"It's so nice outside." Rachel said. "Why don't you and I go sit in the porch swing?"

"I would love to."

As Rachel and Phillip sat in the swing, Rachel began to laugh.

"What's so funny?" Phillip asked.

"I was thinking about the time that I was scared out of my skin as I came on this porch."

"When was that?" Phillip asked as he began to push the swing.

"The day John and I had been into town. John was putting the car in the garage. I was hurrying into the house, because a storm was coming up. The sky was growing dark, and the wind was blowing so hard. A cloud appeared. It was very close to the ground. There was a flash of lightning, and I saw a man in that cloud. The cloud was gone as fast as it came. That was the first time that I saw Haleb, or should I say Doug Holland?"

"I remember that story," he said. "It's one I don't forget."

Rachel squeezed Phillip's hand. "You know to live your life for the Lord is everything. Life has a way of slipping away from us."

"Well, here they come," Phillip interrupted. "It must be Mom driving back. Stephen would never let you see him drive like that."

"My heavens! Does Stephen really drive like that, Phillip?"

"Not often. I won't let him."

Cordilia and Stephen parked the car. As soon as they got out, Rachel and Phillip laughed. Sure enough, Cordilia and Stephen had ice cream cones.

"You two are so predictable," Rachel declared.

Cordilia looked at Stephen and teased, "Predictable! What could they mean by that, Stephen? Did you also predict that Stephen and I would bring you two some ice cream? Of course, you have to put it in your own cones."

Chapter 97
Phillip Wants Time with Rachel

$\mathcal{T}$hat night, as Rachel was preparing for bed, she had a very sharp pain in her chest. Stephen heard her groaning and came to check on her. Entering the room, he saw Rachel holding her chest. Rushing to her, Stephen said, "Mom, are you all right?" He put his arm around Rachel and helped her sit down on the bed. "You sit here. I'm calling the doctor."

With the growth of Todd's Creek came a new doctor to town. Dr. Moore was a cardiologist. He agreed to come to Rachel's house. While Dr. Moore was on his way, Stephen called Cordilia. She, Paul and Phillip were on their way as well. Stephen's heart raced. He could tell his mom wasn't doing well. He sat beside her on the bed. "Mom, you're going to be okay," he said as tears rolled down his cheeks.

"Stephen, I want you to listen to me very carefully. Please remember all the things I told you concerning your birth. You must never forget about Queen Jewel, Shemed, Delilah, Telmar and Peggy."

"Mom, you're going to be fine." Stephen went to the window. "Where is that doctor? Here comes Cordilia, Mom." Stephen went over and gently rubbed Rachel's forehead.

The door burst open. Cordilia, Paul and Phillip rushed to the bedside. "Oh God, Rachel!" Cordilia screamed as she took hold of Rachel's hand. "Dr. Moore should be here any minute. You hang on, do you hear me?"

Cordilia helped undress Rachel and helped her put a gown on so the doctor could check her. "You can't leave me, Rachel!" Cordilia begged, no longer trying to hold the tears back.

"You stop that, Cordilia! You're only jealous because I get to go up Jacob's Ladder first. You're my kindred spirit, and I love you."

"I love you, Rachel," Cordilia answered as she continued to wipe the tears.

"Cordilia, didn't we do it all?"

"And more!" she agreed, as she calmed down somewhat.

"Take care of Stephen for me."

"You don't even have to ask that."

Dr. Moore came into the room. He brought his nurse with him to assist. Cordilia, Paul and Phillip consoled Stephen.

"Cordilia, she's got to be okay," Stephen sobbed. "She's got to!" They held hands and prayed for Rachel as they waited. The bedroom door opened, and Dr. Moore came out. They surrounded him, eager to hear what he had to say.

"How is she, Dr. Moore?" Stephen asked.

Dr. Moore lowered his head. "She may not make it through the night. Her heart's very weak. My nurse will stay with you and Rachel. If you need anything, let me know."

Panicked, Stephen screamed, "Do you mean you're not going to take her to the hospital?"

"I told her we could, but she said no. She wants to be home with you all."

When Dr. Moore left, Cordilia looked at Stephen, Paul and Phillip. "This is about to kill us all, but please try to be strong for Rachel's sake. Paul, call Pastor Miller, Leah, Paula and Chris. Stephen, let's you and I go be with your mom."

After Paul made the call to Pastor Miller, he joined Stephen and Cordilia. "Phillip! Are you coming?" Paul asked.

"I'll go see her in just moment, Dad."

Pastor Miller and Leah arrived in just a few minutes. Chris and Paula were on their way. Everyone was in the room, except Phillip.

Stephen came out to check on him.

He was standing on the front porch looking up toward heaven.

"Phillip!" Stephen exclaimed as he stood beside him, "Are you okay?"

"I need some time with Rachel."

"Come on. I'll go in with you." Phillip turned and looked Stephen in the eye. "Alone!"

Pausing, Stephen knew in his heart that Phillip knew more than he was saying to him. Nevertheless, without asking for details, he relented, "Okay. I'll tell the others."

"Stephen!"

"Yes."

"Look at the sky. Remember what your mom told us about the storms."

Stephen could see the black clouds gathering, and the moaning sound of the wind was chilling.

"You better come in, Phillip. It's lightning."

"Yes! It's time to go," Phillip agreed as they went inside.

Stephen told everyone Phillip needed time alone with Rachel. When everyone cleared the room, Phillip went inside and closed the door behind him.

He walked over and stood by Rachel's bed. When Rachel looked up at Phillip, again she had that strange feeling. Phillip, knowing this, asked, "Rachel, are you still trying to figure out who I remind you of?"

Now very weak, Rachel whispered, "How did you know that?"

"Because I recognize the look I've seen all my life."

Rachel turned her head toward the window. Taking a short breath, Rachel commented, "It sounds like a terrible storm outside."

"It's no ordinary storm, Rachel. I remember that you told Stephen and me about the battle in the heavens every time a child of God dies. The warfare is all the way to the top of Jacob's ladder. There, the angels present you back to the Father."

"I know, Phillip," Rachel assured as she squeezed Phillip's hand.

"The angels have arrived, Rachel."

Slowly, she lifted her eyes and looked at Phillip.

"The Most High is taking you into a different dimension, Rachel. Look around the room. The angels are here."

Rachel turned her head from left to right. Truly, angels had filled the room. In only a whisper, Rachel concurred, "Phillip they're here. They're here!"

"Rachel, God has sent someone very special to escort you home."

Rachel looked up and with a very short breath, exclaimed, "John! John! Phillip, it's John."

"I know, and look who else."

Her eyes brightened when she saw Raptor standing beside John. "How . . . did you know they were coming?"

"King Rayon told me He was sending John and Raptor just for you."

Rachel could hardly breathe. Still holding Phillip's hand, she looked at Phillip and said, "Take good care of Stephen."

Phillip gently stroked her forehead. "You don't have to worry, Rachel. Eri is here."

Her breath almost gone from her, Rachel looked into Phillip's eyes. This time Rachel no longer saw Phillip, but the angel who had stood at her bed many years ago and announced Stephen's birth. Looking deep into Eri's eyes, she said her final words, "My Watcher . . ."

Rachel's eyes closed, and instantly John, Raptor, and the other angels escorted Rachel into the White Stone Kingdom. Rachel finally made the journey she had studied about many years earlier. No longer was she in a transition period of "being changed from glory to glory."

It had been fulfilled in her life. She was changed from glory to be born into a flesh body. Thus, she descended Jacob's ladder. Now, her flesh body had loosed the spirit, and again she was changed to glory. Rachel ascended Jacob's Ladder to be with her God and Creator, who was waiting to welcome her home.

Chapter 98
Calvin's Point

*A*fter the funeral, Cordilia, Paul and Phillip stayed very close to Stephen. They helped get all the legal formalities taken care of. Six months passed, and Cordilia felt as though a part of her had been torn away. She too was beginning to think of Jacob's ladder that she and Rachel had talked about so often.

Stephen and Phillip were at school, but Stephen wasn't happy. He was talking about putting the home place up for sale. The idea of finding a small farm and trying his hand at farming was flooding his mind. He wanted just anything to get away from all the memories.

He had a friend at school who heard him talking about moving away and maybe buying a small farm down South. He told Stephen that his mom and dad left him a small farm, just off the Georgia coast in a very small town named Calvin's Point.

Stephen agreed to go look at the farm. He and Phillip went to Georgia and found Calvin's Point.

Stephen didn't think the farm was so small with its sprawling twenty acres. The home place had only five acres. "What do you think about the farm, Phillip?" he asked.

"The farm is fine. However, you're not Stephen. You're running from the pain of losing your mom."

"So what if I am? I can't stay there and look at memories that are eating me alive."

"What about school, Stephen?"

"I want to take some time off and not have to think about it right now. Phillip, this is a big two-story house. Why don't you move down here with me?"

"We have been through everything together, but this, you will have to do alone. I'll help you move to Calvin's Point if this is what you want, but it's just not what I want. I wish you would reconsider, Stephen."

Changing the subject, Stephen commented, "Look at this porch, Phillip. This is the perfect place for porch swing. Don't you think?"

Phillip put his hand on Stephens's shoulder and questioned him intensely, "Are you sure this is what you want?"

Nodding, Stephen answered, "I'm sure." Stephen had made up his mind. He would be moving to Calvin's Point.

Cordilia and Paul bought the home place from Stephen. Phillip wanted to live there and continue going to school. One of the hardest things Stephen ever did was to sell the place, the only place he had known as home. He tried to act as though he didn't mind, but Phillip saw him wipe the tears away more than once.

The last thing to be loaded in the moving van was the porch swing. Before taking it down, Stephen sat in it one last time, and remembered. Phillip came and sat down beside him.

"I'll really miss you, Phillip."

"Likewise, my friend."

"We've sure had our share of time in this swing, haven't we?" Stephen reminisced as he tried to hold back the tears. "Did I ever tell you the story behind the building of this swing?"

"No, but I would love to hear it."

"Have you ever noticed the carvings on each piece of wood?"

"No, not really."

"Dad told me each marking was a reminder of the victories that Grandpa had won in prayer on his behalf. You know, Phillip, my Dad did the same thing. Look at this," Stephen pointed out as he showed Phillip the markings his dad had made on his behalf. "Look at this one. Dad made it when I had pneumonia. He told me Mom sat up all night holding my hand and checking my temperature. He spent the night sitting in this porch swing, looking into heaven and praying for me. He said that the next morning I woke up and that my fever broke instantly. God had healed me. I want to show you one I helped make with Dad." Stephen went to the back of the swing. Right in the middle of the top board, the letter V had been carved twice.

"Phillip, this one on the right I helped dad make. My first loose tooth had to come out, and I was scared. I begged Dad not to pull it. I remember the whole tooth was connected to one tiny piece of my gum. Dad hugged me and sat me up in the swing beside him. He took a handkerchief from his back pocket and wiped my tears. He explained why the tooth needed to come out. Then he put his arm around me and advised, 'Let's you and I ask God to help calm you and help the tooth to come out so fast that you don't have time to even feel it.' That's exactly what we did. The tooth came out so fast it didn't have time to hurt. Dad clapped his hands and told me what a big boy I was. Then he reminded me, 'Let's give God some praise too.' We said, 'Thank You, Jesus,' and Dad said, 'Come on Stephen. I think you should help with this mark.' So we made this mark together. After we finished the mark, Dad told me the same thing happened when he and Grandpa made the other V. Dad said, 'Stephen, when you have a child, I want you to do the same thing with him or her.'"

"You know, Stephen," Phillip said, "all of my life I've seen that swing but never noticed the carving before."

"Oh well, enough of memory lane. Let's get the swing loaded, and we'll be ready to go. The movers are going to follow us down, so, Phillip, you're in charge of not letting me drive too fast. The driver of the van said that he had never heard of Calvin's Point, and since I was going, he wanted to follow."

Cordilia and Paul came to say their goodbyes. Holding Stephen for one last goodbye, Cordilia told Stephen through her tears that he would always have a home to come to in Todd's Creek.

"Cordilia, I want you to promise me that you and Paul will come visit. It's a big house, so I'll have lots of room." Stephen hugged Cordilia one last time.

"I promise we will visit often."

Stephen smiled, held up his pinky finger, and teased, "Do you pinky promise?"

Cordilia held up her pinky finger, took hold of Stephen's and recited, "I pinky promise."

Phillip hugged his mom and dad and assured them that he would be home in one week. He was going to stay and help Stephen get everything straightened out in the house. Finally, with one more hug, Stephen and Phillip were on their way to Calvin's Point.

The trip went well, and they arrived in good time. The movers unloaded everything. Stephen and Phillip made sure the bedroom furniture was in the right room first. Both the boys were very tired and looked forward to a good night's sleep. They slept like babies, not changing positions all night.

They were awakened the next morning to a knock at the door. Stephen hurried down the stairs to see who could be knocking since he knew no one.

Opening the door, Stephen saw one of the most beautiful girls he had ever seen. At the same time, he had never been so embarrassed. There he stood in his pajamas with his hair totally disarrayed. As Stephen said hello, he rubbed his hand through his hair in a lame attempt to make it lie down.

"Hi! I'm Leann Conners. My mom and dad own the farm adjoining yours." Seeing Stephen was embarrassed, she added quickly, "I'm sorry. I should have waited until later in the day to stop by."

Responding, he said, "I'm Stephen Harris, and I'm glad you dropped by."

"We heard you moved in yesterday. This is a very small town, and everything gets around if you know what I mean. My parents and I want to assist you in your move in any way we can, so if you need any help, just let me know. Here is our phone number. I know you may not have your phone hooked up yet, but when you do, give us a call. I think my mom is making you a casserole to bring by later."

"That sounds great!" Stephen exclaimed, again running his fingers through his hair, unsure of his appearance. "I don't cook very well. Neither does Phillip."

"Oh, so we have two bachelors," Leann said with a grin.

"Yes, that pretty well sums it up. I want to invite you in . . ."

Before Stephen could finish his thought, Leann chimed in, "No, no, that's fine. I better be going. I have lots to do today."

"Thanks for stopping by, Leann."

"Yes, it's nice to meet, Stephen." Leann turned to walk away, and Stephen impulsively stopped her, "Leann, will you be coming over with your mom and dad?"

"Yes, I sure I will."

"Leann!"

"Yes."

"Are you married?" Stephen wondered. He didn't know where his courage came from.

"No!" Leann responded. "Nor am I engaged. I'll see you later." Leann's smile was perfect. Stephen's mouth was so dry that he could hardly swallow. She waved as she pulled away. Stephen managed to throw his hand up, but all he could see was that smile.

"Who was that at the door, Stephen?" Phillip asked as he was coming down the stairs.

"Wow! It was an angel, Phillip. The most beautiful girl I have ever seen." Still gazing out the door, Stephen shook his head and continued, "She will be welcome here any time she wants, day or night."

"Well, are we a little starry-eyed, Stephen?"

"I think so."

"There's one thing I know for sure, Stephen."

"What's that?"

"If she likes you, it's not because of what she saw at the door this morning."

Phillip and Stephen worked hard all day, emptying boxes, and putting things away. Late that afternoon, Stephen saw a car coming down the driveway. Full of excitement, Stephen called to Phillip, "I think this is the Conners. Get down here, Phillip. Hurry! I see Leann in the backseat!"

Phillip smiled in reply, "You better calm down, or you're going to be obvious. Don't forget her parents are with her. You need to make a good first impression. Here they come."

"Phillip, you fixed the tea, didn't you?"

"It's all taken care of. Stop being so hyper, Stephen."

A knock came at the door. Stephen took a deep breath and opened it. There stood an older couple and Leann. "Hello!" Stephen greeted, trying to be on his best behavior.

"Hi, Stephen. This is my mom and dad, Jason and Jamie Conners."

"It's a pleasure to meet you. This is Phillip Dawson, and I'm Stephen Harris."

"I brought you a chicken casserole," Mrs. Conners said. "I sure hope you like chicken."

"Yes! Phillip and I both love chicken casserole."

Mr. Conners was a very quiet man while Mrs. Conners was a very brash, outspoken woman. "Are you boys Christians?" Mrs. Conners inquired a little too boldly.

"Yes, we are." Stephen was quick to answer.

"Well, good! I don't want a bunch of heathens for neighbors."

"Mother," Leann whined, totally embarrassed.

Mr. Conners spoke up. "Don't mind Jamie. She says pretty much what comes to her mind. Try to control yourself, dear."

"I meant no harm, Jason."

"I know that, dear, but Stephen and Phillip don't."

"I don't apologize for being who I am. This is me! You take me or not."

"You're fine, Mrs. Conners," Stephen consoled, just a little surprised.

"Did I tell you that my name is Jamie, young man?"

"Yes, you did," Stephen replied, swallowing hard.

"Then call me Jamie."

"Of course, Jamie, I'll do that," Stephens relented, breaking a sweat.

Phillip talked mainly to Jason and tried to keep from laughing at Stephen, whom Jamie had taken a liking to. The only thing that kept Stephen from screaming was Leann. Before the visit was over, Jamie asked at least ten thousand questions. Most of which she didn't allow Stephen to fully answer.

As the visit ended, Jamie looked at Stephen. "I'll expect to see you at Calvin's Point First Baptist Church on Sunday morning at 10:00 a.m. I'm talking to you too, Phillip."

Phillip smiled and responded obediently, "Yes, Jamie, we'll be there."

Phillip walked out with Jason and Jamie as Leann lingered behind to apologize for her mom. "I'm sorry, Stephen. I should have warned you about Mom."

"No, no. Your mom was fine. A bit brassy, but other than that she was very nice. She reminded me of Cordilia, Phillip's mom. I'm glad you came, Leann."

Leann smiled at Stephen, "So am I. I better go. Mom will be back in for me." They both laughed and said goodbye.

When Phillip came back inside, he was laughing so hard that tears rolled down his cheeks. "What's so funny, Phillip?"

"You. I thought you were going to pass out a time or two."

"Thanks for helping me out, friend." Phillip finally got his laughter under control. When he did, Stephen continued, "What did you think of Leann?"

"She's very nice."

"What do you mean 'she's very nice'? What else did you think?"

"Yes," Phillip said. "She is beautiful."

"That's more like it. Did you see any chemistry or not, Phillip?"

"Stephen, you're acting like a teenager."

"That's because I feel like a teenager." Stephen talked about Leann up until bedtime, and Phillip laughed about Mrs. Conner's abrupt personality with Stephen.

The men worked very hard to finish unpacking and putting away before Phillip had to leave. They found out that the only place in town to buy food was a place called Andy's Market. They had what anyone needed, but the store was smaller than any store in Todd's Creek. It took a total of five minutes to see all there was to see.

Chapter 99
Feeling Alone

*T*he day had come for Phillip to leave. The last thing the men did was hang the swing on the front porch. They put Phillip's things in his car and came back to sit down in the swing. "I wish you would stay with me, Phillip."

"I can't, Stephen. I have to go, but I'll come visit and call often."

"You know, Phillip, we've never been apart. I'll miss you."

"I'll be here any time you need me, Stephen."

"You've always kept me straight. Now who's going to?"

Phillip laughed and suggested Jamie Conners. Stephen punched Phillip on his shoulder and teased, "You got a kick out of that, didn't you?"

Phillip was holding his stomach, laughing again. "Yes, I did. That was one of the funniest conversations I have ever witnessed. I think Leann will help balance Mrs. Conners."

"Thank God!" Stephen exclaimed.

"Stephen, I'll pray for you every day. I want you to remember all that your mom and dad and my mom and dad told you about Shemed, Telmar and the Gray Stone Kingdom."

"I won't ever forget, Phillip."

"More than that, Stephen, I want you to remember what Rachel told you about Queen Jewel saying she would be coming for you."

"How could I ever forget that, Phillip?"

"God is pulling me away from you, Stephen. You're going to face some things, but you must face these things in order for God to bring you to your destiny. God knows about the call on your life, but so does Queen Jewel. Guard yourself with prayer, fasting and the Word of God. You're going to need all of that for what you're going to face and for what you're going to see."

Again, Stephen fought back tears. Phillip's emotions were getting the better of him, too. "It doesn't seem fair, Phillip," Stephen sobbed as the tears flowed free.

Phillip put his arm around Stephen. "What doesn't seem fair?"

"It wasn't enough for God to take Dad. He had to take Mom, too. My insides are screaming. Neither one got to see a grandchild or what God has for my life. Why . . . why?" Stephen groaned in pain.

Phillip's heart ached as he tried to comfort Stephen, his brother.

"Stephen, I want you to remember what your mom told you about Jacob's ladder. I'm going to tell you something I haven't told you that took place right before Rachel died. She saw into a different dimension that night. You know when you're about to die that happens many times. Your mom saw angels fill the room. One angel that God sent to escort Rachel back up Jacob's ladder was very special. It was your dad. Rachel was holding my hand, and she said, 'There's John, Phillip. I see John!'"

"Why didn't you tell me these things?"

"That wasn't the time to tell you. God knew you would need to hear it now."

"Did you see John, Phillip?"

"Yes, I did. Rachel wasn't afraid, Stephen, because it's a natural part of God's plan to bring His children back to Him. When you die, you see many things you don't normally see. I saw your mom being taken from the flesh body that died, but her spirit was set free."

"How could you see? You weren't dying."

"No, I wasn't, but I am a prophet, Stephen. Sometimes that goes with the calling. Not all the time, but sometimes."

"Thank you for sharing that with me, Phillip. You're right. I needed to hear it now."

"I want you to release all the emotions and pain, so God can heal you, Stephen. Don't hold anything in. Release it all. This too is a reason that God is pulling me away for a while. These things only you can do. In the hard times, the warring angels will be there. In the times when you need encouragement, the Holy Spirit, and the ministering angels, will be there. God has you covered, but don't forget to cover yourself with prayer and fasting. Of course, you know to stay in the Word."

"I will. In those times that I feel I need someone to agree with me, I'll be calling my family."

As Phillip started off the porch, he turned and said, "By the way, I forgot to tell you that Raptor came with your dad to get your mother."

A final goodbye and Phillip was on his way back to Todd's Creek.

For the first time in his life, Stephen was alone. There was so much work to do. Stephen hoped this would help the time pass until he adjusted to his new surroundings. Several weeks went by. Many phone calls were made to and from Todd's Creek. Being a very organized, young man, Stephen had everything in its place.

He was attending the First Baptist Church of Calvin's Point and, of course, sharing a pew with Leann. He thought about her night and day. They went out several times and seemed to be hitting it off just perfectly.

Jamie and Jason had invited Stephen to their home often. Like Leann, they too had grown very fond of Stephen.

Phillip, Cordilia and Paul visited a few times and loved the farm. Almost a year had passed, and Stephen had marriage on his mind. He wanted to marry Leann and have a family. Stephen would soon be 26 years old. He wanted children while he was young enough to watch them grow up. He knew all three hundred people in Calvin's Point. His heart was set on marrying Leann and making it three hundred one.

He asked Leann to marry him, but Stephen wasn't sure who was the happiest, Leann, or her mom or dad. They would be married in the spring of next year. Phillip, of course, would be the best man, and Paul and Cordilia would stand with him as his mom and dad.

***

It was early fall, and the weather was gorgeous. The leaves were beginning to turn colors. It wasn't as pretty as Todd's Creek, because there were no mountains. Nonetheless, it was beautiful.

Stephen studied his Bible one late afternoon as he sat on the front porch in the swing. The Holy Spirit led him to do a study on Elijah, the prophet. The first thing Stephen noticed about Elijah was God pulled him aside from everyone, including his family. Stephen felt that part of Elijah. He too felt God had separated him from everyone. He wasn't sure of the reason, but one thing he was sure of was the call of God on his life to preach the gospel. He felt at times like a caged animal who wanted to be loosed. The fire of God was blazing in his soul. It was hard to contain it, but one thing his mom taught him was timing. The timing had to be God's, not his.

The sun was setting, and Stephen could no longer see to read, but still he sat in the swing, looking toward heaven and praying. The wind was picking up, and the clouds were moving faster than Stephen had ever seen. In the distance, he heard the rumble of thunder and saw lightning flash across the sky.

"Well, I guess I'd better get inside," Stephen thought aloud as he stood and stretched his arms over his head, feeling stiff from sitting for so long.

He locked the house up, went upstairs and turned the television on while he was brushing his teeth and preparing for bed. He could get one station out of Atlanta. The reception was a little snowy, but the sound was clear. Stephen couldn't believe his ears when the weatherman said, "It will be a calm clear night with no chance of rain in sight."

"How in the world can he say it will be a calm, clear night? Stephen wondered aloud There's a terrible storm brewing. Don't they have any satellites operating in space tonight?"

Stephen looked out the window. The cloud formation was different from any he had ever seen before. The wind was leaning the trees. "God keep me tonight!"

The last thing Stephen did before going to bed was open the bedroom window just enough to feel the cool breeze and hear the rain pounding the roof—feeling so alone, yet eager to live this new life in a new town.

Stephen was unaware this night was the end of this town the way everyone knew it. This storm was unlike any storm that had ever been or would ever be.

Horses ran in circles around the fence line. Dogs' eerie howls echoed through the empty streets.

Cats hid in corners on porches, their fur raised on their backs. Trees were bending from side to side while the corn in the field lay almost flat from the force of the wind. Streetlights and porch lights were suddenly gone. The only lights that remained were the inconsistent flashes of lightning that lit the sky a deep purple and gray. Taunting jeers and screams from the evil winds bounced off the sides of houses, barns and distant hills, sending a chill throughout the town and all the land.

A green-colored mist filled the valley and entered the heart of the town. It passed the police station and circled Andy's Market as it crept through the streets. As if on a mission, the trails of dampening mist met in the center of town, joined together and began their search for one man. Passing by the high school and several homes, the mist came to a long stretch of open road. The search was over. A long crooked driveway led up to the two-story, white farmhouse. The mailbox had been tossed to the ground, but it still read 77 Harris.

Up the driveway, past the rows of corn, the mist paused in front of the house. Then with great certainty, the mist floated up the east side of the house and seeped through an open bedroom window. Instantly, it circled around the bedroom, making its way over and under everything. The desk that sat by the window. The chest of drawers. The nightstand beside the bed and finally the bed.

This is where the Stephen slept peacefully until the mist transformed itself into the form of a hand that brushed his cheek, causing him to stir. He raised his hand to his face and waved it around as if he were swatting at a fly. Then he rolled over, fluffed his pillow and went back to sleep. WHOOSH! The mist suddenly wrapped itself around the man and seeped through his head. Instantly his peaceful sleep turned into restlessness. He tossed and moaned. Sweat began to form on his forehead and all over his body. He kicked the covers and curled into a fetal position. His body ached and his head pulsed with pain. He kicked and flipped over on his back and threw his arms into the air. He gasped for air. All at once he sat up, eyes wide open and screamed, "Shemed!"

About the Author

Wilma Styles has written eight novels and numerous songs and plays. Her teaching, speaking, and singing ministry brings the voice and heart that has brought healing and inspiration to the congregations that she has ministered to. She believes her source of strength comes from being in HIS presence. Wilma has been the keynote speaker at women conferences in Virginia, North and South Carolina. Her teaching ministry offers hope to the hopeless, healing to the broken hearted, and freedom to those in bondage.

The second book of the trilogy, *Eden's Gate*, is available now wherever books are sold. Wilma is looking forward to the third book of the trilogy *Angels of the Ages* coming out soon—*TRUTH.*

Wilma and her husband Ray live in Inman, South Carolina, where they enjoy their two daughters, three grand-children and three great-grandchildren.

www.ingramcontent.com/pod-product-compliance
Lightning Source LLC
Chambersburg PA
CBHW040930050726
47507CB00022B/273